FIGHTING HER FATHER'S WAR

BOOK ONE

OF

THE FIGHTING TOMCATS

M. L. MAKI

ROSE HILL PRESS, OLYMPIA, WASHINGTON

Fighting Her Father's War
First Book in the Fighting Tomcat Series

Cover design by Megan L. Maki

Photograph by Megan L. Maki

Fighting Her Father's War is a work of historical fiction and speculation using well-known historical and public figures. All incidents and dialogue are products of the author's imagination and are not to be construed as real. Because of the speculative nature of this work, we have changed some timelines of the present, such as the fact that the aircraft carrier battlegroup as described in this book has never existed. Also, we have changed the historical timeline in the present to suit the nature of the work. Any resemblance to persons living or dead who are not historical figures is entirely coincidental.

The views presented are those of the authors and do not necessarily represent the views of the DoD or the United States Navy.

NOTES

When beginning a novel of this type, it is necessary to decide at the outset how to tackle a number of issues. The Navy uses a great deal of jargon, technical terms, and acronyms that are used in speech. Eliminating this techno-speak from the dialogue would remove the character of the story. We decided to leave the language as spoken, with a few exceptions. When ships communicate over radio, each ship has a code name that is used in place of the ship's actual name. To avoid confusion, in some cases, we opted to use the ship's name. Many complex procedures are simplified to keep the story flowing and reduce confusion. Aircraft numbers are based on the bureau (serial) number of the plane, regardless of who's the pilot. The exception is the commanding officer, whose number is always one. Though this may be confusing, the reader should be able to follow the dialogue without the number cue. When events are occurring simultaneously, yet in different time zones, the author chose to adopt Greenwich Mean Time for clarity. In all other sections, local time is used. A number of technical details were changed to prevent revealing classified information.

A note on naval rank structure, in other services an enlisted person is addressed by rank, 'corporal, sergeant', etc. In the navy, sailors are addressed with rate and rank. An E-6 is not normally addressed as petty officer first class. He or she is addressed as MM1, BT1, BM1, etc. The rate is the job classification of the sailor, be that machinist mate (engine room equipment operator), or mess specialist (cook). A more comprehensive list of rates can be found in the glossary or online.

The rank of enlisted sailors is in three groups of three ranks; E-1 through E-3 sailors are non-petty officers. These are new sailors who may or may not have a rate. E-4 through E-6 sailors are petty officers. These sailors are the technical experts and watch-standers who keep the navy running: E-4 is a third class; E-5 is a second class; and E-6 is a first class petty officer. E-7 through E-9 sailors are middle managers; chief, senior chief, and master chief. Chiefs are systems experts who train, lead, and guide, instead of operating equipment. The colloquial for E-7 is chief, for E-8 is senior, and no one calls a master chief, master. Calling a senior or master chief, chief, is not an insult.

There are essentially two types of officers: line officers can command vessels and aircraft; non-line, or limited duty officers, are doctors, nurses, dentists, chaplains, civil engineer corps, or have other specific duties.

Ships are arranged by deck and frame. It's based off the main deck, or longest continuous deck on the ship. For carriers, this is the hangar deck. The main deck is level 1. All decks below the main deck are numbered downward, 2, 3, 4, 5, etc. All decks above the main deck are labeled upward, 01, 02, 03, 04, etc. Every four feet of a ship's length is marked with a frame and frames are numbered from forward to aft. Each compartment (room) is given a third number based on how far it is from the center line of the ship. If the center line passes through the compartment, it is numbered 0. Compartments to starboard have odd numbers, and compartments to port have even numbers. Finally, each compartment is given a letter designation showing its use. Thus, a compartment numbered 03-140-1L is on the level beneath the flight deck, which is the 04 level, 560 feet from the bow, on the starboard side near the middle and is a living area, or stateroom.

ACKNOWLEDGEMENTS

We would like to thank everyone who contributed advice or help on this project. Without your kind help, it would never have happened. Our family cheering section kept up our spirits when it got tough. We especially want to thank our beta readers, especially Michael Mohr, Robert Maki, Penny Sevedge, and Scott Richardson. Your advice, insight, and support made this all possible.

DEDICATION

To our amazing fathers, Kenneth Wayne Maki and William Roy Sevedge,

and to all those veterans, past, present, and future, who have served the

the cause of freedom.

CONTENTS

"Those who fail to learn from history
are condemned to repeat it."

WINSTON CHURCHILL - 1948

CHAPTER 1

USS CARL VINSON
BATTLE GROUP

WESTERN PACIFIC OCEAN

1742 December 19TH, 1990

A F-14 Tomcat sliced the clear blue sky. Knight 211 rolls into a turn and Lt. Samantha 'Spike' Hunt sees the Pacific Ocean far below. The water a darker hue of the blue sky, stretches from horizon to horizon. As the jet rockets past 25,000 feet, she looks back and sees her wingman 500 feet away and smiles, her grey blue eyes alive with the joy of being in the air.

On intercom, "Ok, Puck, we are at waypoint Whiskey. Call it in and remember to watch our back. The XO is out there."

Lt. JG Eric 'Puck' Hawke is the radar intercept officer in the back seat of the big fighter. The dark-haired Sioux says on the radio, "Ghost Rider 201, Knight 211 is 600 knots at flight level 25." Then on intercom, "Spike, I know my job. Remember, we are supposed to do a 1V1 before relieving the XO. Swede is on his wing and he is fucking good. If we get waxed too easy we'll never hear the end of it."

Spike answers, "I got it."

On radio, "Knight 211, Ghost Rider. Bandit 60 miles at 050 and flight level 30. Come to 060 and engage."

Puck on the radio, "60 miles, 060 at 30. Knight 211 is in."

ENS Jose 'Speedy' Gonzales, RIO for Knight 212, Lt. Hunt's

wingman, says, "Knight 212 is high cover." Because the rules of engagement for this action is "one on one", her wingman has to stay out of the fight. They will engage afterward.

Spike rolls the F-14 on its side and pulls in a tight turn, saying, "Grunt." Both pilot and RIO repeatedly squeeze their butt and leg muscles to keep blood in their brains as the turn increases the G load on their bodies.

Straightening her plane's trajectory, Spike says, "Tally-ho." Another F-14 is closing on her Tomcat head to head. The two fighters close at a combined speed of over 1200 knots as they pass in the merge.

Spike says, "Grunt. Burners on," and lights the afterburners, pulling into a climb. Sam smiles, "God this is great. The fight is on."

Puck says, "It's Book. He's climbing to meet us. Turn right a bit to clear him." Spike makes the adjustment, throttles back and extends the air brake briefly, and the other F-14 shoots past them, crossing in a vertical scissors. She has to win this one, but she's up against LCDR John 'Book' Carleton, the executive officer of her squadron, VF-154, the Black Knights, and he's good. She goes to zone 5 afterburner, climbing straight up and spinning the fighter to line up on the other plane. She can tell by his maneuver that he's playing it safe. By the book.

Puck, breathing hard because of the G's they're pulling, says, "Roll and pull to stay inside him."

"I got it," Sam grunts. She sees Book invert into a dive and pulls the stick into her gut, looping over in pursuit. She leaves her afterburners on in the dive to gain airspeed, then throttles back to full military as she levels out. She thinks, "Ok, you're going to scissor, and then I have you."

Puck says, "He's rolling and pulling. A diving scissors. Roll right and pull."

Saying nothing, she whips the 55,000-pound F-14 into a tight barrel roll, then pulls the stick into her belly, "Grunt." She's now below and behind the other fighter. "You can't see me. Got to roll or climb to find me."

Book pulls up, climbing into a loop. Following him, she becomes visible in the turn. As Book crosses vertical, he does a snap roll, reversing back into a vertical scissors.

Puck says, "He's back to the vertical scissors. Get on him." She turns early, trying to stay on Book's six in the vertical scissors, and for a moment, they can't see their opponent below their nose. When he doesn't cross where she expected, she snap rolls and pulls back across vertical, trying to find him.

Puck says, "Spike, he's on our six. Break right." She rolls her bird and pulls right. Book follows her turn. She rolls over the top into a dive trying to shake him. Unloading her wings, she snap rolls right and pulls out of the dive in a twisting climb. Through it all he stays on her.

Then they hear Lt. Lyle 'Packs' Boxter, Book's RIO say, "Guns. Guns. Guns. We got you Spike and Puck."

"Fuck." Spike grimaces.

Puck on the radio, "Acknowledge guns. Good fight Packs."

He replies, "Well fought guys."

Puck answers, "Thank you, sir."

In Knight 224, Books F-14, he says to his RIO, "We got that fucking bitch. Maybe now she won't be so full of herself. Stupid cunt belongs in the kitchen of some east fucking Tennessee cabin making babies for Huck Finn."

Pack shakes his head, "It's 1V1, boss. It's not like we won the Super Bowl. Could you clean it up some, boss? You're doubling my prayer time."

Calming down, Book replies, "Ok. Ok. Sorry for yelling. I just hate chicks taking up billets guys are supposed to fill. You did good."

"Knight 212, this is Ghost Rider, Bandit at 050 and angels 35, steer 010 to engage." Lt. Frank 'Thud' Jackson, pilot of Knight 212, responds and turns his F-14 into the fight. In moments he has taken out Books wingman, Lt. Stephan 'Swede' Swedenborg. "Damn, that was fast," says Puck. Then, "Knight 212, 35 and 010 for point X-ray." Then to Spike, "Thud is high at 7 o'clock,"

"Right," says Spike, and they settle on course and climb to continue their mission. In a moment, her wingman, 'Thud' Jackson is on their wing in loose deuce formation. They fly in silence for a time. "Puck, I know we've only flown together for a month, and we're fresh out of fighter school. And I know this is your first deployment. I get it, but, in a knife fight tell me where they are, not where to steer. Ok?"

"In RIO school, we are taught to tell the pilot where to go so we can use the weapon system."

"That's fine for long range missile attacks, but in a knife fight, I need to fly the plane."

"I still have to warn you about collisions."

"Yes, I know. Oh, forget it."

The sea below fades to a darker blue as the westering sun sets. The two fighters slide gracefully through the air, doing lazy eights at 35,000 feet on far CAP. The engines are just about idling, their vibration a comfortable thrum. As flight leader, Spike's plane is 200 yards ahead and to the left of her wingman's. She loves flying the Tomcat. She loved her E-2 Hawkeye radar plane, but when the Navy opened up a few slots for females to transition to fighters, she had to go all in.

The radio crackles to life, "Puck, Speedy, there's a fishing boat down there dead in the water." Puck on intercom, "Because it's fishing?" Then on radio, "How do you know it's in distress? It could just be fishing?"

Spike asks, "What do you see, Puck?" She straightens out the big jet, making it easier for Puck to track the vessel. "Ok, got it. Yeah, he's right. It's dead in the water." Using the camera mounted under the chin of the F-14, and behind the radar dome, the RIO can see the long distances required for targeting the long-range Phoenix missiles the Tomcat is designed to use. It's also very useful for other things, like inspecting a fishing boat from 35,000 feet.

"Puck, Speedy. It's Japanese, and it looks like they've had a fire."

"Ok, Speedy, I'll call it in."

Spike asks, "Can you get a range and bearing?"

Puck grimaces, "Can I give you a range and bearing? Um, gee, we're tooling around up here in $45 million of the highest tech whiz bang out here."

"We need to give Gold Eagle its location, not ours. Sorry, Puck"

"22 miles at 272," says Puck. Then, switching to strike frequency, "Gold Eagle, Knight 211. We have a Japanese fishing boat in distress 22 miles from our position at 272, request permission for a low-speed flyby."

"Knight 211, Gold Eagle, how do you know it's in distress? Is the flag upside down?"

Speedy comes on the radio, "Gold Eagle, Knight 212. It's Japanese. The meatball looks the same both ways."

"Knight 211, Gold Eagle, send one bird for low-speed flyby, the other stays at angels 35."

Puck says, "Roger, Gold Eagle, Knight 211 out. Ok, Speedy, you go. We've got you on top."

Turning to the west, she angles the F-14 so she can watch her wingman descend, wings spread to keep it slow. The last rays of the setting sun set Thud's and Speedy's plane aglow with crimson and gold against the deepening blue of the sky as they turn on their lights in the encroaching darkness.

A few of minutes later, "Puck, Speedy. Yeah, they're in distress. They're signaling with a light and waving their arms. I couldn't raise them on 16. We best call in the cavalry."

"Roger, Speedy. Gold Eagle, Knight 211. We have confirmation, the Japanese fishing vessel is in distress. We are at their location and standing by."

"Understood, Knight 211. We're sending out a surface unit."

Thud climbs and returns to Spikes wing. Once again, they're making lazy eights in the darkening sky.

Puck says, "Spike, did I ever tell you a F-14 is mighty pretty in the setting sun?"

"They are, aren't they?"

"Speedy, Puck. What's your fuel state?"

"Still have 15 minutes of loiter, Puck. I'm at 11K."

"Okay, Speedy. We have 11 decimal 5. Ten more minutes."

"Gold Eagle, Knight 211. What's the ETA on the surface unit?"

"Knight 211, Gold Eagle. Hewitt should be in sight, but it's still 70 minutes out."

"Roger, Gold Eagle. We have only 10 minutes more on station."

"Understood, Knight 211. One moment."

They wait, still doing lazy eights and keeping an eye on the trawler. "Wish we could talk to them, so they knew help is coming," says Spike.

"Yeah, that would be nice. Fire at sea is terrifying."

"Knight 211, Gold Eagle. Contact Hewitt on 19 decimal 2 and give them a steer, please."

"Roger, Gold Eagle, 19 decimal 2."

"Spike, I found the Hewitt and they're in a hurry. Good.

Switching to 19 decimal 2."

"Hewitt, Knight 211."

"Go ahead, Knight 211, this is Hewitt actual," comes back a female voice.

"Hewitt, Knight 211, come to 242, you are about 50 miles out."

Spike says, "I know her. Well, I met her in Hawaii."

"Knight 211, good job spotting the disabled vessel. Most fighter types don't look down."

"Thank you, ma'am. It was spotted by our wingman, Knight 212."

"Do you have time for a flyby?"

Puck says, "Sorry, Hewitt, we're pretty much bingo fuel. Good luck, and take care, Knight 211 out."

Changing frequency, "Speedy, Puck. Time to head home."

"Roger that, Puck."

They turn, speeding through the twilight, their lights flashing, heading for home. Home for the Black Knight squadron is the USS Carl Vinson, CVN-70, a Nimitz-class nuclear-powered aircraft carrier.

Puck asks, "You said you know her?"

"Yes, I met her on Waikiki. She and Gloria tried to teach me to surf. It wasn't pretty, but it was fun."

"Let me guess, she looks like Margaret Thatcher in bloomers."

"Nope. In fact, she looked pretty good in a bikini."

"Commanders shouldn't wear bikinis."

Spike smiles, "Why not?"

"They are senior officers, and...never mind."

It's full dark as they approach the carrier and flight operations are wrapping up. The flight deck is lit up with yellow lights, just enough illumination for the deck crews to do their jobs.

"Puck, have Thud land first."

"Ok." On radio, "Speedy, Puck. You have the lead."

"Roger, Puck. We go first. Gold Eagle, Knight 212, request to marshal. Fuel state is 2 decimal 7."

The controller in the Carrier Air Traffic Control Center (CATCC) says, "Roger, Knight 212, enter your downwind leg at 210. You'll be landing behind Magic 417."

Puck says, "Gold Eagle, Knight 211. Request to enter marshal. Fuel state is 2 decimal 5."

"Roger, Knight 211, Eagle approach. Enter the downwind leg at 210. You'll be landing behind Knight 212."

"Roger, Eagle."

Spike says, "Puck, here we go. Night landings, I so love them."

"Yes, ma'am. We're at 1, 5 hundred, radar off, board green."

They watch as Thud and Speedy make the break, a sharp 180 degree turn that lines the aircraft up with the stern of the carrier.

"Ok, Puck. Engines are good, gear and flaps down, making the break."

Then, "Gold Eagle, Magic 417 aborting landing. Bird strike."

"Roger, Magic 417. Do you need to eject?"

Lt. JG Mike 'Too Tall' Mohr, pilot of Magic 417 replies, "Negative, Gold Eagle. We're still flying. Canopy is damaged and covered in crap. The ILS is out. I can't see much out of the front of the cockpit, and the wind is a bit intense."

Knight 212 lands, catching the 3 wire.

"Magic 417, we are in blue water operations. There are no alternative landing fields. If you cannot land, I advise you to eject."

Listening intently, Sam say, "Abort landing." She raises the landing gear and trims the plane for flight. "Tell him we'll fly his wing and guiding him down."

Puck says, "Magic 417, Knight 211. We see you. Keep it straight and level. We'll come in on your left wing." Then, "Spike, I'll keep the spacing and you fly the approach."

"Got it, Puck. I can do it. Ok, I've got him."

Puck says, "Magic 417, you're slowly climbing through angels 4. We'll be on your wing in 15 seconds."

"Grunt, Puck," and they make a high G turn to parallel the EA-6B.

"Ok, Spike, I've got the spacing, you watch the instruments."

"Got it, Puck. You have him?"

"Yes, Spike. We're pulling a bit ahead. They're 50 feet behind…30…10…ok, got them. Let's get them down."

Puck says, "Ok, Magic, can you see me?"

Lt. JG Mohr replies, "Yeah, I got you. I'm Too Tall, ok?"

"Ok, Too Tall, I'm Puck, and my pilot is Spike. Let's keep it about 50 feet off my wing and we'll do a gentle turn to the left."

Gold Eagle breaks in, "Knight 211, Eagle approach. What are your intentions?"

"Gold Eagle, Knight 211. We'll fly the ball 50 feet to the left and guide him in. Hopefully, he can see well enough to land once he is close."

"Magic 417, Eagle approach. We advise ejection. What are your intentions?"

"Eagle, Magic 417. Our seats look damaged. I don't know if they will work. We would like to attempt a landing first. If we can't set it down, we will bail out."

"Roger, Magic 417. Do you want the barricade?"

"Negative, Eagle. Knight 211 has to land after us. We will make it, or we won't."

"Understood, Magic 417. Knight 211, landing speed for an EA-6B is 110 knots. The deck is yours."

"Roger, Eagle approach. The deck is ours."

"Too Tall, Puck. How you doing?"

"I can see you fine. It would be better if it weren't for all the blood and guts in the cockpit."

"How are your co-pilot and crypto-tech?"

"Ok, just covered in dead bird goo."

"Well, you tenderized him, Too Tall. He should fry up nice when we get to the boat." On intercom, "We're pulling ahead, Spike."

"Got it. Starting another slow left turn to line up for a long approach."

Puck, "Ok, Too Tall. We're going to take an easy left turn to line up for a long approach."

"Got it, Puck. We're with you."

"Pulling ahead, Spike."

"Got it, slowing to 110 knots." The F-14 starts swaying back and forth, fighting a stall. She raises the nose, giving it a little more power, barely able to see the ship ahead.

"Knight 211, Magic 417, Eagle approach. Call the ball."

Spike on intercom, "Got it."

Puck on radio, "Roger, ball."

Too Tall says, "I can't see it."

Puck on intercom, "We're wobbling a bit."

Spike, "Got it."

"Magic 417, call the ball."

The Landing Signal Officer (LSO) on the flight deck says, "Magic, you're a little high."

Puck starts calling the altitude, "400...300."

Too Tall says, "Roger, ball, 4, 2."

Puck, "200...150."

The LSO says, "Looking good, Magic. Now, cut"

The EA-6B hits the deck, catching the 1 wire.

Spike rolls on the throttle, breaking left, rocketing the F-14 back into the sky. Puck says, "Gold Eagle, Knight 211, pulling up and left."

"Roger, Knight 211. The sky is yours. Mark fuel state."

"Eagle, Knight 211. Fuel is 1 decimal 8. Request to re-enter marshal."

"Roger, Knight 211, come to 210 for the downwind. You're the last bird up."

"Roger, Gold Eagle, coming to 210 for the downwind." The F-14 descends on the downwind leg, makes the break four miles behind the carrier and lines up for the landing. In the deep darkness, the Vinson looks like a dimly lit postage stamp.

"Knight 211, Eagle approach. Call the ball."

"Roger, ball, 49."

The F-14A+ hits the deck in a beautiful landing. The three-wire screaming as it slows the plane to a stop against the power of full afterburners. Power needed if the aircraft misses the wires and needs to get airborne again. The wire slowly pulls the F-14 backwards, as Spike returns the throttles to idle and then raises the hook.

Retracting the wings to the storage position, she slowly bumps the throttles and moves the plane out of the landing zone. A yellow shirt direct them to a parking spot, chains the plane down, and only then, do they signal for engine shut down. Puck and Spike work through the post flight check list as the engines spool down. Their plane captain opens the steps and knocks on the side of the aircraft. Only then does Spike raise the canopy. They disconnect their harnesses and complete the post flight checklist.

Climbing out of the plane, Puck say, "Spike…"

"Yeah, Puck?"

A tall, young, sandy-haired man in a flight suit runs up, "That was amazing flying, Spike. Damn amazing."

"Thank you, Thud. You and Speedy, ok?"

Puck hits the deck at her side, "We best get to debrief. We all know Book doesn't like people running late."

PRI-FLY ABOVE THE BRIDGE

The Air Boss, Commander Charley Forrester, watches them leave the flight deck. He turns to the Mini Boss, "What do you think of women flying fighters?"

The Mini Boss, LCDR John Gooding says, "I'm all for it. How else could you get a blow job from a senior officer?"

"Not from her. You'd get frostbite on your pecker."

"Yeah, but Hoolihan, she's alright."

"There will be none of that here gentleman," says Captain Lee, as he walks up behind them.

An enlisted woman wearing sound powered phones behind them, says a belated, "CAG on deck." The Air Boss gives her an angry look, then says, "Yes, sir."

The CAG, or Commander of the Air Group, is Captain Richard 'Dixie' Lee. He owns all the air squadrons and squadron operations. He gives the two officers a thoughtful look, "Is there a problem, Commander Forrester, Lieutenant Commander Gooding?"

"No, sir."

Lee shakes his head, "We all have a job to do. Let's focus on it, gentleman. I'm up here to tell you we need to double check the tie downs tonight. Meteorology says it will be bumpy. Carry on, gentleman."

CHAPTER 2

USS CARL VINSON, 03 LEVEL AFT

2103 December 19TH, 1990

Spike, Puck, Thud, and Speedy walk through the crowded warren of corridors below the flight deck on the 03 level to their squadron ready room. For the aircrew of the Black Knights the ready room is home. As they enter, six officers are already seated and a tall, graying man in working khakis and a gold leaf on each collar is standing at the podium. He gives them the stern look of a displeased schoolmaster as they come in.

"Hey Spike, do we need to change your call sign to Pathfinder?" asks a grinning curvaceous red-haired woman.

"Gloria," sighs Sam.

LCDR Carleton at the podium says, "That's enough. Okay, attention to the debriefing. Lieutenant JG Hoolihan?"

The red-head, Lt. JG Gloria 'Hot Pants' Hoolihan, says, "Well, sir, a pretty standard mission. Launch and climb to 35, went out to point Yoke and orbited with no contacts. The Stoddert requested a high-speed flyby on the return leg, and with the captain's permission, we obliged. Came home, trapped, no excitement."

"Anything to add, Ensign Stanley?"

Ensign 'GQ' Stanley, Gloria's RIO, says, "That's about it, sir. The light breaker popped on launch, and I put in a gripe on the radar because the joy stick is a bit loose, but otherwise, routine."

"Ok, Lieutenant Harden?"

Lt. JG John 'Gunner' Harden says, "Hot Pants pretty much covered it." Some of the guys snicker and Gunner gives them a stern look, continuing, "Straight forward CAP mission. We have a hydraulic leak in the right main gear that the guys are fixing tonight."

"Lieutenant Jacobs?"

Lt. JG Wally 'NOB' Nelson, Gunner's RIO, says, "Gunner and Miss Hoolihan covered it, sir."

"Ok, next flight. Lieutenant Hunt, how did your flight go?"

"Very well, sir. Launched, climbed to angels 25 on our way to X-ray. Did the 1V1 with the unit we relieved, then loitered. We were 25 minutes into loiter when Ensign Gonzales spotted a Japanese fishing vessel in distress. We reported it, investigated, and they sent in the Hewitt to render aid. Returned to base, Ensign Jackson trapped, then we trapped after Magic 417. They had a little trouble getting down, sir."

"Oh, come now, Lieutenant. We needn't be modest. Let's include the heroics of the night."

"Heroics, sir?" Sam cringes inside. Please no.

Carleton gives her a long look, "That will do. Everyone dismissed. Lieutenant Hunt, a minute please."

As everyone else files out, Eric walks up to the podium with Sam. Carleton glances at him and says, "That will do, Lieutenant Hawke." Eric shrugs and leaves.

Carleton turns back to Sam, "That is a 45-million-dollar aircraft that you were showboating with out there. Wing gliding with an EA-6B! What were you thinking?"

Sam looks down, silent.

"Well, come on."

"Sir, I was not showboating. A colleague was in trouble. I had to help."

Carleton shakes his head, "One misstep, one error, one slight misjudgment, and I'm writing home to your parents right now. Do you understand, Lieutenant? Do you?"

Someone clears their throat behind Carleton and Captain Lee says, "No, Lieutenant Commander, I would be writing that letter. That was the most beautiful bit of flying I've seen in a long time. Gutsy as hell."

Carleton says, "Sir, if something had gone wrong..."

"Nothing went wrong, Commander." Lee turns to Sam, "Lieutenant Hunt walk with me. Excuse us, Commander." Lee turns and walks out of the door.

Sam says, "By your leave, sir." He says nothing and she turns and follows Lee.

As they walk through the ship, crewman step aside and Lee greets them as they pass, shaking hands as he goes. "Captain Johnson wants to see you on the bridge. He asked me to fetch you. How are you doing, Sam?"

She finally exhales, "I'm good. How are you, Rick?"

"Ok, busy. But that's a good thing. You okay with Carleton?"

"Yeah, I'm okay. I'm used to it."

He stops and turns toward her, "If you were having problems would you tell me?"

"Sir, he is just sore because I got on his six earlier in 1V1."

"You beat him?"

"No, I over anticipated and he got me."

He smiles, "Spike, you're one hell of a pilot. Hell, you've been on my six before. If he gets out of hand, tell me, ok?"

"Yes, sir."

"Ok, I'll leave you here. Take care."

She watches him walk away, "You too, Dixie," and starts the

five-story climb to the bridge.

BLACK KNIGHTS CO'S OFFICE

LCDR Carleton knocks, then walks into Commander James 'Pappa' Holtz's office. "Captain Lee seems to think it was a great idea to have a green split tail pilot showboating with a 45-million-dollar airplane. That bitch is going to be impossible now."

Holtz shakes his head, "Why are you pissed? I mean, she pulled it off, didn't she?"

"No, boss. She just got lucky up there. That's it, she is lucky. What the hell does the CAG see in her anyway? I think her name should start with a 'c', not 'h'."

"Book, rein it in. Understand, damn it, I don't like women in uniform any more than you do. I think women in uniform are a hazard to navigation. We don't need a whole bunch of hormones flying around the ship when the shit hits the fan. It's going to be nothing but trouble."

"Then why don't you get rid of her?"

"You can't just fire someone because they don't have a dick, Book."

"Why not? All you have to do is take away her flight cert, simple as that. She can't fly. She goes away."

"Why in hell would I do that, Book? She has a better landing record than you do. She's a stone-cold bitch, don't get me wrong. She just doesn't make mistakes. Look at it like this, Book. The Navy has changed. Warfare has changed. Women are flying aircraft now, and that's not going to change. I hate it, too, but I deal with it. If she makes one little itsy-bitsy mistake, I'll send her home on rails. But, until then, you shut up and put up with it. Book, you're never going to make commander with an attitude like yours. You have to shut your mouth and do your fucking job."

"I do rein it in in front of her. But, you and me, we can talk, right?"

"Yes, we can talk, which means most of the time I talk and you shut up," Pappa pauses. "You know she was an E-2 driver before she went to jets. Captain Lee wrote her recommendation to fighter school. I heard they deployed together in the Med."

"Oh, I see! So, the CAG has a piece on the side," says Book.

"You just stop that talk! It ain't no such thing. If word got around that's what you were thinking, Book, Lee would have you cleaning shitters the rest of the cruise. Besides, anybody stick their dick in that, it would freeze to ice and shatter into shards."

Book finally laughs, "So true."

"You know she got her call sign, Spike, at the fighter training squadron. When she flew E-2's, they called her "CIB". It stood for 'cold intellectual bitch.'"

"Did she know that?"

"From what I heard, she carried it like a badge of honor. Book, just keep off her ass and let me deal with her, ok?"

"Okay, boss. But, I don't like it."

THE LADDER TO THE BRIDGE,

2141 HRS (1141 ZULU)

Lieutenant Hunt, climbing the ladder, hears over the 1MC, "Flight quarters, flight quarters. All hands to your flight quarter stations to receive a medevac helo." Finally, she reaches the bridge and stops before entering. The bridge is the navigational brain of the ship. It is filled with watch standers in pressed dungarees. This is the commanding officer's domain. Where airdales rarely come.

Lt. Warren, the Officer of the deck (OOD), stands next to the captain's chair briefing him, "The Long Beach has a wounded sailor, partial amputation of a hand. Camden has a helo up returning from the Stoddert and has offered to make the transfer. Long Beach and Camden are coming alongside and medical has been informed."

Captain William "Hoser" Johnson says, "Very well, Lieutenant Warren. Mind the helm closely while we have the ships alongside."

Lieutenant Warren is a nuclear power officer who normally runs the 1 Plant Reactor Electrical Division. He smiles, "Yes, sir. Shall I call a master helmsman?"

"No, that won't be necessary."

A petty officer walks up behind Lt. Hunt, and says quietly, "Ma'am, you have to request permission to enter the bridge," then raises his voice, "Request to enter with dispatches."

The OOD says, "Enter."

Sam says, "Request to enter and speak with the Captain."

The OOD looks her over, cocks his head, and says, "No flight suits on the bridge."

Captain Johnson looks up, "I'll waive it this time OOD. She's the 14 driver who helped the 6B onto the boat."

The OOD shrugs and says, "Enter," then to the lee helm, "Ahead 2/3rds."

The lee helm repeats, "Ahead 2/3rds at 080, aye, sir."

Johnson says to Sam, "Grab a cup of coffee and the cookies are good, Lieutenant."

"Thank you, sir. I'm sure they are, sir."

"Go ahead. One cookie won't ruin your figure."

Watching the approaching ships through the windscreen, he says, "That was some nice flying, Lieutenant. I flew '4's off the Enterprise in 'Nam, and qualified on the '14 when the Navy transitioned. Tell me, how did you guide him down?"

She can see out the windscreen the vista of the flight deck, aircraft tied down for the night, and the USS Long Beach steaming alongside only 1000 yards away. Sam turns back to the Captain, in rigid control, "My RIO handled the positioning of the EA-6B, sir. All I had to do was fly the bird, sir."

"Yeah, that's what I thought. So, not only good at flying, but good judgment, too. Who's your RIO?"

"Lt. JG Hawke, sir."

"Is this our first tour in the F-14?"

"Yes, sir."

As they watch, a Chinook settles onto the Long Beach's flight deck, just as lightning strikes near the battle group. The OOD interrupts, "Captain, you might want to look at this."

A large web of lightning begins flashing above the ships, spiraling down towards the sea, a tornado of blue white light. As the lightning web slowly gets closer, the winds gust up, and the Vinson flight deck crew run out onto the deck, preparing for the Chinook.

THE AUSTRALIAN OUTBACK

2141 (1141 ZULU), December 19TH, 1941

Inside a three-story room, 100 feet on a side, stands a metal column. On the column is a sphere with a spike. The spike tapers to a fine point just short of a closed retractable roof. On the opposite sides of the room are two banks of electrical capacitors, each in its own cage. In a corner is a small glassed in control room. Inside, two men face each other.

"Dr. Heinlein, let's see what his Majesty's government has spent all this money on, shall we?" He gestures to the device, "Just what does this thing do?"

"General, have you not read the briefing materials?"

"Yes, but I thought it something out of a H.G. Wells novel and not to be taken seriously."

"Herr General, we are at war. This," waving at the room, "will win the war and crush the regime of the horrible man, Hitler. Tonight, we make history."

"This is personal, Dr. Heinlein?"

The doctor gives the general a measuring look, "Yes, Kristallnacht. My uncle and two of my brothers were killed. I barely escaped. The monster must pay."

A technician approaches, "Doctor, all is ready. The final capacitor is charged."

"Very good, Stephen, inform the others it is time to come to the control room." He steps up onto a platform containing an electrical console with a mass of gauges and instruments on three levels. He motions to the general to join him as the technicians file into the room and find their places at consoles facing the device. The control room glass goes all the way to the ceiling, shimmering with a golden sheen.

"Would you wish the honor of throwing the main switch, Herr General?"

Stepping down from the platform the general says, "No, Doctor, it is your device. The honor should be yours."

"Stephen, open the roof, please." The technician pushes a button, motors spin up, whining, and the roof panel slowly opens. "Gentleman, all gauges reading correctly?"

"Yes, Doctor, all the readings are correct. The capacitors are at maximum. The skies are clear. We are ready," answers Stephen.

"Very well, gentlemen, we look forward to our future." He throws the switch. The banks of capacitors release all of their power into the device at once. Even protected by the Faraday cage of the control room, the men's hair stands on end. Static electricity dances over their bodies, running around the room in a terrifying display. Only the general does not pass out, but even he must hold onto the console to keep from falling.

BRIDGE, USS CARL VINSON

2152 (1152), 19 December, 1990

Captain Johnson grabs the ship to ship radio, "Long Beach, this is Vinson actual, ground that bird." Grabbing the hand mic, "Clear the flight deck and all weather decks. All hands seek shelter immediately."

Then the lightning meets the sea.

An enormous static charge builds in the ships surrounded by the lightning tornado. A Tesla coil of energy strikes the Vinson's flight deck dead center and the static electricity discharges, running from person to person, structure to person, in a brilliant dancing hell. Sam is driven to the deck, her hands frozen fists, unable to break her fall. She sees Johnson hit the deck, going to his knees, electricity dancing up his torso, the look on his face more that of surprise than pain. Then the world goes black.

NUMBER 2 REACTOR AUXILIARY ROOM, USS CARL VINSON

2141, 19 December, 1990

When nothing is going on, it's not uncommon for watch standers in the power plant to congregate to talk. One of those locations in the RAR is the generator flat upper level. As the lightning begins, men are gathered around Senior Chief Harvey, the standing Engineer Watch Supervisor. EMCS Harvey gives a shit about his guys and always does his best. But, the gym, where's that? So, he's a little out of shape and the stairs are a bit difficult for him. Tonight, he's made it up to the generator flat to talk to his guys about the last propulsion plant drill set and what they could do better. But, as usual, it quickly devolves into where the next port of call is, which is Subic Bay, the Navy's forward base in the Philippines. His ample frame in the only chair, the four men are on Vidmars drinking sodas.

"What's Subic like, Senior?" asks MM2 John Nolan.

"Well, the last time I was in Subic the girls cost, oh, about ten bucks. Now, you want to watch where it is you go dip your wicks, if you hear me. My first time, I got the clap, not that I'm proud of it. But that's the way it was. So, what I'm sayin' boys, if your gonna hump, you better wrap your stump. And you better be careful where you decide to spend your money. What I do is, I walk into the bathroom. If it's clean, I figure that's the kind of establishment I could spend some money and some time. If the bathroom is a shithole, you can pretty much figure everything else is. There's other things to do in Subic besides drinking and fucking. Shopping is good, and cheap. It's fairly safe 'cause the locals don't like sailors getting rolled. It's bad for business. Not that you're going to be stupid or anything, but only bring the amount of money you want to spend, and keep it in your front pocket." Grinning, "Were I you, I'd wrap a twenty around your crank."

"Now, why would we want to do that?" asks MM3 Shirley.

"Well, it's an old trick taught me be a gunner's mate I knew. You see, you put your twenty down there and every time a girl goes reaching for your crank you realize all she's after is your money." Grinning, he leans back, enjoying their laughter.

Then lightning begins sparkling on the reactor compartment bulkhead, just a small flash, then two, fairly quickly building into a stream of light and energy in the RAR. EMCS Harvey drops the front of his chair down, startled. "What the hell is that? Boys, back to your stations!" The lightning builds as the sailors' scatter to their watch stations, most not making it. Senior Chief feels pain building in his chest, pulsing with the lightning dancing in the compartment. Clutching his chest with his right hand, he holds his left hand up, watching St. Elmo's fire running along his fingers. The last thing he sees as he falls to the deck is an intense web of lightning hitting a locker on the outboard wall, pulsing into a sphere of light, then flashing out of existence as the light in his eyes fades and goes out.

DR. HEINLEIN'S LAB, AUSTRALIAN OUTBACK

2157 (1157 ZULU), 19 December, 1941 (PRIME)

As the lightning storm wanes, the device is smoking, but otherwise undamaged by the discharge. One of the cabinets is on fire and a pall of smoke fills the room as the men come groggily to their feet. "Gentlemen, fire extinguishers," barks the general.

Dr. Heinlein comes to, looking around, "Mein Gott!" He looks up and gets to his feet, "Shall we see what the future has brought us, Herr General?"

They all go to the military vehicles parked outside in the compound of metal-sided and roofed buildings baking in the desert sun. It only takes a few minutes to drive the five miles to the secondary facility. Here, standing outside, is a much smaller device. It is undamaged. They look around and see scrub vegetation, red dirt, the tracks of small animals. There is nothing else, nothing.

Dr. Heinlein looks around dismayed, "No! No! This cannot be!"

CHAPTER 3

CHITOSE AIR BASE, HOKKAIDO, JAPAN

2157 (1157 ZULU), 19 December, 1941

Ichiro Nagasawa walks out of his ground floor office and surveys the skies. An aeronautical engineer and test pilot with Mitsubishi Heavy Industries, he is up from Tokyo supervising upgrades on the F-15J fighters on the base. He has never experienced such a severe lightning storm and is not surprised that the city's lights have gone out, but it is a strange and eerie sight to see only blackness.

Hearing the sound of a prop plane above him, he looks up to see a Mitsubishi Zero attempting a landing, then pull up and fly overhead. He realizes he did not make a mistake, it is a Zero. The profile is unmistakable. The Zero flies off south and Captain Hachirou Oshiro, the duty officer with the 203rd Fighter Squadron joins him, "That was an amazing storm, Nagasawa-san. It shook my bones."

Ichiro says, "I thought I saw a Zero fighter. It seems improbable one would fly here."

LEICHFELD AIR FORCE BASE, 20km SOUTH OF AUGSBURG, GERMANY

0135 (1157 ZULU), 19 December, 1941

Captain Louis Mossberg, USMC, is the first to recover as the lightning storm subsides. From the shelter of the wing of his F/A-18 fighter he watches his ground crew come too. Stepping out, all the tall black man sees is clear blue skies. "That storm passed fast, I've never seen anything like it." Then he sees a formation of single propeller aircraft approaching. One peels off and dives toward the runway, guns blazing. "Mother fucker, take cover guys," and dives for cover.

"What was that, Captain?" asks his plane captain.

Staring in disbelief at the iron cross on the Messerschmitt 109, he says, "Hell boys. Hell. Let's see if we can get this bird into the air."

NIZHNY TAGIL INDUSTRIAL CITY, USSR

1657 (1157 ZULU), 19 December, 1941

As the lightning storm fades away, General Yuri Kryukov walks onto his office balcony, marveling how such a fierce storm could fade so fast. Commander of the 14th Combined Arms Army posted at Nizhny Tagil, his is an enviable assignment. His location near the factory, his connections in Moscow, and the fact his unit tests the newest tanks and armored vehicles means he's in a position to move up, gaining both power and privilege. But this storm worries him.

Looking out over the industrial city and the drill fields below him, he realizes something is very wrong. The city beyond his field is gone, just gone. Nothing but trees. There are no drab industrial apartments standing in row after row. Turning, he runs into his office and grabs the phone just as a red-faced lieutenant colonel runs in, gasping for air. The two men stare at each other in dismay.

USS CARL VINSON BATTLE GROUP, WESTERN PACIFIC

2157 (1157 ZULU), 19 December, 1941

The static dissipates and Lt. Sam Hunt comes too on her side, staring at the Captain's chair. All her muscles scream as she struggles to rise. Grabbing the chair, she uses it to lever herself up and shakes her head to clear her sight.

The Captain pushes himself up and croaks out, "Mind your helm!"

Sam sees the helmsman on his back and the wheel turning. Looking up, she sees the 90,000-ton carrier drifting toward the Long Beach on the port side. She launches herself to the wheel and turns it right, praying she's doing it right.

The Captain struggles to her side and points to the rudder position indicator, "5-degree right rudder." Turning the rudder, she says, "Yes, sir."

He makes his way to the OOD station and grabs a mic and shouts into it, "All stations, damage report." Then to Sam, "Rudder amidships, steady as she goes."

"Yes, sir," turning the rudder back to zero degrees.

Then the Captain barks, "Back full emergency!" Sam looks at him, bewildered, and Johnson grabs the Engine Order Telegraph, ringing it back and forth, then to Back Full, "Turn the dial to the bell I order, ok?"

"Yes, sir, the bell you order." Then the response comes in form the engine rooms.

Johnson says, "Good, the engine rooms are awake."

The lee helmsman manages to get to his feet, holding his hand against his head, "What just happened?"

Sam says, "It doesn't matter. Are you the helmsman?" The ship begins to shake with the backing bell.

BMSN Jeremy Turnkey replies, "No...no, ma'am. He's there," pointing at the unconscious form of a man on the deck. "I'm the lee helm. I do the engines, ma'am."

"Fine, take the throttles."

Johnson orders, "Right standard rudder. Oh, Lieutenant, that's 10 degrees, and all stop."

She nods to the order.

Johnson says, "Lieutenant, I need verbatim repeat backs."

"Yes, sir, right standard rudder, sir, and all stop." She turns the wheel as the lee helm orders all stop. "Sir, rudder is right 10 degrees and engines are at all stop."

"Very well."

The Vinson has nearly stopped moving, but the Camden and the Long Beach are still moving ahead and are coming closer together. Johnson grabs the ship to ship radio, "Long Beach, Vinson actual, you're drifting close to the Camden. Mind your helm, sir."

"This is Lt. Phillips, sir. The captain's unconscious."

"Then order back full and put your rudder amidships."

"Yes, sir."

"Camden, this is Vinson actual. Are you awake over there?"

A scratchy voice comes back, "What the hell just happened?"

"It doesn't matter right now. Mind your helm!"

The voice comes back, "Shit!"

Johnson sees Lt. Warren get to his feet, "Welcome back OOD, please check the fleet to our stern, sir."

Warren says, "Yes, sir," and wobbles out to the Aux Con to look aft.

Then, Johnson says, "Ahead 1/3rd." He picks up the VHF, "All units, Vinson actual, report."

"Long Beach has helm and steering." The rest of the ships in the group report in, all except Hewitt.

CHAPTER 4

ENGINE ROOM 1, USS LONG BEACH

2157, 19 December, 1941

"Wake the fuck up," yells MM1 Carl Colbert, Leading Petty Officer and Engine Room Supervisor in 1 Main, kicking one of his watch standers.

"Shit man, what the hell happened?" asks MM2 Maki.

"Just wake the fuck up and stand your watch, idiot. Let the brass figure it out."

Maki stands, rubbing his head from the clocking it took on the remote operator for the main sea water inlet valve. "But, what happened, Carl?"

"Listen up, dick weed, lightning hit all over the place, we got static cling from hell, and you're still not fucking standing your watch. The EOS is not responding, so set the emergency throttle watch."

"Yes, sir," and moves to the throttle panel in the enclosed operating station.

"Oh, don't make me hit you."

"Sorry, MM, um, sorry Carl." Taking control of one main, he quickly shuts the ahead throttle and starts opening the astern throttle. "The Bridge ordered back full emergency, boss." His loud shout can be barely heard over the running machinery where Colbert is now looking for the distilling plant watch.

"Then answer the fucking bell! God damn, I'm surrounded

40

by fucking idiots!"

The main engine rumbles as more and more steam dumps into it, forcing the shaft to stop spinning forward. For a second the shaft is motionless before it begins to spin astern. MM2 Maki shouts, "Shouldn't we start a second condensate pump?"

"Of course, we should start a second, oh shit, Dub…" Colbert runs down to lower level where he finds the Lower Level Watch, MM1 Walters, unconscious on Lube Oil Flat. Running forward, he starts the second pump as the level in the hot well rises nearly out of sight. Running back to Dub Walters, he hesitates. Walters is a big guy with a well-known temper. You don't kick Dub. Kneeling next to him, he gently shakes him awake, then turns and runs back to the upper level.

As he reaches the top of the ladder, he sees the TG DU watch walking from behind the turbine generator, sleepy eyed and confused, "Yo, dude, what happened?" Colbert grabs him by the shirt front and continues running into the control room. MM3 Jerry Small loses his footing and finds himself being dragged behind the running LPO. "Yo, dude, owe, shit, hey, shit, dude, owe, shit, owe, HEY DUD!" Colbert stops and looks at Small, realizing he's dragging him. With a confused look, "Man your watch, 'Dude'," and pushes him backward.

Then the 1MC announces, "USS Long Beach, this is your Captain. I'm not sure just what happened, but I believe we were hit by an EMP. At this time, I'm taking the ship to General Quarters. I want all watch standers to investigate the status of their equipment and report any casualties immediately to combat. Stay sharp!" And the 1MC sounds the familiar alarm, 'Gong. Gong. Gong.'

AFT SWITCH GEAR ROOM, USS HORNE

2157 December, 1941

EM2 Hanks comes to, slumped over his panel, with lights

flashing everywhere. Looking up, his face whitens, "Oh fuck, oh fuck, oh fuck. What did you do, Davy?" He picks up the phone and growls central control. Getting no response, he trips 2 breaker saying, "There, at least now the diesel will start." He can hear the rhythmic thumping start back aft. He tries central control again. Finally, someone comes on the sound powered phone, "Shit, what happened? Is this aft switch gear?"

Hanks replies, "Aft switch gear, we lost the aft half of the loop. Both of the turbine generators in number 2 engine room tripped out. I've started the aft diesel.

Lt. JG Indio says, "Understood EM2. We all passed out. Stand by."

Captain Rodgers comes up on the 1MC, "Horne, this is the Captain. We've lost steering control. Get off your asses and restore steering. Let's get hopping, folks."

As the diesel comes up to speed, the voltage automatically picks up the vital loads, including aft steering. Hanks picks up his coffee cup, finding only grounds, "Damn." He raises it in a salute, "Here's to you, Captain Jackass. Always on the problem five minutes too late."

NUMBER 2 ENGINE ROOM, USS FIFE

2157, 19 December, 1941

As the lightning fades away, a young sailor lies crumpled at the base of the ladder out of the engine room. Watchers sway to their feet, their brains slowly clearing. GSM2 Lance Smith sees the collapsed man and recognizes his friend, GSM3 Jamie Hernandez, "Hey, Jamie. JAMIE!" Smith runs over, grabs Jamie's shoulder and starts to turn him over. He then sees Jamie's head tilt at an impossible angle and stops, "Call medical! Somebody! Call medical, Jamie's hurt!"

His division officer, Lt. JG Laura Wakefield, grabs the phone and reports what turns out to be one of the only two fatalities from the storm. "Smith, you stay with Hernandez, ok?" She touches the young man on the shoulder, "Don't move him. Don't move him at all. But, you can touch him and let him know it's alright, ok? Help is coming. I have the engine room." GSM2 Lance Smith can only nod his head, tears streaming down his face.

BRIDGE, USS CARL VINSON

2228, 19 December, 1941

Captain Johnson puts up the VHS and picks up a phone, "Charley, can you get a bird up?"

CDR Charles Forrester, the air boss replies, "Sir, what the hell just happened? It was the damnedest thunderstorm I've ever seen."

"Charley, I think it was an EMP. The Hewitt isn't reporting in. We need to search."

"Sir, if it was an EMP shouldn't we check our electronics first? I don't want to launch someone to their death."

"You're right, damn it to hell. Ok, a surface search. Get your people going."

Admiral Ren walks onto the bridge as the boatswain at the lee helm announces, "Admiral on the bridge."

"Sorry, Will. I was, um, taking a nap. Did I hear right? The Hewitt is missing?"

"Evening, Admiral. Yes, sir. We all took a nap. Hewitt hasn't reported in, and all the ships have personnel injuries."

"Ok, first, tell all ships to stand down from General Quarters and tend their wounded. Does our radar work?"

"Yes, sir."

"Then presumably Long Beach and Horne have theirs as well. Let's light up the skies as we head back to Hewitt's last known position and start our search. Is there any word from Washington?"

"Not yet, sir. Lieutenant Warren, is anyone awake in radio?"

"Checking now, sir."

A corpsman shows up, "Medic on the bridge."

Johnson asks, "Over here, only one corpsman?"

"We're swamped, sir."

Johnson says, "Boatswains Mate of the Watch relieve the helm."

The BMOW says, "Relieve the helm, aye."

To Sam, "Ma'am, I'll relieve you on the helm."

Gratefully, Sam says, "Thank you," and steps away from the wheel.

BMOW, "Helm relieved. No course given."

Lt. Warren, back on the bridge, says, "No comms with radio, sir."

Turning to Lt. Hunt, Captain Johnson asks, "Could you take a message down to radio for me?"

"Yes, sir."

"It's to be sent 'Navy immediate, SITREP. Carrier Group 72 has been hit by a probable EMP. Damage assessment is on-going. Mission degradation is unknown. USS Hewitt is missing."

Writing the message down in her pocket brain, a small note-book, she asks, "Is there anything else, sir."

Warren says, "Sir, I need her full name and rank for the deck log."

"Yes, of course. Lieutenant, if you run into the DCA, I still need a damage report. And have radio call me here when the message is sent."

"Yes, sir," She turns to Lt. Warren, "Lt. Samantha Leigh Hunt,

VF-154."

Radio is located on the 03 level, amidships, so Sam goes down the ladders from the 07 level. As she does, a corpsman, running to another casualty shouts, "Make a hole!" She swiftly steps aside as he passes down the ladder. Then a lieutenant commander raises a hand to stop her, "What the hell just happened?"

Continuing on her way, she says, "Good question, sir. I'm on my way to radio to send a message for the Captain. Please stand aside."

"Well, what does it say?"

"Please ask the Captain, and stand aside."

Giving her a measured look, he steps aside. Pushing on, Sam arrives at radio, which has a cypher lock with a small grill and a buzzer for service. No one goes into radio, except radiomen. She pushes the button and seconds pass before the grill opens. A grumpy voice says, "We're a little busy in here, come back later," and the grill slams shut.

She jabs the button, over and over, then pounds on the door. Finally, the grill opens again, "I don't care if you are an officer, things are busy in here. Go away!" and starts to close the grill again.

"I've a message from the Captain. You're not answering your phone."

"Oh, oh, I'm sorry, ma'am."

"Are you ready to copy?"

'Uh, yes, ma'am, go ahead." She delivers the message, eyeing RM1 Denton behind the grill. "I don't know when we'll be able to send it out ma'am. All of our radio communications with higher are lost. That is why we are so busy."

"All of it?"

"Yes, ma'am, all of it, except local VHF between ships."

"You're talking about the conventional bands, right?"

"Well, yes, ma'am, all the secured lines of communication are down. We don't even have a satellite carrier signal."

"Pass me a phone."

"Yes, ma'am," passing her a phone through the grill. "I'll have to dial from here."

"Ok, dial the Captain's chair on the bridge."

"Yes, ma'am," and dials the phone.

From the receiver, "Bridge, Captain speaking."

"Captain, this is Lt. Hunt. I'm at radio. We have a situation, sir. The satellite signal is gone, and they're unable to pick up any traffic on the secure bands."

"I'm not terribly surprised. Our satellites are supposed to be hardened against EMP, but obviously the pulse took them out. Tell them to try sideband. Captain out."

She hands back the receiver, "The Captain says to try sideband. I would also try shortwave and any other frequencies that might work."

"Ok, we'll try, but it seems like everything is fried in here," and slides the grill shut.

Shaking her head as she walks away, "You've got to at least try."

CHAPTER 5

BLACK KNIGHT SQUADRON READY ROOM, USS CARL VINSON

2250, 19 December, 1941

Lt. Samantha Hunt heads for the Black Knights ready room a few frames aft of radio. When she walks in, the room is filled to capacity with all the pilots, RIO's, and some enlisted. Standing at the podium are CDR Holtz, LCDR Carleton, and the squadron ops officer, Lt. Stephan "Swede" Swedenborg. Holtz sees her and motions her over. "You were talking to the Captain when all this shit happened. Any idea what's going on?"

"Well, sir," then lowering her voice, Spike says, "Can we talk about this in private, sir?"

"Right now, doesn't seem a really good time for niceties."

"Right," she takes a deep breath, "Yes, sir. I was on the bridge when it happened. Sir, I don't know how much I should tell you right now."

"I don't understand. How about all of it, and let me make my own judgments." Holtz motions her to follow him and leads her into his office.

"Thank you, sir."

Once inside, he turns, "I just want to get to the bottom of this."

Sam sighs, "I don't know if the Captain is ready to tell everybody about this, and I don't want to break his confidence by saying anything without his permission."

"Okay, okay, I see. But we need to know at least if we're under attack."

"Okay, sir. The Captain thinks it may have been an EMP. It was a huge lightning storm. There was St. Elmo's fire on the bridge. It knocked everybody to the deck, and the helmsman was still unconscious when I left. I had to take the helm, sir. It was bad."

"Okay, continue."

"When I left the bridge, we had control of the ship, and the Captain sent me to radio with a message. The problem is… we lost contact with the satellites."

Holtz stares at her, "Lost contact with the satellites? The Captain may be right about that EMP. Fucking Russians. If it is that, we need to figure how many planes can still fly. Fuck, we could already be at war. See, that's why I needed to know."

"Sorry, sir."

Holtz brushes it off, "You were worried about pissing off the Captain. I understand. We need everybody, and I mean every-body, pilots and enlisted both, checking out our birds. If we were attacked, we need to be ready."

"Yes, sir."

Walking back into the ready room, Holtz says, "All right everybody, listen up. We road through a hell of a lightning storm, so, I want a full court press inspecting the birds. This means all hands, officers and office pukes, everyone down to the hangar bay and up on the flight deck. I want the status on every bird and immediate notification when a bird is ready to fly. Let's get busy, folks."

MAIN CONTROL, ENGINEERING DEPT., USS CARL VINSON

"All right people, what's going on with the power plant?"

asks the Reactor Officer (RO), Captain Klindt. He cocks his head, looking expectantly at Load Dispatcher, EM1 Zimmerman.

"All four turbine generators are up and running in a Gold Eagle four TG line up."

Damage Control Watch, HT1 Sandusky reports, "Damage control parties out and no damage reported at this time. Material condition Yoke set."

The EOOW Lt. Naihi reports, "Split and crit, sir. There is a medical emergency in 2 RAR. All four main engines making turns for 10 knots, one through four DU's up and making good water. Catapults secure at this time."

"Very well, report same to the bridge. Who is the personnel casualty?"

"Senior Chief Harvey, sir."

"Oh, damn," Klindt passes a hand over his face, "Load dispatcher, we just went through a huge electrical event and you're telling me we have no grounds?" He shakes his head, "Okay, EOOW, you have the watch. I'm going up to brief the Captain. If there is any change or an update on Harvey's condition, let me know."

FLIGHT DECK, USS CARL VINSON

2340, 19 December, 1941

On the flight deck, most of the access ports on Spike's F-14 are open. Electrical and mechanical personnel are checking the multitude of components it takes to make an F-14 fly. Spike is head down in the aft cockpit, her feet on a ladder. Puck has the radome on the nose open. He says, "Okay, Spike, I got the line connected. Do you have a signal yet?"

"Yeah, Puck, it's starting it's wake up cycle."

"Good, just let it warm up and see if it starts right."

A cool tropical breeze blows across the flight deck, making it both pleasant and difficult to work. AD3 Cervella, his head and shoulders inside a rear landing gear bay, drops his wrench, and it clangs across the deck. Grumbling as he retrieves it, "Sir, can't this wait 'till daylight? There's this big ball of light that comes up in the morning making flashlights irrelevant?" Puck disengages from what he is doing and just looks at the petty officer. Dejected, Cervella says, "Yes, sir. I understand."

A soft chuckle comes from the cockpit and Spike says, "Okay, it's warmed up. Stand clear and see if it tracks."

Puck says, "Full right. Up. Down. Full left. Looks good, Spike, on to the IFF."

CDR Holtz walks up, "How's it going guys?"

Spike lifts her head, "Just finished the radar, sir. Now working on the IFF. What's up?"

"Think she'll be ready to fly by morning?"

"Yes, sir."

"Can the ground crew finish it?"

Spike raises an eyebrow, "Yes, sir, they can."

"Good, you two have the Ready Five in the morning. Get some sleep."

"Yes, sir. Okay, Petty Officer Cervella you got it. Sorry."

As Spike and Puck walk into the island, Sam asks, "Are you alright, Puck? You've been quiet, even for you."

Puck stops and faces her, "Lieutenant, am I a member of your flight team, or just a passenger on YOUR plane? We are SUPPOSED to work together. You don't listen to me in a dogfight. You go haring off to rescue a fellow airman, which was a good call, but you didn't even talk to me about your plan. You either just assume I got it figured out, or you don't give a damn what I do back there. I can help, Spike, but you gotta let me."

She goes cold inside, standing rigid for the ass chewing. When he finishes, he looks at her for ten brutal seconds. When she says nothing, he turns and walks away.

ADMIRAL'S CONFERENCE ROOM, USS CARL VINSON

Captain Johnson sits at a conference table with Admiral Ren and his chief of staff, Captain Van Zandt. They listen as the Admiral's intel officer attempts to explain what just happened. LCDR Giles says, "Sirs, we have lost all communications with Hawaii and Washington. The satellite antennas are not even picking up a carrier wave. The sideband isn't picking up any threat orders or warnings. Radio has completed a system diagnostic and the problem is not on board. A number of crew members have suffered minor injuries due to the lightning storm. We have two fatalities, one on Vinson, and one of Fife. Both reactors are up and functioning normally. Squadrons and AIMD are inspecting aircraft as fast as they can. By morning, approximately 20% of the air wing will be available for flight. By tomorrow afternoon, the remainder should also be available. So far there are no reports of damage to the aircraft, at least none that can be directly attributable to the storm.

"Also, our ordinance department is inspecting missiles and control systems. Overall, we're in pretty good shape, except for the lack of communication. The battle group, except for the Hewitt, of course, rode out the storm pretty well. The two fatalities were, an older chief of an apparent heart attack on the Vinson, and a petty officer from a bad fall on the Fife. The crews are recovering and I expect they will take the loss hard. We should have a memorial service.

"None of the ships have any communication outside our group. We cannot raise the Hewitt. We will be in the area she was last reported to be in 45 minutes. Also, the LORAN radio navigation system and GPS satellite system are both non-functional. Tests of the equipment on Long Beach and Horne have the same result. All the equipment seems to be functioning, but it's like none of the satellites are transmitting anymore."

"Very well, Commander. That pretty much sums up our status, but what caused it? I saw that storm and it was unlike anything I've ever seen before," says Admiral Ren.

CMDR Giles replies, "Sir, I have no idea. I've not been briefed in on any weapon system used by any nation that would have the footprint we saw. My only thought is that it must be an EMP to be able to take out the satellites. No storm anywhere could've done that."

Captain Johnson nods his head, "Admiral, Commander, it seemed to me as well that an EMP is likely, but we must not rule out a large solar flare, either. The flare would need to be huge, but I believe it would be possible."

Ren says, "That's a point, Captain. But all the satellites? It seems unlikely."

Giles says, "Captain, with all due respect, I should point out that the storm occurred at night. We were facing away from the sun. How could a flare on the other side of the world affect satellites in this hemisphere?"

Ren says, "The truth is, gentlemen, we don't know. Within the realm of what we know, we must assume our nation was attacked. That being the case, I want the ship and its battle group ready to fight as soon as possible. Another thing, no solar flare, or EMP, or anything like it, could sink the Hewitt."

Johnson nods again, "Yes, Admiral, it's damn strange. I will have my ship ready as fast as possible."

"Well then, if you will excuse me, I have a few more messages I can't send to write. I believe we both have letters to write to the families. But, how in the hell can we notify them?" Ren shakes his head, "Good day, gentlemen."

LT. SAMANTHA 'SPIKE' HUNT'S STATEROOM, 03 LEVEL FORWARD

0055, 20 December, 1941

Sam, showered and dressed in P.J.'s, robe, and slippers, enters the stateroom she shares with Lt. JG Gloria 'Hot Pants' Hoolihan. The curvaceous red-head studies her friend as Sam hangs her shower stuff, slips out of her robe and slippers and climbs into the top rack. "Sam, are you alright? You can't still be upset about Book jumping on you. He's a jack ass."

"That's not it," Sam's voice flat and tight.

Gloria puts down the novel she's reading, "Well then, what is it?"

Sam, a tremble in her voice, says, "I think I fucked up. It's Puck. He let me have it big time."

"Oookay, about what?"

"He thinks I don't trust him. That I'm not being a team player. He said something very interesting. He feels I might be thinking he's got it together so well in the backseat that I don't have to talk to him. He's feeling frustrated because I'm not communicating."

"He said all that? I haven't heard him put that many sentences together since we came aboard."

"Yes, it was shocking. I, ah, I couldn't even speak. I just stood there frozen, making it worse."

"Sam, is he right?"

"Yeah,...yeah, he's right. I just didn't realize...."

"You know, Sam, you really gotta lighten up some. You drive yourself so hard that you don't lift your head, look around, and see the people you're working with. I don't know Puck as well as you do, but he seems like a good guy."

"He's a great guy."

"Then what's the problem?"

"I don't know..."

"You know, Sam, I met Admiral Haggarty once when I was at UCLA. She gave a speech for us ROTC pukes. You recall who she is?"

"Yes, the first woman to make Admiral, something to do with electronics."

"Yeah, well, she said something really good, you know. Really good advice. She said there can be only two kinds of women in the Navy, either you're a bitch, or you're a slut. The guys in the Navy won't let you be anything else. She told us that it's good to be a bitch, because a bitch gets things done. But you have to be a little bit of a slut, now and then, because that keeps the guys motivated."

"Yeah, but I don't know how. I just...I give everything. I just can't do it."

"Come on, Sam, it's me. I'm not saying go spread your legs on the mess decks and take all comers. I'm just saying flirt a little bit. You need to be a little less bitch, and a little more slut."

"That's for girly girls. I'm not one of them."

Gloria thumps the bottom of Sam's mattress and leans out to see her, "Hey, are you saying I'm a girly girl? Well, what of it. It ain't such a bad thing. You know there's more than one way to get things done around here, girl. It seems to me; your way isn't working. Hell, I know I got half the ship slavering over me every time I walk out of this door. Am I fucking any of them? No, I'm not. But it's useful, a smile here, a wiggle there, and the guys are working damn hard to keep me happy."

Sam cracks up, "Gloria, you always seem to do it like a lady. How do manage that?"

In fake southern accent, Gloria responds, "Oh, I do declare. Is the southern belle asking me how to act like a lady?"

"Nooo," laughing.

"The real point is you and Puck. Do you like him?"

"Yeah, I do. I'd like to be friends. He feels like someone you can trust. I'll apologize tomorrow."

"Honey, you best do a little more that apologize. I'd listen to what he has to say."

"I thought I was, but apparently not. It's been an eye-opener."

"You know, Sam, you dodged the question back there. Do you like him?"

"I said yes. What are you talking about?"

"No, you said you wanted to be friends. That wasn't the question at all, and you know it."

"Oh, I couldn't tell you."

"Come on, Sam, we're all grown up big girls here, haven't you ever had a boyfriend?"

"Yes, I've had a few boyfriends. It never went well."

"Well, duh. It's almost impossible to find a decent guy who'll put up with a woman loving jets."

Sam laughs, "No kidding."

"I'm lucky. I've got my Jerry. He has his own life and he puts up with mine. When we're together it's awesome. It's just so great to cuddle up with my head on his shoulder and trace lines on his six-pack with my finger. He's a hunk."

"I've never heard it called that before."

"So, your mind is capable of going into the gutter. I didn't mean it that way. I was talking about cuddling. All the other stuff is none of your business. So, you've never had a boy-friend like that?"

"No, they were all control freaks. I know how to pick them."

"That brings us back to the question of Puck. You have no-ticed he's a hunk, right?"

"Yes, Gloria, I've noticed. He's good looking and really well-built, and all that stuff," Sam replies flatly.

"Ah, so it's okay that Sam notices that Puck's a hunk, but it's not so great when Gloria does."

"What!"

"You sound a little testy."

"No, it's...it's okay. If you want to make a move on him, it's fine with me."

"Well then, I have a question. Is he called Puck because it's one inch long and three inches wide?"

Sam cracks up again, "No, he got it in primary flight school roll call: Hawke, E., so, Puck."

"Well, I guess that's not as lame as being miss-named after a tv seductress."

"At least my call sign now isn't as bad as my last one."

"Okay then, you going to leave me hanging?"

"It was C.I.B., for cold intellectual bitch."

"That's awful, kind of accurate, but awful."

"It's alright. Anyway, I'll do what damage control I can to-morrow. I didn't mean to hurt him. I didn't realize I was. For him to get that angry...well, anyway."

"Okay, honey, just work on your inter-personal flirtation skills. I'll set up a remedial course."

"Gloria, go to sleep."

CHAPTER 6

USS CARL VINSON, PRIMARY FLIGHT CONTROL

0600, 20 December, 1941

The early morning quiet is interrupted by a common call, "Flight quarters, flight quarters. All hands, man your flight quarter stations." The flight crews, groggy from a long night working on aircraft and testing systems, wearily drag themselves from their racks, put on their flight deck uniforms, and head out to work. Some swing by the mess decks and grab a bite, for others there's not even time to eat.

It's still dark as the Vinson gently turns into the wind. The rest of the battle group are spread out, searching for the destroyer Hewitt. Long Beach closes up behind Vinson as the plane guard. Cables are tightened and aircraft pre-flight inspections are completed as the flight deck slowly comes alive. All of it visible from the lofty heights of PRIFLY. The air boss, Charley Forrester, is normally a friendly and calm man, but when monitoring the flight deck, he's an absolute tyrant for safety. An aircraft carrier is one of the most dangerous places on earth and only the most brutal discipline keeps the herd of 18 year-olds running around on it safe. "Good morning air department, shake a leg out there and look alive. Shake out the cobwebs and keep your heads on a swivel. There were a lot of people on the flight deck last night, so keep a sharp eye out for FOD." He picks up another handset, "Captain, air boss, I recommend another FOD walk-down."

"Order it, Captain out."

Changing handsets again, Forrester says, "FOD walkdown, FOD walkdown. All hands not on watch lay to the flight deck for FOD walkdown." Sucking FOD (Foreign Object Damage) into a jet engine can lead to a bad day for all involved.

And the day's routine begins.

SAMANTHA AND GLORIA'S STATEROOM

There is a loud knock on Sam's door, "Flight briefing in 10 minutes, Spike."

"Got it, thank you." She drags herself out of her rack and notices Gloria is already up and out. She puts on her flight suit and fills her pocket with flight stuff: granola bars, utility tool, folding knife, and spare underwear. Done, she walks to the ready room on the 03-level aft of her stateroom. She can hear a helicopter spooling up on the flight deck above. It will be the plane guard helicopter. Always, a helicopter is the first to take off and the last to land during flight quarters. If any pilot gets in trouble, the helicopter is there to fish them out of the sea.

When Spike gets to the Black Knights ready room there is already a handful of pilots and RIOs, but she beats Puck in. Odd, he's always gets in first. Collecting a cup of coffee, she sits in one of the comfortable chairs at the back. Generally, she's careful with how much coffee she drinks before a flight, but one cup should be okay. Puck walks in, catching her eye. As she nods to him, Speedy and Thud arrive with platters of fresh chocolate chip cookies. The fragrance of chocolate wafts through the room. There is no faster way to disrupt a briefing.

'Pappa' Holtz grabs a cookie, "Well, if you're gonna be late for briefing, this is a perfect excuse."

Speedy says, "Late, skipper? We're just on time."

"Okay, okay, just sit down. Now, first mission launches in 30 minutes. Lieutenant Commander Carleton and Lt. Boxter will have that one. I want Swede and Ghandi flying your wing. You will both have TARPS pods. Your mission is to overfly Quenioc Atoll. There is a LORAN station there. The Captain and the Admiral want you to overfly the station, take some good pictures, and figure out if it looks operational. The intel lieutenant here will give you the particulars and pictures of the atoll. You will be carrying a light air-to-air load to give you better legs." The intel lieutenant hands out the information as the skipper continues.

"I want everyone to remember, GPS is down. You must actually navigate." He gives them all a stern look. "The Tomcatters are going to be far CAP to the north and west. There will be a Guardian E-2 up and four flights of S-3s doing a concentric circle search for the Hewitt. I want everybody airborne today to keep their heads on a swivel looking for debris and sailors in the water. Also, in support of that, fly no higher than angels fifteen, clear? Okay, questions?"

"Any word from Washington, or the rest of the fleet?"

"No, Book, nothing yet, and that worries me. All of you, I want you to think about what's going on. We're not sure why the loss of communications, but the folks upstairs believe it's foul play. That means we may be at war status and not know it yet. Keep your heads on a swivel. We don't want to be caught with our pants down. Any more questions?"

"There is nothing in the briefing papers about radio silence, but you said we may be on a wartime footing. Sir, shouldn't our flight be under radio silence?"

"Good question, Swede. I'll talk to the boss and get back to you guys before you launch. Anything else? Okay then, Spike?"

"Yes, sir."

"In about 45 minutes, I want you and Thud on ready five.

You will be flying bureau number 501 and 626 because your normal birds aren't ready yet. You will have the normal air-to-air load out; AIM five fours, AIM nines, and AIM sevens. I think they will want you on the bow cats, but I'm not sure yet. Make sure you keep your radios on and pay attention to what's going on out there so you know what to expect if you're launched. You'll be ready five until ten hundred, then the Tomcatters take over. Any questions?"

"Have we found anything wrong with any of the planes?"

"Good question, Puck, and no, we have not. At least nothing related to a lightning storm."

"Sir?"

"Go ahead, Spike."

"So, we're not on a wartime footing, but we are preparing just in case. We have to stay sharp, not expect that anyone we encounter is the enemy, but be prepared."

"Yes, Spike, that's about it."

"Sir, the point I'm trying to make is that we can't allow our actions to be over-ridden by disbelief."

"What do you mean?"

"We have been at peace for a long time, most of us. If we are at war, we need to think like we are at war, not be trigger-happy, but be ready. That's what I'm trying to say, skipper. It's a lousy position to be in. An enemy we may face could already know we're at war and the benefit in reaction time."

Book rolls his eyes and smiles at Packs.

Holtz nods his head, "Unfortunately, the rules of engagement stand as put out by the Admiral at the beginning of the cruise: you cannot initiate hostile action until fired upon, or hostile action is initiated upon you. The Admiral may change the orders, but for now, they stand. Any more questions?"

"So, the short version, sir, is after they shoot us down, we can shoot back. Got it, sir."

"I understand, Speedy. You don't have to like it, but you do have to do it. Any more gripes? Let's get it all out."

Speedy asks, "Sir, can we get a new inflight movie?"

"Any real questions? Okay, then, fall out, man your planes."

FLIGHT DECK NEAR CAT 1

Ready five is a kind of pilot coitus interruptus. Your plane is on the flight deck, its pre-flight check done and everything is ready to go, and there you sit. You can't take off. You can't go anywhere. You just sit. After a few minutes you begin to pray for World War III to break out, so you have something to do. It's not like you can play checkers. You can read a small dime novel if you can find a corner of the cockpit to stuff it into should you actually get to take off. After all, you can't throw the thing over the side of the airplane like a cop would with late-night stake out doughnuts and coffee, because that's FOD on the deck, which can foul an engine and cost a pilot his life. So, there's not much of anything you can do, but just sit.

Of course, F-14 pilots and RIOs have the lap of luxury. They have someone else to enjoy the prison with them, which is at least someone to talk to. This is the reason why military buddies know everything about each other: their likes and dislikes, little Susie Rottencrotch whom they took to the prom, what their daddy's farm grows, or doesn't. Nothing is secret, because, after all, you are bored.

Spike and Puck walk three quarters the length of the carrier before climbing out onto the flight deck. In the ready room they were polite and cordial, but as they walk in silence, the tension grows. They get to their F-14 near the bow catapults and begin the pre-flight with the help of their plane captain. They inspect the flaps, the fuel, and the myriad things that have to be checked before they are allowed to take off. After they're in the plane, there's nothing else to do but sit there.

They try to relax. Harness straps are off and helmets set aside. The canopy of the plane is fully open, allowing the wind to cool them, at least a little bit. In the tropic temperatures it takes no time at all before they are sweating. The cockpit of an F-14 on ready five is also the most private place two people can talk on the entire ship. With 5,500 crew crammed on board the carrier, privacy is a premium.

"Puck?"

"Are we going to talk?"

"Yes, we should. I'm sorry how I treated you."

"Apology accepted, ma'am. I was out of line, as well. For that, I'm sorry."

'No Puck, you were right, and call me Spike, or Sam, or whatever, not ma'am."

"We still haven't solved the underlying problem."

"Explain to me what you mean, please."

"You don't listen to me in the air. I need to be your RIO, not a passenger. We're only as good as we are together, Spike. That's the deal. We have to do it together."

"I think I understand. What is the right way to do this? My last RIO drove me nuts."

"Who was he?"

"Jerry 'Butch' Carter. He kept telling me where to fly like I'm blind. He would scream at me."

"Is that how you got your call sign, 'Butch' and 'Spike'?"

"Yeah."

"They teach us in RIO school that we are to tell you where to go when we see a threat."

"I don't like it. Just tell me where the threat is and what

they're doing."

"Okay, but how do I do that succinctly? That is why they say to give you instructions rather than descriptions. It's more succinct."

"Yeah, I see that, but I know how to fight the aircraft. I can feel what the other guy is doing and outwit him. I just need to know where they are and I will know what they are doing."

"How do you know?"

"There are only so many options. The other guy is limited by the same physics we are. If he is diving on us, I pull into it because he can't turn that fast. When he is climbing, we cross so I can see him in the turn. It's like that. If I can understand what the other guy is doing, I can beat him. When you give me directions, I can't feel the fight. I can't tell what I should do."

"You don't trust me to know? I understand how to fight the plane, too."

"I'm not saying I don't trust you. I just...Puck, I can do this. I beat Dixie two of two when I stopped listening to Butch telling me where to go and just trusted my instincts. Can we at least try to find a language that works?"

"Yeah. It has to be short, like three or four word."

"Okay, let's start with zones. If it is from the side forward, I probably see it. If you think I don't, say front, okay?"

"And if they are coming in from behind, I say, like, 'High. Right. Diving.'"

"That works. If you give me a disembodied number like 'five', I know it is a clock position. If you put an object in front of it, you are giving a number like, 'Migs, two.'"

"So, if I say, 'Mig, high, right, crossing,' you would know what I mean?"

"Yes. There is a Mig coming in from the right on a course that crosses ours at a high angle of attack. That would be perfect."

"Okay, I can do that. But, if I tell you to break, then it means there is no time to explain."

"Fair, I'm good with that. Look, I know I come across as cold. I'm sorry, but I do."

"Spike, on the ground, you come across as cold and controlling. In the air, you're a different person, you come alive. Cold isn't the problem. The problem is teamwork. We have to work together."

"Yes, I want to work together. I'm sorry I come across as bossy and controlling. I don't want you to think I'm talking down to you."

"Is that what people say? They're idiots. You're smart and a great pilot. I don't care if you talk down to me, just talk. Okay?"

"Okay, and thank you. You're awesome at your job, too. I also need you to keep a running commentary about where Thud is. With that, and giving me what the enemy is doing, I can fight the plane. If you need something for a missile shot, just say what you want, like '10 right 5 up for sparrow.' Something like that."

"All right, then. Also, the next time you're going to do some of your pilot heroics, let me know what you're going to do, so I can help, if there's time. We pulled off helping Too Tall land, but it was off the cuff and pure luck. We had enough time to talk about it. We should have talked it over."

'You're right, I just threw orders."

"Yes, and there is a time for that. One thing you do really well is warn me when you're about to crank on the G's. It allows me to reposition myself so I can operate everything without problems."

"Well, if I didn't, I'd end up hurting you, or have you pass out.

That's not an option."

"Not an option, but a possibility. Anyway, I had a great instructor when I was learning the RIO trade. He talked about conversations like these with our pilots. I don't think he ever thought I would be having one with...well, that it would play out the way it has."

"Say it, Puck."

"Okay...it's the girl thing. Don't get me wrong, I think you're a great pilot, and I have no issues with women in combat. Thing is, when you start criticizing a woman about interpersonal relations, well, it gets complicated."

"You were really pissed last night, weren't you?"

"Yeah, I was too pissed for my own good."

"I see."

"Do you?"

"Okay, spell it out. I don't do subtle."

"Now there's a revelation. Okay, you're prickly. I know you're prickly. Hell, everybody knows you're prickly, but you're a good pilot. You've got skills. Book was way out of line chewing on you like that, then, I piled on like an ass."

Spike stays quiet.

"Spike, if we're going to make this work, then I need to call you on your shit, AND, you need to call me on mine."

"Yes. You're right. But I'm really going to need your help, because I'm not good at this. Please?" Then she smiles, "So, hear anything on the radio, Puck?"

"It's quiet as a tomb."

"Wonderful."

"Book and Swede ought to be over the island, excuse me, atoll, about now."

IN THE AIR SOUTH WEST OF THE VINSON BATTLE GROUP

0755, 20 December, 1941

Two F-14s soar over the blue gray ocean, wings full forward, idling at their most economical speed. They're in loose deuce and flying lower than normal, and the low altitude eats up their fuel. But even with that, the F-14 has the range for this trip. Book asks, "You see anything down there, Packs?"

"No, sir, nothing but rolling ocean. Um, hey sir, Swede is waggling his wings."

"Okay, I see him. He's breaking right. Um, alright then, let's give him the lead."

Swede's plane spirals toward the ocean.

"What does he see, Packs? You need to have the sharpest eyes out here, okay?"

"Understood, sir. I have it now. It looks like a periscope. Yes, sir, a periscope for sure. I'm barely making out the shadow of the submarine, too."

"Well, that's interesting, but not what we're looking for."

Book waggles his wings to get Swede's attention and gently turns to climb back on course. Swede comes back on his wing and they continue on toward the atoll. As they get closer, the overcast begins to break up and slowly blue skies replace the gray gloom. Ahead and to the right a mass of clouds rises above the others, like an ice cream among fluffy cotton balls. They turn towards the cloud mass knowing that's the sign of land. The two aircraft slowly orbit the atoll at 1,000 feet, their Tactical Airborne Reconnaissance Pods (TARPs) turned on. They study the atoll, comparing it to the map they'd been given. "Sir, I'm pretty sure the Loran station should be right there on that bit of high ground. That's the location on the map, but I don't see the station."

"Look closer, Packs. It's got to be there, even if it's broke."

They circle the atoll again, "Sir, like I said, it just isn't there. It's like it was taken apart a long time ago and jungle grew over it. There's no indication of the road, or the pier."

"Okay, I'll just fly closer, so you can get a better look."

"No, sir, it won't help. I have the camera at its widest angle. I could see a basketball down there. This camera is designed to identify aircraft at 130 miles. It's just...not there, sir."

"Well, we're about bingo fuel. Let's head back. We'll let the intel folks figure this one out."

Book waggles his wings to get Swedes attention and climbs to just below the clouds once more for the return flight. They are quiet as they carefully scan the horizon and the ocean below for signs of the Hewitt. Then Swede waggles his wings again and turns west. "What the hell has he seen this time?" asks Book.

"I've no idea, sir, but I'm looking."

"Damnit, Packs, I'm tired of them getting the jump on us. It doesn't look good for the XO to be following some hot shot around the sky."

"Understood, sir. I think I see it, it's a twin-engine prop plane with a large bubble canopy."

"We're bingo fuel, no time to fuck around," and Book comes alongside Swede's plane and hand signals for a return to base line course to the ship.

CHAPTER 7

ADMIRAL'S CONFERENCE ROOM, USS CARL VINSON

1145, 20 December, 1941

Captain Johnson and Admiral Ren are having lunch. "Well, William, no sign of the Hewitt. There's not even an oil slick."

"I know, sir, it doesn't make sense. Whatever is going on, ships don't just disappear."

"Have we got anything from signals intelligence?"

"Again, sir, nothing makes sense. They picked up a little chatter on short wave, but most of the talk is about Pearl Harbor and Europe, and it doesn't really make any sense."

"I understand, William. To quote Sir Arthur Conan Doyle, 'once you eliminate the impossible, whatever is left, no matter how improbable, must contain the truth.'"

"Okay, but where does that leave us, sir, up the creek without a paddle?"

"It leaves us lacking a lot of information. The temptation is to continue the mission as ordered. It is tempting because it doesn't require a decision. It's also stupid. The situation has changed and a good leader acknowledges the change and adapts. Whatever hit us, it probably hit the Philippines, and pretty hard. I'm starting to think we may have more luck if we pull into Yokasuka, but I don't want to run home with our tail between our legs."

"I understand, Admiral. I think, though, the first decision we need to make is to accept the loss of the Hewitt and continue on. I think the search we did today is due diligence. We covered over 1000 square miles without even a hint of Hewitt."

"Have we debriefed the pilots that overflew the atoll?"

"They just landed, sir. It will be a few minutes, and a half an hour, or so, for the film."

"We need to get some good minds on this, William. I'm calling an all captains meeting for this evening, say 1900, in my conference room. Another point, let's put together a brain trust. You know what I mean, collect up some of the pocket protector crowd, and throw in a few odd balls that think outside of the box. Let's see what they come up with."

"Yes, sir, I know just the people."

USS CARL VINSON, 03 LEVEL, AFT EXERCISE ROOM

1325, 20 December, 1941

Samantha is running on a treadmill facing the aft bulkhead, Gloria is running next to her, head phones on, quietly singing as she runs. Sam, also with headphones on, is more aware of her surroundings, and looking behind her spots two male sailors watching them. She gives them a cold stare and they move along. Gloria asks, "Was your butt burning, or something?"

Sam smiles and shakes her head, "No, situational awareness."

"How did you and Puck get along on ready five?"

"We're working it out."

"He hasn't promised to show you his totem pole, has he?"

"Gloria!"

Unabashed, Gloria chuckles, "Just thinking that's one way of knowing for sure how that gorgeous man got his call sign."

BLACK KNIGHTS READY ROOM

1410, 20 December, 1941

Captain William 'Dixie' Lee walks from the squad room into CDR Holtz's office. "Hey, Dixie, what's up?"

"The admiral wants to put together a brain trust to figure out why we lost comms, and the other things that are happening right now. They meet at 1700 in the RT class room. I want Lieutenant Hunt on it."

"Okay, I'll pull her from the flight rotation."

"That's not necessary. This will be a collateral duty. She stays in rotation."

"CAG, you sure have taken to women in flight suits. May I ask why?"

"Jim, we were on the FDR together with the Sundowners. You're a damn fine pilot and you need to get your head straight about this. You cannot turn back the clock. Women are serving in uniform, and that's the way it is. Truth is some of them make damn fine pilots, so as soon as you can overcome your thick-headedness about the whole thing, the better. Savvy? The brain trust meets at 1700 tonight in the RT classroom."

HANGAR BAY TWO

1630, 20 December, 1941

Spike is in the cockpit of her F-14 with the procedure check list up on the dash. Under her breath she says, "Okay, flame out right engine." She quickly moves her hands through the control sequence from memory, and says, "Descend to less than 14K. Commence relight, back to level flight." She looks at the book, "Okay, remember the speed." She sits quiet for a moment, "Misfire." Her hands move through the motions as she says, "Arming switch, pull away." She looks at the book.

Chief 'Mosey' White, standing beside the plane, asks, "What

are you doing?"

Startled, she looks down, "Um, practicing, Chief. Making sure I remember all the immediate actions for problems in the air."

He shakes his head, "Can we talk about Airman Siemens?"

"Yeah, sure, Chief," and she climbs down and closes the canopy.

"Walk with me, LT."

Sam says, "He was trying to put an access panel in upside down. I can't just sit by while he screws up his job."

"Lieutenant, sometimes you need to let people learn by making mistakes. By correcting Airman Siemens too soon, he now feels you don't trust him."

"I don't."

Exasperated, Chief White says, "I know. Me either, but you can't show it. Give him time to grow into the job."

Shaking her head, she thinks: Shit, I have to fix this place and now you are part of the problem. "What are you trying to tell me, Chief?"

"Lieutenant, is this your first time running a division?"

"I was QAO for VAW-122, but that was only a couple of first classes and a chief."

Mosey smiles, "Ok, LT, what is your job in this division?"

She thinks for a moment, squares her shoulders, and says, "I'm in charge of the men and responsible for maintaining their training, quality of work, and military bearing."

"No, that is not your job. That's my job. Your job is to learn from me. Legally, you're in charge, but functionally, I am. My job is to mentor you through the mine fields of leadership. Are we clear?"

Sam tightens her lips, narrowing her eyes, thinking: Chief, you work for me. "Just what are trying to say, Chief?"

"Ok, I want to be clear about this. I've been in the Navy 16 years. I've been a chief for seven. You are not my first division officer. We can basically do it two ways, and I've done it both ways. Either you can be a cooperative student, or you can fight me. Cooperative is easier, but regardless, I will win. You will either learn what you must, or you will fail, destroying what appears, from this point of view to be a promising career. Okay, how is it going to go?"

Feeling her chest tighten, Sam thinks: Either I fight the chief and all of command or I trust him. How can I trust him? Can he see how messed up I am? I have to get it right. Have to... Have to trust him. Sam takes a deep breath, "Chief, I don't want to fight you. I never intended that. I...I know I'm wet behind the ears."

"Shit. Wet behind the ears? I haven't heard that since...um. Where are you from, ma'am?"

"Tennessee, east Tennessee. I was raised on a farm."

"Okay, good. Farm people generally have a bit of common sense. Now, what do we do about Airman Siemens?"

"Obviously, I don't have a clue. I wish I did."

"That's fine. You're learning. What you do is give him the same maintenance on your bird. It is coming up, I checked. Don't tell him your sorry. That comes off as weak and indecisive. A leader must be decisive, even if he, or she, is wrong."

After a deep breath, "My bird?"

"Yep, nothing says I trust you like asking someone to fix the aircraft you fly."

"I thought we both agreed not to trust him?"

"We don't. AD1 will follow after him and sort him out, making sure everything is squared away with positive reinforcement, not negative. Get it?"

"Yeah, okay Chief," nodding her head.

"How long have you been in the Navy, ma'am?"

"Six years, Chief. I've been on a Med cruise with the Blue Tails, but this is my first WestPac."

"Okay, we'll be hitting Subic first for Christmas. I recommend you stay on the base at night, or get away from Olongapo. The guys are going to be misbehaving, and it makes things awkward."

"Awkward?"

"Um, imagine walking down a dingy third world shithole street and stumbling onto, say AD1 with a hooker on each arm...awkward."

"Understood, I'll stay on the boat."

"Nah, just on the base at night. There's a nice O club, or so they tell me, white table clothes, the works."

Sam laughs, "Right, Chief."

"You're a bit rough around the edges, ma'am, but you listen and you seem to have a level head. You're gonna work out."

"So, I pay attention, and if I can't figure something out, come straight to you."

"You're getting it. Every discipline decision should be a joint one."

"Right, Chief. Thank you."

They see a line of airdales waiting in line at a closed door. Chief asks, "What are you doing?"

Lori 'Sass' Givens, from Sam's division says, "We are waiting for shoe issue, Chief. Some petty officers were here too, but they had to go on watch."

White and Sam struggle not to laugh. White says, "Guys, go back to work. That's a fan room and the ship doesn't issue shoes."

Lori says, "But, Chief, they said."

White says, "I know, Givens, it's an old trick that black shoes like to pull on unsuspecting airman. Get back to work."

AD1 Gellar approaches, "Ma'am, the Captain wants you to go to the RT classroom at 1700."

Sam looks at White, then back to Gellar, "Do you know why?"

"No, ma'am, I just know it's below the reactor department office, starboard side, aft of the mess decks. I've been looking all over for you."

Sam says, "Thank you, Gellar. I'd best get going."

CARL VINSON REACTOR OFFICE

1650, 20 December, 1941

Captain Klindt steps out of his office and looks at the two men in front of him. "Okay, folks, the captain has called on us to figure out what the hell has been going on after the lightning storm. He asked for my most creative thinkers. Unfortunately, they are all on watch, so I'm stuck with you."

They chuckle, and MM1 Shawn Hughes asks, "Sir, will we be off the watch bill?"

"You would like that, but, no can-do. Tell you what, I'll keep you off the evening watches, and if we can figure this out correctly in less than 24 hours, you will stand no duty in our next liberty port, but we have to be both accurate and complete. Meet the rest of the team at 1700 in the RT classroom."

"Who else is attending?" asks ETCS Scott Richardson, the Reactor Controls Senior Chief.

"You two, Lt. Warren, myself, and some others."

REACTOR TRAINING CLASSROOM

1700, 20 December, 1941

An unusual group of people sit around a table in the RT

classroom. There is MM1 Hughes, ETCS Richardson, and Lt. Warren from the reactor department; Lt. Hunt, Lt. JG Mike 'Too Tall' Mohr, both pilots; and a crypto-tech, CT1 Kevin Barr, who is huddled up in a conversation with RM1 Phillip Denton, from radio. The two occasionally look at the others as if they are interlopers on their private conversation.

Too Tall sits near Sam, looking uncomfortable, "Lieutenant Hunt?"

"Yes?"

"I didn't get a chance to thank you for helping me last night. There is no way I would have found the boat without you on my wing."

"No problem, Too Tall. I'm glad we were there."

"Any idea why we're here?"

"None."

Lt. Warren speaks up, "The RO asked us to come down here as part of a brain trust. I assume he wanted you guys to join, but I have no idea why?"

Captain Klindt walks into the room. Warren says, "Attention on deck!" and the all stand up.

Klindt says, "Carry on, and please sit down. Coffee and cookies are coming down so we can all be comfortable. But first, I want to sort out one thing. I want everybody to take their hats and put them over there on the shelf."

Hunt stands up, takes off her ball cap, and puts in on the shelf. Mike Mohr slowly stand up and follows suit. MM1 Hughes stays seated, "Captain, why are we doing that?"

"Nukes, God, I love them, and I hate them. They always have to question everything. MM1 just do what I ask and I'll explain" By then the rest have also put their caps up and Klindt spins his ball cap in his hands and sets it up with the others. As Hughes finally puts his cap up and sits down, a mess specialist comes in with cookies and a carafe of coffee. "Thank you, Petty Officer Lovejoy, we appreciate the refreshments. Please, put them on the table and excuse us. Thank you, again."

Klindt waits for him to leave, looking over his motley crew. "The Captain had me set up this brain trust to figure out what has happened during the lightning storm. All of the hats are over there, and so are our ranks. We are equals around this table. No idea is a bad idea. No suggestion is a stupid suggestion, and I expect to hear from all of you.

"This is the format we are going to use: first, discussing what information we actually have. That is, what we really know. Next, having put that on the table, with no analysis whatsoever, we're going to brainstorm and put all the ideas out there that everyone comes up with on this team. Having done that, we will start evaluating which of the ideas actually meet with all the known criteria. We are authorized to recommend missions to the Captain and the Admiral to gather more information if we need it. But, we need to move fast with this, because it's possible we're at war right now." He pauses and lets that statement sink in.

"This job is a very relevant one for the safety of every man and woman in the battle group. Okay, first order of business, does anyone volunteer to be the clerk and write all this down?"

Nobody makes eye contact and all hands are studiously below the table top. Klindt smiles slightly and Sam chuckles. After a short wait, Klindt says, "Excellent, thank you Petty Officer Hughes for volunteering. Your initiative earlier is paying off now."

"Hey, wait a minute, sir. I'm a lousy clerk. I can't even type. If we are all equals in this room, why shouldn't an officer do it?"

"Because, Hughes, as your department head, I'm concerned with your personal development."

"Yes, sir." Shawn pulls out a notebook and pen from his shirt pocket and prepares to take notes.

"Okay, a brief introduction from each of us, so we all know with whom we are working. Keep it relevant. Save the slow walks on the beach stuff for another time. I'll start. Craig Klindt, masters in nuclear physics from MIT, qualified on five different types of reactors and did a tour at Bettis. Last command was CO of the Virginia, a CGN. Lieutenant Warren, you're next."

"I'm John Warren, ME in double E from UW, first plant."

"Maybe in English, John."

"Um, yes, sir, masters in electrical engineering from University of Washington, Electrical Division Officer in number 1 power plant, sir."

"Lieutenant Hunt?"

"Samantha Hunt, bachelors in aeronautical engineering from Cal-Tech, former E-2 Hawkeye pilot, now F-14 pilot with VF-154."

"Lieutenant Mohr?"

"Mike Mohr, bachelors in mechanical engineering from Oregon State, minor in math. I spent three years designing robots for DARPA before I joined the Navy in a moment of insanity. I fly the EA-6B and wan involved in the design and pre-design for the threat upgrade to the B. I'm a Red Flag graduate. Oh, and I hate walks on the beach, sand gets everywhere."

"Senior Chief?"

"Scott Richardson, PhD in electronics engineering from MIT, and Reactor Controls Division Chief." He gives Klindt a long look, "And no, I do not want to be an officer."

"Understood, MM1 Hughes?"

"I gotta a degree from the school of hard knocks and a minor in bullshit. I'm just a mechanic, sir."

"Not hardly, you are LCDR Sander's go to guy. You did a freeze repair seal on the fly in number 2 Reactor Auxiliary Room to get us underway on time. You're an exceptional mechanic, and no good at bull shit. Petty Officer Denton?"

"I'm Phillip Denton. This is my fourth deployment and first brain trust. I'm a radioman, so ninety percent of what I do is classified. I'm not going to be of any help."

Klindt stares at him, "You do recall Captain Johnson's briefing of just an hour ago. We are all cleared in within the context of our agenda, and RM1, I set the agenda, so spare us the ritual dick beating, okay?"

"I understand, sir, but it has to be cleared through DoN."

"Yep, let's just get them on the phone, shall we? The lack of comms is most of why we are meeting. Petty Officer Barr?"

"Yes, sir, Kevin Barr. I have a MA in linguistics from Columbia, with minors in math and music. I speak a handful of modern languages."

"Which languages, Barr?"

"All of them, sir."

"Is it a long list?"

"I read, write, and speak German, Polish Swedish, Spanish, and French from birth. I'm pretty good in Russian, Romanian, Suomi, Norwegian, Italian, Portuguese, Hindi, Hebrew, and Greek. I can get by, a bit, in Chinese, Japanese, and Arabic. Oh, I also, speak, read, and write ancient Sanskrit, Hebrew, Latin, Greek, with related Aegean languages, Sumerian, and a bit of Egyptian."

Warren asks, "Isn't that everything?"

"No, sir, I'm thinking of expanding to Native American languages as well. Hopi is fascinating and Mayan is out of this world. No one can read it."

Warren looks bemused, "Why are you in the Navy? I would think you'd have been grabbed by, um, No Such Agency."

"Turned them down. Didn't want to live in a cubicle 24-7."

Mohr says, "You live in a box here."

"Yes, sir, I live in a box which is traveling the world and I get to practice for free."

Klindt says, "Okay, then, let's go over what we know. Let's start with you, Denton. What do we know?"

"We know we have no communication with any other U.S. Military force worldwide. We have no satellite connection and no GPS or Loran."

"Clerk, are you taking notes?"

"Yes, Captain."

"Barr?"

"He about said it, sir. We've picked up some signals on side band, but I do not know the encryption. We don't always pick them up, either."

"What about the flight over the atoll?"

Hunt says, "Nothing, sir. When they overflew the island, uh, atoll, there was nothing there, overgrown jungle, no buildings, no antennas, nothing, sir."

Barr asks, "One of the fighters noticed another aircraft on the way back. Have we identified the aircraft yet, ma'am?"

"The pictures were a little grainy, but it appeared to be a Japanese patrol plane of World War II vintage, some sort of restored aircraft."

"What else?"

"The Hewitt is still missing," says Warren.

"True, with no indication whatsoever about what happened to her," says Klindt.

"The Hewitt had a girl captain, maybe she decided to go to

the mall," says Hughes. He glances at Sam and she just shakes her head.

"Are there any other details we can glean from this? What I mean is, I believe we know a lot more than we think we do. There's knowledge that just doesn't have a context yet."

Richardson says, "Well, sir, we know we went through one hell of a lightning storm, and I've heard that not one single electrical component anywhere on this ship, or any of the ships, aircraft, anything, was damaged." They all nod their heads.

"Put that on your list, clerk."

"I am, sir, I may be a monkey mate, but I can actually write pretty fast."

"What else, guys?"

Hunt says, "A suggestion, sir, maybe we should whiteboard this, so we can all look at it."

"Thank you for volunteering, Hunt." She smiles, gets up, walks to the board and lays out the points already discussed.

"Just a question for clarification, did I understand you right? There's no communication with the satellites, not even a carrier wave?" asks Mohr.

"Yes, sir, that's it," says Denton.

"The nights have been pretty clear, has anybody gone out and actually looked for one? Then we can aim our antenna exactly at it and see if it's just a weak signal," says Mohr, looking around the table.

Barr asks, "How do we find the satellite? Aren't they a long way away?"

Sam grins at Mohr as he smiles, "You know Petty Officer Barr, you're damned smart, but you need to crawl out of your box once in a while and look up. We're pilots, we see things. Satellites can be seen at night. They trace across the sky. They probably have a record on board somewhere as to where various satellites are at any given time to make it easier. The geosynchronous ones are sometimes a little hard to find."

"How do you find something so small, that far away?"

Sam, "It's the only fast-moving star up there."

Mohr adds, "Yep, it's like this: you see there's this huge burning ball out in the sky way out there that some of us call the sun. I know you guys hardly ever see it, but, it's still out there, believe me. Anyway, it shines on objects way out there in outer space, and the objects are shiny with things like, oh, I don't know, solar cells to create electricity, they reflect the sun's rays. So, you see this glinting, glittery thing sailing across the night sky, pretty amazing, huh?"

Klindt finally says, "Mohr, do you have a sarcasm button I can dial down?"

"No, sir, it's pretty much stuck on wide open all the time."

Hughes says, "I have a solution for that, Captain. It's called duct tape. It generally dials down the attitude quickly for uppity officers."

Sam goes, "Ow!" And Hughes grins.

"Okay, gentlemen, let's get back on topic. Mohr, your idea is a good one and we will implement it tonight. Meanwhile, let's continue."

Hughes say, "You techno-weenies said something about picking up other frequencies and stuff. What kind of music stations have you drawn in?"

Denton stiffens, "We haven't really been looking for music. We're not supposed to tune in music channels on the radio."

Sam smiles, "I know you guys in radio follow specific rules and regulations, but we've just been hit by an extraordinary event. Please think outside the box. AM, FM, not just short wave, not just sideband, all the low frequencies, we need to look at everything."

Hughes adds, "This is bull shit. There's no fucking way you techno weenies don't listen to the radio. Do you think we're all fucking idiots? You guys got the most expensive receiver in the world. You can't tell me you don't use it."

Klindt, "Colorful observation, Hughes, colorful, but astute. If we're going to get to the bottom of this, we need the truth. So, gentlemen, to what have you been listening?"

Denton's expression sours, and he lowers his head, then looking up, he says, "Sir, we sometimes pick up stuff out there. AM is pretty short range, but sometimes it bounces. FM is pretty much line of sight, so we're not picking up any of that. The AM channels we are picking up have been mostly oldy, moldy stuff."

"What?"

"Well, mostly big band and jazz from the States. I haven't even found Rush Limbaugh, and he's huge."

"Is that about all of the relevant facts? Anything else, anything?"

Sam, "So, what we have right now is:

Freak lightning storm that caused no damage.

Loss of communications via satellite and all other high frequency comms.

Hewitt is missing.

Loran station could not be located.

Old airplane of possible Japanese origin.

Old music on AM frequencies.

Klindt, "Looks like a good list to start, so let's brain storm what it means. I'll go around the table, each of you pick a possible cause for one or more of the issues we are facing. You're first, Lieutenant Warren."

"Sir, I think it could've been an EMP. An EMP could've caused…"

"Hold on, Lieutenant, just ideas first. Later we analyze. You're next Senior Chief."

"Looking at it, sir, a solar flare could effectively act exactly like an EMP, and could cause some of our problems, if not all of them."

"Hughes?"

"The Russians have a secret weapon they fired at us that functions similarly to an EMP or solar flare."

"Denton?"

"I've got nothing, sir," he shrugs his shoulders, "mass hallucination?"

"If that's it, it's been a downer of a trip thus far, Barr?"

"I don't know, sir. We're in the wrong part of the ocean for the Bermuda Triangle."

"I know, but the idea is tempting, isn't it. Mohr?"

"Well, sir, Spock would say it's irrational, but I would say we've left our own space time continuum."

Hughes says under his breath, "Shit, I'm a nuke, and I don't even know what that means."

Sam asks, "You don't read science fiction, Hughes?"

"No, ma'am, I'm more Field and Stream."

"Back on task, people, Hunt?"

"Well, sir, Mohr has a point, but what if there was an EMP, but it was directed only at the satellites? But, that doesn't explain the lightning storm, the Loran site, or the Hewitt. I got nothing."

"This is the part where we just bring up ideas. We don't bring them up and knock them down. So, your idea is a directed EMP?"

"Yes, sir, at this point."

"That leaves me, and I would have to say we don't have

enough information, but based on what we do know, some sort of electrical flux, like a Tesla coil. But, that's too lame. So, I'm going to vote for time travel."

CHAPTER 8

I-7 JUNSEN CLASS JAPANESE SUBMARINE

1816, December 20, 1941

Commander Hirotaka Chiba could not believe his luck. It was the largest American carrier he had ever seen, and it wasn't even zig-zagging. With his six forward firing torpedo tubes, he just has to wait as this monster ship steams right into his firing solution. "Flood tubes 1, 2, 5, and 6. Set depth to 20 feet."

Submarine fighting is a patient job. The amount of time needed to load and fire torpedoes, forces patience. Commander Chiba mumbles, "Haste leads to death, and worse, failure." Then loudly, "Stand by to mark bearing."

"Yes, sir," says Petty Officer Sato Nishimura.

"Distance is 26,000 meters. Set torpedoes to slow. I want them all on the same bearing. They'll spread enough on the way."

"Yes, sir, setting torpedoes to slow," repeats the phone talker.

"Ready, mark."

"Bearing 312, Commander," says Sato.

"Bearing 312, set, Commander," says the Firing Chief Officer, Chief Isidro Hataki.

"Fire 1, 2, 5, and 6."

"Firing 1, 2, 5, and 6." The sub shudders as compressed air

forces a slug of water to expel the torpedoes, one aft of the other. Four deadly Type 93 Long Lance torpedoes speed at 35 knots toward the Carl Vinson.

USS BENJAMIN STODDERT, DDG-22, SONAR ROOM

ST2 John Givens is on watch with just one and a half hours left and looking forward to a shower and the Louis L'Amour novel he's reading. It's good, and he is so bored. The sonar equipment aboard Stoddert is archaic by 1990 standards. It's sensitive and it works, it's just clunky. Sonar is located in the bowels of the ship, between the forward emergency diesel generator and the magazine for Mount 51. To make matters worse, the air conditioning doesn't work down here, making it muggy and warm.

And so, he sits, bored, listening to the noises of the ocean. Then he hears a distinctive woosh, then a buzz. He doesn't believe it. He's trained for this for years, but never actually, for real heard it. Then he hears it again, then twice more. With a trembling hand he grabs the phone to combat, "Combat, sonar, contact bearing 284, range 24,000 meters, designate Sierra 1. Torpedoes in the water, say again, torpedoes in the water. I count three, no, four, four torpedoes in the water, bearing 284, range 22,000 meters and closing on the Carl Vinson at 35 knots."

STODDERT'S BRIDGE

CDR Kevin Douglas, commanding officer of the Benjamin Stoddert, is a stocky man, and as is his habit on the bridge, stands near his chair, legs spread to compensate for the movements of the small ship. He uses his chair as a desk for sorting the papers needing his attention. When he hears the call from sonar, the papers are quickly forgotten. Shouting, "Go to General Quarters," he picks up the phone to sonar, "Sonar, Captain, are you certain they are torpedoes?"

"Yes, sir, 100% positive, it can't be anything else."

"Do you have range and bearing to the sub?"

"Approximate, sir, now at 282, at 26,000 meters."

"Right, Yankee search and confirm."

Soon the distinctive 'boo waa' sound of active sonar is heard throughout the ship. After the second pulse, sonar is back on the phone, "Captain, sonar, confirm target Sierra 1 is 282, at 24,000 meters. Confirm inbound torpedoes."

Captain Douglas picks up the ship to ship radio and announces to the whole carrier group, "carrier group 72, this is Stoddert actual. Torpedoes in the water, say again, torpedoes in the water inbound to Carl Vinson. Relative bearing on you is 265. Carl Vinson, I recommend violent maneuver to starboard. Benjamin Stoddert is engaging."

USS CARL VINSON, RT CLASSROOM

"Time travel, sir, you've got to be shitting me," says Hughes.

Denton and Barr nod their heads in agreement with Hughes and Mohr says, "Could be, could be, I wouldn't rule it out."

From the 1MC, "Gong. Gong. Gong. General quarters, general quarters, all hands man your battle stations. Up and forward on the starboard side, down and aft on the port, now, general quarters. Gong. Gong. Gong."

As everybody scrambles to clear the room, Sam starts wiping the board. Klindt barks "Wipe the board," then realizes she already has. Turning to Hughes, "Your notes to me," reaching for them.

CARL VINSON BRIDGE

Captain Johnson orders, "Emergency ahead flank!"

The lee helm repeats the order, rotates the engine order telegraph to indicate the ordered bell, and when the engine room responds says, "Emergency ahead flank, ordered and answered, sir."

The conning officer acknowledges the lee helm as Johnson is on the 1MC, "Carl Vinson, we have just been fired upon by a submarine and are taking evasive maneuvers. I need you to focus on setting zebra second deck and below. Prepare for a rough ride. This is not a drill, all hands to stations."

The whole ship shakes as the engines spool up, with massive amounts of steam dumping into the turbines, causing the ship to accelerate through the water. The 260,000-shaft horsepower the engines produce accelerate the 90,000-ton carrier, just not quickly.

Johnson goes to the starboard bridge wing and looks out, surprised to see the streaks of white in the distance. With binoculars he watches the torpedoes closely, timing his maneuvers. He sees Stoddert fire an ASROC missile launched torpedo, then orders, "Left full rudder, back two thirds on engine one and two."

USS BENJAMIN STODDERT, DDG-22, BRIDGE

It's really busy on the Stoddert, a Charles F. Adams class guided missile destroyer commissioned in 1964. For twenty-five years this plucky ship has sailed the waves, seeing action in Vietnam, and recovering Gemini and Apollo space capsules. She rolls to starboard and accelerates, "Lee helm, tell the engine room I want every ounce of power they have. I don't want to hear about limitations, restrictions, or anything else."

"Aye, sir, you want every ounce of power and no limitations."

"Helm, amidships," says CDR Douglas, and picks up the 1MC. "Good evening Stoddert warriors. I know I just called general quarters, but I want all the repair lockers to muster in the forward or aft deck house. I want all hands, except aft steering and engineering to muster to main deck and above. We don't have much time, so let's hustle, folks. We're driving into harm's way. Today and always, I'm proud to be your Captain, Douglas out."

The ship to ship radio sounds with Captain Johnson's voice, "What are your intentions, Stoddert?"

As the Stoddert accelerates to 33 knots, placing itself between the torpedoes and the Carl Vinson, Douglas answers the call. "Doing our job, sir. Please stand by to pick up my crew. It has been an honor to serve with you and your fine vessel, Stoddert out."

STODDERT, 2ND DECK FORWARD IN A PASSAGEWAY

The crew scrambles to follow the Captain's orders. Every escort ship sailor knows it is expected of them to place their ship in harm's way to protect the carrier. Like most people, they don't really believe that day will ever come. The zebra fittings slow things down a bit until the crew relaxes them so they can get by. Still, most of the 354 men serve below decks. There is no way they can all make it out on time. The fear is palpable, but they stay calm. ET3 Donny Stakes from Nebraska, finds his best friend, FC3 Karl Smith from Saginaw, Michigan, ahead of him trying to go up a forward deck hatch as they abandon repair locker 2 in second division berthing. Karl's a big strong guy, but a bit overweight, and Donny says, "Hey, Karl, bet you wished you'd taken a few less trips through the buffet now."

"Why is that, wise ass?"

"Sharks like their meat tender and well-marbled."

"At least I'll float. You don't have a pond big enough to learn how to swim in Nebraska."

STODDERT ENGINEERING LOG ROOM, 3RD DECK NEAR

SONAR

In the log room, the main office for engineering department, YNSN Wallace Sealy, from Detroit, is busy reviewing requisitions, oblivious to what is happening around him. His headphones are plugged into a Walkman in his pocket and all he knows is the violent maneuvers are making it hard for him to stay in his chair. And, the racket is ruining his music. MM2 Owen Brown, from the Bronx, is sweeping for stragglers and finds Sealy, "Hey! YoYo, what the hell are you doing?" He pulls the headphones off Sealy.

"Hey, man, what the hell? The Cheng isn't in. Try later."

Brown yells, "Hey Bub, get your ass outa here. There's torpedoes in the water inbound aimed right at your dumb ass. Get moving!"

AFT STEERING

Aft steering exists in case the bridge loses steering control. MM3 John Baker is on the sound powered phones, standing watch with BMSN Mitchell Blumm from Tennessee. They can feel the aggressive movements back here, and see the swinging rudder arms as the ship maneuvers. Even with the running hydraulic pumps, they have no problem hearing the captain's orders. On the phones, Baker hears BMSN Dupree, the port lookout say, "Four torpedoes, there are four torpedoes coming at us. They were shot at the bird farm, but the captain is maneuvering us in the way."

Baker asks, "How do you know? You can't see torpedoes anymore like back in World War II."

Dupree says, "I can see these."

As reality sets in, Baker says, "Hey, Mitchell, I left my cap in the rope locker in the aft deck house. Could you go get it for me?"

"Your hat is on your head."

"No, man, my lucky hat."

"I'm not supposed to leave."

"Yep, and I also know I want you out of here. Go. Just go get my hat. I can run this and no one will know."

Blumm starts walking to the door going forward and stops, "You don't have a lucky hat. What are you up to?"

"Listen, dumb ass, do what I say, ok? Just do it. Go up to the aft deck house, fucking now."

Blumm, confused, follows his instructions and walks through the water tight door, dogging it behind him, then walks through the aft EDG area. He is shocked to see it empty. The EDG is manned for GQ. He continues forward to engineering berthing where repair locker 4 normally musters, expecting to get into trouble. No one is there. When he makes his way to the ship's aft passageway, he finds crew milling around. His division officer, the First Lieutenant, is trying to get people organized and headed for the mess decks. The div-o says, "Good to see you, Blumm. Muster with the port life rafts. We're going to need them, so stay squared away, ok?"

NUMBER 2 ENGINE ROOM

MM1 Oscar Hammond is the Machinist Mate of the Watch (MMOW), the senior guy in the engine room. He's from Roanoke, Virginia, having served in the Navy for sixteen years, all of it on tin cans. He likes the responsibility and the autonomy of a small crew because there's not enough khaki for a lot of micro-managing, and a first class generally has some pull. Listening the captain's announcement, nobody has to tell him the score. The captain is preparing to sacrifice the ship.

He looks at the six watch standers for whom he is responsible, the youngest is the messenger watch, Fireman Greg

Newburg from Oregon who's only seventeen. "Boys, I want everyone on the upper level. Newburg, you're the messenger, which means you can leave. Get your ass topside."

"But, Ham, I'm part of the watch team. If...if you are all staying, I should too."

"Like hell, kid. I say go, you go. You got the brave gene, but you seem to lack the smart gene, get out of here. Now!" Hammond watches the dejected kid leave, relieved that he listened.

The lower level watch, MMFN Kevin Jacobson, poking his head up the ladder, witnesses the exchange between his LPO and the messenger. "What's up, Ham?"

"Just get over here." He gathers his crew, confused because they didn't hear the Captain, "We've got torpedoes inbound. The captain's expecting to lose the ship. Flash gear on, and remember how to get out of here. Everyone else is up on the main deck. Oil temperatures good?"

The turbine generator, distilling unit, and lower level watch all nod yes. Main engine watch, MM3 Calvin Taylor, says, "My engine is a bit hot because of the bell."

"Make your adjustments, then get back here."

CHAPTER 9

STODDERT, FIRE ROOM 1

BT2 Olly Larson is at the aft burner front on the lower level between the two boilers. It is the unofficial hang out in the fire room. His brother, BT1 Bob Larson, is the Boiler Technician of the Watch (BTOW). As the senior guy, they are all looking to him for answers. "Guys, this is no drill. Sounds like we're going to take a hit. The old man will warn us to brace, so remember what to do: bent knees, mouth open, grab onto something solid. After the hit, check and make sure the boiler is on line. They'll need the steam to fight the ship."

The upper level watch, BT3 Donny Petrakis from Miami, Florida, asks, "What if we're hit in the fire room?"

"Well, my Greek friend, then it's been nice knowing you, because we'll be meeting our maker."

STODDERT, BRIDGE

It's a slow-moving ballet. The Vinson picks up speed, kicking its rudder over to the left to push the stern, with its delicate shafts and rudders, away from the oncoming torpedoes. The Stoddert is racing parallel with the Vinson, placing itself between the torpedoes and their intended target. CDR Douglas orders the lee helm, "All stop. Order the men to evacuate the engine and boiler rooms." He picks up the 1MC, "We're about to be hit by two or three torpedoes. Stay braced until the last torpedo hits. If it's necessary to abandon ship, the carrier group has been warned to pick us up. I would like to thank each and every one of you. I'm proud to be your captain. Now brace for shock. Brace for shock."

A huge geyser of water shoots out from near the bow, just forward of the 5-inch gun. Stoddert rises up on the bow, heeling over to starboard.

SUPPLY DIVISION BERTHING ABOVE SONAR

ST2 Givens is the last to evacuate sonar. He's running through the water tight door into 2nd division berthing when the torpedo hits and explodes 30 feet behind him. The explosion crushes the bulkheads around the forward EDG, sonar, and the log room. Givens manages to stagger to his feet, and through the smoke and darkness, feels his way aft on the tilting deck.

NEAR MOUNT 51

ET3 James Stakes is caught on the weather deck hanging onto a bracket, and is blown off his feet. His friend, FC3 Carl Smith, is braced near the port water tight door when the explosion hits. The door slams open, breaking his right arm. They end up on the deck only feet from each other as water pours down on them.

NUMBER 2 ENGINE ROOM

As the bow settles, the second torpedo hits engine room number 2 in the aft of the boat. The engine room crew had just started evacuating, but MM3 Calvin Taylor, was on the far side when the order came down. He just makes it to the front of the engine when the torpedo hits. The explosion, in microseconds, creates a bubble in the hull that shatters in a storm of molten shards and shrapnel. They fly into the pristine white and terracotta engine room, breaking steam lines and shattering sight glasses.

The main engine takes most of the blast, but MM3 Taylor is killed instantly. As the steam lines rupture, the area now rapidly filling with seawater, is filled with 600-degree steam, scalding those not killed in the blast. FN Newburg was in the aft escape trunk, un-dogging the hatch above him, when the torpedo hit. He managed to hang onto the ladder rungs in the trunk, which protected him from the worst of the blast. Pushing the hatch open, he crawls onto the main deck with minor burns and ringing ears.

Stoddert's roll, 30 degrees to starboard, makes it hard to walk. Debris and wounded are everywhere. The windows of the ships store are shattered, and bubblegum, candy, socks, and razors are underfoot. Steam is escaping from cracks in the deck.

The Chief Engineer (CHENG), LCDR Duane Hubler, is a huge man, six feet eight inches tall, his unruly red hair is a beacon in the chaos. Wearing an oxygen breathing apparatus (OBA), he muscles his way aft, picking up crewman and getting them off the hot deck. He gets to Newburg and motions toward the engine room blast door. Newburg shakes his head and shrugs. Hubler pulls open the blast door, a blast of steam comes out, and he starts down into hell.

As he descends, he finds a crewman on the ladder, picks him up, carries him out, and goes back down. Newburg sees EM2 Westing, terribly burned and gasping for air, and gently helps him aft.

MM1 Hammond was the only one of his watch team to get his emergency escape breathing apparatus (EEBD) on. The plastic window is fogged and hazed from the heat, so trying to remember where each watch stander was, he starts his search. Walking toward the main engine, he finds the decking gone. Then he finds a man and pushes him toward the ladder out. He finds the lower level watch by bumping into him, and guides him to the ladder. His skin burns whenever he touches steel, and on a warship almost everything is steel. With iron determination, he takes one step after another, maintaining awareness of his location from years of standing watch in the same engine room. Finally, he realizes he has to leave, and blindly walking to the ladder, bumps into his CHENG. Hubler gently picks him up like a child and carries him out to the weather decks where the rest of his watch team lies on the heaving deck.

As soon as Hubler sets him down, he struggles to remove the EEBD hood, but his hands aren't working right. Newburg gently pulls off the hood, and Ham can see his watch team lying on the deck, burned and fighting for breath. Hubler says to Newburg, shouting in his ear, "Fireman, you gotta take care of them. A helicopter is coming, make sure you don't leave them."

"Yes, sir," Newburg nods, determined.

Hammond struggles to stand. His lungs are seared, but he tries to mumble his thanks anyway. Hubler gently pushes him back down, "You need to rest, Hammond. You did good, now rest." The CHENG stands up and walks forward.

NUMBER 1 BOILER ROOM

With the ship rolled thirty degrees starboard, the third torpedo hits right under the bridge. Down in the bottom of the ship, where the torpedo strikes is the 5-inch gun auxiliary magazine. The blast can be felt on the weather decks of Carl Vinson a mile away.

Number 1 boiler room is just aft of the gun magazine. When the forward bulkhead collapses, it shatters the forward wall of the 1-A boiler, releasing a cloud of super-heated steam into the space. Upper level watch, BT3 Petrakis, is burned and blinded by the steam, but still struggles to get out of the plant. A hand touches his, then grabs him with enormous strength. He finds himself being carried up to the main deck passageway aft of the wardroom. As the steam clears, he recognizes the CHENG. Hubler shouts into his ear, "Can you make it from here, BT3?"

"Yes, sir."

Steam is roaring out of the fire room. It's obvious there are no other survivors. "You're alright, Petrakis. I need to flood the other magazines. Get to the weather decks and get ready to abandon ship." Hubler turns and leaves. Petrakis starts looking for a way out. Moving forward, he finds himself in the wardroom. Totally lost in the unfamiliar space, he turns back aft. The decking under him buckles and he stumbles to a knee. Fire and escaping steam are everywhere. Staggering to his feet to get his hands and knees off the hot deck, he starts to move, disoriented. All he knows is, he's on the main deck above the fire room. When he looks up, he can see a glimmer of sky, looking down he sees a buckled crack, and the movement of the ship shows him the truth, the bow and stern are moving separately. He watches the gap open and realizes the Stoddert has broken in two.

Through the smoke and steam, Donny Petrakis watches horrified as he recognizes MM3 Peter Gant from engine room 1 grasping at handholds, stumbling toward the gap. Between the bow and stern sections is a meat grinder. He tries shouting, but his lungs are so burnt with steam and smoke he can barely breath. Gant is only three feet from him, when his feet catch on something and he falls. Gant outweighs Donny by about 80 lbs. and a good 7 inches, but Donny grasps a transformer mounted on the bulkhead and leans out, catching Peter's hand. Determined, he keeps Peter from falling into the gap and drags him across onto the bow section.

Donny gets them through the wardroom and out onto the weather deck aft of mount 51 just as the bow starts to point to the sky and roll onto its starboard side. Holding on to a stanchion, they can see their stricken ship, the stern higher than the bow, but already starting to settle. No one seems to be in charge of the crewmen on the bow, and they see several of them jump off into water ten feet below.

They turn and see the shattered bridge above them and someone inside waving at them and realize it's their captain. They look at each other and start climbing the steep deck toward the bridge. They can hear Commander Douglas saying, "Abandon ship. All crew, abandon ship." With the bow now pointing up at a 45-degree angle, they are now using the bulkhead as a deck and looking down at Douglas. He's holding on, wedged between his chair and bulkhead. Both of his legs are fractured, the bones sticking out at odd angles. He has a splinter of steel sticking out of his chest and his right arm is missing just below the elbow. His face is burned, and his blonde, curly hair completely gone. He sees them, and calmly, gasping for breath, says, "Son, you executed...your duty...now, get the hell off this boat."

"Sir, we can get you, too."

Closing his eyes, fighting the pain, Douglas says, "No, damn it. I'm done for. Go."

Then the bow goes under and a wave catches them, washing them off their feet, and they're in the water. They watch their captain calmly smile as he is swallowed by the sea.

IN THE WATER

ET3 James Stakes struggles to inflate his Mae West, but it has a hole in it. He doesn't even remember the explosion, he just woke up in the water. Giving up on the vest, he sees another sailor in the water. He, contrary to his friends' jibe, can swim quit well. As he gets closer, he recognizes his friend, Karl. Karl is floating in a perfectly functioning life preserver, unseeing eyes open to the night sky. As he grabs hold of his friend, James realizes that Karl is missing his right hip, leg, and torso. Holding onto him, he sobs. Of all the dumb ass things to say, he had to make a crack about his buddy's weight, and now he's gone.

FAN TAIL

The XO, LCDR Charley Curtis is trying to get the sailors on the fan tail organized. He has them assembling a 'J' type eductor, to dewater the ship. He has a machinist mate working on a gas- powered dewatering pump. He also has sailors tending the wounded and helping get men in the water back on the boat. But, the stern is separated from the bow, which is floating off to starboard with just twenty feet left, proudly showing the number 22. The CHENG walks out on the fan tail, legs spread, carrying a sailor. He carefully sets him down, and using a bollard for support, looks around.

He walks to the XO, "What the fuck are you doing, Charley? We don't need the eductor, we need life rafts. Throw that over the side and rig life rafts. We're going down."

"The captain hasn't ordered abandon ship. I'll be damned if I will without an order."

"The captain is on the bridge. The bridge is over there sinking. Now, if you haven't fucking noticed, the 1MC is down. When I was up forward, I heard the captain give the order, okay?"

"You don't have to disrespect me in front of the troops, CHENG."

"I only disrespect you when you're being a fucking idiot. The rafts?"

"Yeah, CHENG," Curtis turns back to the men, "Start rigging rafts."

Having sorted out the fan tail, Duane Hubler turns away and goes back inside the ship to look for more sailors.

CHAPTER 10

FLIGHT DECK, USS CARL VINSON

1822, 20 December, 1941

Instead of her normal GQ station in the ready room, Lt. Sam Hunt and her squadron are on the flight deck making sure their aircraft are secure. With the severe maneuvers, they don't want to lose a plane over the side. When the torpedoes struck the Stoddert, everyone stopped to watch. Like a train wreck, they couldn't look away. For Sam, time stands still. The fourth torpedo misses the both ships, passes astern and runs itself out.

Then the captain announces on the 1MC, "Carl Vinson, the destroyer, Benjamin Stoddert, has been hit by multiple torpedoes and is going down. All helicopter crews to the flight deck. All hands prepare to receive casualties. Medical, initiate the mass casualty bill. Flight quarters." Then comes the familiar call, "Flight quarters, flight quarters." A call that's repeated on all ships that have helicopters.

I-7, JUNSEN CLASS SUBMARINE

Commander Hirotaka Chiba hears the explosion, feeling the rumble through the sub's hull, and knows his torpedoes struck a target. He looks at Sub-lieutenant Michio, who's timing the attack. Michio says, "Too soon."

Chiba raises the periscope, surveying the damage, "A large vessel, cruiser perhaps, though too few guns."

Sonarman 1st Class Ichiro Nakamura says, "Captain, I hear sonar. High frequency pinging at 30 degrees."

Chiba turns the periscope to 30 degrees, "There is nothing close." He revolves in a 360-degree search, seeing only American ships with his kill. Perhaps they will slow to render aid. He may have another opportunity if he is shrewd.

Nakamura shouts, "Captain, the sonar is close, and I hear high speed screws, a torpedo!"

"It will miss, Petty Officer, no need for excitement," assures Chiba. But, it doesn't miss. The Mark 46 torpedo uses its own sonar to locate the Japanese sub and home in. Nearly 100 pounds of high explosive detonates against the hull of I-7. The overpressure kills everyone on board instantly, crushing the center like a tin can, shredding the hull. As it starts its long dive to the bottom, the body of Sonarman 1st Class Ichiro Nakamura floats to the surface.

USS LONG BEACH BRIDGE

On the bridge, Captain Tenzar surveys the Stoddert. The Long Beach, a one of a kind nuclear powered missile cruiser, commissioned in 1961, is six miles astern of Stoddert and closing. She lacks her own helicopter, but as a flag ship, her radar and communication center are as sophisticated as any, save the Ticonderoga class ships. Tenzar quickly sees a problem and picks up the ship to ship, "Carl Vinson, this is Long Beach actual."

"Long Beach, this Carl Vinson actual, go ahead."

"We need to increase our ASW. The Fife and Jarrett are better suited to that role. Recommend Vinson continue on, escorted by Horne, Fife, and Jarrett. Long Beach will render aid and co-ordinate the rescue efforts."

"Agreed, Long Beach. Be aware the effort involves fourteen plus rotary."

"Understood." As he hangs up the radio, he sees a geyser of water to the west, so big it occludes the horizon. He picks up the 1MC, "Long Beach, the Benjamin Stoddert has been hit by torpedoes and is sinking. We have sailors in the water. We are lead vessel, so I need all hands on deck. Relax general quarters, there isn't time to secure. Muster the rescue and assistance detail in the gymnasium. Initiate the mass casualty bill. Boat crews, man the boats. Flight quarters, flight quarters. Paddles, we'll be landing the helo's with little or no wind."

The crew of the Long Beach leap into action, running to their assigned stations, ready for something to do. There will be plenty.

CARL VINSON FLIGHT DECK

The flight deck crews scramble to get all eight Sea Hawks airborne. The helos are pulled away from the island, quickly pre-flighted, and moved to their take off spots. Eightballer 1, 331, and 737 are the first off the deck with the only three SAR swimmers on the ship. No one ever planned for something like this. Next, Eightballer 223 and 876 leave with an extra flight engineer as acting SAR, leaving the last three pilots desperately searching for qualified swimmers.

Lt. JG Sandra 'Cargo Britches' Douglas, pilot of Eightballer 416, runs toward the island looking for anyone she can rope in and sees Hunt and Hoolihan, "Hey, Lt. Hunt, you know where I can get a swimmer? My bird needs one."

Sam looks at Gloria, who smiles, "You got two, now." The three women run back to the waiting helo. The rotor is already turning as Sandra climbs in the right door and motions them into the back. In the door of the bird is AB1 Gil Thompson. He grabs a harness in each hand when he sees them run up. He quickly puts a harness on Sam, and has a hand between her legs, snaking the straps into place, when her gender dawns on him, "Um, sorry, ma'am," and turns red.

Over the noise of the rotor, she says, "Just get it done." He finishes getting Sam harnessed up and turns to Gloria, "Um, ma'am?" Gloria smiles, "Come on, guy, I'm not shy. I'm here to help." Nervously, he puts her into the harness, then explains to them how to use the rescue hoist and sling, gives them their helmets, and shows how to plug into the intercom. He then closes the door and runs to the next bird.

The yellow shirt in front of the bird puts his hands over his head, and Sandra takes her up, hovers, and climbs away. Looking down, Sam sees a group of men, with swim fins on their backs, heading for the remaining helos.

Heading out to Stoddert, Sandra asks, "Ok, girls, what squadron do you belong too?"

Sam answers, "VF 154, the Black Knights."

"Okay, you can swim, right?"

"Yes," Sam drawls.

Then, "Gold Eagle, Eightballer 416 out with Lt. Douglas, Lt. Lowandowksi. SAR swimmers are Lt. Hunt and Lt. Hoolihan from VF 154. Please inform their command."

"Roger, Eightballer 416. Acknowledge Lt. Hunt and Lt. Hoolihan are your SAR swimmers. We will notify. Good hunting."

Then, "Good, now listen up. Here are CB's rules for not getting dead. The hoist operator never takes their eyes off the guy in the water. The hoist is simple to use, and once it's out, push it all the way out. Then it is up, down. Hook up to the bird or the hoist before opening the door. You don't open the door or use the hoist without my permission. The swimmer MUST make certain the ground touches the water first, before they enter the water, so they don't get dead. Once you're in the water, you pick up one person at a time, unless you're riding with them. If they are unconscious, ride them up. The hoist operator has to ignore the cargo while she is running the hoist. If they die, they die. If we lose crew, we are out of business. If you can, give us some healthy ones first, so they can buddy care. It's dark, so use your fucking strobe, and I will use the light. Hand signals for the swimmers: one hand straight up means I'm okay, one hand with raised thumb means ready for pick up, hand waved side to side means you're in trouble. Don't git in trouble. By the way, the big toothy fish are not friendly. If you get the chance, shoot to kill. Otherwise, kick, punch, and fight. I like guns, they make a girl strong. Questions?"

"No, succinct and to the point," says Sam.

"I'm good," says Gloria

"Okay, here comes our first customer. Draw straws, I don't care."

Sam looks at Gloria, "Shall I go first?"

Gloria nods, hooks up to the bird, and Sam hooks to the hoist. Gloria says, "Ready."

"Ready back here," says Sam.

"Somebody needs to remove their helmet and put on the swim cranial. Head phones don't like water."

Chagrined, Sam swaps out her headgear, and indicates they're now ready.

"Open the door."

The down wash from the helo whips the otherwise calm seas as Sam rides the cable down. A tail of cable hangs below her to ground the helicopter. Without that ground, her body would be the ground wire between the water and the electrical potential of the helicopter.

She's lowered into the water near six sailors. She swims toward them, shouting, "I need one of you in good shape." The nearest sailor shakes his head, and they start moving someone out of the center of their circle. "Listen, healthy first to take care of him," and grabs a sailor and gets him into the rescue sling. She lifts a thumb and up he goes. The remaining men push the sailor they're protecting toward her and she sees his head is a mess of blood and his eyes are swollen shut. When the harness returns, she gets him into it and rides up with him, helping him into the helo.

When he's secure, she continues bringing up the rest of the men. When they are all aboard, Gloria tells Sandra, and they move on, searching. They position over two men, and Gloria says, "My turn." Sam makes sure she's secure and lowers her down. She drops in next to ST2 John Givens who's holding YNSN Seely from behind trying to use the one life jacket to keep them both afloat. Then Sam sees movement at the edge of the light. Leaning into the cockpit, she shouts, "Gun!"

Lt. JG James 'Smooth' Landowski hands her his 1911. She leans out, seeing Gloria hooking up Seely, and sees movement again. A fin breaks the surface, she takes aim, and fires at the base of the fin. A crazy shot, but the third one hits, and the shark twists away, turning the water red. Gloria gives the thumbs up, her eyes huge, and Sam hoists the man up. She gets him out of the rig, and lowers it to bring Gloria and Givens up as fast as possible.

Once they're in the helicopter, Gloria hooks herself to the bird, pulls in the hoist, and shuts the door. "What's next?"

Sam tells Sandra, "We've one that needs medical attention, now."

Sandra replies, "Okay, on our way." She banks left, heading to the Long Beach, which is slowing to a stop near the stricken vessel. The big ship's spotlight is on the water, and she's lowering boats. Sandra heads for the fan tail with its flight deck. As they approach, another SH-3 takes off, skating to the left before pulling up and away. "Long Beach, this is Eightballer 416 coming in with one seriously wounded, eight passengers total."

"Roger, Eightballer 416, make your approach from the starboard side. Winds are calm."

Sandra slows the helicopter to a hover about 10 feet above the deck on the starboard side, skates to the left, lowers power, and smoothly eases the bird onto the flight deck. Leaving the engines running, she says on the intercom, "Open the door, girls, and get them all out." They slam the door open and gently lower the wounded sailor into the arms of Long Beach sailors. As he's carried away, the rest are helped out. "We're good to go," says Sam.

"Long Beach, Eightballer 416, request to take off port side and return to the hunt."

"Eightballer 416, Long Beach, take off and exit port side. Good luck."

With every helicopter in the battle group out, the sea is bright with spotlights searching for men in the water. Eightballer 1 is loading sailors off the very back of the fan tail of Stoddert, hovering with 1 wheel on the deck. It's a gutsy thing, as the ship is on fire and the missile magazine could cook off at any time. But the helicopters can only hold eight, and as they leave, a few sailors, trying to get on, fall into the sea.

Sandra sees four men around a body on a piece of debris at the stern. She puts Sam just outside the group, and three of the men let go and swim toward her, grabbing her and the hook, panic in their eyes. Sam shouts "GET OFF! One at a time!" and dives below, breaking contact. CG pulls up and moves the hook to where she surfaces. They all swim toward her again, and she sticks up one finger. The best swimmer gets to her first and she gets him into to the harness, gives the thumbs up, and dives again.

As she surfaces, the hook is on the way back down. She's getting the closest man into the rig, when the remaining one grabs her across the throat from behind and puts his head on her right shoulder, dragging her under. Sam lifts her right hand and punches him in the nose with the back of her fist. He grabs his abused nose, letting go of her, and soon one more is rising toward the helo. She then hooks up the last of the three, now patiently waiting his turn. "Um, sorry."

"Well, remember, we're here to help, okay?" Sam then re-orients and swims to the last two. BMSN Mitchell Blumm motions her to take the wounded man on the debris first. All of MM3 Baker's exposed skin in burned, blistered, and swollen, and as she checks him, he moves and gasps. So, very carefully, she hooks him into the harness. As she hooks herself in to ride up with him, Blumm makes the sign of the cross over him, his words lost in the noise.

Then it's one more trip down for Blumm, and back to the Vinson for Baker and more fuel. Eightballer 416 lands on the Vinson, spot 5. Gloria and Sam carefully lower Baker onto a waiting stretcher. Puck, who's helping unload helicopters, looks in their bird, "Hey, what are you two doing in there? You're soaked."

Sam looks at him, "Working."

"They're letting you swim SAR?"

"Yes, second load. We're going out again."

"Do you need any help?"

"We could use some water."

"Will do," he runs to the deck edge, coming back as they are finished the refuel and hands her a cloth bag. "Here you go, girls. Bag lunches, too. You need the energy."

Sam say, "Thanks." She looks into his eyes and smiles, then slams the door shut as CB runs up the engines for takeoff. As they fly back to Stoddert, Sam opens the bags and distributes the booty. There are containers of juice and four bag lunches with sandwiches, crackers, and fruit cups. Ravenous, they eat the food, gulping the juice between bites.

It takes twenty minutes to return to Stoddert. It's lit up with flames, helicopter spot lights, and the search lights from the Long Beach. CB shines the light over the sinking stern section and sees some sailors huddled near the missile launcher. One of them waves his arms. CB says, "Customers," and brings her bird in as close as she can onto the up-tilted fan tail. Black smoke whips around the helo when Sam opens the door. Getting out, they walk down the slanted deck, finding FN Newburg, MM1 Hammond, and the rest of the engine crew. Newburg the only one on is feet.

Sam checks Hammond and he croaks, "Them first." She shakes her head, scoops him up, her left arm under his back and her right under his knees, and forces her way up the slanting deck. He looks her in the eyes, grimacing in pain. She smiles as she carefully lays him in the helicopter, and he mouths the word, "Angel."

She meets Gloria and Newburg carrying one of the burned men on the way back. Gloria shouts, "They're all alive." Two more trips, and they're all aboard. Sam says to CB, "Burn victims, Vinson."

They fly to Vinson, land on spot 3, and off load the men. Puck, again, gives them food and water.

The survivors are now scattered out over a large area, moved by wind and current. Lt. Michael 'Moose' Rock calls, "Eight-baller 223 to any empty bird. I've found a bunch two miles north of the Stoddert."

"Roger, Moose, Cargo Britches is inbound."

As they approach the area, other helicopters are also picking up sailors. CB sees three men in the water and comes to a hover. Sam goes down again. In a way, it's better in the 85-degree water. On the cable, the down draft beating on her wet flight suit, she is very cold. She swims to the nearest man, ET2 James Stakey, clinging to the body of FC3 Karl Smith. She tries releasing James's grip on his friend and get him into the sling, "You have to let him go!"

"No! No! He's my friend, my friend!"

So, she goes to the third man and realizes he's missing from the waist down. She starts back to Smith and another man pops out of the water. Pointing to the dead man she'd just left, he says, "Take the dead, too."

"We're running out of time trying to save the living. You pick him up, I'm trying to save the living."

"Listen, lady, you have to pick up the bodies, otherwise people keep dropping SARS on them. Just do it."

"Who the fuck are you?"

"I'm a fucking SEAL lieutenant. Are you going to listen to me? Who the fuck are you?"

"Lieutenant, help me get the live guy away from his friend, then we'll pick up the dead, okay?"

In response, Lt. Issa swims one stroke to James, gets behind him, and slides his arms inside James', opening his arms up. He turns him 90 degrees and pushes him towards Sam. She grabs him and hooks him up. "It's alright, we'll get your friend." As James rides up, she looks around for the SEAL, but he's gone. She recovers the two bodies, riding up with the last one.

Gloria says, "Hey, Cargo Britches, these last two are dead."

CB says, "Okay, the body bags are in a pouch behind the seat."

Looking for more men, they overfly Stoddert's stern on the way back. There is only the transom and a few feet of ship still visible. Air bubbles and oil and debris are surfacing all around it as it slips under the water. CB says sadly, "Well, there she goes."

CHAPTER 11

EIGHTBALLER 416 AT 100 FEET, SEARCHING FOR SURVIVORS

2238, 20 December, 1941

They're all silent as CB hovers for a moment, then she pulls up on the collective, pushes the stick forward, and they continue their search. "Eightballer 416, this Eightballer 737."

"Go ahead, Eightballer, 737."

"I found a large group of survivors 16 miles north of the Long Beach, can you help me out, Cargo Britches?"

"Sure, Dim Bulb, I'm on my way."

Gloria asks, "How did you get stuck with 'Cargo Britches'?"

CB laughs, "Because, I deliver the goods."

"Um, you mean in the sack?"

"It's been said."

"Damn, and I thought 'Hot Pants' sucked."

"Yep, at least your call sign implies you have them on. I'm used to it. We're almost at Dim Bulb's position, so get ready."

"We're ready, if you're willing," teases Gloria.

"Come on, Hot Pants, don't push the metaphor too far," says CB.

Sam asks, "Do we want to know about 'Dim Bulb'?"

"He isn't stupid. In training he burned up a tranny and had to auto-gyro. Said he couldn't see the warning light 'cause it was too dim and the alarmed failed to sound. Turned out he was right. Okay, open the door, let's get to work."

As Gloria lowers on the harness, she can see Eightballer 737 departing with a full load of survivors from the raft below. Navy rafts are large orange inflatables with tent-like hoods to protect the occupants. There is one access opening and CB puts Gloria in the water right next to it. LCDR Charley Curtis pokes his head out of the hatch and shines a flashlight in Gloria's eyes, making her flinch, "Hey, shine that somewhere else!"

"Sorry," and he moves the light, then realizes she's a woman. "Who are you?"

"Does it matter? I'm a Valkyrie taking you to the promised land."

"You're an officer. You're not supposed to be a SAR swimmer."

"You're an officer, too, which means, you're not supposed to be an idiot. Do you want to be rescued, or not?"

"Yes, of course."

"It would be easier to harness people up from inside the raft, so, request permission to come aboard."

"Yes, yes, of course, Lieutenant, and I'm not an idiot."

Gloria climbs in, "That's not how it looks from here, sir. Who's first?" When no one answers, she grabs the first enlisted man near her, puts the harness on him, and does the thumbs up out the opening. LCDR Curtis sits back fuming. Soon she has all five enlisted hoisted out. Finally, it's just her and Curtis. She hooks them both up and they ride together.

As they reach the door, Sam pulls them in, then takes out the 1911 and shoots the raft. Curtis shouts, "What the hell are you doing?"

"Making sure no SAR swimmer has to dive on an empty raft, sir. You know, jumping out of an airplane is a dangerous thing." She stows the gun, then disconnects him from the harness and sits him down. "Welcome aboard, sir. How are you feeling?"

He looks quizzically at her, then Gloria says, "Somewhat sorely used."

"Well, you just had your ship blown out from under you, sir, of course, you do. I just want to make sure you're alright, so I know the level of care you need."

"Yes, yes, I'm quite alright. Please, just tend to the men."

"Of course," looking closely at his eyes, Sam sees they are unequally dilated, an indication of concussion. "We're you hit on the head, sir?"

"Just a bump, please, tend to the men."

CB says, I've spotted another one, back to work."

Sam changes to the swim cranial, hooks to the hoist, and says, "I think he may have a concussion, Gloria."

As she descends, she sees one body floating face up. She swims to him, hooks him into the harness, and as there are no other men in the water, rides up with him. It isn't until they're in the helo with the door closed and in the red interior light, that she notices his uniform is different. His rank insignia is on the shoulder, rather than the collar, and the coarse fabric is different from American cotton uniforms. She looks at Gloria, grabs a body bag, and puts him in it as quickly as possible. Then she changes to her crew helmet and hears CB ask, "Are we full up back there?"

"Yes, CB, pretty much, no serious injuries," says Gloria.

"Okay, we're going to the Long Beach, then."

Sam says, "We have one body for the Vinson after the Long Beach."

"What's the deal?" asks CB.

"He's not one of ours. I think he's Japanese, like really Japanese, from Japan."

"Oh, okay, the Vinson it is for all of them. Oh, shit. Guys, the TACAN isn't working."

"Oh, shit," Sam and Gloria say together. The TACAN is the homing beacon used to find the carrier.

"In a nutshell, we're lost, but we've got plenty of fuel." She switches channels, "Long Beach, this Eightballer 416, TACAN is down. Can you give us a steer?"

"Eightballer 416, Long Beach, climb so we can establish radar contact."

ON CAP ABOVE CARL VINSON

Lt. JG Frank 'Thud' Jackson says, "Eightballer 416, this is Knight 212. I have you 35 miles north by northwest of Long Beach. Are you returning to Long Beach or Carl Vinson?"

"Thank you, Knight 212. We're heading for Carl Vinson. Can you give us a steer?"

"Eightballer 416, after some rudimentary calculations and minor trigonometry, I'm pretty sure you should go 087 degrees, and you'll find the Vinson in about 50 miles."

CB asks, "Gloria, Sam, do you know this guy?"

Sam says, "Yeah, it's Thud, my wingman. Wonder why Speedy isn't talking?"

On radio, CB says, "Knight 212, Eightballer 416, thanks a million." Then, "That guy deserves a kiss."

Sam and Gloria laugh.

"What's so funny, guys?"

Sam says, "Un, he's so shy, he'll run in the opposite direction as fast as his legs will carry him. Great pilot, best wingman in the world, doesn't do females very well."

"Oh."

Her copilot finally says, "A guy who won't try to get you in the sack, CB? Now, I've seen it all."

"Behave, Mr. Ski. You haven't seen anything yet."

They've flown for about 20 minutes, then CB says, "I think I see the Fife. There must be a carrier around here somewhere." On radio, "Gold Eagle, this is Eightballer 416, request to marshal."

"Eightballer 416, Gold Eagle, approach at 087, make your altitude 500 feet and report when you have us in sight. You'll be landing on spot 1."

"Roger, Gold Eagle, spot one, report when in sight." On intercom, "That Thud is good. They didn't change my course."

"Yes, he reads technical manuals for fun," says Sam.

"Might just have to look him up for that kiss, oh, there it is," and switches to radio, "Gold Eagle, Eightballer 416, I have you in sight, approaching the bow to land on spot 1."

"Roger, Eightballer 416, you're cleared to land. Once chalked and chained, you will spin down your engine."

"Did we get them all, or do they just not want us flying around without a direction finder?"

"Maybe both," says Smooth.

CARL VINSON FLIGHT DECK, SPOT 1

0022, 21 December, 1941

After a long night flying, Cargo Britches still makes the landing look easy, kissing it in without a bump. While the engines are spooling down, Sam and Gloria unload their passengers. Even after their ordeal, because they were in a life raft, most of them are ambulatory. They save the Japanese body for last. Sam tells the Vinson sailors taking the body from her, "The Captain needs to know about this one. Take it to medical and inform Captain Johnson a Japanese sailor is on the boat."

She and Gloria finally climb out of the chopper and shake hands with Cargo Britches and Smooth. Turning to go, they see their XO, LCDR Carleton walking toward them. Gloria says, "Now what?"

Even over the noise of the flight deck, Carleton can be clearly heard by all four of them, "Just what the hell do you think you were doing? You want to be the fucking hero? You're pilots, not fucking SAR swimmers. I'm writing you both up for conduct unbecoming an officer."

Sam slumps, exhausted, "Really, sir?"

"You have a discipline problem, Lieutenant, and I'm going to nip it in the bud and end your career."

The two women, soaked to the skin, covered in blood and diesel oil, thirsty, hungry, and exhausted, look at each other. Sam says, "Yes, sir. Request permission to go below and clean up. And sir, fuck you very much, sir!" Not waiting for a reply, Sam walks away.

Gloria looks after her friend, smiles wryly, and says, Sir, you might have missed the fact that we were saving lives. I thought lives mattered, sir!" and follows Sam below.

FLIGHT DECK AT THE ISLAND

When they get to the hatch on the island, they bump into Chief White, "Are you two, okay?"

Sam smiles, "Yeah, thanks, Chief."

"I checked, neither of you are on rotation tonight or tomorrow morning. I got the division. Get some sleep. You too, Hoolihan. I'll tell your Chief."

FEMALE HEAD, 03 LEVEL, PORTSIDE

The female junior officer stateroom area is a small group of six staterooms. Four of the six hold two officers apiece, and two have six each. The shower area, where Sam and Gloria are cleaning off layers of gunk, has only three stalls and push button shower heads. Water is precious on a Navy ship, so Hollywood showers, where the water runs continuously, are not allowed. They have no trouble hearing each other, "Do you think Book will actually write us up? It's stupid," says Sam.

"I think 'Book' is really short for 'stupid'," answers Gloria.

"What will we do? All I've ever wanted to do is fly." In her exhaustion, her head is spinning.

"He might write us up, but it won't go anywhere. He'll just come off as an idiot. I've known guys like him before, and so have you. He wants us to fail."

"An Admiral's mast will do that. All it takes is the request being made, and we're done."

"We won't get a mast, hon, no way."

BLACK KNIGHT COMMANDER'S OFFICE

"I'm finally going to get those two. They departed their duty station without orders. They had no business out there risking their necks doing someone else's job. While they were out hot-dogging, Hunt missed a flight call. I'm going to put them back in the kitchen where they belong, uppity bitches. Hunt told me... she said 'fuck you' to her superior officer. That can't stand, it's insubordination. The way Hoolihan looked at me," he pauses, "she won't be smug in front of the admiral."

Holtz wearily raises his hand to stop the tirade, "Book, just drop it, it won't fly, and you should know that."

"I'm writing her up, anyway."

"I'll disapprove it."

"I thought you hated them, too?"

116

"I'm trying to save your sorry ass. CATCC told me they were out there. That's why I pulled them from the rotation. It won't wash."

"Jim, this will fly. No one wants them here."

"The Navy does, now drop it."

EIGHTBALLER COMMMANDER'S OFFICE

"I'm telling you, sir, their XO was really pissed. Those ladies saved the lives of some forty sailors tonight. They were amazing, and he's going to write them up. We have to do something."

"Sandra, what do you want us to do?" asks CDR David Yankee Crocket, OIC of the Eightballers Detachment on the Carl Vinson.

"I want them put in for medals."

"They don't work for us."

"They did when they were in the back of my bird."

"Okay, write it up."

CHAPTER 12

SAMANTHA AND GLORIA'S STATEROOM

0500, 21 December, 1941

Sam is jarred awake by a knock on the door, "RT classroom in 30 minutes." Rolling over, she looks at her clock, 0500. Groaning, she crawls out of her rack, finds her footing, and tries to stretch the pain out of her cramped muscles, "I need Motrin."

Gloria sleepily asks, "Flight call?"

"No, honey, go back to sleep." She gets dressed, swallows a couple of Motrin, gets a quick bite and coffee in wardroom 3, and makes her way to the RT classroom. She's the last one in.

RT CLASSROOM

"Grab some coffee, Lieutenant." Gratefully, she gets another cup of coffee and sits down. Captain Klindt continues, "The situation has changed. We will be briefing Admiral Ren and all the captains in two hours. We need definitive answers. John, why don't you take the white board, and MM1 Hughes, you're still the clerk. John the following facts:

Freak lightning storm that caused no damage,

Loss of communications with satellites, an all other high frequency comms,

Hewitt is missing,

Loran station could not be located,

> Old airplane of possible Japanese origin,
>
> Old music on AM frequencies."

Sam speaks up, "Add the attack on the Benjamin Stoddert and a Japanese sailor's body recovered from near where the attacking sub was sunk."

Klindt asks, "We recovered the body of a Japanese sailor?"

"Yes, sir. Not sure he came from the sub, but he was wearing a Japanese Navy uniform. I fished him out of the water."

Warren asks, "What were you doing in the water?"

"SAR swimming. It isn't relevant. Trust me, he's Japanese."

Lt. Mike Mohr says, "Sir, don't forget the torpedoes were the old WWII straight line, leaves bubbles type, not modern guided ones."

"Right, put it all on the board," waiting for Warren to finish.

"Next list:

> EMP, short of electro-magnetic pulse,
>
> Solar Flare,
>
> Russian secret weapon, similar to EMP,
>
> Mass hallucination,
>
> Bermuda triangle,
>
> Alternative space time continuum,
>
> EMP directed only at satellites,
>
> Time travel."

After a moment, Klindt says, "Okay, now, no matter how seemingly ridiculous, let's take each theory and check off how many facts fit them. EMP – one, maybe two, maybe three. Solar flare, the same. Russian weapon, again, the same. EMP at satellites, it's all the same thing. Right, all these amount to the same thing, some electro-magnetic disturbance and none of it explains what is happening down here. Mass hallucination, anyone want to take a crack at that?"

"No, all of us? All the techies? I don't think so," says Hunt.

Hughes adds, "Hallucinations can't burn or kill. I helped move guys from the flight deck to medical. No way."

"Next, the Bermuda Triangle. Never mind we're half a world away from Bermuda, and I don't think we're near the Devil's Triangle here in the Pacific. What do you think?"

CT1 Barr says, "Sir, I asked the bridge watch. They said Lt. Hunt was on the helm. Did the compass swing randomly?"

"It was the first time I ever steered a ship, but I don't recall the compass ever changing except when we changed course. I was on the helm after the storm. And I really need to get my SWO."

Barr nods his head, "I talked to the helmsman in medical. He's partially paralyzed. He said it was steady until he got knocked out. I know the gyro compass in combat never moved. Always, in Bermuda Triangle stories, they say the compass spins. Also, we're not lost. We found the atoll fine, and the Quarter Masters had no trouble getting fixes. We are not lost, so I don't see the Bermuda Triangle working."

"If I recall, it was you that came up with it," says Klindt.

"Yes, sir, but I realize it doesn't work."

"Okay, that leaves alternative space time continuum and time travel. Lt. Mohr, would you agree that ASTC is essentially the same as time travel?"

"Well, no, sir, the concepts are totally different. With time travel, you go back in your time stream creating all kinds of paradox. In ASTC, and I love the initialism, a new time line is created, avoiding paradox."

Hughes sighs, "Oh my God. Geek alert."

Klindt says, "Okay, conceded. But if we're experiencing one or the other it would look the same. We could not be aware of our own paradox."

Hughes moans, "Oh no, it's contagious."

Sam is staring, her eyes unfocused. Warren asks, "Hunt, are you okay?"

She shakes her head, "My God, if we've traveled back in time, they are all gone."

Klindt asks, "Who's gone, Hunt?"

"Everybody, sir. Everybody. Our families no longer exist."

Stunned, they look at each other in silence. Hughes shakes his head, "Yeah, but it's just a theory. There's just no way we could travel back in time."

Mohr replies, "Um, it works for the facts we have."

"Yeah, like that count down movie, but that stuff just don't happen," say Hughes.

Exasperated, Mohr says, "All I'm saying, is it works. You have a better explanation that fits the facts, then give it."

"Gentlemen," Klindt interrupts, "We have to brief the Admiral and a slew of captains in about an hour. Let's WORK the problem, not BE the problem. Does time travel actually work to answer all the facts?"

"Yes," says Mohr, "It works if we are now in World War II. That would, or could, explain everything. No GPS, coms, or Loran, they didn't exist then. The Stoddert, the non-homing torpedoes, the Japanese sailor, and even the patrol plane are explained, if we went back in time."

"If we have, then denial is fatal," says Hunt, looking at Hughes. "We already lost the Stoddert because we couldn't figure it out."

Barr says, "There is a problem with all of this. What time is it? Heck, what day is it" Has the war just started, or is it almost over? That matters."

"He's right, how do we figure it out?" asks Sam.

"First, do we all agree that time travel is the most plausible, if seemingly preposterous explanation?" asks Klindt. They all nod their heads. "Okay, now how can we determine the date?"

Denton asks, "Celestially?"

Klindt says, "That can tell where we are, if we know when we are, or, when we are, if we know where we are. It can't do both."

"How do you know so much about navigation?" asks Denton.

"My last ship, the cruiser Virginia, I was her captain. A skipper has to know where he's going."

"I can tell if we've dropped the bomb yet, or not," says Warren. "We do an internal dose count on the dead Japanese. That would make me a believer."

"How does that tell us anything?" asks Barr

"Good idea," says Hunt.

"I don't get it. What if he wasn't near the bomb site to get irradiated?" asks Barr.

Hughes smiles, "He doesn't have to be. We all have higher dose counts then he will."

"I'm not a nuke," says Barr.

"Hughes is right. Because of all the testing since 1945, it is ambient. We all have elevated radiation counts, which the Japanese won't have. Warren, Hughes, see to it. We'll catch you up when you get back," says Klindt. He looks at the remaining five, "Can we narrow it down further?"

Richardson says, "History books? Overfly an island, like Tarawa, where the photo was taken on a specific date. If the Japanese hold it, then we're before that date."

"We could try to get somebody on the short wave and ask," says Denton.

Klindt says, "What would we tell them? Most people know what day it is."

"I don't know, maybe say I'm a ship wreck survivor on Gilligan's Island?"

"Why don't you say you're a private sail yacht and you've lost track of time. Keep it simple," says Sam.

"Okay, that's better than Gilligan's Island."

Richardson asks, "Did people sail around in private yachts back then?"

Mohr answers, "Yeah, it happened, though it was rare. My step-dad is a sail boat nut."

Klindt picks up the wall phone and dials the bridge, "Sir, it's Klindt, I would like to send Petty Officers Denton and Barr up to radio to raise someone on short wave... Yes, sir, it's worth breaking radio silence. Thank you, sir." He turns to the petty officers, "Boys, up to radio with you, and practice a good lie."

"Now, folks, we are testing our theory. Good. While they're gone, let's talk about what we ought to do should it be true."

"Sir, anything we do will change history. That's not good," says Sam.

Mohr tilts his head, "We sank a Japanese submarine, and have one of its sailors on ice. That already changes history."

"Point."

"I agree, that ship has already sailed. Now what?" asks Klindt.

Mohr says, "We kick some Japanese ass, sir, then report to higher."

"Who, Roosevelt?" asks Richardson.

"Why should we fight first, Mohr? I'm not sure we should expend irreplaceable assets until higher has a chance to think it through," says Klindt.

"Well, sir, this is what I'm thinking. Picture yourself as, say Admiral Nimitz. We show up and say 'Hi, we're this kick ass ship from the future here to help.' And he's like, 'cool, but what can you do?' Much better if we say, 'Hi, we're a kick ass ship from the future and look at what we've already done," says Mohr.

"Good point."

"Shit, I have a good history of WWII in my stuff for some light West Pac reading. May I go get it, sir? We'll know where they are. Know, not guess," says Richardson.

"Light reading?" says Sam.

"Yes, I'm not a wing wiper. I'm way past 'see spot run'," says Richardson, as he leaves to laughter.

DOSIMETRY OFFICE

0550, 21 December, 1941

It was actually easier to move the body to dosimetry, than to move the big radiation detector to the body. Hughes and Warren carry the body bag to the dosimetry office, trying to ignore the stares from the crew. The engineering laboratory tech, MM1 Klegman, stops them at the door, "Hey, hey Hughes, what the hell are you doing?" You can't bring a body in here. Hell, you aren't allowed in here. Get the hell out…"

Lt. Warren cuts him off, "Stow it, Klegman. We've got orders."

Hughes unzips the bag and smiles at Klegman. Klegman gets a good look at the dead Japanese, who's swollen and a dark red from the pressure that killed him. He retches, motioning them out, "I don't care. Get it the hell out ahere!"

Muscling past him, they get the body into the small office and Hughes says, "Listen, Klegman, he's kinda heavy and sorta squishy. Are you going to fire up the internal monitor, or should I just set him in your lap while I do it?"

Klegman turns green and howls, "Sirrrr?"

Warren says, "The orders are from the RO. Now, are you going to run your machine, or hold the body?"

Klegman starts setting up the internal dose detector. Hughes says, "Come on, man. Hurry up. I think he's leaking into the bag. Oops, I'm losing him!" Klegman starts to answer, raises his thumb, indicating the machine is ready, and sticks his head in the trash, vomiting violently.

Hughes and Warren maneuver the body so its chest is against the tester. Klegman, head still in the trash can, says, "You hafta open his shirt an...oh, um, ya hafta dry him off. Sea water will, ugh, oh man, throw off the test."

Hughes mutters under his breath, "ELT pussy. He oughta clean the oily waste tank sometime." He and Warren struggle to get the shirt open while still holding the body, then he uses chem wipes off the desk to clean the now bare chest. They put the body against the test plate and Hughes says, "Hey, Vomitus! Turn this fucker on."

The ELT lifts his head long enough to push a button, gets another look at the dead sailor's face, and goes another round. Between dry heaves, he says, "When the light turns green, tell me what it reads."

It takes about 45 seconds before the light turns green. Hughes says, "It reads 9 counts."

Klegman says, "That's not right. It should be above 20. About 20 is background." His curiosity getting the better of him, he looks up. "Hug...it was calibrated this morning by Sherry and she's pretty careful. Sorry, guys, I need to calibrate it again. Remove the, um, move him away." Klegman puts in place a test source and runs a check. It comes out okay, and he notes the calibration card. He changes sources and gets the same result. "Okay, um, let's do it again." Forty-five seconds later, it still reads 9. "This isn't right," he mumbles, as Warren and Hughes exchange a look.

Lt. Warren says, "Thank you, Klegman, you've been most

helpful."

"But the machine isn't reading right, sir."

"We have to get the dead guy back to the morgue, thank you, Klegman." To Hughes, "Let's go, the RO is waiting."

CHAPTER 13

RADIO ROOM, CARL VINSON

0550, 21, December, 1941

"You should make the call, you're the radio operator," says Barr.

"Which is why I shouldn't. Any competent radio operator would know what day it is," replies Denton. "Anyway, you speak all those languages. Let's put them to use."

"Okay, I can do that, alright."

"Just keep to the story and someone will bite."

Barr sits at the console, "Okay, here goes." He gets on the radio and transmits in French, "Hello? Hello? Could anyone help me? I'm lost."

A reply in an Australian accent comes back, "VK6769 to unknown station, you shouldn't be playing with your father's radio."

Barr switches to heavily accented English, "My father is, sir, he's morte, sorry, dead. And I am lost."

"Good, you speak English. Your dad teach you?"

"Yes, sir, my father is, was a sailor and we've been sailing since I was little."

"You're on a sail boat?"

"Yes, sir, somewhere east of the Philippines. I can read the chart and I can use the sextant, but I can't do the tables because I don't know when it is to use the declination tables.

My father taught me."

"You need the date?"

"Yes, sir."

"How old are you, son?" Barr looks up at Denton, panicking. Denton hold up one and two fingers.

"I'm twelve years old."

"Do you know the Japanese are invading the Philippines?"

"No."

"Head way east before heading south. Get to Brisbane and we'll take care of you. And son, it's December 21st, 1941."

Barr's voice cracks for real, "Merci, si'l vous plait."

RT CLASSROOM

0645, 21 December, 1941

Lt. Warren and MM1 Hughes are the last two back. Hughes says, "Sorry boss. We changed clothes to get the dead guy funk off us."

Klindt nods as they sit down, "No problem. What did you find?"

Warren says, "The guy is pre-1945. He had 9 counts, which is 11 counts lower than background."

Klindt says, "Good. We now have a body of evidence to bring to the meeting. I know this sucks, but we need to focus on what is in front of us. I'll do most of the talking, but expect some tough questions. Give them your best, and remember, 'I don't know' is an answer."

"What did we miss?" asks Warren.

"The date is December 21st, 1941. Richardson has a couple of good histories to guide us, and, well, we are out of time. Let's go."

THE AUSTRALIAN DESERT

21 December, 1941

A Ford sedan and an army truck pull up to a complex of dilapidated old buildings. John Dunham leaves the car, followed by Major Walter Prescott. Dunham looks around, incredulous. "What happened here? Professor? Professor?" He runs toward the largest building.

Major Prescott tells the soldiers in the truck to dismount. "My God, man, what happened here? A few days ago, it was pristine. Men, fan out and look for survivors." Grumbling, the men search the complex.

Dunham and Prescott enter the large building, its door unlocked and partly off its hinges. As they pull it open, it falls with a crash. Walking in, Dunham says, "Major, this is where the cyclotron is."

"What is it? I mean, really, what is it?"

"In essence, it's a time machine. It sends a signal that has tremendous power, which draws objects back in time."

"Did it work? This place is changed, but I don't see any futuristic military equipment. Where is it?"

"Most of the power plant equipment is gone. It looks like it was removed a long time ago. The cyclotron is pretty much intact, though. There is no sign of an explosion in the transmission room. Let's check the office and control room."

Circuit panels are in place, but the control consoles are missing, only wiring sticking out of the floor to show where they stood. Prescott says, "What a mess. Mr. Dunham, you worked with the professor, what could have happened?"

"I don't know. The receiving antenna is five mile south of here. The reaction must have been must larger than anticipated."

"Then let's go recover our prize."

"I don't get it. Why didn't they maintain this place? What happened here?"

They hear a shout, "Major, come out here. You need to see this."

Back out under the blazing sun, they follow Corporal Stackhouse to the south side of the complex. There is an old car, small and boxy, the tires tucked within the body of the vehicle instead of having proper fenders. Most of the light blue paint is gone, the windows cracked and hazed by the heat and blowing sand. The corporal points to the grill. It is then they see the word 'Toyota.'

ADMIRAL'S CONFERENCE ROOM, 03 LEVEL

0700, 21 December, 1941

Admiral Ren, Captain Johnson, and all the captains of the battle group, are sitting at the table. Captain Klindt, at the podium, surveys their faces; Captain Tenzar of the nuclear cruiser Long Beach, Captain John Rodgers of the guided missile cruiser Horne, Commander James Lamoure of the Spruance class destroyer Fife, Commander Robert Hilton of the guided missile frigate Jarrett, Captain Dwight Edwards of the supply ship Camden, and Ship's Master Donald of the supply ship USNS Henry J. Kaiser.

With the brain trust behind him, Klindt begins, "Gentlemen, our conclusion is we've traveled, either back in time, or into an alternate space time continuum. The supporting facts are...."

Rodgers of the Horne breaks in, "Rubbish, pure garbage. Captain Johnson, is this what passes for intel over here?" Captain Johnson just holds up his index finger and lets Rodgers continue. "It sounds to me like Klindt is writing a novel, rather than investigating facts. Do you have anything of actual value to add to this fantasy convention, Captain Johnson?"

"Good, my turn. I asked MY people to come up with a conclusion that meets ALL THE FACTS. Captain Klindt, please proceed."

Klindt explains the facts and conclusions of the brain trust, "I know it sounds fantastical, but it is the only conclusion that supports the facts we have, sir."

"Rodgers says, "This is stupid. There is no way you're right."

Johnson says, "Captain Rodgers, obviously you and your crew have worked out an alternative reason for the Japanese to have attacked United States vessels with WWII torpedoes. If so, quit holding back, and spill it. Meanwhile, I would ask the Captain to be mindful that THIS captain has no patience with posturing and nay saying. We have lost friends, a ship, and are out of contact with higher, so, Captain Rodgers, add something constructive, or stow it."

Rodgers glares at Johnson.

Admiral Ren says, "Well, Captain Rodgers, do you have a theory to counter that of our brain trust?"

'No, sir, but this is stupid," Rodgers says through clenched teeth.

Admiral Ren says, "Very well, then, thank you, Captain Rodgers. Now, Captain Klindt, do you or your people have any idea how this happened?"

"Sir, we know, what, when, and where, but how and why are eluding us so far."

"It's a start. Please, freshen up my history. Who is Pacific Fleet now, and what are the Japanese up to?"

Klindt points to Richardson, "Admiral Nimitz is already in charge. The Japanese will invade Wake Island on the 23rd, and our Marines surrender after about five hours of fighting. The Japanese invade Luzon tomorrow, the 22nd. They already have some islands in southern PI. They are pushing down

Malaysia toward Singapore, and Pearl Harbor is recovering. We have seven aircraft carriers in commission, most of them in the Pacific Theater, eight, counting the Carl Vinson, sir."

Ren says, "Thank you, Senior Chief. Okay, people, ideas. What is our next move?"

Johnson says, "We need to make contact with Pearl."

Klindt says, "We're out here, let's do something."

Lt. Mohr says, "We need to kick some ass, sir."

The officers chuckle and Ren says, "Thank you, Lieutenant, I agree. But first, Captain Johnson, how do we make contact?"

Johnson replies, "Not sure, sir. We can't just call on the radio, they wouldn't believe it. We are way out of range to fly there. I guess, fight first, report later."

Commander James Lamoure of Fife says, "Sir, we are critically short on ASW with Stoddert and Hewitt both gone."

Ren says, "True. We have what we have, though. You're ASW commander, how do we work this problem?"

"Sir, we need to fly more helo sorties to make up, and we need to zigzag to screw up their targeting."

"That will mess up flight ops, but I see your point." He picks up a wall phone, "Ren here, start zigzagging 10 degrees from base line as soon as everyone gets the word." He hangs up, "Next, do we know where their fleet is? I want to sink some aircraft carriers."

In the silence, all eyes turn to Senior Chief Richardson, "The invasion of PI is the biggest thing happening in the next few days, with more than 100,000 Japanese soldiers landing. I have found only one carrier, the Ryujo, in the area. There is mention of a third carrier division, but I can't tell what ships are in it. According to accounts, more than 300 Japanese aircraft took part in the invasion. They had to come from somewhere, maybe Taiwan. It's the best I have, sorry."

"Thank you, Senior Chief," Johnson says. "Sir, could we hit PI, then Wake on the way back to Pearl?"

Ren asks, "What's the size of the Japanese force attacking Wake?"

Richardson says, "The Japanese had about 2,500 men, 2 carriers, with some cruisers and destroyers."

Ren asks, "How about the fleet attacking PI? Do we know where they are at?"

Richardson replies, "The book is vague, and I'm still researching. According to one map I found, they attacked from the South China Sea off Lingayen Gulf. With the short legs of WWII planes, they would have to be within about 300 miles of Luzon."

Ren says, "Okay. Seems to me the fight in PI is more important than Wake. We hit PI and then, if we can find them, we hit the forces around Wake."

Captain Tenzar of the Long Beach asks, "What about paradox, sir."

Klindt replies, "As Lt. Mohr pointed out when I brought it up, we've already sunk a Japanese sub. So, that ship has sailed."

Ren says, "This isn't a war we expected to fight, gentlemen, but it is the one in front of us, and we have our duty. I know it's a lot to take in and believe, but, under the circumstances, we have to try." Turning to Klindt, "One last thing, sir, are we going to be able to go home?"

Klindt looks at his team, and Lt. Hunt says, "What do you mean by going home, sir?"

"I mean, back to our own time."

Hunt says, "We don't know, sir. We don't know how we got here."

Tenzar, "Admiral, what would you recommend we tell our crews? I prefer the truth, but this truth is hard to swallow."

"Hard or not, the crews deserve the truth as we know it. Break it to them nice, maybe after a good meal and ice cream. Until the captains make their announcements, this meeting is classified."

Hunt says, "Sir, they will know something is up."

Ren smiles, "That is true, Lieutenant, but it is harder to get pissed with a bowl of rocky road in front of you."

She smiles, comprehending, as the senior officers' nod.

Ren says, "Okay, dismissed. I have an alpha strike to plan. Captain Lamoure, get your ASW plan on my desk soonest. Captain Klindt, I want your brain trust meeting once a day. Try to keep ahead of this. Thank you."

HOKKAIDO JAPAN, ARMY INTELLIGENCE STATION

21 December, 1941

Ichiro Nagasawa is tied to a chair in a room with bare walls, save for a picture of Emperor Hirohito. There's a table with another chair facing him. His right eye is nearly swollen shut and he has welts on his torso. Finally, the door opens, and his interrogator walks in with a major. The uniforms are from WWII, as is the attitude of his jailors. The major sits down in the empty chair, and his interrogator, a captain, walks behind Nagasawa.

"Mr. Nagasawa, what year were you born?" asks the major.

"I told the captain, 1947. Why did you arrest me?"

"Please, Mr. Nagasawa, where did you attend university?"

"The Massachusetts Institute of Technology in Cambridge, Massachusetts. I completed my master's degree three years ago, in 1987. Why is this important?"

"Mr. Nagasawa, I ask the questions. What did you do before going to university?"

"I was a fighter pilot with the 305th squadron out of Hyakuri.

I flew the F-4 and F-15 fighters. I was a test pilot for the F-15J when we received it from the Americans. I do not understand why this is important?"

"You tell me the wonderful planes at Chitose were given to us by the American government?"

"No, of course not, we bought them."

"How much did we pay for them?"

"I'm not sure, two billion Yen a piece, or so."

The captain says, "Cannot be. We could buy three battleships for less."

The major hisses at him to be silent, "How long has Japan flown the beautiful planes at Chitose?"

"We've had jets since 1953, but we've only had the F-15s since 1978."

"How long has Japan and America been friends?"

"This is ridiculous! Have you lived under a rock? Since we lost the war."

"And when was that? When did we lose the war?"

"After the Americans destroyed Hiroshima and Nagasaki in August, 1945."

"You mean we gave in after just two cities were bombed? That cannot be true!"

"You're serious? You do not know? How can that be?"

"It's is December 21ˢᵗ, 1941, Mr. Nagasawa. You tell me how it is you are here?"

Ichiro stares at him, shocked. "That cannot be! My wife, Kaoru, my little Kenji!" He bursts into tears, hanging his head.

"It is, Mr. Nagasawa. Can you explain why?"

Looking up at his tormentor, despair in his eyes, "No, I have no idea how such a thing could happen. There was a large lightning storm, such as I have never seen before. After the storm cleared, I recall seeing a Rei-san A6M abort a landing, which I thought was odd. Chitose is exclusively a military field. I went back into my office. I tried to call...I tried to call home. I couldn't get through, so I continued working at my desk. Then your soldiers arrested me."

"You know how to fly the planes at Chitose?"

"Yes, of course."

"You know how they are built?"

"It's why I went to school."

"You will fly against the Americans so we may defeat them."

"No."

"I was not asking."

"I care not. We should beg forgiveness of the Americans before they reduce out islands to radioactive cinders."

"We could force you to."

"No, you cannot. I have no family to threaten. You can beat me. You can starve me. You can put a gun to my head. I will not contribute to the destruction of the home I love. We cannot defeat the Americans. For every aircraft we shoot down, they build two; for every ship we sink, they build three. They will have nuclear weapons soon, if they do not now."

"What is this weapon you speak of?"

"One bomb, from one aircraft, will obliterate a city in a ten-mile circle. In my time, the Americans have thousands of them, more than anyone in the world."

"And how many do we have in Chitose?"

"None, we do not use them. We do not have them. They are terrible beyond comprehension."

"If they are so horrible, then why will you not help us defend our home from them?"

"If you carried a bucket, could you stop a tsunami? With a shovel, could you stop an earthquake? It's as much folly trying to stop the Americans."

"You would rather die, than fight?"

"I will die either way. Can you imagine watching a child slowly die as her skin rots and falls off? Her face disfigured by burns? Skin draping like curtains from her little arms? It is the nature of atomic weapons."

"You have knowledge we need. Perhaps, we may expand our territory, as we must, and then sue for peace. It is the plan, after all."

Ichiro hangs his head for a moment, then looks up, "I do not know how it is I have come back in time. It bewilders me. But, if I did, is it not conceivable that some American Air Force base did as well?"

"Yes, that is why we need your expertise."

"Even now, they could be loading nuclear bombs aboard their aircraft and preparing to attack us. It would be a disagreeable mission for the Americans from 1990, but not as much as it would be for a Japanese."

"Mr. Nagasawa, already we are at war. No matter your wishes, that cannot change. Help us end it well. Save that little girl you spoke of. What is it you need to be convinced?'

Ichiro is silent, then says, "I need to speak to the Emperor. That is my price. If I may speak with the Emperor first, only then will I help."

CHAPTER 14

MEDICAL DEPARTMENT, USS CARL VINSON

1152, 21 December, 1941

Sam and Gloria are walking in Medical down an athwart ship blue-painted passageway. Hanging on the wall are the pictures of all the corpsmen who have received the Medal of Honor. It's generally quiet, but today, those working here are even quieter, but the moans of the wounded can clearly be heard. Then they hear, "Get out. I will take care of your friend, now get out." A doctor in scrubs escorts Fireman Newburg out.

Newburg says, "Sir, I was ordered to stay with him. ORDERED! All the others died, sir. Ham has to make it."

Sam says, "Hey there! Have you had anything to eat?"

"No, ma'am, but I'm fine. I can wait."

Sam says, "No, you can't. Come with me." Then to the doc, "I've got him, sir."

The tired surgeon says, "Thank you, Lieutenant," and walks back into Medical.

Newburg sets his feet, "NO!"

Grinning, she asks, "Rank, name?"

He looks her in the eye, "Newburg, Greg, Fireman." Then, in recognition, "Ma'am, are you the ladies from the helicopter?"

Sam says, "Yeah, and you need some coffee and something to

eat, Fireman Greg Newburg. This is Lt. Hoolihan, and I'm Lt. Hunt. Let's get you fed."

Taking his arm, she starts him moving as she talks, "Who ordered you to stay with your friend?"

"My CHENG ordered me to. He saved my life. He saved Ham's life. He saved all our lives. He told me, he said, 'Fireman Newburg, stay with these guys.' I did. When all the people left the ship, they didn't help me. They said to jump, but Ham and the guys, they couldn't jump, so I stayed. And...and...and then you came. You brought the helicopter and it was like a miracle. God brought you angels to save us. That's what Ham said."

Sam glances a look at Gloria, "Is that your friend in surgery?"

"Yes, um, Ham is not really my friend. Um, he's my LPO. Me being his friend would be like being your friend, ma'am. Um, begging pardon. I'm just a fireman."

"You're a very brave fireman, and I'm honored to know you."

Taking off their covers as they enter the mess decks, they head for the chow line. Gloria asks the crew waiting in line, "He's off the Stoddert. May we cut?"

The sailors make room, and Gloria nabs a tray for Newburg and they start down the line. "What do you want?" asks Sam.

He looks surprised that they're actually in line, "Um, a slider, please, and um, fries, and corn, please." The mess attendants fill his plate as Gloria points to his choices, getting plenty of ketchup for his fries. Sam takes him to a table with his tray, and Gloria joins them with three coffees. Newburg starts eating, then notices they aren't. "Um, ma'am, aren't you eating, too?"

Sam says, "No, Greg, we've already eaten."

Between bites, Newburg says, "I'm not brave like you said. Ham and the CHENG, they are brave. Ham, he didn't even want me down there, like I wasn't good enough. He said I wasn't old enough to shave, so I needed to go topside. Why would he do that if I was brave?"

Sam looks him in the eye, "He said that to save your life."

Newburg starts to cry, "Me, and now I'm crying like a baby. He stayed down there. He was the last guy out, 'cept maybe the CHENG. And he saved me, too. Ham is the brave one."

Sam sees how carefully he's holding his slider, "Have the corpsman looked at you yet?"

"I'm fine. The others, they need help, but I'm fine. Just a couple of little burns. No worse than I get all the time just working."

"Answer the question, Fireman."

"Um, no ma'am. They've just been pushing me away from Ham and the others. The others didn't make it." He starts crying again, lifting a hand to wipe his tears.

As he does, Gloria gasps, "Greg, show us your hands." He puts them out, palms up, and they see several blisters, the largest as big as a silver dollar.

Sam asks, "How do they feel?"

Newburg shrugs, "They hurt some, but I've done worse. Steam is hot, you know."

"How old are you, son?"

"Seventeen, ma'am. Been in the Navy seven months."

Gloria says, "Finish up, you need to get those burns looked at."

When they return to medical, they see a corpsman in black BDUs carrying a tray of supplies into a ward. Sam says, "He has burns on his hands that weren't treated, can you check them, corpsman?"

HM1 Larry 'Munchkin' Shockley, the SEAL corpsman, says, "Sure." To Greg, "Let's see your hands."

Greg shows them, "No big deal, like I told them. I had worse."

"They need cleaned and bandaged. If you let burns like these go, they can turn septic and cost you your hand or your life." Then to Sam, "I have him, ma'am. Is he one of your airmen?"

"No, he's off the Stoddert. One of our pick-ups last night."

"Oh, he was with the burn victims. That explains why he's been underfoot. I'm sorry, um, sorry we didn't tend to you. What's your name?"

"Newburg, Greg, Fireman."

"I have him, ma'am. We have to attach him to a unit. Shall I give him to your squadron?"

"Sure, that fine. It's VF-154." She grins at Newburg, "You're officially a Black Knight."

HANGER BAY 3

1230, 21 December, 1941

Chief White gives out assignments to the division and asks, "Anything to add, Lieutenant?"

"Just this, things have changed after the Stoddert. Keep every bird as ready as we can, fueled, armed, and ready to fly. I can't say anything more now. Chief, a word?" and walks away from the group. "Chief, we have a new member in our division, Fireman Greg Newburg. He's is in medical right now getting his burns tended."

"Where did we get him, Stoddert?"

"Yeah, Hoolihan and I picked him up, with most of his watch team, off the fan tail, just before she sank. Most of them didn't make it."

"Understood. It was a gutsy thing you and Lt. Hoolihan did last night, LT, a fine thing." He smiles, "Aye, ma'am, I'll send someone to fetch him."

"Thank you, Chief."

Then they hear, "All hands, this is the Captain. The sun has crossed the yard arm and I think it's a good time for ice cream. Stand down for the afternoon, unless otherwise assigned, and grab a bite of goodness on the aft mess decks courtesy of the wardroom. That is all."

BLACK KNIGHT READY ROOM

1330, 21 December, 1941

Sam walks in and all eyes turn to her. Holtz is doing paper work, some of the guys are playing Hearts, and others are watching Raiders of the Lost Ark on site tv. Thud is leaning back reading a book, as is Puck. There are a couple of tubs of ice cream open on a table and most of the guys have a bowl in front of them. Ensign Robert 'Bo-Bo' Bolen, says, "Well, if it ain't the Admiral's girl Friday."

Sam tenses and looks around, realizing they are all looking at her.

"Stow it, Bo-Bo," says Holtz

Samantha squares her shoulders and walks over to Puck. "Why, Boss, worried she might just tattle and ruin your chance for an eagle on your collar?"

"No, I'm worried you've pulled too many g's and now you're thinking with your ass."

Sam sits down next to Puck, and he asks, "Any word on what's going on?"

Looking straight ahead, she says, "I can't say until the Captain makes his announcement, sorry."

Gloria walks in, all smiles, looks around and sees Sam. She kneels on the chair in front of her friend, "So, what's going on?"

"Can't say, Gloria."

The 1MC comes on, "Good afternoon, Carl Vinson, this is the Captain. I hope you're enjoying your ice cream. Now, I need you all to listen up, because this is a difficult announcement. As you know, three nights ago we experienced a severe lightning storm. Since then, we have been out of communication with Washington, D.C. and Hawaii. We have tried to re-establish comms to figure out what happened. Some believed the storm to be some type of attack. After the sinking of the Benjamin Stoddert it seems likely. I can now explain in part what happened. I cannot explain how or why, but I can explain what and when. The Stoddert was sunk by three Japanese Long Lance torpedoes fired from a WWII Japanese submarine. The reason the Japanese fired on us is because the date right now is December 21, 1941. Crew, you heard right. December 21, 1941. I do not know how that storm brought us back in time, but I do know it did. Because it did, we are now in a state of war with Japan, Germany, and Italy. I want each of you to focus on your duties and keep working safely. Trust that we will keep you informed and take care of you as best we can. Thank you, Captain out."

The ready room is quiet, the Bo-Bo says, "Bull shit. Tell me, Hunt, what shit is the CO smoke'n? He has to be smoking something."

"He's not."

Book looks up from the game of Hearts, "Come on, Hunt. Give. Why does the Skipper think we are in WWII?"

Sam looks at Holtz, "Sir?"

"Go ahead, Lieutenant, explain," replies Holtz.

Sam walks up to the front white board and writes down the reasons from the brain trust. She has everyone's complete attention. Next, she writes down the supporting evidence. As she finishes, Thud raises his hand. She nods, and he asks, "So, the Hewitt was outside the storm."

"Yes."

Bo-Bo raises his hand, "Oh, teacher, teacher, does this mean I can date Marilyn Monroe?"

"She's like nine years old, dumb ass," says Swede, "now, stow it. I want to hear the grownups talk."

Sam asks, "Questions?"

Papa says, "Just about a thousand, but the most relevant is: what does the Captain plan on doing?"

"He wants us to wrap our heads around being in World War II. I'm not able to say much more than that."

"Hey, guys!" chortles Lt. JG Lorne 'Jedi' Luke, "We're gonna get to shoot down some Japs. Hell, we'll all make ace. Even nerd boy, Thud, might shoot something down."

Thud shrugs his shoulders and goes back to reading.

"Quiet down!" Papa looks at Sam, "He mentioned to you what he is planning to do, but you don't think you have permission to say. Am I close?"

She makes eye contact with him, and lowers her gaze before saying, "You're very close, sir."

"Okay, I take it he wants to go kick some ass. I don't care where, yet, just that we will attack."

"Yes, sir."

Papa looks out over his people, "Okay, ladies, I want every bird A-1 ready. I know we just checked them. Check 'em again. Keep your eyes on the prize, people. I want to be able to launch everything as soon as we are given a mission. That means get out there and get to work. Let's go, people."

As they leave, Puck and Sam lock eyes briefly, and Papa calls out, "Lieutenant Hunt, a moment?"

"Yes, sir," and turns back.

"You need to decide who you're working for. It's bullshit that you are keeping secrets from me. I can't have it. So, what's it going to be, Lieutenant? Are you going to trust the man who writes your FITREP, or play I got a secret?"

Sam takes a deep breath and slowly exhales, looking him in the eye, "Sir, this isn't about secrets, this is about the chain of command. When the Admiral and the Captain both tell me that what I know is classified and it doesn't leave the room, what am I supposed to do?"

"You're supposed to shut up about it to everyone, but me. Is that clear enough?"

"Interesting, sir."

"Are we clear?"

"Oh, we are clear, sir."

"Where are we going to strike."

"Fine. The Philippines, sir. The Japanese are invading the Philippines right now. We are going after their carrier and support ships."

Looking at her, thinking, he says, "What's the deal between you and Lee? I've known the Captain for a long time. He likes you for some reason. Why?"

"I don't know, sir."

"He's single…you two got something going on? I don't care about the regs. I just want to know."

Sam presses her lips tightly, then, "NO, SIR! That's an insult to your commander."

"Okay. Okay. I'm just asking. He does like you, that is clear enough."

"Has it occurred to you that he is following orders from higher to support integration of women into the Navy?"

"Yeah, but that's not it. It's a puzzle, and I hate puzzles. It doesn't make sense, you're just not that good."

She looks up, clenching her teeth, and makes eye contact again, "Sir, thank you for that vote of confidence."

Startled, he says, "I don't mean it meanly, it's just the plain truth…um, is that all you can tell me, Lieutenant?"

"Sir, could you please talk to Admiral Ren or Captain Johnson to get your information, instead of forcing me to break my orders."

"Um, I see your point, Lieutenant. Okay, you're dismissed."

"Thank you, sir."

PASSAGEWAY OUTSIDE OF BLACK KNIGHTS READY ROOM

Lt. Hunt walks out of the ready room in a controlled fury, nearly running into Lt. Robert Issa, UDT/SEAL. She says a curt, "Excuse me," and moves to go around him.

Issa raises a hand, "Lieutenant, could we talk?"

She finally recognizes him as more that an obstacle. He's the guy who chewed her out in the water. Instead of a wet suit, he's wearing black BDUs with Lieutenants bars and the SEAL trident. "WHAT!"

"Lieutenant, we talked in the water last night, right?"

"Yes," forcing herself to calm down.

"I, um, owe you an apology. I was an ass, and I'm sorry."

She takes another deep breath and lets it out slowly, "Apology accepted."

"Are you okay? You seem really pissed."

"I just had an unsettling discussion with my commander. I'm sorry if I was short with you."

"Oh, I have those about all the time. I understand. And, Lieutenant, if I couldn't handle one pissed off lady, I wouldn't be much of a SEAL. Can I invite you down to the squad by for a cup of coffee and a chat?"

Sam smile, and totally ignoring her orders, says, "Yes."

The SEAL squad bay is on the 01-level aft of elevator 4. As he shows her in, she pauses; there is cammo netting, guys lounging in hammocks, and piles of equipment in green bags and boxes, everywhere. On the far wall is a map of the region with pins and notes scribbled on it. Under the map is a large table with twelve chairs. One guy is in a chair reading a novel with his feet up on the table, and another is sleeping on it. Three guys, one of them a Chief, are breaking down, cleaning, and re-assembling what look like AK-47s. Issa says in a loud voice, "Welcome to my home. Guys, this is Lt. Hunt. We met in the water surrounded by bodies." He looks back at her, "You said you're a '14 driver, yes?"

"Yes."

They all look at Sam with interest. "The coffee is over here. Hey, Broke Dick, get off the table."

Sam grins, "Is he always this nice to you?"

Broke Dick stands up, all six feet six inches of him, "No, ma'am, yes ma'am, I mean, Broke Dick is my name." The guys laugh.

"Okay, like Spike is mine."

Issa asks, "How do you like your coffee?"

"Black, no sugar."

He hands her a cup with a SEAL trident, "Broke Dick missed a drop zone during parachute training and hit a young elm tree square in the...."

Sam winces, "OOWE!"

"Anyway, that's how he got his name. How did you come by 'Spike'?"

"My first RIO," she sits down, "He was excitable, like the cartoon character, Butch. So, Spike. What do they call you?"

"'Abdul', because my family is from Lebanon." The guys gather around like kids listening to their adults talking.

"Lebanese, I see."

"You're good in the water."

ET 3 Gerry 'Meat' Monahan says, "I bet she was."

Sam grins as Issa cuffs him upside the head, "As a swimmer, Meat. Stow it."

She chuckles as the young SEAL explains, "I'm just saying, sir, she is undoubtedly a good swimmer." Then she laughs, shaking her head.

Issa, realizing he needn't fight this battle, says, "She had the balls to SAR swim without any training, so yeah, I'm sure she is."

"So, you guys are awfully relaxed after the Captain's announcement," comments Sam.

"SEALs are pretty single-minded," says Issa, and the Chief, Mark 'Fang' Fronzak finishes, "Yep, if they can't drive it, eat it, drink it, fuck it, or shoot it, they don't care."

"Oh my," says Sam.

Meat asks, "Is it true? Are we going to get to fight World War II all over again?"

Sam says, "Looks like."

Meat high fives a teammate, "Cool!"

Issa says, "Yeah, but what about our families back home? My wife was pregnant with our second."

"My God, I'm sorry," says Sam.

"Yeah, but it isn't like they're dead. It's more like they never existed. My wife isn't even born yet."

"Neither are my brothers. If I remember correctly, my parents aren't even married yet."

Meat says, "Don't date your dad. That would be weird."

Chief Fronzak says, "True, Meat, but your grandma is probably looking pretty hot right now."

Sam puts her head in her hands, laughing, as Meat replies, "I'll kick your ass for that! That's just sick."

Fronzak, laughing, says, "You can't kick that high, and besides, that's no way to talk to your elders. I could be your grandpa."

Issa laughs as Fang and Meat start wrestling, saying, "You see, SEALs are generally not deep thinkers. Give us a mission we can do and we'll figure it out."

The combatants bump into her chair, and she says, "Really."

Issa, seemingly uninterested in the fight, answers, "Yep, pretty much. You want deep thinking you have to talk to a nuke. As for us, if you absolutely have to kill someone overnight, call us."

Sam laughs, "I'll remember that."

Chief Fronzak pins Meat to the floor, "If you can't respect your elders, you're gonna respect your betters." To Sam he says, "Ma'am, if you or any of the other ladies want self-defense training, I want to start a class."

"I started learning Aikido in college. Do you know it?"

Issa says, "Chief knows them all. Anything in a Gi."

"I'll think on it and ask around." Then to Issa, "You know, Lieutenant, right now the Japanese are invading the Philippines, Britain is being bombed, and the US has just started a two-front war." She looks him in the eyes, "My dad was a Marine on Guadalcanal."

"My grandpa is fighting the Germans with the British in Arabia, I understand. Come down for coffee and entertainment any time, Lieutenant."

Laughing, Sam says, "Definitely for the entertainment."

As she gets to the door, Meat finally says, "Okay, okay, Chief, I give."

CHAPTER 15

HANGAR BAY 3

1410, 21 December, 1941

Lt. Hunt's power plant and air frame division are busy instal-ling a repaired engine on Bureau number 467 when she joins them in hangar bay 3. "Hey, LT, wanna get your hands dirty?" asks AD1 Robert 'Bobby' Gellar.

"You bet. What are we working on?"

"Just swapping out a re-furb. We are about thirty hours early, but it looks like things might get busy."

"Always good to be ahead on maintenance," and stooping over, she gets inside the engine bay of the F-14. With the lower engine cover hinged out of the way, there is plenty of room for most jobs. There are always those jobs, however, that require long arms and deft fingers. Standing up inside the bay, she sees ADAN Louis 'Deep Fried' Siemens struggling with the Amphenol; the plug connector which sends the engine instrumentation signals for engine status and com-mands from the throttle. "Deep Fried, how are you doing?"

"Okay ma'am, am I doing it right?"

"I'm sure you are. Let me see." She reaches in and traces the wire bundle, "Okay, you got it. It needs to attach here," and clicks the wire onto the hanger.

"Thank you, ma'am."

"You are doing well, Deep Fried. Are you ready to plug it in, Bobby?"

"Just a sec., LT. We're almost done with the mount." His tongue slides back and forth out of his mouth as he reaches in to lock the forward ball mount into place. The powerful GE engine transmits its force to the aircraft with just one ball joint. The makeup of this joint is critical. It transmits all 27,000 lbs. of force from the engine to the airframe. A ball joint failure is catastrophic. "Go ahead, LT."

She reaches up between the engine and the airframe to plug the aircraft Amphenol to the engine. As she feels the click of the plug locking into place, she hears MM1 Hughes say, "Uh, Lieutenant Hunt, Captain Klindt wants the brain trust to muster in the RT classroom in about 10 minutes."

AD1 Gellar can see the TLD (radiation dosimeter) on the nuke mechanic's belt, "Hey, glow worm, back off on the aircraft. You might cross contaminate it with your zoomies."

"Shove it, wing wiper. I'm too busy to kick your ass right now."

Sam makes sure the connection is secure with a couple of tugs and climbs out from underneath the plane, "Gentlemen, really? Ten minutes, MM1." He nods, "Okay, gives me time to clean up. The Amphenol is connected and checked. You got it, Gellar?"

"Yes, ma'am. Why you hanging out with nukes? It's like slumming or something."

She grins, "It's an officer thing. You wouldn't understand, Bobby."

RT CLASSROOM

The brain trust is all in their seats, waiting for Klindt. Senior Chief Richardson has a stack of books in front of him. As they sit down, Hughes says to Sam, "You know, that first class of yours was acting like he's in need of a calibration, ma'am. I have that PQS signed off and would be glad to help out."

"What do mean, Hughes?"

"Well, ma'am, I have completed the 'Kick Ass Instructor' PQS, and I'm willing to adjust his attitude down to a more reasonable and respectful level."

She chuckles, "Hughes, get over yourself."

Mohr asks, "Where did you get your 'Kick Ass Instruction'? Was it formal, or on the job?"

Surprised, Hughes says, "OTJ of the best kind."

"Okay, I received mine from Okinawan Kenpo and Kobudo," affecting and Asian accent, "Your path is slow because your head is thick, Grasshopper."

Everybody is laughing as Klindt walks in and Warren says, "Attention on deck."

They all stand up, still laughing. "Carry on, and what did I miss?" asks Klindt.

Mohr says, "I was just explaining to Hughes the intricacies of true 'Kick Ass Fu' mastery."

"Well, I'm glad we're starting out on a light note. Admiral Ren, Captain Johnson, and Captain Lee will be down to talk to us in a bit."

The laughter dies, "What about, sir?" asks Warren.

Klindt turns to Richardson, "Have you learned anything from those books?"

"Yes, sir, the Japanese are invading the Philippines, as we speak. They hit Lingayen Gulf tomorrow morning. They will be attacking Lamon Bar in a couple of days."

"Okay, let's find out where Lingayen and Lamon are. I brought down some maps. Denton, Barr, please set them up over the white board."

Sam asks, "What books do you have for reference, Senior?"

"I have Empires in the Balance: Japanese and Allied Pacific Strategies to April 1942; Japan at War: Illustrated History of

War in the Far East 1931 – 1945; The Rising Sun in the Pacific, 1931- 1942; and Admiral Halsey's Story: Politics and Strategy of WWII. I'm looking for Japanese Aircraft of the Pacific, but it is checked out to a Frank Jackson. Anyone heard of him?"

"He's my wingman, and I think he's almost memorized it," says Sam.

"Can you get it from him?" asks Richardson.

"Sure, but you know, the truth is he should be here. He knows more technical stuff about WWII than anyone. He practically eats it for breakfast."

"Call him," says Klindt, "I'll let the CAG and Captain know when they get here."

Sam goes to the phone and calls Thud at his division office, squadron QA. As she hangs up, CDR Holtz walks into the classroom and motions to Hunt to come with him.

Klindt asks, "Can I help you, Commander?"

"No sir, I need my lieutenant doing the work she is supposed to be doing, that's all."

Sam freezes, stunned, as Klindt asks, "Your name, sir?"

"Commander Holtz, Captain. I'm her squadron commander."

"Pleased to meet you, Commander Holtz. I'm Captain Klindt, the Reactor Officer. Commander she is right where I, Captain Johnson, and Admiral Ren need her to be. What do you need that trumps all of us?"

"I'm sure it's of no concern to you, Captain."

"It is very much of concern to me, sir, and my team here has much to do, so, please, Commander, say your piece so we can move forward."

"Why do you even need her? She isn't anything special. I have a dozen pilots her equal. She's competent in a plane, sure, but Einstein she isn't"

Sam stands frozen, wishing she could disappear. Hughes tugs her sleeve and whispers, "You have to work for that asshole?"

Klindt says, "Commander, you are out of line, sir. Perhaps, we should step outside."

Holtz nods, "Okay, fair enough."

Klindt walks across the small hallway to the Reactor Training Division office, opens the door, and invites Holtz in. To the petty officers in the office, he says, "Gentlemen, could you give me a moment?"

"Yes, sir," and they leave.

Klindt spins a chair around and sits, motioning to Holtz to do so as well, "Okay, Holtz, I am going to make this succinct. Hunt is a diamond. She is an excellent officer with a good attitude. Why are you trying to turn her into coal?"

"I take it you have drunk the women in combatant roles kool aid?"

"Are you stupid, Holtz. It is 1941. Where are we going to get qualified male pilots, and male nukes, and male flight deck personnel to replace the women we have now. How I feel about it is irrelevant, though, I believe it is working out pretty well. The problems come from dinosaurs like you, not from the women."

"When the 1941 Navy and congress finds out we have women serving in combatant roles, they are going to have a cow."

"Holtz, women flew aircraft in WWII. They built ships, aircraft, and guns. They were nurses on the front lines. Just like our conversation right now, the problem was not the women, it was the shallow men who had to degrade and diminish women in order to think better of themselves. Are you that kind of bully, Holtz? Are you the kind of guy who will demean or harm Lt. Hunt so you can feel superior to her?"

"No, no, I just…I don't want her to believe she is better than she is. Overconfidence can kill."

"Yes. Overconfidence can kill careers, too. I will be briefing Admiral Ren, Captain Johnson, and Captain Lee in about five minutes. What should I tell them about you?"

Panic rising in his voice, he says, "Um, uh, can we work this out? It isn't personal. I have treated her fairly and will continue to do so. Okay?"

"She continues to work with my brain trust. I receive a whisper about the most minor mistreatment of her, or any other woman under your command, I will consider it very personally. I am watching, Commander. We need every pilot we have, but we do not need every leader we have. Am I clear, Commander?"

"Yes, Captain."

"Okay, get out of here. I have work to do."

As Holtz climbs up the stairs to the second deck, he sees Captain Lee approach and waits for him. "What are you doing here, Papa?"

The Admiral and Captain Johnson come up behind Lee, and Holtz says, "Um, just had a quick word with, um, the Captain. Excuse me," and walks away.

The three officers walk into the classroom and Warren says, "Attention on deck," they all stand.

Sitting down, Ren says, "Carry on. The reason I called you together was to figure out what happened to us. You have done that very well, and I thank each of you for your work. Now, our battle group is moving to help the men defending the Philippines. Our Ops crew will plan the attack. What we need from you is an idea of where the enemy is, what their order of battle is, and how well their weapons function.

"There are a lot of sticky questions. Should we communicate with the American forces in the Philippines? If we do, how should we do so without tipping our hand? We also need to think about what to do next? How should we report to Admiral Nimitz? I need to the fight the enemy in front of me, but I want to be at least one step ahead. That is where you come in."

Klindt says, "Okay, guys, let's brief him first on what we face in the Philippines. Chief Richardson."

"Yes, sir. Admiral, Captains, the Japanese are invading the Philippines starting tomorrow morning at Lingayen Gulf, near the north end of Luzon," pointing at the map. "They will be attacking Lamon Bay in two days right here. They have the aircraft carrier Ryujo, which is one of their smaller ones. They also have carrier division 3, but the only carriers I found in that division are for seaplanes. There may be another bird farm in that group, but if so, it is a small one. I have accounted for all the others. They have five heavy cruisers, five light cruisers, and twenty-nine destroyers, with some smaller or tender type ships. Most of the aircraft involved are flying from Taiwan, in this time called Formosa. There'll be aircraft from air fields captured in the south, a total of approximately six hundred planes. The Navy fighter is the Zero. The Army fighter is the Nate. Lt. JG Jackson will be better for briefing about the aircraft. Lieutenant?"

Thud stands up, and says from memory, "The A6M Zero was a very good fighter in its day. Top speed of about 300 knots and a range of sixteen hundred miles, but it climbed slowly, even for the day. You don't want ever to get into a turning fight with the Zero. They carry two 20mm and two .30 caliber machine guns, so they definitely can bite. They are fragile, though. The Japanese didn't much consider pilot safety, which cost them dear toward the end of the war. The Nate was in most ways an inferior plane. Slower, at 270 knots, and not able to turn as tightly, but it is simple to operate and maintain. It didn't even have retracting landing gear. It had a way shorter range of 680 miles and its guns were two .30

caliber. Its climb rate was a bit better than the Zero's, but only marginally. Not nearly as effective, still flying as slow as they will be, they will be able to easily turn inside us.

"The Japanese have a number of bombers. All are twin engine, and as fast as their fighters. The fastest was the Sally, at nearly 300 knots. One thing to keep in mind about the bombers, though, is they have rear facing guns. Something we are not used to facing. Also, all of them are capable of operating off airfields way worse than what we can."

Johnson asks, "Can we use sidewinders against them?"

"I don't know, sir. A sidewinder can track a C-2 easy enough, but the C-2 still has a turbine engine. With a piston engine it's doubtful. I would load AIM-7s and plenty of gun ammo. Using guns, we'll have to slash and dash, sir."

Ren asks, "Slash and dash? I was an E-2C pilot."

"Yes, sir. Fly through the formation quickly, taking shots as you can, without getting on their six."

Ren then asks, "How many troops do they have on the ground?"

Richardson says, "About 130,000, sir, but they will be spread out and some are in reserve on the ships. We think there will be about 40,000 to 50,000 at Lingayen Gulf. That would probably be the most bang for the buck, sir."

"Are we going to focus on troops, aircraft, or ships, sir?" asks Warren.

"Corregidor," says Hunt.

"Yeah, the last stand, then the Bataan Death March," says Hughes.

Ren says, "You're right. I'd like to sink flat tops, but you're right. Saving men is the priority. This is why this group is valuable. Okay, I will get the strike folks moving that way. Can you put this information in writing for them?"

"I'm already on it, sir," says Hughes, "I'm the clerk."

Johnson asks, "Do we contact the American forces?"

Mohr says, "We have to. They will have planes in the air. We don't want blue on blue."

"We should be able to sort out the American planes," says Lee.

"Yes, sir," says Mohr, "but what about them shooting at us?"

"Exactly," says Hunt, "We'll need their frequencies. Do you think you can find their frequencies, Denton?"

"Yeah, sure, I'm pretty sure I already know them. What I can't do is break their encryption. We'll have to transmit in the clear."

"Richardson, so do you have anything in that lovely stack of books?" asks Hunt.

"No, ma'am. That would be in my other pile of books. I did find a couple on WWII encryptions, but I haven't had time to go through them yet."

"Chief, each to his expertise, cough 'em up," says Barr.

"Okay, whether in the clear or encrypted, they cannot be expecting us. What do we say?" asks Ren.

"Call ourselves Rogue squadron, sir, and the Japanese carrier the Death Star 1," says Mohr.

"Anachronism, Mohr, anachronism, it needs to be something in their cultural reference," says Hunt.

"Buck Rogers?" says Warren.

"Superman?" suggests Denton.

"Batman?" says Barr.

"Mickey Mouse?" suggests Mohr, "It makes a sort of sense."

Through the laughter, Ren says, "I just can't see debriefing Admiral Nimitz about the movements of the Mickey Mouse Patrol."

Hunt says, "We're the Gold Eagle, why not just use that."

Ren says, "I can't see why not."

"They are going to see us, sir," says Hunt. "Our existence will get out."

Klindt adds, "That makes things easier when we brief in Admiral Nimitz."

Ren says, "Gold Eagle it is. We contact them in the clear, or encrypted, if we've broken the code. We make contact by radio with the first American air unit meets ours. Hopefully, it will be at or after zero hour to protect the surprise. We hit the Japanese hard, with a focus on transports and troops on the ground, after that we take out the ships as we can. The call sign for sinking the flat top will be Death Star Down. The crew will like that.

"After this attack, we head to Hawaii by way of Wake island, where we will hit their naval units, if we can. We'll be needing fuel. Start thinking on how we should report to Nimitz. I don't want anyone shot, stabbed, or court martialed. Thank you all." He stands, and when they also stand, he shakes everyone's hand and leaves.

On the 1MC, "Commence propulsion plant drills."

Klindt says, "I need to go, they are playing my tune."

CHAPTER 16

CAPTAIN LEE'S OFFICE, 03 LEVEL, STARBOARD SIDE

1800, 21 December, 1941

CDR Holtz knocks, and enters when he hears Captain Lee say, "Enter." Lee looks up as Holtz walks up and stands at attention. "At ease, Commander, sit down, coffee, cookie?"

"Yes, sir," and sits down.

"As I recall, sugar, no cream," and hands him a cup with an oatmeal cookie.

"Thank you, sir."

"We're in private, Jim. What's on your mind?"

"Well, sir, I was wondering, what is the deal between you and Lt. Hunt."

"It's really none of your business, Jim. We are not having, nor have we ever had an affair, it that's what you're asking."

"I know that, she was clear on that. It's just you and I have served together a long time, and I just don't get it."

"So, you asked her?"

"Well, sir, in truth, I about demanded it. She didn't say anything except to ask you, so I'm asking."

Lee pours himself another cup of coffee, "Jim, when we are in private, call me Rick. We're old shipmates."

"Yes, sir...Rick. The thing is, you of all people should know I don't believe women belong in the cockpit of an airplane, or hell, for that matter, anywhere in the military. They just take up a slot better taken by a man. I thought you felt the same, but you don't. Not with her, anyway. It's even rumored that, well, that you and Hunt spent some time together and that you put in a letter recommending her for jets. I know you well enough, and from her reaction, I know it's not romantic, but Rick, what's going on?"

"What happened down in the RT classroom, Jim? I know you weren't touring the ship."

Holtz looks into his cup, "I tried to pull Hunt out of the brain trust and Captain Klindt read to me from the book. He made it pretty clear that Hunt is under his protection. He even called me a dinosaur. The thing is, why is she so important? You wanted her on that brain trust. You recommended her for jets. I know Carleton is an ass, but it was you that pulled him off her after the EA-6B thing. What's the deal?"

Lee stares into his cup, "Lt. Hunt helped me through a really bad time, and has been discreet enough to keep her mouth shut about it since."

"On the Kennedy?"

"Yeah, it was her first deployment and I was commander of the Bounty Hunters."

"I can't imagine you needing her help with anything."

"Well, I did. We were in Rota, and I was a mess. I was barely functional. I went on the biggest bender of my life. I spilled my guts to her, and she listened. She talked me through a terrible time, and then poured coffee down me, and walked me around until I was semi-sober, and got me back on board. After that night, she never said a word about it to anyone. Not a word."

"I can't imagine you drunk. I have never seen you drunk. We went on some benders together and it always you getting me back."

Lee chuckles, "Yeah, I did a lot of that."

"What could possibly cause you to drink like that?" Please, Rick, I just want to understand."

"You're still the same, like a dog with a bone. Can't let it go. It isn't an endearing trait, you know, but you know how to keep your mouth shut." Lee smiles at him, "Like that accident in VF-111."

"Yeah, when Tri-pod took a hooker up in his F-4," Holtz smiles.

"If I tell you, it would cost me my career. Hunt knows, but I don't think anyone else does. Well, one guy."

"Thank you."

"Don't thank me 'til I'm done. You might regret it. Remember when we were in the Sundowners?" Holtz nods and Lee continues, "I went through my divorce then. We got back from deployment, hostage crisis. Anyway, I get back and my wife is gone, and she's taken our daughter, Melanie. She just moved away, no warning. I stopped getting letters from her, oh, maybe halfway through deployment, but I thought, well, maybe something happened, maybe she lost my address...I don't know. A desperate man has desperate thoughts. Anyway, I chased her down in Minnesota.

"When Rhonda took Melanie away like that, it broke something in my daughter. She was my special girl, only eight years old. I loved her so much. Rhonda knew that, so she campaigned against me. Rhoda kept moving and changing her name and my daughter grew up thinking her dad was a monster. I never stopped believing in...I never gave up, but it was hard, Jim, damn hard.

"My ex contacted me when Melanie turned eighteen. She'd dropped out of school and run away. I took leave, all I had on the books, looking for her. God, did I look for her. Then, ten months later, she shows up on my doorstep. I don't know how she found me, but she did. She was strung out on, God... I don't know what. I cleaned her up, got her into rehab, and I did good by her, Jim, I really did. I had a daughter again and life was wonderful...for about a year.

"She was haunted, looking over her shoulder, you know? She wouldn't talk about it, but I knew her past was bothering her. I tried to give her all the love she missed. I did. One day, I come home from work and the door is smashed in, the house wrecked, and no sign of Melanie. I called the police and they told me she was in the hospital.

"Her past had caught up with her in a big way. Her old pimp found her. He raped her and beat her. He beat my daughter to death. The doc just shook his head when I told him...I told him I'd give her my kidney, my spleen, my heart, hell, I'd give her my life. He just said that nothing could be done.

"I held my daughter in my arms and watched her die. She said, 'Daddy, I'm sorry.' But, damn it, Jim, she didn't have anything to be sorry for.

"There was this black guy there, at the hospital. He found Melanie on the side of the road and got her to the hospital and called the cops. He stayed with her, Jim, this old guy. He didn't know her at all. Didn't know me, but he stayed and he prayed with her. I owe that guy. I owe him a lot.

Taking a deep breath, then a sip of coffee, he continues, "Lt. Hunt is the kind of woman Melanie could have been. She's the kind of woman I wish my daughter had the chance to become. The first time I saw her...the face, the hair, she looks so much like Melanie. The same quirky smile, when she ever does smile. She was good to me. She could have, well, you know, but she didn't. That's worth something. And Jim, she has drive. She has a dream, and she believes in it. And you know what, I believe in it too. I'm glad they gave her a chance."

"But can she fly? Can she fight? I understand, but if she can't, she's going to get someone killed."

"Well, when she was in the training squadron I came through

San Diego after Command College. I arranged to fly against her and Thud. I and a member of the aggressor squadron were planning to clean her clock. You know, teach her something. She waxed me, Jim. It wasn't even close. So, the next time we meet, one on one, she had me with guns in about 30 seconds. Thud is good. But, really, she's even better. We swapped around, because by then I'm thinking this old man has lost his edge. She got a sidewinder on the instructor in about 20 seconds. She's good, Jim. I have three kills from Vietnam, and I say she's good.

"I'm not asking you to give her any favors, and I'm not asking you to give her a ride. I'm telling you, Jim, give her a chance. She deserves a shot. And by God, she's gonna get the shot my daughter didn't. You wanted to know. You wanted to know, Jim, why I care about this girl, well, now you do."

"Please tell me they found the guy. Please tell me he's rotting in prison."

"No, Jim, he isn't rotting in prison. He's rotting in the ground. I don't want this talked around. I'm only saying this because we're friends, but I killed that son of a bitch."

"You shot him?"

"No, Jim, I killed him with my bare hands. When my hands got too bad, I used a hammer."

"Did the police, um, did anybody find out?"

"I think the cops knew. I know the detective did. He told me he was absolutely, positively certain it was a Mexican gang. Then he suggested I wear gloves for a few weeks."

"Does Hunt know?"

"Yeah, she knows."

SAM AND GLORIA'S STATEROOM

0230, 22 December, 1941

There's a knock, and "Hunt, Hoolihan, brief in 30 minutes."

Gloria, groaning, rolls out of her rack, "God, I hate early morning flights."

"We're going to war, Gloria."

"Yeah, but why can't we kill Japanese at a reasonable hour. Isn't there a Geneva convention or something on that?"

Sam laughs as she rolls off the top rack and drops to the floor, grabs her gear and heads for the bathroom. Gloria follows, her hair in wild disarray, trying to get it out of her eyes. "You're perky. You hiding coffee?"

"No, wish I was. You okay?"

"Yeah, if I stop grumping, then it's time to worry. How about you?"

"I'm great."

"Last night you looked like hell. Why the change?"

"We're going to war, Gloria. I realized last night that if we do this right, my dad might not go through so much hell on Guadalcanal."

"Oh, well, if we get dressed fast enough there may be coffee in our future, and breakfast. We can be well caffeinated while we save the world."

BLACK KNIGHT READY ROOM

0300, 22 December, 1941

Spike and Hot Pants are almost the last ones in. They find seats with their RIO's, Puck and GQ. Thud is in animated conversation with Speedy directly in front of them. He turns, holding a large book. "Hey, Spike, this book says the Long Lance torpedo used liquid oxygen. A few shots at a torpedo could cause a surface ship to explode."

"Wow, Thud, we might be able to destroy a ship with guns. Good to know."

CDR Holtz walks to the podium, "Okay, everyone, listen up. Assignments are as follows: Book, you will lead flight two with Bo-Bo, Johnny, and Gunner. I will lead flight one with Glow Rod, Jedi, and Bug. Swede, you will lead flight three with Spike, Hot Pants, and Thud. Now, I have asked Thud to brief us on the opposition aircraft we can expect to face. Thud."

Thud starts, "The primary naval fighter is the A6M type 21 Zero. It has a top speed of about 300 knots, a climb rate of 3000 feet per minute, and a service ceiling of 33,000 feet. It has trouble in a dive. The control surfaces are too small and at high speeds has difficulty pulling out of a dive. It has two forward mounted .30 caliber machine guns and two 20mm cannon. The 20 mm could screw us up good, but they only have 100 rounds. The fuel tank is behind the pilot inside the fuselage. The tanks do not seal, so a couple of hits there, and it's bye, bye Zero. Don't get in a turning fight with a Zero. They had the best turning rate of any fighter in the war."

Bo-Bo snickers, "I was just wondering if the Japanese carried sling shots, too. It worked for David."

Thud replies, "The British army disregarded the Zulu warriors as primitive, and the Zulu wiped out whole units of British regulars during the Boer War. Just because the equipment is inferior, doesn't mean the pilots are."

Holtz adds, "Just listen up, Bolen, so I don't have to write your mama explaining why Bo-Bo got a boo-boo. Continue, Thud."

"The KI-27 Nate is inferior to the Zero in every way except climb rate. They are easy to tell apart because the Nate has fixed landing gear. Top speed on the Nate is about 275 knots and the service ceiling is about 32,000 feet. The Nate will still out turn us, so we are better off going vertical. Most of the bombers are two engine types. The American Army Air Corp will probably have B-25 Mitchells in theater and they look a lot like a G2M Nell bomber. So, be careful what you shoot at. The rest of the Japanese bombers will have a single vertical stabilizer, which could possibly be confused with a C-47. What we know as a DC-3."

"Won't the big meat ball on the wing give it away?" asks Gunner.

"Don't be an ass, Gunner. He's trying to help," says Gunner's RIO, Wally 'NOB' Nelson. Thud ignores them and continues, "The Japanese started the campaign with over 600 aircraft of all types and about 200 of those are fighters of both types. Zeros outnumber the Nates, and the Zero has that 20mm cannon. Another thing, the bombers, including the single engine KI-30 Anne, are mounted with rear facing guns. If possible, the best approach angle is from the rear and below, or head to head and low. Of course, that won't happen with torpedo bombers, they generally fly on the deck."

Thud stops and looks at Holtz, who asks, "Questions?"

Chris 'Klutz' Brandt, Bo-Bo's RIO, asks, "Do these old prop planes even count as a full kill? Hell, we'll all be aces before the day is out, even the girls."

Hot Pants says, "Spike and I will equal or better the count of any of you, Chris, except Thud. I bet he'll be the squadron lead ace."

Klutz says, "Is that a bet? What's the bet?"

Hot Pants says, "If you lose, you all have to wear a pink bow on your uniform until we hit port again, or any of you sad sacks catch up with us."

Holtz says, "I agree, and if any two of us outscore you, then, you two have to wear a tie."

Spike and Hot Pants look at each other, "You're on, except, you can't leave out Swede either, as he's flying with us."

Holtz says, "Deal. Do you all agree?" All the pilots nod. "Okay, then, Book, Flight 2 will make the run with the 12 A-6 Intruders of VA-52 Knight Riders, engaging troops, transports, and the fleet of Lamon Bay. You will fly the east coast of PI and avoid contact, unless attacked, until after the A-6's attack. Once the Intruders expend their ordinance, you are to escort them back, and you are free to engage at will to accomplish the mission. Consider it a fighter sweep while covering the A-6s.

"Swede, you will approach from the east as well. Overfly Luzon, escorting 12 F/A 18s of VFA-22 Red Cocks. Your mission is to cover them while they engage the Japanese at the forward edge of the battle and the invasion beaches. I will be leading the escorts for the attack on the Japanese fleet with the 12 F/A 18s of VFA-146 Blue Diamonds. I will also have a flight of four from the VF-33 Tomcatters. Two Tomcatters will be covering the E-2C Ghost Rider. Two will be covering the refueling planes, and another four will be doing a fighter sweep between Taiwan and PI. Questions?"

Swede asks, "How many friendly aircraft are in theater?"

Holtz looks at Thud, and he says, "There is supposed to be ninety-one P-40 Warhawk fighters and thirty-four bombers, but I'm not sure what type and I have no idea how many are left."

GQ asks, "Are we going to have Dust Off available when one of these guys hits the silk?"

Holtz says, "Not at first, so you'll have to escape and evade. Once the skies are relatively clear, we'll send in helos, any more questions?"

Thud raises his hand, "Yes, Thud?"

"Will I have to wear a pink ribbon, too, when you guys lose?"

"Nope, you're playing for the other team today." Everyone laughs, "Okay, lets break and go to Wardroom 3 for the final brief."

As they walk out, Thud says to Spike, "So, me and Speedy

we're thinking..." and Spike gives him a wry grin. Thud continues, "Not like that, Spike. We're thinking how to go after Zeros. What if we did opposed barrel rolls like this," flying his hands through the air. "One of us takes the lead, you of course, and you do a barrel roll, say to the left, and I'd be a couple of hundred feet behind and barrel roll to the right. As we roll anything that comes into our sights with guns or the AIMs, we engage. We would be going way too fast for any of them to get on our six, and we could weave in and out and blow them away. We don't want to get into a turning fight with them. That would be worse than getting into a turning fight with an F-16."

"You're right, but we should make the barrel rolls away from each other, less chance of a collision."

"Yeah, I see that. I thought if I was behind, that wouldn't be a problem, but then it's harder to track the tangos. Okay, away from each other. So, what do you think?"

"It might work, Thud. I like it, kind of an updated offensive thatch weave."

WARDROOM 3, 03 LEVEL FORWARD

0345, 22 December, 1941

Big pilot briefings have always been held in one of the wardrooms. It's called a formal briefing, but it's actually conducted more informally. The crews jostle around and give each other a hard time while waiting. They all seem to be in a good mood. As Spike walks in with Thud, she over hears an F/A-18 pilot, Rick 'Jail Bait' Funk, talking to Swede, "You know, going to briefings is kind of like being married."

Swede asks, "How's that?"

"Well, you have to sit around and talk about it all the time, instead of just going in there and getting it done."

Spike chuckles, and Swede says, "You're such a bonehead."

Spike and Swede go to sit with their RIOs and wingmen. As they settle in, Admiral Ren, Captain Johnson, and Captain Lee walk in. Someone shouts, "Attention on deck," and everyone stands.

Admiral Ren says, "Carry on. Carry on. Captain Lee, you have the floor," and the admiral sits down.

Captain Lee steps to the podium and goes over the three-pronged attack plan, explaining the duties of each squadron. "The objective is to sink all the enemy naval forces with a focus on transports, disrupt the landings, and pound the troops already on the ground. Sinking the Ryujo is, of course, a priority. The code phrase for sinking the carrier is 'Death Star Down'."

When the laughter dies down, Lee says, "Lieutenant Jackson could you come up and brief us on the Japanese forces in theater?" Thud walks forward and nervously repeats the same brief he gave his own squadron a few minutes ago. Then Lee asks each of the squadron commanders to explain how they intend to execute their part of the plan. When they are finished, Lee says, "Questions?"

An F/A-18 pilot, Elijah 'Way Low' Cruze, of the Blue Diamonds, asks, "Given we will not be getting resupplied, is it wise to expend Harpoon missiles against WWII ships?"

"It's what we have and we'll use them. It's much better than losing any of our own ships. I've had quite enough of that," answers Admiral Ren.

Lt. Hunt asks, "Sir, are the escorting F-14s going to carry any air to ground ordinance?"

"No, I see the F-14s as primarily air to air. However, as long as there are ships floating out there I would just as soon you didn't come back with any ordinance. Is that clear?" That comment starts a happy rumble and several people say, "Yes, sir!" Thud and Spike lock eyes.

One of the Red Cock pilots, Lt. JG Laramie 'Six Gun' Morrison asks, "Are we going to have any S-3s available for refuel?" The F-14 pilots chuckle, as the F/A-18 has notoriously short legs.

Admiral Ren says, "Yes, we will still need ASW, but we'll keep a few gas stations orbiting below the E2C. They will be dispatched as needed." Pausing a moment, he looks out at the eager faces, "Okay, folks, a lot of you are thinking this is going to be like shooting fish in a barrel. I'd like to wipe that thought from your mind. It may be propeller planes vs jets, but do not forget, you are going up against some of the best fighter pilots that ever lived. As we always do in training, the dog fight is against the other pilot as much as it is against the other plane. Now, let's go out there and kick some ass." The men erupt, cheering.

As they file out of the wardroom, Swede motions to everyone in his flight to join him, "When we tangle with the Zeros, remember to fight them in the vertical and don't get in a turning fight. Thud is right, turn with a Zero, you lose. And, we'll be dealing with ack-ack, so don't ever fly a straight line. Remember to keep talking to each other. There will be sixteen planes flying together, so we need to pay special attention to avoid collisions. Keep your eyes out of the cockpit."

CHAPTER 17

FLIGHT DECK, USS CARL VINSON

0430, 22 December, 1941

A carrier flight deck is at its most chaotic when launching an alpha strike, a maximum effort by all aircraft and crews. It's the kind of attack the Navy did against the Japanese carriers at Midway. As the ground crews prepare the aircraft, the pilots and RIOs pre-flight their birds. Each thinks about their chances of returning, but pilots are not a fatalistic lot. To do their job well, they have to believe, without doubt, that they are the best SOB in the sky. However, when there are sixty-four aircraft flying toward the same objective, the possibility of something going wrong is there. Getting them all in the air is not less dangerous, the timing has to be exact.

KNIGHT 211, SPIKE AND PUCK

Spike and Puck strap into their bird with the help of Airman Joe 'Handy' Washington. He's their plane captain, responsible for putting every switch and mechanism in its proper position, so it's ready to fly. Part of that is making sure the pilot and RIO are correctly strapped in. As he checks Spike's straps, he kisses the fingers on this right hand and taps them on the forehead of her helmet. Spike gives him a puzzled look. He just smiles and shouts over the noise of the flight deck, "For luck." She smiles and gives him a thumbs up.

When it's time, Spike is directed to close the canopy and proceed to CAT 2. Thud's plane is behind her. It's organized chaos. The folks in Flight Deck Control move scale replicas of the aircraft on a scale replica of the flight deck, called an Ouija board, to make sure each craft has room to get into position before it is moved. The order of movement is determined by the fuel and ordinance load out of each plane and the distance to their target. The yellow shirts perform the movements choreographed in Flight Deck Control by waving hand signals with yellow flashlight wands. Nothing moves without the direction of a yellow shirt.

The flight deck crews have to keep their heads on swivels as more and more planes start their engines. The blast from a jet engine can send a person tumbling down the deck, or blow them off the deck into the water. It's even more dangerous in the predawn darkness.

Spike's '14 is directed forward by a yellow shirt. Then she's told to turn, and she is passed off from one yellow shirt to another until her plane is aligned with catapult. At the right point, they signal to stop and lower the 'T' bar that engages the catapult. Then, they draw the catapult forward a bit, until it's tight to the 'T' bar. Then the jet blast deflector is raised. She keeps the engines idle, waiting, watching the yellow shirt controlling her launch. His right hand is holding a green light wand straight over his head and his left is holding a red want behind his back. As long as the left hand stays behind his back, things are good. If he shows the red wand, the launch is aborted.

Crewman crawl under the plane, installing a hold back bar designed to prevent the catapult from moving until there is enough pressure to prevent a cold shot. When the catapult fires without enough force to get the plane airborne, that's a cold shot, resulting in a destroyed aircraft, and wet, pissed off crew. It's also a quick way to die.

The hold back bar is installed and checked, and the ordinance flags are pulled. As each crewman runs out from under the aircraft, they give the thumbs up, showing the catapult officer their check was good. When the last crewman is clear, the catapult officer lowers his hand to chest high, the signal to run up her engines. Once the engines are stable at full military power, she looks over her instruments, "And, we are green. How are we looking, Puck?"

"All systems look good, Spike."

After one final look at her instruments, making sure the engines are at full power and the temperature readings are good, she turns on the navigation lights, salutes the catapult officer, and returns her hand to the stick, pulling it back a bit into flight trim. The launch officer leans over, lowering his hand to the deck with a straight arm, and then points his arm to the bow, his wand straight forward. That's the signal for the catapult operator in the booth to push the button that actually fires the catapult. The F-14 is accelerated down the 252-foot long catapult, pushing the aircraft to its take off speed of 175 knots. It shoots off the bow of the Vinson, its tail dipping as the nose comes up, and they fly. The feeling of falling is disconcerting, but normal. It all happens so fast, their senses and even the instruments can't keep up. A catapult launch is really a leap of faith.

"Knight 211, airborne, climbing to angels 30, course 200 for assembly point 'Whiskey'," says Puck to Gold Eagle.

"Roger, Knight 211. Good hunting," replies the air traffic control center.

On the intercom, "Are we still green, Puck?"

"Yes, Spike, we look good. Are you going to try that thatch washing machine idea Thud came up with?"

"Yeah, I think so, if we can. It has merit."

"Okay, when we're in it, I'm going to focus on avoiding collisions. You'll be using the guns, anyway."

"True."

"If you need my head in the plane for radar work, just say so, okay?"

"Yes, Puck, not a problem."

"We're going to be talking to each other, right? Like we said?"

"Yes, Puck, we're going to be talking. I'm sorry if I seem distracted just now. We've a lot of young hotshots out here, and they're not taking the dangers seriously."

"Got that, thank you. God, it's good to be back in the air."

BACK ON CAT 2, KNIGHT 212, THUD AND SPEEDY

"Speedy, is the board green?"

"Si, Senor Thud, we are ready to launch into the big blue."

"Roger that, Senorita."

Thud completes the procedure and salutes the catapult officer. There's a strong kick in the ass as the plane accelerates to 175 knots. They reach the end of the flight deck and settle a bit as the wings take the load. Thud gently pulls back on the stick and the aircraft begins its climb. In a calm voice, Thud says, "Yee Haw.

ASSEMBLY POINT WHISKEY, KNIGHT 211

The Vinson launched her planes 400 miles north east of Luzon, and 400 miles east of Formosa. Point Whiskey is 100 miles south of the battle group and is where Gold Eagle Strike 3 is assembling; Swede's flight of F-14s from the Black Knights and the F/A-18s of the Fighting Red Cocks. Spike is making lazy left turns with Swede and Hot Pants ahead, above, and to the inside of the turn. She can see the sun beginning to rise at this altitude, but the ocean below is still in darkness. Spike says on intercom, "God, there are a lot of birds on this."

Puck replies, "My first alpha strike. Thud is high and behind."

"I know, Puck."

"Just starting into the rhythm."

"Okay, we're going to talk. We're going to work together, Puck."

Five thousand feet above them, the E-2C and S-3s are orbiting, escorted by four Tomcatters. One thousand feet below, the Red Cocks are assembling. Five thousand feet below them Gold Eagle Strike 2, with Book's four F-14s, the A-6's of the Knight Riders, and two EA-6B's of the Wizards, are assembling.

On the radio, "Knight Flight 3, Beefeater 1, Beefeater squadron is assembled and ready," says LCDR Jeremy 'Frosty' Winters, the skipper of the Red Cocks.

"Roger, Beefeater 1, we are ready as well. Frosty, you have the lead," replies Ghandi, Swede's RIO.

"Okay, gentlemen, lock your 'X' foils in the attack position and accelerate to attack speed. Descend on me," says Frosty.

On intercom, Puck says, "God, there's always one."

"I don't blame him. I'd probably do the same thing," says Spike.

"Yeah, may the force be with you."

"And also, with you," replies Spike. With the '14s above and behind the '18s, Spike has a great view as Luzon becomes a smudge on the horizon. The Hornets are flying in elements of two in a loose chevron as they descend, their lights visible against the dark ocean. Forty miles east of Luzon, they pull out of their dive at 400 feet, and start their turn west. On the radio, "Ground search on," says Frosty, turning on his synthetic aperture radar for mapping ground features. As they approach Luzon over Baker Bar, they climb to avoid the coast range which can reach 5,000 feet.

KNIGHT 212

Approaching the mountains, Thud says, "Speedy, snow in PI?" The light from the rising sun behind them glints on the snowy peaks.

"Si, Senor Thud, it snows in Mexico too, when you get high enough."

"I think I see some lights to the north," says Thud.

"I think that's Dipaculao according to the map. We are on track."

"I will be bumpy as we cross the mountains."

"Si, Senor, I will hold on."

KNIGHT 211

Passing over the first peak, it does get bumpy. The Hornets dip into the valley between two peaks, the Tomcats on over watch above. The sun rising slowly behind sets the whole world on fire. Puck says, "Aircraft to the northwest at 25 miles, maybe six, Spike."

"Okay, get the word out."

"Tallyho, bandits northwest at 25 miles."

Ghandi says, "Roger, Puck, we see more to the south. Split elements and engage. We got the southern units." Spike and Thud roll their '14s onto their right side, pulling back on the stick.

"Time to go to work, Spike."

"Yeah, turn on the radar."

Puck says, "Speedy, illuminate."

Spike asks, "Okay, what'cha got?"

"Eighty tangos passing north to south at 3000, 15 miles," then to Speedy, "You guys engage the north four with AIMs."

On intercom, "Spike, I have lock, 10 miles."

"Okay, two sparrows."

Puck on radio, "Fox 1, Fox 1," as she pickles off two AIM-7 Sparrow missiles; a Mach four medium range air to air missile, its own seeker head can guide it, but it is more accurate using the powerful AWG-9 radar on the '14 for initial guidance. To keep the radar on target, they keep flying toward the oncoming planes. But at Mach 4, it only takes the sparrows 7 seconds from launch to detonation. They follow the missiles in at 550 knots, clearly seeing the explosion as one of their missiles hit. Pucks says, "Bulls eye! Splash one Zero." A moment later, Thud's missiles fly home as well and two Zeros fall from the sky.

ZERO FIGHTER

Warrant Officer Tadashi Hisakawa has flown the A6M fighter for three years. From the small village of Akita in northern Japan, where his father is a chemist, his whole family was proud of him joining the Navy, and even more so when he was selected to be a pilot. The A6M is his first love, and his experience in China with the 11th Air Fleet, makes his confidence high. Then he sees his squadron mates blown from the sky in front of him. He sees two bomber size aircraft moving so fast, he can't believe it. He raises the nose of his plane and pushes the throttle forward to attack. As they close, he sees a sparkling just to the left of the cockpit, and realizes they aircraft is shooting at him. It's his last thought as eight 20mm rounds hit and shred his aircraft.

KNIGHT 211

Spike lines up on one of the remaining Zeros, "Guns, guns." A quick burst and the plane explodes, "Got it."

"Thud, low and right." To her right and below, another Zero

explodes, courtesy of Thud. She climbs vertically, slowly rolling inverted, to see below.

Speedy says, "Scratch one Zero."

Puck says, "Thud, below, behind and right."

Then they hear GQ, "Fox 1, Fox 1," as he and Hot Pants engage the southern targets.

The sky fills with aircraft as the Red Cocks start their bomb runs to the west. Puck, seeing fighters to his left, "Tangos, 10 low at 15 miles, heading for the Red Cocks," on the radio and intercom.

She rolls the plane and pulls, "Grunt." Diving, then rolling upright in the dive to engage.

Puck says, "Shit, Spike, it's like ants at a picnic. They're everywhere."

"I know."

"Thud, behind, and to the left."

On the radio, GQ says, "Guns, guns, splash one. Shit, yeah, splash two."

Spike lines up a pass on two Zeros flying across her front in close formation. "Guns, guns," firing two quick zips of the 20mm, then pulls and rudders hard over, "Grunt." Both Zeros explode. She banks hard to the right, looking for more, "Grunt," and pulls the stick to her belly.

They hear Speedy on the radio, "Crossing over you, Spike, you got one six high," as they engage a Zero attempting a dive on Spike. Then "Guns, guns, nailed him, your clear, Spike."

"Thanks, Speedy."

On the radio, Gandhi says, "Fox 1, Fox 1, Frosty, there'll be a few leakers." Frosty says, "Roger, Gandhi. Beefeaters circle north. I'm dropping smoke on the forward edge of battle, keep it low and fast."

Spike says, "I'm going to yo-yo."

"We will yo-yo, Speedy," then on intercom, Puck says, "Thud right, behind."

She pulls the stick back to the right and hits rudder, climbing and rolling over the top, looking for more targets. Ahead a line of six G3M Nell bombers pass left to right about four miles away, at about 500 feet, their distinctive twin tail and the meatball on the wings making the identification easy. Spike drops out of the yo-yo, lines up on the Nells and dives.

"Thud still right and behind."

On the radio they hear GQ, "Fox 2, Fox 2," as Hot Pants fires two AIM-9 Sidewinders. The Sidewinder is a short-range heat-seeking missile. The thermal seeker locks onto the hot exhaust coming off Zero's engine cowls, but her target turns to evade and the missiles lose track. "Shit, guns, guns, sidewinders don't work."

Speedy says, "Spike, we're engaging Zeros to the south, the bombers are all yours."

Spike says to Puck, "I'm wrong. We need to protect the Red Cocks." She flies past the Nells and hits a Zero crossing low. Then pulls out just above the forest canopy. "You're right, Spike. Thud is a couple of miles back."

On the radio, Frosty says, "Cluster, then napalm, make your pass, Beefeaters."

Puck says, "The '18s are about 30 miles west, looks like they found targets."

On the radio, Speedy says, "Shit, they're everywhere. Guns, guns, splash two."

Spike rolls left, climbing, "Puck, where's Thud?"

"Roll over the top, I think he's five o'clock low."

She completes the Immelmann and now faces east into the rising sun. Puck says, "Got him on radar, 12 miles, and he's in the shit. Ready tone."

"How do you know we're not targeting Thud?"

"Zeros can't go 600 knots, shoot, damn it. One missile," then on radio, "Thud, we're cleaning your six."

"Roger, Fox 1," says Spike. The missile flies true, hitting a Nate fighter as it dives on Thud. The exploding fighter hits its wingman, and Puck says, "My God, a twofer."

Spike laughs, "Sorry, Puck. Let's get with Thud."

"Okay, Spike." On radio, "We're coming up behind you, Speedy. How're you doing?"

"It's like we knocked over a bee hive," says Speedy, as Thud rolls to his right, rudders down, firing his guns at a Nate, hitting it, completes his roll, then hits another, "Splash 1."

On her way to Thud's position, she sees a KI-30 Anne bomber flying just above the jungle, she rolls over in a dive, fires the 20mm, splashes the Anne, then turns to join her wingman. Pucks says, "Splash 1."

Thud has another Nate in his sights, when it suddenly turns and dives toward the ground. He cannot line up without risking going into the ground himself. Speedy asks, "Can't get him. Can you, Puck?"

Spike inverts, rudders over, and leads the fighter, firing a quick burst. The Nate explodes. Puck says, "Yep, got him," as they roll back upright, starting their climb from just above the trees.

On the radio they hear Gandhi, "Where are you, Puck?"

"We are north and east of the invasion beach about 10 miles."

"Okay, we're south of you. Keep to the north quadrant and we'll stay south."

"Roger, Gandhi."

"Grunt, Puck," says Spike, as she engages two Zeros trying to roll in on Thud. "Guns, guns." The lead plane staggers in the air as the left wing just falls off and the plane drops into the jungle. The other dives into the trees, then they see a fireball. Puck says, "Splash 2." On intercom, "He crashed, does that count?"

"Don't know," and pulls the '14 level, "Anyone bothering the '18s?"

"Turn right so I can see."

"Turning right."

"Twenty aircraft, angels 2 and 300 knots, heading their way. They're 40 miles out, Spike. We need to close."

"Okay, tell Thud to form on us. Accelerate to attack speed," she smiles.

Puck says, "Speedy, twenty bandits at 40 miles, form on us."

On the radio, Gandhi asks, "We've cleaned up south, heading toward the '18s. What do you have, Puck?"

"Engaging twenty bandits from the north."

Thud comes up on Spike's wing, and on radio, Speedy asks, "Afterburners?"

Spike says to Puck, "Yeah, Hit, zoom, then thatch weave."

"Roger, Speedy, light 'em up." On intercom, "He's 8 left, Spike."

The adjustable wings roll back to 68 degrees as the fighters quickly accelerate past the speed of sound. Something they've never been allowed to do over land. The booming shock wave is heard for miles. On radio, Gandhi says, "Okay, Puck, we're coming, too."

Puck says, "We have four more AIM-7s, Spike, let's use them." The incoming Zeros are arranged in two groups of ten, one higher than the other. "Okay, Puck."

"Speedy, hit the high group. We'll hit the lower, then we'll zoom through them and thatch."

"Roger, hit high. Zoom. Thatch."

Gandhi says, "We'll hit 45 seconds after you. As we fire, we'll tell you to zoom."

Puck says, "Roger, Gandhi." At 900 knots, it doesn't take long to eat up the distance.

Speedy says, "Roger, Gandhi, make like an astronaut."

At 15 miles, Puck says, "Good tone. Fox 1, Fox 1, Fox 1, Fox 1." Spike pickles off all four missiles, "Rolling off burners, Puck."

Puck on the radio, "Burners off." Both pilots throttle off the fuel guzzling afterburners. Then on intercom, "Thud, right, behind."

Spike says, "Switching to guns."

The two aircraft are still faster than the speed of sound, but slowing as they follow their missiles in. The first and third missiles find their target, the second fails to lock, and the fourth's Zero turns violently into the missile and jinks up, causing the missile to lose lock. On the radio, "Splash five meatballs," says Speedy, "two for you, three for us."

"Grunt," says Spike, as they pull through the formation. Spike climbs to line up on a Zero, shoots it in the belly, then spins violently to avoid the explosion, then has to break right to miss another. The Zero is way too close to shoot, as they pass canopy to canopy, missing each other by feet.

ZERO FIGHTER

Lt. Kenzo Koizumi saw the missile flying at him and turned by instinct. Born the son of a regional magistrate in Fukui, a small town on the shore of Honshu, west of Tokyo, he's been a pilot for six years. Working his way up to flight leader while fighting the American Flying Tigers, with four kills, he his respected by his colleagues and commanders. The huge fighters approaching his formation are flying faster than anything he has ever seen. As big as bombers, he knows they are not. After he jinks up, he turns to dive at the enemy planes, but they are past him too fast. He pulls out of his dive at about 800 feet, looks up, and sees another of his A6M Reisen destroyed. The new planes soar above them like a bird of prey. Knowing he cannot match their speed, he rolls back into the fight anyway, calling on the radio, "TAKAO, Flight 73 leader, the Americans have a super weapon, fast planes that shake the air. They kill like sharks among tuna."

KNIGHT 211

As she and Thud clear the formation, Puck says, "Thud, right, Spike."

Spike says, "Thatch, rolling left."

Puck relays, "Thatch rolling left, Speedy."

"Acknowledged, thatch, rolling right." The two F-14s roll apart and dive into the scattering Zeros. As she rolls in a Zero climbs to meet her, a quick burst of the 20mm and its engine bursts into flames. They pass each other and she can see the shocked look on the pilot's face, he's covered in blood, his mouth agape. Puck says, "Thud's closing, pull a little right to miss him."

"Ok." And as they pass, Thud misses them by only a few feet, rocking in their jet wash.

"Speedy calls, "Puck, we adjust to you. If we both adjust, we die."

"Understood, my fault, Speedy."

"No problem, rolling in." They do the weave one more time, and Thud gets a Zero.

Then on radio, Gandhi, "Spike, Thud, zoom, Fox 1, Fox 1."

Thud and Spike level out, pull their sticks full back, and the '14s rocket up. Spike says, "Burners," and lights them to maintain her speed of 600 knots. Puck relays the order, and Thud follows, closing back into a loose deuce.

On the radio they hear, "Death Star Down, say again, Death Star Down." Gandhi says "Good, we got the carrier."

"Swede, this is Frosty, we are sans ordinance and bingo fuel. RTB."

Gandhi says, "Roger that, Frosty. Keep it on the deck and we'll catch up to you after we clean up a bit."

ZERO FIGHTER

Lt. Koizumi, flying just above the jungle canopy, has managed twice to evade rockets fired by the Americans. His confidence growing, he knows his command in Takao need to know how to beat the American super planes.

CHAPTER 18

KNIGHT 211, OVER LUZON

0715, 22 December, 1941

Spike rolls level at 25,ooo feet and 500 knots, "Burners off." Rolling onto their right side to see the carnage below. She realizes they're over the Lingayen Gulf, about a quarter mile ahead a puff of black smoke appears, then another, closer. "What the hell is that?" Another appears only few hundred feet away.

Puck says, "Shit. Climb." Then, "Climb, Thud, we're over water. It's ack-ack from the Japanese ships."

Spike says, "Damn," and climbs past 30,000 feet, and circles back east, the ack-ack detonating below.

"Hey, Puck, those ships are shooting at us," says Speedy.

"How uncivilized of them."

Then, Gandhi, "Knight Flight 3, mark your fuel state."

Puck says, "10."

Speedy says, "9 decimal 8, we are muy Bueno."

GQ says, "10 decimal 2."

Spike says to Puck, "Remember what Thud said about their torpedoes?"

"Yeah, I like it," then on radio, "Gandhi, GQ, they use lox for their torpedoes. We want to go after the destroyers." Then on intercom, "We have about 150 rounds of 20mm. You best shoot careful."

"Okay, I will."

Gandhi asks, "Brother Swede wants to know how you plan to engage the destroyers?"

Puck says, "Guns, Gandhi."

"Okay, we'll shoot a couple of AIM-7s first, to get their attention. Pull out going east and we'll form up and go home."

Puck, Speedy, and GQ say, "Roger."

Gandhi says, "One each, GQ," then they both say, "Fox 1," and two AIM-7 Sparrows fly toward the destroyers.

Spike says, "Okay, Puck, let's get 'em." She noses down the '14 into a near vertical dive and Thud follows. The wings automatically go back as they accelerate and pass the speed of sound. Not needing afterburners, or even a high throttle setting, as they exchange altitude for speed. They see the missiles hit home on two destroyers. As they pass 5,000 feet, they see the flash of tracers, the rounds missing. The F-14s pull seven g's coming out of the dive 1,000 feet above the waves, and descend to 100 feet as they close their targets. They line up their gun reticules on the torpedo launcher amidships and fire.

JAPANESE LIGHT CRUISER JINTSU

Seiichi Ueno has proudly served on the Jintsu since completing his training two years ago. Proud of his gunnery skills, he aims the 76.2mm anti-aircraft gun at the planes flying toward them. His gun's range is only 7600 meters, so he waited and aimed. When the aircraft are in range, he fires, a round every three seconds. But the fuse setter is setting the rounds to detonate too late, "Set the fuses faster!" Then the planes levels out at 100 feet above the water, and his stomach knots as one of them flies straight at Jintsu. He sees the sparkle as a gun fires at them, first falling short, then hitting amidships. Then it is gone from sight. He swings his gun to port, trying to reacquire the enemy, thankful no bombs were dropped, when a violent explosion shakes the Jintsu.

KNIGHT 211

Spike turns right, climbing out, "Grunt. Where's Thud?"

"Right, quarter mile."

Then, she turns back left, seeing ack-ack near, she rolls, turning right again, "Grunt." Thud pulls back onto their wing in loose deuce, and a few seconds later they're flying 2,000 feet over the invasion beaches, well clear of the anti-aircraft fire.

Puck says, "My God! Spike, turn left and look at the ships we hit!" Rolling to the left, she can see over her left shoulder. The cruiser she hit is breaking in half and sinking. Thud's destroyer is burning end to end, and as she watches, rolls onto its port side and settles at the bow. The two destroyers hit by the AIM missiles are on fire, but still afloat.

She breathes, "Oh, My God!"

On radio, Speedy says, "That's for the Stoddert, you sons of bitches!"

Gandhi says, "Damn fine shooting. Economical climb to angels 20 and we'll form up. Steer 020."

Frosty says, "Beefeater flight is feet wet," as they all climb over the Pacific on the way home.

The flight back to the Vinson is quiet, Spike and Puck alone with their thoughts. Every warrior wonders what they will do when they face combat for the first time. Training is an attempt at preparing, but until the bullets fly, no one really knows. Now, both Sam and Eric know, and it's tempered with a feeling of deep loss. No rational human can take the life of another without cost. They have taken many lives today, and as the adrenalin burns out, it hits home.

KNIGHT 212

"Oh, my God, Jose, did you see that cruiser go up?"

Forgetting the accent, Speedy says, "Holy shit man! You are awesome."

"No, man, we were awesome. Damn, how many kills? I know we are aces, but damn."

"I don't know, Thud, I kinda lost count."

"Did you see many ejection seats? Oh, damn, damn, Speedy, they don't have ejection seats. God man, how many people did we kill today?"

"It was our job, Thud. It was us or them, you know that."

"Was it really? Not one of those guys could catch us, or really even hurt us. We just killed them. Just like that."

"What about the guys in PI they were trying to kill? We saved American lives today, Thud."

"I know, I...God, man. It still feels like murder."

USS CARL VINSON FLIGHT DECK

0805, 22 December, 1941

Thud and Spike each catch the three wire when they land. They idle their engines and lift the hooks as the yellow shirts direct them to a spot near elevator 2. Then they spool down their engines as the purple shirts pull fuel hoses toward their planes, and red-shirted ordinance crew wheel more missiles to under their wings. 'Handy' Washington climbs the steps to the cockpit, "Hey, LT! Did you get any? They're going to send you back up, but you have time to pee."

"Thanks for the heads up. Okay, Puck, head break." They guys have a tube and cup installed so they can urinate in flight, but they've never managed to design one for women. Some female pilots wear adult diapers and others take potty breaks when they can. Spike and Hot Pants both wear diapers, but will never give up the chance to use the head and both un-ass their birds to use the facilities. In the female head, Gloria asks, "You okay, Sam?"

"I'm...I'm fine. You?"

"Not nearly as happy as I thought I'd be. I'm mostly tired and kind of sad, you know?"

"Yes."

"I don't care about the stupid bet anymore. What kind of sick bitch I must be to bet about killing people?"

"You had no idea, none of us did. You can't beat yourself up about it. Think about all the men on the ground you probably saved."

"True, but it's still terrible, and, I think we're good at it. We're good at killing planes. In the middle of it all, my blood was up, and thank God, GQ stayed calm and kept me from getting stupid. How are you and Puck managing?"

"Good, actually."

"He's still not pissed at you?"

"We worked it out, so I think we're good, but I'll ask. We seem to be doing pretty good up there."

Gloria flushes, "Better not keep the boys waiting too long. They might decide to two-time us and fly behind someone else."

Sam chuckles, "No, I don't think so."

HEADQUARTERS, 11TH AIR FLEET, FORMOSA

0815, 22 December, 1941

Lt. Koizumi briefs his commanding officer, Colonel Tetsuo Oshiro, "Colonel, the American aircraft are large, too large to be fighters, nearly as large as a bomber. They flew as a falcon among sparrows. They had to be a fighter. They could climb like a rocket, and we're armed with one machine cannon and rockets. The accuracy of the rockets defied belief. Nearly everyone found their target. It seemed to steer right at me. Had I not turned suddenly at the last moment before impact, I, too, would be lost. That is the key to defeating them. Though they are exceedingly fast, they are not maneuverable. We can exploit that weakness."

"How, Lieutenant?"

"We change our formation, sir, and we use surprise."

"I have reports that they have mounted radar on their aircraft. It will be difficult to surprise them."

"Do we know where they came from, Colonel?"

"I believe they came from a large aircraft carrier. A submarine reported sighting one before attacking. The submarine is missing."

"We must attack it, Colonel. It is their weakness."

FLIGHT DECK,

0820, 22 December, 1941

Spike climbs back into her plane, ignoring the chaos around her. Launching and landing planes at the same time means only catapult 1 and 2 are available, so they wait to launch. They can hear flight control on the radio communicating with the rest of the aircraft.

Book, in Knight 221 is on approach. The Landing Signal Officer is talking him in, "You're high. You're high. You're high. Wave off. Go around."

Bo-Bo lands next, then 'Jail Bait' Funk in Beefeater 611 launches from Cat 2. Lt. JG Tommy 'Wingnut' Urland of the VF-32 Tomcatters is next to land, catching the coveted 3 wire. Next, Swede launches from Cat 1, and Book comes in for his second approach. "Knight 221, call the ball."

"Roger, ball, 49," says Packs, Books RIO.

"You're good, you're low, you're low, power, power, bolter, bolter." Book hits the deck late, missing all four wires. Using full afterburner, he gets back in the air.

Thud launches from Cat 1, a few seconds before Hot Pants launches from Cat 2. Spike lines up on Cat 2, "are we good, Puck?"

"We are green."

She gets the signal and runs the engines up to full afterburner, the fighter straining against the hold back bar. A final instrument check, she salutes, and grabs the stick. A moment later they are airborne. As she climbs out and turns west, she hears Book finally trap. They climb straight to the assembly point 100 miles southwest of the carrier. As they approach assembly point Zulu at angels 30, Puck says, "Okay, I got the others in left orbit at 30 miles. If you steer two degrees right and drop 50, we can tuck right in."

"Roger, that. Thanks Puck," and adjusts her course.

ASSEMBLY POINT ZULU

0856, 22 December, 1941

"Welcome back, brothers and sisters," says Gandhi. "Today we have the distinct pleasure of a fighter sweep. We're to fly south along the west edge of the archipelago down to Mindoro Island, south of Manila, then back up the east side. If it flies with Meat Ball Airlines, we splash it. Loose deuce, 5 miles separation, my element will lead, Spikes will trail. Questions?"

"Do we need your permission to engage?" asks Speedy.

"Stick with your wingman and try to spread it around, so we all have ammo on the return leg. You're otherwise free to engage."

They roll out of the turn, flying south and west, slowly

climbing to angels 35. As they overfly the northern Philippines, the sky is blue, with puffy clouds. The emerald islands below set as gems in the lapis lazuli sea. Spike breathes, "Beautiful."

"It is. It's almost impossible that a couple of hours ago we were fighting just over there."

"See anything?"

"Four '18s working over the invasion area and some '14s are north bound off to the east. "It's quiet."

"Good, any word on how our forces down there are dealing with us?"

"Haven't heard anything, Spike." They approach Lingayen Gulf and see the remaining naval vessels, some firing at them. They maneuver away.

Gandhi says, "Not our mission, guys. Maybe if we have some missiles left on the return leg."

They pass over the Panasinan Peninsula, and continue down the coast, changing course to due south. As they overfly Cabangan, with Mt. Penatubo to their left, GQ says, "Four bogies, 65 miles at ten o'clock low. Looks like their near Manila."

Gandhi says, "Roger, GQ. We'll meet them. Puck, stay at altitude as over watch." The four fighters turn southeast and the lead element descends.

Puck says, "Okay, got them on camera. They're not Zeros. I can't tell the markings. They're head on."

The lead '14s gain speed as they descend, wings back. Spike and Thud are cruising at 450 knots, conserving fuel and falling behind. Spike opens up her throttles to stay with Swede and Thud follows suit. As the vertical separation between the elements grows, Puck says, "Gandhi, they're friendly. I see the star."

On radio, Speedy says, "I confirm, Gandhi, the bogies are Papa

Four Zero's, American fighters."

Gandhi answers, "Roger, weapons tight. Let's meet them, GQ. Keep some separation so our wash doesn't crash 'em. Puck, sweep the frequencies, let's see if we can talk."

Puck asks, "You want me to talk, right?"

Gandhi says, "Nope, brother Swede wants them to hear Spike's sweet southern drawl."

Spike, on intercom, "Okay, Puck, what frequency?"

Gandhi says, "Invert, let's pass above them and give them a good look."

Puck says, "Got it, 116.4. Wonder if someone else has already made contact?"

Spike goes to frequency 116.4, "American fighters hold course and speed, we're friendly."

Swede and Hot Pants are near the speed of sound as they pass 500 feet above the P-40 Warhawks. Gandhi says, "Reverse Immelmann and form up on each side, brakes out." They dive in a loop, reversing course, and bleeding speed with their air brakes extended."

"Unidentified planes, this is Major Curtis Army Air Corp Far East, identify yourselves and state aircraft type."

"Guess, they didn't contact anyone, Puck," drawls Spike.

"Nope, it's up to us."

"Tell Swede we have contact."

Puck relay's the message and Gandhi says, "Okay, tell Spike to put on the charm. These guys look a little shaky," and Swede and Hotpants pull to each side of the P-40s.

Puck relays Gandhi's orders, and Spike takes a deep breath, "P-40 flight, this is Knight Flight 3, hope you didn't root for the Yankees."

"Knight Flight, this is Major Curtis. Who am I talking to?"

"You're talking to Lt. Samantha Hunt, US Navy. How'd your boys do yesterday?"

"Since when does the Navy let women serve? Is this a joke?"

"This is not a joke. Observe the aircraft on your wing. By the way, your welcome for this morning."

"What type of aircraft?" asks Curtis.

"These are F-14 Tomcats."

"Never heard of it, Grumman?"

"It sure is."

Another voice breaks in, "Navy aircraft, this is Commander United States Army Forces Far East. State your name, rank, unit name and number."

"Sir, I am Samantha Leigh Hunt, Lieutenant, US Navy, Black Knight Squadron, VF-154, sir."

General McArthur replies, "Lieutenant Hunt, you and your flight are to land at Manila, immediately."

"My apologies, sir, we are unable to land at Manila. The airfield is unsuitable for our aircraft. We are carrier based."

Gandhi tells Puck, "Admiral Ren is coming on line. He'll have an E-2 in position to relay soon. We're supposed to keep them talking. Oh, and do not agree that we are under their command." Puck relays the information to Spike.

"Sir, my commander will be on the line in a few minutes. May I please ask your name?"

"You're speaking with General Douglas McArthur, Lieutenant. Who is your commander?"

"Admiral Richard Ren, US Navy, Commander Carrier Group 72, sir."

"Never heard of him, and I've never heard of that group. I would have certainly heard of him. Who is his reporting senior?"

"We serve under Admiral Nimitz, sir."

"The Admiral would not send a unit to help me yesterday, what made him change his mind?"

"Can't say, sir." Matching the speed of the P-40s, the flight is now back together flying at 25,000 feet at 350 knots. The '14s flying with their wings forward.

Gandhi says, "We are to do one low level fly by over Manila and the General's headquarters, then continue our mission. We'll swing west and descent due east."

Admiral Ren comes on the line, "Lieutenant Hunt, thank you. This is Admiral Ren, Commander Carrier Group 72. Who am I speaking with?"

"This is General Douglas McArthur. What is your rank, Admiral?"

"Rear Admiral, General. Please understand, General, we do not have the fuel to remain long and I need to report to Admiral Nimitz soon. I'm glad we had the chance to render aid and hope you can make a successful stand against the Japanese from here. I have authorized a couple more strikes today, then we must leave."

Gandhi says, "Time to make a flyby, folks. Immelmann, and shift to diamond formation. Hotpants right, Spike left, and Thud behind and below. Execute."

"What aircraft carrier are you flying from?" asks McArther.

The pilots in the P-40s watch as the Tomcats just lift up, climbing 2000 feet in seconds as they execute the Immelmann. "The Gold Eagle, General. I know it is new to you," replies Ren.

At the top of the Immelmann, Gandhi says, "Rotate," and they roll upright.

"Thank you for your assistance, Admiral. It is appreciated. How long has the Navy allowed women to fly?"

Gandhi, "Spike, Thud, barrel roll over us and come to right chevron as we dive. Execute." Spike pulls up, rolls and comes down on Hot Pants right wing. Thud pulls up, rolls and comes down on Spike right wing just as Swede start the dive toward the city below. Gandhi says, "Brakes out," as they accelerate in the dive.

Ren answers, "That one is kind of complicated. I'll just say it was a very wise decision. We have several successful female pilots. The one you just talked to made 14 kills this morning."

Puck says, "Shit, Spike, we're double aces."

McArthur asks, "When did you graduate from the Naval Academy, Admiral?"

Gandhi says, "Shift back to diamond formation as we pull out at 500 feet. Thud, you are high, behind. Then we'll settle down to 200 feet. As we pass over the field, I want a 360-degree right roll, and we'll climb out at 80 degrees on four different headings. We'll climb east, Hot Pants north, Spike south, and Thud west. Speedy, you'll have to call the break. We top out at 5000 feet, with 200 feet altitude separation as we cross. We'll be at 4600 feet, Hot Pants at 4800 feet, Spike at 5000 feet, and Thud at 5200 feet. We'll then form up south and continue climbing out, going back into a diamond."

They all reply, "Roger."

Ren says, "Another complicated question. Where are my aircraft?"

McArthur steps out on the patio overlooking the airfield, the radio still in his hand, "They are diving toward the city very fast. I cannot hear them."

Ren says, "Because they are traveling at the speed of sound."

"They are in a diamond...MY GOD!" The '14s execute the roll and climb out as planned. Swede's plane going nearly vertical over the headquarters building making the entire complex shake. As he hears the sound over the radio, Ren says, "Welcome to the new way to wage war, General."

"What aircraft was that?"

"That, General, was the F-14 Tomcat, the best interceptor and fighter in the world."

CHAPTER 19

KNIGHT FLIGHT 3, OVER LUZON

1047, 22 December, 1941

Knight Flight 3 is back in formation and south bound, continuing on mission. On radio, Speedy says, "That was so cool. We rocked Manila Bay. In our time, we'd get in so much trouble for that."

Gandhi replies, "War changes everything, Speedy. Let's stay focused on the mission, my man. It's time to make the left turn."

On intercom, Spike says, "Puck, I just talked to General McArthur."

"I know. Are you okay? You don't want his autograph, do you?"

"No, Puck. I just hope I didn't screw it up too bad."

"I don't think you did badly. He seemed to be a little nicer than I thought he'd be."

"Yeah, Puck, how do you feel about what we did this morning?"

"How do I feel? I feel that your flying was amazing. I think we're coordinating better. We can smooth things out some still."

"Yeah, we did pretty well. I know we were saving a lot of people, but I've never killed anyone before."

"You did well, Samantha. We did what we had to do. It was

our job, but I can understand your regrets. I can even understand it if you feel sick. It's a normal response."

"I do feel a little sick. Are you okay, Puck?"

"Yeah, I'm okay."

Their flight continues uninterrupted. On the north bound leg, Gandhi calls, Ghost Rider, this is Knight Flight 3 requesting a tank for 100 miles south of assembly point Whiskey." The E-2C Hawkeye radio operator replies, "Roger, Knight Flight 3, Arco 2 and 3 are being dispatched. Contact them on 19 decimal 7 at angels 25."

"Roger, 19 decimal 7 at 25, Knight Flight out."

GQ says, "Gandhi, we have enough fuel to make it. Are you close?"

"Do you have enough fuel after 10 minutes of combat? Just being prepared."

ON THE FLIGHT DECK

1122, 22 DECEMBER, 1941

LCDR Carleton is climbing into the cockpit of his repaired F-14, when CDR Holtz puts a hand on his back. Book hops down, as Holtz asks, "Book, are you okay? You had a close call."

Book says, "Yes, sir, I'm fine. Just a bit of bad luck, that's all. I need to get back out there. No way, those two are going to win."

"I've got the results back from intel. Spike has fourteen kills and Hot Pants has six. How have you done?

"Fourteen kills? How is it those bit...those b..., those two manage to line up every stupid pilot Japan has in front of their guns?"

"I don't know, Book. Maybe they're actually good pilots."

Book shakes his head, "No way, just dumb luck."

200

"We'll dumb or not, I'll take luck any day. Don't go out there and do something stupid, okay?"

"I won't boss. I know I'm a better pilot, that's all. And I'm going to prove it."

"That's what I mean. Focus on the mission. You have nothing to prove."

"You don't think I can do it? You're on the side of the, um, those girls. Ain't no way I'm gonna wear a pink ribbon. You'll see." Book climbs into his jet.

ABOVE LINGAYEN GULF

1150, 22 December, 1941

"Do you think they'll let us blow up more ships? There isn't anything else out here," asks Puck.

"Probably," replies Spike. "Wonder how they're doing down there? Do you know about Corregidor?"

"Yeah, I know. If we can hold PI, everything changes." On radio, "Hey, brother Gandhi, can we kill some Japanese ships? There are nine destroyers just sitting there."

Gandhi replies, "I'll check with higher. How did you blow up those others with just guns?"

Speedy says, "Target their torpedo launchers. The long lance torpedo used liquid oxygen."

"Okay, I'll check." He comes back after a minute, "They say only two AIM-7s each. Puck, Speedy, show us how it's done and we'll follow you in."

"Roger that, Gandhi." On radio, "Ready, Spike?" The two fighters dive toward the destroyers, descending to 10,000 feet and accelerating to 800 knots. They approach in a diving curve that puts them side on to the destroyers. Jinking to avoid the ack-ack coming from the ships, they line up on the torpedo launchers amidships. Puck says, "I have a good target. We have tone, one missile." On radio, "Fox 1," as Spike fires the missile.

A moment later, Speedy says, "Fox 1." and one more missile fly toward the destroyers.

All missiles hit, but not the torpedoes. The AIM-7 does a lot of damage, but is clearly not mortal, unless the torpedoes are hit. Spike turns in, on the deck, and lines up on the first destroyer where her missile hit aft of the torpedo launcher. At three quarters of a mile, she fires a quick burst, and the torpedoes explode as she climbs out.

JAPANES DESTROYER AMAGIRI

Michio Inoue watches in horror as the cursed planes fly toward them. He's standing his post on the forward port side of a type 26, 25mm anti-aircraft gun. "When the American's come close enough...just let them get close," he thinks. While still miles away, he sees smoke coming from behind them and thinks they've been hit by the larger caliber guns already firing. He realizes his error when a rocket flies toward the destroyer Fubuki, ahead of them. The first explosion seems not too bad, then a second later there's a second explosion which blows the guts out of the Fubuki. The ship lifts from the water and crashes down, split in two, as the fire ball grows.

Commander Kazuo Tsukino on the bridge of the Amagiri orders the helm hard over, trying to miss the wreck of the Fubuki. Then, to the stern, the Nokaze blows up. Michio looks back, then looks through his sights. He orders his gun crew, "give me rounds," as he starts firing.

As the aircraft close, he sees the sparkling of gun fire. Desperate, he fires his gun, but in seconds they are out of range. "One rocket each? How could it be?" he thinks. Then he sees through the pillars of smoke and flame two more planes. He holds down the fire paddle, pouring rounds at the diving planes. Then he sees more rockets. Fire balls erupt on Hama-kaze and Makinami.

The jets circle in for another pass, using their guns. Four destroyers go away.

Inoue realizes, as the Americans fly away, that their ship is alone. All the other destroyers, save his, are gone. He hopes he has at least damaged the aircraft that killed so many of his fellow sailors.

He hears his commander, "Petty Officer Inoue, cease fire. They are out of range."

He shouts back, "The Americans are demons."

"We must attend to our mission. It falls on us."

NORTH EAST OF LUZON

1215, 22 December, 1941

After the attack on the destroyers, they head for the refueling point. On radio, "Knight Flight 3, this is Arco 2 standing by to give you guys a drink. Refueling course is 015 at angels 25, speed is 420 knots. Just step up to the bar and we'll buy you a round. Drogue is out."

Gandhi says, "Okay, flight, call your numbers." After they've all reported their fuel weight, Gandhi says, "Knight 309 has 8 decimal 2. Thud, Hot Pants, you're first. Can you get us to 9k, Arco?"

Lt. Fred 'Piper' McCrimmon, flying Arco 2 says, "Sure thing, Knights, we can get you all to 9 decimal 5, but don't ask us to do the windows."

Gandhi replies, "Much obliged, Arco." Thud lines up on Arco 3 and Hot Pants behind Arco 2. Flying well behind, Swede and Spike wait their turn, then take their place.

KNIGHT 224, APPROACHING ASSEMBLY POINT ZULU

1225, 22 December, 1941

Book, seething as they climb toward Zulu, "Packs, ain't no way those bitches going to beat our score. Can you believe this shit? Fourteen kills."

Pack says, "Let's just keep our head in the fight man. Focus on the kill in front of us."

"That's the thing, it's like the sky is swept clean of Japanese. There's nothing to kill."

Then they hear, "All units, Ghost Rider 207, raid warning west. I have multiple bandits coming out of Taiwan."

Book says, "YES! Ask for a steer, Packs."

"Ghost Rider, Knight 224, give me a steer toward the bandits."

"Knight 224, Ghost Rider, come to 294 and climb to angels 35."

"Roger, Ghost Rider."

Bo-Bo is a few miles behind them and they hear, "Knight 467, Ghost Rider, steer 308 and climb to angels 35 to join your wingman."

"Roger, 308 to 25," replies ENS Chris 'Klutz' Brandt, Bo-Bo's RIO.

"Felix Flight 3, Ghost Rider, steer 315 and climb to angels 35."

"Felix 3, roger."

"All units, Ghost Rider 207, be advised, raid one out of Taiwan is one hundred, say again 1,0,0, inbound at angels 30."

Book says, "Shit, Packs, it's a target rich environment. Hell, yeah! And we're the first in."

They hear combat control on the Vinson say, "Diamond Flight 2, Gold Eagle, discard air to ground and make your course 310 to intercept." LCDR Sean 'Lobster' Fitzgerald, XO of VFA-146, Blue Diamonds flying at Zulu says, "Roger, Gold

Eagle. Okay, boys, hang onto the bombs until we are well clear of Zulu. There are aircraft below us, full military in loose deuce."

SOUTH OF ASSEMBLY POINT WHISKEY

Well to the east and south, Swede and Spike are just finishing refueling when they hear the raid warning. Puck says, "Thanks for the drink."

"No problem, Knight 211. Exit low and slow." Spike eases the throttles back releasing the drogue, inverts and pulls away.

Gandhi says, "Got all we're taking. There's Japs to fight."

Arco 2 says, "Good hunting, Knight 309. Stab one for us, release slow and low." Swede throttles back, inverts in a snap roll down.

Gandhi calls out, "Ghost Rider, Knight Flight 3, tanked and needing a steer."

"Roger, Knight Flight 3, Ghost Rider, come to course 268 and make your altitude 35."

KNIGHT 224, CLOSING THE ENEMY

1242, 22 December, 1941

"Knight 224, Ghost Rider, the lead elements are twenty miles to your front, illuminate and engage."

Pack says, "Roger, Ghost Rider, tallyho." Then, on intercom, "Shit, there's a lot of them, and they're moving around a lot."

Book says, "Lock on, I don't want complaints. We fire missiles, then follow them in for gun attacks."

On radio, ENS Wally 'NOB' Nelson, RIO for Knight 626, asks, "Sir, we have Hornets, Felix and Knight 3 inbound. Do we engage or wait for support?"

Book says on intercom, "Fuck no! These kills are ours. Tell them to get busy."

Packs says, "We engage gentleman."

Packs and NOB call out, "Fox 1," as they close to 10 miles. Book says, "Tell Ghost Rider to keep Swede's crew in reserve, okay?"

Packs says, "Yes, sir," then, "Ghost Rider, Knight 224, recommend keeping Knight Flight 3 in reserve. They are probably short on fuel."

"Knight 224, Ghost Rider, understand."

From Strike control on the Vinson, "Knight Flight 3, Gold Eagle, mark fuel state and load out."

Gandhi says, "Each unit of Knight Flight 3 has approximately 9 decimal 4 and a full load minus one sparrow."

"Knight Flight 3, Gold Eagle, we are sending Arco 4 and 5 to fill you up. Meet them at 50 miles west of our position and stand by for leakers."

Knight Flight 2 start reporting kills as about half of their missiles hit. Book finds himself head to head with a Zero in a high speed game of chicken. As they close, he sees flashes from the wings as the Zero opens fire. Book inverts and dives without firing a shot. As he rolls upright and starts to climb, a Zero passes front of him, climbing and showing its white belly. He takes a quick shot and hits the fuel tank. He has to climb at 9 g's to avoid the explosion. He fails to warn Packs, who passes out.

As Packs comes to, "Warn me, man. Damn Where is BO-Bo?"

"It's Bo-Bo's job to find us." A Zero crosses again, and he fires, missing.

KNIGHT 467

'Bo-Bo' Bolen is 1000 feet below his wingman trying to avoid a collision. He's been taking potshots at passing Zeros. He hits one and it explodes. "Klutz, where's Book?"

"I dunno, man. They're everywhere."

"Find him, Klutz, we gotta cover him."

Lt. Sean 'Lobster' Fitzgerald says, "Tallyho, we're in the fight. Guns only, gentlemen. We have friendlies in there," and the six Hornets join the fray. The Tomcat folks love to disparage the Hornet because of its short legs, slower top speed, and smaller payload, but it's a very agile fighter. In a gun fight, agility matters.

Bo-Bo says, "Hold on," as he pulls up and spins to miss a Zero. He finds another in front of him and fires, taking off the left wing at the root.

"Shit, good shooting," says Klutz.

"Thanks, where's the boss?"

"He's a thousand feet up and kind of behind us."

"Can I climb?"

"Yeah, go." Bo-Bo pulls the stick back, saying "Grunt." He's pulls 9 g's, standing the fighter on its tail. A Zero passes cockpit to cockpit only a few feet away. "Shit, man. That was close. Warn me about traffic, damn it!"

"Sorry, dude, I didn't see him."

"Open your fucking eyes, dude."

"I'm trying."

"Fucking, try harder. There he is." Book is chasing a Zero in a tight circle. He pulls around, straightens out to line up a shot, and the Zero turns inside, out of his sights, and the dance repeats. "Hey, boss, break left and we can take him."

Book says, to Packs, "No damn it, my kill."

Packs says, "Just cover us, Klutz." Then to Book, "Where are the bombers?"

Klutz on radio, "Hey, boss, these are all Zeros and Nates. Where the hell are the bombers?"

Lobster says, "Gold Eagle, Diamond 272, Raid one is all fighters. There are no bombers in this fight."

"Diamond 272, Gold Eagle, acknowledged."

Book to Packs, "Bombers or no bombers, let's just kill them."

"There's one rolling in on us."

"Tell them this is the main fucking attack."

Bo-Bo cuts across Book's path, engaging a Zero that was lining up ahead of Book. "Gimme room," says Book, diving back in again. This time a Zero anticipates his moves and puts several .30 caliber rounds through his wing. "Shit, we're hit. Fuck! Not again."

Klutz shouts, "Book's hit! Book's hit!" Bo-Bo rolls in, putting rounds in the Zero which explodes. Klutz says, "Book, hit the burners and get clear."

Book says, "I'm still flying. Tell them, I'm still flying."

Packs says, 'We're still flying and the plane seems fine." Another Zero tries to pull into their plane and Packs says, "Break right!" The huge '14 rolls right and pulls into a tight turn.

Klutz says, "Book, you're losing fuel."

Lt. JG Shawn 'Lizard' Todd, 'Papa' Holtz's RIO, says, "Book, Papa says take it to the barn. Bo-Bo, you escort."

Packs says, "Roger, Lizard. RTB." To Book, "Papa says we go home, Book. We gotta go home."

Book accelerates out of the melee and flies toward the signal that tells them where the ship is, "Fuck, fuck, fuck. I'm going, Packs. What shitty luck."

A6M REI-SEN "ZERO", LT. KENZO KOIZUMI

Lt. Koizumi sees the wounded American pull out of the fray and knows his wingman must follow. He rolls his fighter around, almost upside down, pulling in a tight turn, he fires a burst of 20mm and sees it trace across the big grey plane. The left engine explodes, bringing a smile to Kenzo's face. As he thought, they can be destroyed. Then he sees the canopy blow off and the two pilots rocket out of the crippled craft. "What is this?" He circles, avoiding other aircraft, and sees the parachutes deploy. Continuing the circle, he machine-guns the air crew, making his kill complete.

KNIGHT 626

NOB, Gunner's RIO, shouts on the radio, "Bo-Bo's hit. Clean ejection." On intercom, "Come on, Gunner, break right and kill the bastard."

Gunner says, "I'm in, watch traffic."

As they pull around, NOB shouts, "He fucking shot them! The mother fucker shot them!"

Lizard says, "The boss says to stay calm, NOB. Focus on the fight."

NOB says, "He murdered them."

"I know, NOB, you and Johnny hang in there. We're in bound with Jedi and a couple of Tomcatters."

ZERO FIGHTER

Lt. Koizumi wheels below the fighters, looking for another target. He now knows how to kill the big planes, and he knows they use rocket seats to escape when hit. "Cowards." He sees one of the big planes dive on him and he pulls up, twisting right to break their line. The plane flies past below him. It has been a good day.

KNIGHT 626

"Don't fight him, Gunner, just shoot and scoot," says NOB.

Lizard asks, "Which one is he, NO? The boss says to stay

calm, okay?"

"I'll dive on him," says Gunner. "Fuck, he's good."

CHAPTER 20

BOMBER RAID, NORTH OF USS CARL VINSON

1346, 22 December, 1941

KNIGHT FLIGHT 3

On radio, "All units, Ghost Rider 2, raid warning north, designate raid 2. Knight Flight 3, steer 010 and engage. Beefeater Flight 1, discard air to ground and follow Knight Flight 3. There are 120 tangos inbound at 250 knots on the deck."

Gandhi says, "Alright, brothers and sisters, illuminate. Full military and descend."

Swede says, "Let's welcome Frosty and see what he has."

"Right," on radio, "Frosty, Gandhi, good to have you with us. How many birds?"

"We've got five, couldn't wait for six."

"You have missiles?"

"Sparrows and sidewinders."

Gandhi, "Save the sidewinders for bombers, it's too easy for the fighters to break lock. Brother Swede wants us to attack in battle spread, shoot our sparrows, then follow them through the formation, and climb out for your shot. You guys him them right behind us and break right. Give us 15 miles to clear your missiles."

"Gandhi, Frosty, will do."

Then, "Gandhi, this is Dixie. I have four more 18's a few miles back. I like your plan. We'll hit 'em and break left 15 miles behind the Beefeater flight."

"Thank you, Dixie, good to have you. Twelve miles, target bombers and light 'em up."

Puck says, "Fox 1, Fox 1, Fox 1, Fox 1."

The others follow suit and the missiles shoot past the escorting Nate fighters, hitting the Nell and Betty bombers behind. The bombers can't escape. Missile after missile hits as Knight Flight 3 follow their missiles in. Puck, "Splash three."

Speedy, "Splash two."

GQ, "Splash two."

Gandhi, "Splash three. Hit them and climb out."

With the low altitude, they can't zoom through, instead, they pull out of their dive, nearly head to head, and take a snap shot with guns as they climb out. The enemy fire misses them, and the only one to score a hit on a bomber is Thud, who as he pulls out, does a barrel roll and hits a Nate, too. Gandhi says, "Hey Thud, show off." As the four fighters climb out at steep 60 degrees, they hear the Beefeaters calling off, "Fox 1, Fox 1."

At 10,000 feet, Gandhi says, "Level out. Invert and reverse Immelmann." Then, Dixie, "Fox 1, Fox 1," as Frosty calls, "Break right."

Gandhi, "Knight Flight 3 rolling in. We'll hit them with missiles, then guns."

Tracers reach out from the bombers as they dive. A Nate climbs in front of Spike to protect the bombers. She fires a 20mm burst and does a barrel roll to miss the explosive debris. Mid-roll, she sees another Nate trying for Swede. It's below his field of view, so she adjusts her roll and fires, and misses. The Nate pulls vertical, still trying for Swede, the aggressive maneuver costing him his airspeed, but he's getting his nose on Swede. Spike, still in the barrel roll, "Grunt," and hits the airbrake, pulls the wings forward while pulling the stick into her belly, and throttling back her engines. They pull 9 g's, but have the shot. She squeezes the trigger and the Nate explodes as the 20mm rounds hit. Then, it's full right aileron, elevator down, right rudder, and full military on her left engine. The F-14 whips into a right snap roll that should be impossible for so large a jet.

Puck, "That maneuver was awesome, but my chiropractor is going to hate you."

"Sorry."

"No problem, you warned me, and it's all good."

Spike and Thud are out of sparrows, so they fire two side-winders each as they close to three miles, "Fox 2, Fox 2." One of Spike's missiles hits the left engine of a Betty, the other fails to ignite and falls into the sea.

Speedy, "Two sidewinders failed to ignite. Switching to guns."

Swede and Hot Pants missiles each score another Betty. Then Spike says, "What the hell?" And takes a quick gun shot at a bomber, which bursts into flames. Then they climb in a barrel roll, firing at another. The second bomber pulls up, causing Spike to pull negative g's in a reverse barrel roll, which she changes to a snap roll and adds power to pull away. Once in normal flight, Spike says, "What the hell? Who taught these guys to drive?"

Puck says, "Last I checked, I think they're the enemy. And, Spike, that was amazing flying, thank you."

Gandhi, "Knight Flight 3 is out. Clear field, Beefeaters."

"Gandhi, Frosty, Roger," and the Beefeaters roll in.

Then Gandhi says, "60 degree climb as before. Brother Swede wants a status. Be we good?"

Puck, "Yep."

GQ, "We might have been hit, but it feels okay."

Gandhi, "Level out and I will give you a good look. Spike, check Thud, then they can check us."

Puck, "Speedy, you have rounds through the left intake, check us."

Gandhi, "GQ, you have holes punched into the right elevator and right vertical stabilizer. My brother says you are done, finished, and completed for this day. Please give us a look."

GQ, "Gandhi, you're clean. We don't want to leave."

Speedy, "Puck, you're good. Gandhi, we're fine."

Gandhi, "You two escort each other home."

Speedy, "Our bird is flying great. We can stay."

GQ, "Do we have to hold hands? Our bird is flying fine."

Gandhi, "Our brother ain't asking. He says, take it to the barn."

"Roger," say Speedy and GQ in unison, and reluctantly, they head back to the Vinson, and Spike forms up on Swede as his wingman.

Puck, "What's next, boss?"

Gandhi, "We stay in the fight while our fuel lasts. Let's go."

Swede breaks left in a smooth 3 G turn, and she follows. The bombers have scattered into smaller formations, so they line up on six Kate torpedo bombers. Gandhi, "Okay, Spike, combat spread, through and pull, rolling in."

Puck, "Roger," and Spike flies alongside Swede. Now, it's nothing but dogfighting: one on one.

USS CARL VINSON

Speedy, "Gold Eagle, Knight 212 requests marshal for Knight 212 and Knight 894. Both birds are damaged."

"Roger, Knight 212, do you need the barricade?"

"Negative, Gold Eagle, we just have a few holes."

"Understood, Knight 212. Proceed downwind at 284. You land after Magic 1."

Magic 1, an EA-6B flown by LCDR Mark 'Faster' Harder commanding VAQ-133 Wizards detachment 2, traps as Thud makes the break.

"Knight 212, call the ball."

"Roger, ball, 51."

Thud, "Hang on, compadre."

"Si, Senor."

His '14 slams into the deck, catching the 3 wire. After parking, he high fives Speedy, then they climb down. Walking around their bird they see that four rounds hit, passing through the left intake from the cowl back to just forward of the engine.

As Hot Pants is parking her plane next to theirs, Speedy says, "Shit, we're lucky, man."

"Nah, just good."

"Good, hell, I'll take lucky over good. What do you think, .30 cal. rounds?"

"Think so," and Senior Chief walks up. AOCS Bruce 'Fluffy' Bond is a large black man with huge shoulders that strain his white long-sleeved t-shirt and float coat. The float coat says 'SAFETY'.

"Sir, what the hell did you do to your airplane?"

Thud, "Just a little boo-boo, Senior, from a Betty dorsal gun, I think," then falls quiet. Bo-Bo and Klutz aren't coming home.

KNIGHT FLIGHT 3

Swede and Spike roll in on the Kates, a brief burst of gunfire and their RIO's both say, "Gun, guns. Splash one."

Spike sees they are only a few miles from the battle group,

215

"Damn, Puck, we're close."

Puck, "You're right. Let's kill these fuckers before they get fish in the water."

They roll in on the last four, splashing two more, and circle back in. Then, Puck sees the flash of missile fire from the USS Horne. He realizes there is no change of bearing, and shouts, "Missiles in bound! Chaff, chaff, break left!"

Swede and Spike hit the chaff and turn violently into a dive, avoiding the telephone pole sized missiles flying right at them. The missile radar reflects off the metal fragments in the air, breaking lock, and the SM-1 missiles pass above them. Puck, "Navy ship, cease fire, cease fire, you're shooting at friendlies."

"This is Horne actual, who am I talking to?"

Gandhi, "This is Knight Flight 3, two Foxtrot one fours. You fired on us, sir." Then, "Thanks, Puck. Let's get the last two."

"Roger."

"My apologies, Knight 3. Status of inbound raid?" asks Captain John Rodgers of the USS Horne.

Puck, "Splash one."

Gandhi, "Splash one." He looks around and sees the Hornets have cleaned up the rest of the incoming bombers, "The Japs are swimming their way to hell, sir. You are clear."

Puck, on intercom, "We're getting a little thirsty, Spike. Time to land or get a drink."

"Yes, Puck."

Puck, "Hey, Gandhi, we're bingo fuel. How are you?"

"Getting thirsty, too. Let's head home. Gold Eagle, Knight Flight 3 requests marshal for two foxtrot one fours, coming in thirsty."

"Roger, Knight Flight 3, enter marshal, you are behind Beefeater 611 and 332."

They enter the pattern behind Lt. JG Rick 'Jail Bait' Funk and ENS Walt 'Meat Head' Jones.

ON THE DECK

Hot Pants and GQ do their own walk around with Senior Chief Bond. Their F-14 has eight holes in the right elevator and four in the right vertical stabilizer. Fluffy, says, "Damn it. Why are you coming back with holes in your plane? My beautiful planes deserve to stay pristine and unsoiled, like a, um," he looks at Hot Pants.

"Fluffy, there is one hell of a lot of lead flying around up there. At least, we brought them home."

IN MARSHAL

"Knight 211, call the ball."

"Roger, ball, 48," and drops to the deck, catching a rocky two wire, ending eight hours in the air. Swede, behind her, catches an okay one wire. They are directed to park with their tails sticking out over the water. As they are positioned, they open their canopies. Pulling off his helmet, Puck asks, "You okay, Spike?"

"Yeah, tired and hungry. How are you? Good catch on those missiles. Thank you."

"I'm okay. It was a hell of a day's work, and, you're welcome."

Their plane captain, helping with her straps, "You okay, Lieutenant? How many kills?"

"I'm not sure. How's the ship?"

Joe 'Handy' Washington says, "No hits. No hits on any of the battle group. Did we win the bet?"

"I don't know, Joey. Can you help me up, please?" He helps her climb out of the cockpit and down the steps to the deck. Puck wave him off, climbing stiffly out of the plane. Once he's on the deck, he runs his hand along the side of the fuselage, pats it, and says, "Good Horse."

Spike smiles, "Would you two like a moment alone?"

Surprised, he says, "No, um, all good. Let's get to debrief. I see coffee in our future." Smiling, Spike hobbles to the head.

2000 FEET ABOVE TAKAO, FORMOSA

1525, 22 December, 1941

Lt. Kenzo Koizumi wipes his face, again. Part of his canopy is shattered and his face is bleeding from many annoying cuts. But, his Zero is still flying. He takes a pass over the runway before landing as his radio was destroyed by the same cursed American rounds that hit his canopy. Looking down he sees a nearly empty airfield where there once was a mighty air fleet.

He flies the downwind leg, praying his landing gear will extend. As it locks in place, he smiles. On his final approach he is much more relaxed. He lines up over the field and flares to land. As his main gear touches, he senses something wrong, a grabbing on the right side. Adding power, he lifts the right wing a bit, and the plane straightens out, but he has to land. As he touches down again, the right wheel grabs and spins the Zero nearly 90 degrees right. Then the tip of the wing touches the ground, and the plane flips up on its right wing, and it crumbles.

He ends upside down, hanging from his harness. Cursing the US Navy, he releases the latch and falls a few feet onto his shoulder. Hearing a fire vehicle approaching, he struggles to free himself from the wreckage. Finally, he's free and able to stand, but not before he's sprayed down with foam.

CHAPTER 21

BLACK KNIGHT SQUADRON READY ROOM

1418, 22 December, 1941

The atmosphere in the ready room is quiet and somber as Spike walks in. No one is playing cards or goofing off. Instead, their talking in hushed voices waiting for CDR Holtz to arrive for the debrief. She walks over to Puck, Speedy, and Thud, passing Book at the podium. She has to step over Swede's long legs in the aisle. As she reaches her seat, they all hear on the 1MC, "Good evening, Carl Vinson, this is your Captain. I regret to inform all of you that we lost four planes today. We have recovered Lt. JG Larry Stone and Ensign John Dover of the Blue Diamonds, and Dover was wounded. Of the Knightriders, Lt. JG Peter Greer and Ensign Larry Lewis successfully ejected over the jungle, but we have not yet recovered them. That mission is ongoing.

"We lost Ensign Robert Bolen and Ensign Christopher Brandt of the Black Knights. Both were killed in their parachutes. It is the nature of warfare that people are lost, but acceptance of this reality does nothing to diminish the pain of losing a friend. Ensign Robert 'Bo-Bo' Bolen was 26 years old, born of a military family, his father serving as a Master Sargent in the Air Force. He graduated from the University of Colorado and was a member of the Black Knights for only five months. Ensign Christopher 'Klutz' Brandt was 27 years old. He was the first person in his family to join the military and graduated from Rochester Colgate University. He joined the Black Knights with his pilot five months ago. In those five months, they impressed everyone with their hard work and dedication. They were comrades, colleagues, and friends. They successfully engaged seven aircraft before being hit, and so they died aces. The loss of Ensign Bolen and Ensign Brandt tempers what has been, otherwise, a very successful day for Air Wing 9 of the Carl Vinson team.

"We broke the back of the invasion force, downing over 300 aircraft, sinking one aircraft carrier, one battleship, six cruisers, and nineteen destroyers, as well as other craft. As I am sure most of you realize, resupply is going to become a critical problem soon. Admiral Ren, therefore, has decided to withdraw once all aircraft are recovered. Our next stop is Wake Island, where we hope to intercept an invasion fleet. After that, we will make our way to Pearl Harbor. I cannot guarantee a port visit as we will have to see what happens once we report to Admiral Nimitz. You have all done an exemplary job, and I expect, we will continue to do so. That is all. Captain out."

Pucks looks at Spike and smiles, offering her the seat next to him. "I see you're not hobbling anymore."

"Yeah, I got the stiffness out." She surveys the room, "Puck…"

Book pacing at the podium looks at Swede, "You think you are hot shit, sinking destroyers."

"I haven't said anything, Book."

Book continues, not hearing him, "Yeah, you and the pink flight, that's what we should call it, the PINK FLIGHT."

Swede says, "Just drop it, Book."

"Fuck you, hillbilly. I ain't gonna wear no fucking pink ribbon."

Hot Pants says, "Who cares about a stupid bet."

Book, "SHUT UP…YOU…STUPID…BITCH! Both of you, just shut the fuck up."

Spike looks at him, surprised, and Swede says, "Book, you're out of line, man. Rein it in."

"Fuck you, Swede. You think you are hot shit. Well, you're just lead pimp in the pink flight."

Swede stands, "Book..." All of Flight 3 stand up.

Ignoring them, Book continues, "That's right, a pimp. What's it like getting blow jobs from your subordinate pilots?"

Swede takes a step forward, "Commander Carelton, stop, now!"

Spike quickly moves ahead of Swede, putting a hand on his shoulder, "Let him rant, Swede. He's upset, okay? We all are." Book walks toward them, scowling.

Swede says, "You're right, Spike."

"Do you make them swallow, pimp, or do you shoot all over their hair?"

Turning to Book, Sam says, "It's ok, Book. We are all upset about Bo-Bo and Klutz."

Book yells, "BITCH!" and hits Sam with a wicked right cross to the chin. She falls back and to the side, Puck running to catch her, and they both fall.

Swede's right hand leaps up, hitting Book in the mouth, driving his head back. Book staggers back, sitting down hard on the deck. Thud, Speedy, and Gandhi close on Book, while Gloria goes to Sam and Puck. Book struggles to his feet, bleeding from a cut lip, "I'm going to destroy you for that."

Calm, Swede says, "Okay, well, I might as well get my money's worth." He hits Book again with a cross to the cheek. Book staggers back, bumping into Gandhi, who keeps him standing. Book throws a chopping right jab, hitting Swede in the chest. Then, Swede spreads his legs and hits Book twice in the stomach. The two stand, toe to toe, throwing punches on each other.

Puck, "Are you alright, Sam?" as he helps her to her feet.

Rubbing her jaw, "Yeah, Eric," then to the two men, "GUYS, KNOCK IT OFF!"

Packs grabs Thud, pulling him away from the melee. Thud looks at him, "You aren't fighting for him, Packs? He's wrong."

Packs answers, "He's my pilot," and swings at Thud.

Sam steps toward Swede and Book, "STOP! Just stop."

Puck wraps her from behind, "Let them fight it out, Sam. It's been coming for a while."

Thud slips a blow from Packs, "This ain't about loyalty, Packs. He hit Spike."

Packs turns, blind-siding Gandhi with a blow to the arm. Gandhi moves out of the hit, grabs Packs in a wrist lock, and flips him to the floor. "Book's out of line, and you know it."

Packs, "He's my pilot," as he struggles against the arm bar Gandhi has him in. Work it as he might, he cannot move.

Thud, "Packs, this isn't about loyalty, man."

Swede and Book continue, toe to toe. Swede pounding blow after blow to Book's belly, and Book landing hit after hit to Swede's face and shoulders. Then, Book tries a knee to Swede's groin, and Swede twists, taking the hit on his hip, and getting in an uppercut that snaps Book's head back. The crushing right uppercut staggers Book, and Swede says, "You're done, Book. Don't make me finish this."

Sam steps in, "Guys, stop it. Please, stop it."

Book steps back, wiping blood off his mouth and breathing heavily. Swede turns to Sam, "Are you alri…" Book charges and Swede swings a cross to Book's jaw, and he crumbles to the deck.

From the door Holtz shouts, "KNOCK IT OFF!"

Swede steps back and Book rolls onto his knees, retching.

The others move back, clearing a path for Holtz. Gandhi lets loose of Packs. Holtz looks over the scene, "Swede, what the hell just happened?"

Swede tears the rank insignia off his uniform, hands them to Holtz, and sits down. Book still on his knees, says, "He...he struck me. You saw it yourself. I want him in the brig."

Holtz shakes his head, "Everyone, sit down. Book, Book, I saw you both fighting. But, why? Why would Swede...?"

"What does it matter why, he did it."

Gloria says, "Carleton hit Sam first, and Swede was defending her."

Book says, "Shut up, cunt. No one is asking you."

Holtz, "Stow it, Book. Another word out of you and I'll hit you myself."

Swede finally says, "He hit her, boss. He was way out line. If I'm going to the brig, he ought to, too." He looks at Book, "If you're charging me with assault, I'm charging you with assault and sexual harassment."

Holtz says, "Settle down, Swede. I thought it was something like that. What did he say?" No one answers, then, "Spike, what did he say?"

"He called Swede a pimp and said Swede was getting blow jobs from his pilots. He was spoiling for a fight, sir. When I tried to calm him down, he hit me."

"Is that what all of you heard? What you saw?"

They all nod, and Puck says, "Spike was trying to calm him when he hit her, sir."

Book now on his feet, turns to Puck, "You helped him! All of you helped him! You're gonna go down, too."

In a cold tone of voice, Puck says, "Carleton, I haven't hit you, yet."

Holtz says, "Enough of that, Book. Are you trying to court

martial my whole squadron? Just be quiet and let me think." Then, "Did anyone other than Swede hit you?"

"No, only him."

"The problem, Swede, is once he leveled charges at you, you can't counter charge. The UCMJ doesn't allow it." Then to Book, "Are you sure you want to press charges? It will tear up the squadron and we're in a shooting war."

Book says, "Damn straight. He's going down. Then they won't have their protector." Book turns to Spike and Hot Pants, "We lost two good MEN today. Why couldn't we have lost you two instead?"

Puck balls his fists, his face darkening, "You evil son of a bitch."

Gloria opens her mouth in shock, then puts her face in her hands. GQ puts his hand on her shoulder, lips tight.

Gunner says under his breath, "What the fuck man?"

The silence in the room deepens until the only sound is Gloria crying.

Spike grits her teeth, eyes narrowed, and looks around. Some of the men meet her gaze, but others look away. "Fine. He hit me. I'm charging him with assault."

Holtz asks, "Not sexual harassment?" She shakes her head.

Thud, crimson, looks at Speedy, who's scowling, "Commander?"

"Go ahead, Thud."

"Commander, I want to place charges on Lieutenant Commander Carleton, sir."

Confused, Holtz asks, "What for?"

"For sexual harassment and conduct unbecoming an officer, he accused me of having homosexual sex with Lieutenant Swedenborg, sir."

"He did?"

"Yes, sir. He said Swede was getting blow jobs from ALL his pilots, sir. I'm one of those pilots."

Holtz sits down, putting his head in his hands.

Spike, holding Gloria, looks at Thud, shocked.

Book says, "Oh my God. It's high time we got rid of Swedenborg and his pussy pink flight."

Holtz glares at Book, "Shut the fuck up, Book." Then to his RIO, Lt. JG Todd, "Shawn, call the masters at arms. I've got to call the CAG and the Captain."

ADMIRAL'S CONFERENCE ROOM, ONE HOUR LATER

LCDR Carleton, Lt. Swedenborg, CDR Holtz, Lt. Hunt, and Lt. JG Jackson are all in their dress blues waiting for the Admiral and Captain to come in. Because of the rules of non-judicial punishment, a chaplain and the Chief Master at Arms are required to be present, as well as the accused person's supervisor. The requirement for the chaplain is a holdover from the days when a commanding officer could issue capital punishments such as the cat 'o nine tails, keel hauling, hanging, or hanging from the bows. The chaplain is there to offer last rites to the condemned. The CMAA is there if the commanding officer orders confinement to the brig, or even bread and water.

The accused has the right to ask witnesses to be present, but the CO is not obligated to allow the witnesses to speak. The accused cannot ask for counsel, as the proceedings are non-judicial, but he can waive the NJP and ask for court martial. Not normally a good idea. Court martial convictions are felonies.

"Attention on deck!" and Admiral Ren, Captain Johnson, and Captain Lee walk in wearing working khaki.

Ren says, "Master at Arms, I will hear the case against Lieutenant Swedenborg first."

The CMAA says, "Lieutenant Swedenborg is charged with one count of Article 90, Assaulting or willfully disobeying a superior officer."

Ren asks Swede, "How do you plead?"

"Guilty, sir."

"No excuses about extenuating circumstances?"

"No, sir, I hit him."

"Why?"

"Because, sir, he hit Lt. Hunt. Before that he accused me of taking sexual advantage of my subordinate officers, sir, and selling their services for money."

"He said that?"

"He called me a pimp, sir. That's what a pimp does."

"Setting the assault aside for now, the gist is, he impugned your honor?"

"Yes, sir, but he also impugned the virtue of three officers under my command."

"Is it honorable to strike a superior officer, Lieutenant?"

"No, sir."

"So, in defense of your honor, you yourself impugned it."

"No, sir, but that's not how I see it."

"Neither do I. Do you feel your actions were in defense of Lt. Hunt?"

"Yes, at least, to begin with. The truth is, Lt. Hunt was sucker punched. Otherwise, she could have defended herself with no help from me. Sir, he was spoiling for a fight. He said all that stuff to start a fight. I should have known better. It pissed me off that he hit her and that was the final straw. After that the fight was on. I could have tried to hold him down, or something, but by then my blood was up. I'm sorry, sir."

"I'm sorry, too. You admittedly struck a superior officer. For that offense, you will be reduced in rank to lieutenant junior grade, suspended for three months, and continue in flight status.

Swede says, "Yes, sir." Salutes, does an about face, and is directed out of the room by the CMAA.

Admiral Ren says, "Master at Arms, please read the charges against Lieutenant Commander Carleton."

The CMAA says, "Two counts of Article 92, failure to obey an order or regulation; one count of Article 117, provoking speech or gestures; two counts of Article 128, assault; and three counts of Article 133, conduct unbecoming an officer and gentleman."

Ren asks, "How do you plead, Lieutenant Commander Carleton?"

Carleton says, "Not guilty, sir. I was defending myself from Lieutenant Hunt and Lieutenant Swedenborg."

"You were defending yourself? According to the reports I read, she was trying to calm you down."

"She raised her hand to me. I thought she would strike me."

"And how do you explain your aggressive and inappropriate comments before the encounter?"

"I never intended to include Lieutenant Jackson in my comments?"

"Your intent is irrelevant. You said what you said."

"Then, sir, how is it I have three counts?"

Ren says, "One count of conduct unbecoming for tonight, the second for other night when you yelled at Lieutenant Hunt and Lieutenant Hoolihan for saving lives, and the third for several nights ago when you berated Lieutenant Hunt for helping Lieutenant Mohr. So, two counts each time for disobeying the general orders of the Navy, and for disobeying the orders given to you by your commanding officer. One count for each female officer, but you're right, that would be five counts. So, note it in the charge paper, Master at Arms. Any more questions, Lieutenant Commander Carleton?"

Turning pale, Book says, "No, sir."

Ren continues, "I would say you made a regular ass out of yourself, Lieutenant Commander. This is your opportunity to attempt to redeem yourself. Have you anything to say?"

Carleton says, "Sir, why did the Navy ever think women should fly jets? It's 1941 now, and it's illegal, and I believe it's wrong. The Lord never meant a woman to do a man's work. The Bible says so. Besides, I was just saying what everyone else is thinking."

Turning red, Ren says, "Jesus also said, 'Love one another as I love you.' Did you forget that scripture, or do you only read ones that let you be an asshole? I find you guilty on all counts. You're busted to Lieutenant Junior Grade, taking a half month pay, times two, and giving you four days of bread and water to think about what you've done. If it were practical to court martial you, I would. You are also going to be transferred to Captain Lee's staff. I would pull you from flight status, but we need every pilot, even an idiot like you. I'm ordering you to have no contact with any of the aircrew involved in this, except as part of your official duties. If I hear about another outburst from you, I will throw you in the brig to rot. Do you understand?"

Carleton lowers his head to hide his anger, "Yes, sir."

"Good. Master at Arms, get him out of my face."

As the CMAA leads Carleton away, Ren looks at the remaining officers, "Commander Holtz, you need a new XO, but this isn't the time or place. Can you handle your squadron without one for now?"

"Yes, sir, I can."

"Okay, I have one question, Lieutenant Hunt, why didn't you or Lieutenant Hoolihan file charges of sexual harassment? He was way out of line."

Sam swallows, trying to find her voice, and Thud says, "If I may, sir?"

"Yes, lieutenant, go ahead."

"Because they're girls, and neither want to be accused of causing trouble. They work really hard to get respect, and I think, if they filed sexual harassment charges against Lieutenant Carleton, they would fear they would lose what respect they have with the guys."

Ren is quiet, then he says, "I understand, son. I hope, though, that after their performance in the air today, they get that respect. They've earned mine. Commander Holtz, I don't envy you your job. Okay, dismissed."

CHAPTER 22

11TH AIR FLEET HEADQUARTERS, TAKAO PREFECTURE, FORMOSA

0630, 23 December, 1941

Lt. Kenzo Koizumi stands at attention in the office of Vice Admiral Nishizo Tsukahara. He sips his tea, reading, and looks up, "Lieutenant Koizumi, you have done very well to shoot down one of the American planes. You are the only one of my pilots to do so, though, many were able to hit them with guns. Why were you successful?"

"Fortune favored me, Admiral. All of my fellow pilots are excellent aviators."

"Yes, they are, however, as you analyze your movements, what gave you the advantage?"

"I was always moving, sir. Never did I fly in a straight line. When I saw an opportunity, I did not hesitate."

"We have lost a great number of aircraft and pilots today. I do not wish to lose you, but you have been recalled to Japan. May you continue to serve the Emperor with distinction."

ENGINE MAINTENANCE AFT OF HANGAR BAY 3

0810, 23 December, 1941

Most of the space between hangar bay 3 and the fantail belongs to the Aviation Intermediate Maintenance Depot, which is part of the ship's force. It's also home to the power plant divisions of every squadron on deployment. Functionally, each squadron gets a corner for their tools which are stored in large multi-drawer cabinets called vidmars.

The Black Knight Air Frame and Power Plant Division belongs to Lt. Hunt. This morning they're working on a General Electric F110-400 turbofan engine, preparing it for turnover to AIMD for testing. Three people are working on the engine, the rest are standing around talking. Sam is leaning against a vidmar reading the QA report on the engine they just wheeled back to AIMD. There, they fire the engine out the stern, often adding a knot or two of speed to the 90,000-ton vessel.

Greg Newburg, her new airman off the Stoddert, walks in, and without looking up, Sam asks, "How is MM1 Hammond, Greg?"

The rest of her crew look up, knowing his friend is still in medical. "He's ok. The corpsman says it's going to take a long time. He started walking a bit today, though."

AD1 Gellar says, "LT, if we're going to keep your pet fireman in the division, shouldn't we give him a call sign?"

Grinning, "Hmmm, you're right. What should it be? What defines you?"

Newburg answers, "I don't know. Does everybody have one?"

Gellar says, "Yes, I'm 'Bobby'. Travis over there is 'Plow Boy', Joe Cervella, with the scope, is 'Mouth', Lt. Hunt is 'Spike', Chief White is 'Mosey'. We all have names.

Joe says, "He's a bit young to be a man, let's call him 'Fireboy'."

Gellar says, "Nah, he's an airman, now."

AD3 Ernest 'Hip' Gnosis says, "He got off the Stoddert before she sank. Let's call him 'Sinker'."

ADC(AW) Paul 'Mosey' White walks in, "No, he's not a sinker. Let's call him 'Bobber'."

"No Chief, that's too close to 'Bobby'."

"Then maybe we ought to call you 'late', Gellar. Where are those QA reports?"

"LT has them, Chief."

"Okay, and seeing as you don't like 'Bobber', let's call him 'Duck', 'cause they float and fly."

Joe says, "So do you seagulls."

"Yeah, but seagulls shit on everything. Newburg's all right. I like 'Duck'. Is that okay, Newburg?"

Greg says, "Yes, Chief, um, 'Duck' is fine."

Watching them, Sam realizes just how good White is with their people. Watch and learn, she tells herself, watch and learn.

Joe says, "What the hell? I didn't get a choice."

Gellar laughs, "That's because you ARE a mouth, Mouth." The crew laughs, then settles down to work. Duck grabs a broom and starts sweeping. Sam straightens the report before she hands them to White. He leans toward her and whispers, "Keep them busy," and leaves.

Joe asks Sam, "So, it's all true about going back in time?"

"Yeah, Joe, those were real WWII Japanese planes we were fighting."

He puts the borescope back down into the engine, inspecting the fans. Starting to tremble, he yanks the scope out, and stands up. "Shit man! I'm never going to taste my momma's lasagna or her tiramisu again. Oh my God, her tiramisu."

Bobby says, "Lock it down, Cervella."

"Fuck you, Bobby. You ain't never had my momma's tiramisu. You probably couldn't tell tiramisu from pound cake."

"I said, lock it down. We're all kinda fucked up about this and I don't need your crap."

Joe gets red in the face, walks over, and puts his face in Gellar's, "Really? Really? You're a fucked up..."

Sam steps in, "Gentlemen! That's enough! We are all hurting here. We are not taking it out on each other."

Joe turns to her, "Why not, ma'am? He's pushing me."

"And you're pushing back."

"Ma'am, you just don't understand. I mean, my family's close. I mean really close. Like Italian close."

"Yes, yes, I do understand, Joe, we're all we have now. This... these people around you, they're your family now."

He stands in front of her, not meeting her eyes. A tear slips down his cheek, and he curls his fists tight, struggling to keep his feet still. Puck starts to walk into the engine maintenance room, sees the confrontation, and stops just outside, watching and listening. Sam says, "I bet your momma's tiramisu is so good it'll make your heartbreak, just like my Nana's peach pie."

"Ma'am, it's just, well, my family is close, like real close."

"You're worried about them, aren't you?"

Without thinking, he reaches for her, his tears falling, and with a painful sob, wraps his arms around her, his head on her shoulders. Gellar says, "Umm...?" Sam gives him a sharp look and shakes her head, holding Joe and letting him cry. The rest of her people quietly go about their business, watching. AD2 Argyle 'Socks' McCrimmon picks up the borescope and continues inspecting the engine. ADAN Lori "Sass' Givens picks up a rag and wipes down a work bench. Bobby shakes his head and goes back to his paperwork. Duck keeps sweeping.

Sam holds Joe until he cries himself out. When he runs out of tears, he looks up straight into her eyes, "I'm sorry, ma'am."

"Shhh, it's alright. Are you okay?"

"Yeah, I think so, ma'am. Ma'am?"

"Yes?"

"Ma'am, you're alright."

"Why thank you, Joe. I appreciate that, now go to the head and clean up."

Puck quietly turns and walks away.

As Joe leaves, ADAN Louis 'Deep Fried' Siemens asks, "Ma'am, if we're family now, does that mean I can't date Lori?"

"In your dream, Deep Fried, in your dreams," says Sass, making them all laugh.

Sam says, "Please excuse me," and leaves. She walks swiftly to her stateroom on the 03 level, well forward from the power plant area. She walks past people in the narrow passageways without seeing them. She walks by Gloria, who starts to say something, then sees Sam's eyes, and lets her go. In her stateroom, she locks the door, goes to her desk and collapses into her chair, sobbing. "God, this is hard. I think I got it right. Joe needed me. I think I need them as much."

BLACK KNIGHTS QA OFFICE

0830, 23 December, 1941

Thud Jackson is wearing a clean flight suit and pacing back and forth in front of his desk. An office so small, that he can only take two steps before he has to turn. He looks at his watch, again, and finally there's a knock on the door. He quickly returns to his chair, picks up a piece of paper, and says, "Enter."

A pretty blonde female ensign walks in, "You wanted to see me, Lieutenant?"

"Ensign Severn?"

"Yes, sir, Penny Severn, sir."

"We had three AIM-9s fail to fire yesterday, Ensign Severn. Do you know what's wrong with the missiles?"

She comes to attention, "No, sir, I was not aware of a malfunction, sir."

Thud gentles his voice, "Ensign, a bad missile could cost us a pilot and a plane."

"Sir, is that what happened to Ensign Bolen? Oh God! Oh God!"

"No, Ensign, no, he did not call Fox 2 before he was hit. Because of all the good guys up there, we were only using guns. I had two missiles fall off my plane, though, when I tried to fire them, and I came back with a hole in my plane."

"I'm sorry, sir. We'll take every missile down to parade rest, sir. It will not happen again."

"I know what went wrong, Ensign. Your crew failed to hook up the Amphenol's properly and they shook loose in flight. I checked the rest of them when I got back, and some of them were loose."

"Okay, okay, sir, I'll find out who screwed up."

He raises a hand, "Just remind your people to be careful, okay?"

"I will, sir, it will never happen again."

"Okay, um, I...by the way, I'm Frank Jackson. They call me Thud."

"Not because your missile fell off, I hope," Severn laughs.

Startled, he laughs, "No, it's, um, oh never mind. Thank you for coming up."

SAMANTHA'S STATEROOM

0930, 23 December, 1941

Sam cries herself out. She goes to the head to clean up and splash cold water on her face. She runs her fingers through her hair and leaves to go back to work. Captain Lee, leaving his stateroom a couple of frames aft, glances at her, then stops and looks more closely, "How are you, Lieutenant?"

"I'm fine, sir, how are you today?"

"Do you have a minute to talk?"

"Yes, sir, I do."

They walk further aft to his office, just off CATCC. They walk through to the inner office, "Book is on ready 5. In here." He ushers her in and closes the door, then pours them each a cup of coffee, and sits down. "I know, normally, it's taboo to shut a door when male and female officers are alone in an office, but I think we need the privacy. You are not okay, and we both know it. Talk to me."

"I don't know what to say."

"You lost your family, you've had your first taste of combat, you had a ton of pressure put on you as part of the brain trust, you had to deal with a hostile chain of command, you lost two co-workers, and you had your XO wish you dead, that about cover it? These last few days have been tough. If you're fine, then you're not human. Your eyes are puffy like you've been crying. I'm not an idiot, Samantha, but I am your friend."

Her tears start up again, and she puts her face in her hands. He grabs a handful of tissues and gives them to her, then sits back and waits. After a bit, she blows her nose, wipes her face, and looks up. "Airman Cervella cried in my arms. I have to be strong for my people. I have to be strong. I can't keep breaking down like this."

"Your guys are vulnerable, too, Sam. They need you. They need you like I, well, like I did. Now that Carleton has been transferred things should smooth out some, I hope." He pauses, "I'm not pretending that it isn't hard. It's damn hard. Stuff worth doing generally is."

"Rick, my wall is down and I can't get it back up."

"You mean your C.I.B. wall?"

"Yes...I feel...I feel raw."

"I hope this doesn't sound cold, Sam, but you're better off without it."

"When do I stop feeling raw?"

"You have to live through it, experience the pain and conquer it, and make it our own. It takes time. You're strong and you can do it, Sam. Just know, it gets better."

"All those people I'm responsible for, what if I fail them?"

"You will. We all do. Just do your best every day. At the end of the day, you have to hope you've got it more right than wrong. Remember, you're not alone."

"Right, it just feels like it." She looks at him, "You know what triggered Cervella off? His mother's tiramisu. At that moment, I could taste my Nana's peach pie. I almost lost it then."

Lee chuckles, "It's always something. I was thinking back to my dad's hunting cabin. He let us kids taste whiskey for the first time after we got our first deer. We have to hold things together, Sam, if the officer corps falls apart, we lose everything."

She smiles, "You're right. All I wanted was to be an astronaut."

He smiles, too, "I wanted to be an ace. As of today, I am, and so are you. The stars might still be in your future, Samantha. Things are going to happen much more quickly."

"Right, well, we have to survive first."

Lee shakes his head, "Nope. We just have to our job the best we can. Whether we survive or not is up to the guy upstairs. Don't forget Him, Sam. He looks after fools and aviators."

"You've you got a point."

"Okay, now, you're doing better. Now git. This old codger

still has a lot of work."

"Yes, Rick, thank you." Sam carefully closes the door behind her as she leaves, smiling.

HANGAR BAY 3

1000, 23 December, 1941

Book and Packs walk up to ENS Wally 'NOB' Nelson, who is inspecting the inside of an open radome of a '14, "Hey, NOB, ya got a minute?"

"Sure, Book, what's up?"

"I see you're wearing a pink ribbon. Those broads must be really proud of themselves."

"We're all wearing pink ribbons, Book. We lost the bet and a bet is a bet. You two should be wearing one, too."

Packs says, "Not me. I will not play their game. No way."

Book says, "Packs is right. No fucking way. The bitches must be insufferable."

NOB shakes his head, "You got it wrong. The ladies didn't say a word. The guys, well, pretty much we all decided it was the right thing to do."

Packs says, "Now, they're ladies?"

Book snorts, "A lady doesn't take a job away from a man."

NOB presses his lips tight, "Still on that kick, Book? Why don't you preach it somewhere else? I have work."

"Are you going to shut us down like that?"

"Yeah, Book," looking him in the eyes, "I guess I am. When are you going to let it go?"

"Never."

NOB turns back to the radome, "Like I said, I got work to do."

As they leave, they hear the whoosh and shudder of a catapult launch.

CHAPTER 23

POWER PLANT OFFICE AFT OF HANGAR BAY 3

1045, 23 December, 1941

Lt. Hunt sits at her desk doing the never-ending paperwork in the office she shares with the DIVOs from three other squadrons. Lt. Warren walks in, "Are you busy, Lieutenant?"

"Yes. Are you going to save me from all this paperwork, Lieutenant?"

"I guess so, Captain Klindt wants the trust together in about 10 minutes."

"Oh, thank you, Lieutenant," then to Chief White, "Chief, can you finish reviewing our inventory? I need to go."

"Yes, ma'am, I got it."

She picks up the phone and calls Thud.

HANGAR BAY 3

Sam is walking across toward hangar bay 3 when Thud catches up with her, "Hey, Spike, I think I made a jerk out of myself."

"How so?"

"Well, I called the ordinance division officer up to QA because of those missiles that failed to fire."

"Okay, well, what happened?"

"I told her they didn't fire because her guys didn't hook up the Amphenol's right."

"Is that what happened to the missiles? Sounds like you did the right thing."

"Yeah, but she's a girl. She's Ensign Severn, and I chewed her out like for five minutes before I even introduced myself."

Sam laughs as they get to the ladder down, "Why is it so important that you introduce yourself before you chew her out?"

"Well, it was just rude of me. My mom would kick my butt for treating a girl like that," as they walk aft to the next ladder.

"Thud, it's ok. It was in the line of duty. Was she cute?"

As they walk into the RT classroom, Thud turns beet red, "Um, well, uh, shit, Spike, that's not fair."

Sam chuckles.

Captain Klindt asks, "Do you want to share, Lieutenant?"

"Not really, sir, just a Thud moment."

"Okay, let's get back to work. First, the early morning invasion of Wake that was supposed to happen, didn't. We picked up radio chatter from Wake, and there is no mention of an attack. There is still a Japanese invasion fleet out there somewhere and they may still be planning to attack. We need to know where it is. Also, the command wants to know, what day is it?"

Mohr says, "I thought we worked that out, it's December 23rd, 1941."

"That's the date, what day of the week is it? The chaplains would like to have Sunday services, you see. It's sort of a tradition."

They all look at each other, and Mohr asks, "We wouldn't happen to have a 1941 calendar lying around?"

Chuckling, Klindt says, "No, Mohr, we don't.

Sam says, "Maybe Senior Chief can find it in one of those books of his."

Richardson looks at her, "Am I the only one who can read?"

Thud says, "Are you all kidding? The math isn't that hard."

Sam says, "Enlighten us, oh great one."

Thud turns red again, but plows on, "We all know the attack on Pearl Harbor happened on December 7th, 1941. Sunday, December 7th, 1941."

Klindt rolls his eyes, as Mohr hits his forehead with the heel of his palm, "Duh, and we're a brain trust?"

Then Klindt says, "Thank you, Lieutenant Jackson. That makes today Tuesday. It will be an eleven day transit to Pearl at a speed of advance of 18 knots. We need to conserve fuel. Christmas will be on Thursday, and the Captain is planning a stand down and party. We need to be looking for the enemy carrier group on the way. But, we should reach Pearl on January 2, 1942, so we need to plan how to contact Admiral Nimitz on the first."

Sam asks, "Two things, sir. When is the memorial for the men of the Stoddert and for Bo-Bo and Klutz?"

"The chaplains are planning it for this afternoon, part of why we needed to know the day of the week."

Denton says, "My math has us arriving on the third, sir."

"You forgot to subtract a day for the date line. I've been doing this navigation thing for a while."

"Yes, sir."

Mohr says, "We also need to figure out where our fleet is right now. It would suck to be attacked by our own guys"

Klindt says, "True, so we need to plan an approach to Pearl that avoids other fleet units while still looking for the enemy. Radio is listening close for mention of Wake. It's clear the Japanese are doing something different. What do you think it means?"

Mohr says, "It could be they are redirecting the Wake task force to look for us."

"If that's the case, we want to be the first ones to make contact. Did the Japanese use their radar much in WWII? I'm sure they had it."

Richardson says, "Sir, actually, few Japanese ships had radar. Carriers did, as did many cruisers, but I don't know if they would have it on. Just like now, turning on radar is a beacon for attack."

"Okay, what was the range of their radar?"

"It doesn't say."

Thud asks, "Is there a picture so we can get the rough dimensions?"

Richardson says, "Yeah, I saw one in here, why?"

"With that information, we can get a rough range. If we keep an E-2 up, we will find them before they see the plane, if they illuminate."

Sam says, "Why don't we send out a far cap with an E-2 with radar on to cover a wide swathe of ocean? If we find them, we hit them. If they pick up the E-2, they still don't know our location."

Klindt nods, "Sounds reasonable. Everyone like it?" They all nod, "Okay, we still need to figure out how to contact Nimitz. Is there anything else on the table?"

Richardson says, "Yes, sir, we need to start thinking resupply."

"There really isn't any. Horne, Camden, and Kaiser can get refueled with diesel from this period of time, but they don't have any JP-5."

"Exactly, sir, which is why we will need to have it made.

They don't have any of the missiles, electronics, jet engines, etcetera that we will need. So, we'll need to create the technology to resupply the ship and do it fast."

Klindt says, "Shit, you're talking about a whole new industrial revolution, aren't you?"

"Yes, sir, exactly."

Barr says, "It took decades to learn how to build this stuff."

Hughes says, "Never mind the nuclear power plant needs, they're great, but they need specialized maintenance that no one knows how to do."

Warren says, "Not true, we do."

"Sir, have you ever inspected generator tubes? Ever refueled a reactor? Me neither."

Klindt interjects, "One thing at a time, folks. This ship has twenty years of fuel left, so we have time to work that out, and Hughes, I have refueled a reactor before."

Sam says, "The point is, guys, we don't have to re-invent the wheel. First, we have to contact Nimitz, all the rest is moot for now."

Klindt says, "Okay, we start thinking about how we'll drag the 1940's into the 1990's and talk about it in another meeting. Right now, let's divide the problem: Richardson, you tackle electronics; Mohr, you have JP-5; Hunt, you have jet engines. That's your division, right?"

"Yes, sir."

"Warren, you tackle nuclear maintenance. You'll need to fly over to Long Beach and figure out what kind of shape they're in. Denton, Barr, I need a report from you about upgrading all the crypto and communications. We can't assume that what was used in WWII is secure any more. Hughes, you have metallurgy. We need a lot of stainless and titanium. Did they even make what we need in '41? You will need to talk to Hunt about metal requirements for making and repairing aircraft. Is there anything else?"

Thud asks, "What do you want me to do?

Klindt says, "Sorry, Lieutenant Jackson, forgot you were here. Do you know anything about missiles?"

"I know someone who does, but I just pissed her off."

"Well, buy her some chocolate and say you're sorry. We will need new missiles soon. Questions?"

When no replies, he continues, "Okay, where is the fleet?"

Everybody looks at Richardson, who sighs and digs through his books, "I'm not sure. It's too soon for Doolittle. I think Halsey had the fleet kicking butt somewhere. They did a lot of raiding after Pearl. There will be pickets off Pearl, though, no matter where the main fleet is."

"See what you can find. Okay, how do we avoid the pickets?"

"A diversion, sir?" asks Thud.

Mohr says, "Not a good idea. After Pearl Harbor, any hint of trouble will have the place on full alert."

Warren asks, "What are we going to do when we get there? It would be a lot easier to sneak one boat or a few helicopters in then to get the whole battle group close."

"What's the maximum range of our helicopters?

Thud answers, The SH-3's we fly have a safe range of about 250 to 300 miles. The SH-60's on the Fife and Jarret have a bit shorter range, but carry more weight."

Sam says, "Um, sir, I have a solution to your problem of sneaking in."

"Okay, good. Is it simple?"

"SEALs sir, Lt. Issa's team. Sneaking ashore is what SEALs do."

"Okay, I like that idea. Could you give him a call? We still need to figure out how to get them in and out."

Sam calls the SEAL team office as Warren says, "If we had a

sub, it would be easy, but we don't."

"If frogs had wings, they wouldn't bump their asses on the ground. Focus on what we do have."

Mohr asks, "Where were the radars placed at Pearl in WWII?"

Richardson says, "I found the fleet."

"Where?"

"One carrier group is returning from an aborted attempt to aide Wake Island, and the other is patrolling west of Pearl looking for the Japanese. The one aiding Wake may bore on if the Japanese don't invade."

"Damn, right where we need to go. What about the radars?"

"I saw that somewhere, give me a minute."

Lt. Robert 'Abdul' Issa walks into the room wearing black BDUs with subdued rank and SEAL patches, "So, what is this about, Lieutenant?"

Klindt stands and offers his hand, "Good morning, Lieutenant. I'm Captain Klindt, the Reactor Officer. I asked Lt. Hunt to call you down here. How is it, an F-14 pilot has come to know a SEAL?"

"Well, sir, we met in the water the other night and had a nice chat over a dead guy. What do you need, Captain?"

"We are planning how to make contact with Admiral Nimitz. Please, sit down."

"How about on radio?"

Mohr says, "Already thought of that, it won't work."

"Why not, we have all the codes, don't we?"

Barr laughs, "Hell no, codes never make it into the history books."

Issa says, "Okay, I'm starting to not like this plan. What do you want us to do?"

Klindt says, "Get in, make contact with Nimitz and get him

out here for a look."

"Okay, I have some questions. First, where does he live?"

Thud says, "Nimitz House on base." They all look at him, "What? I don't spend all my liberty in a bar, okay?"

Issa says, "Hey, there's nothing wrong with bars."

Klindt, "Okay, so how do we get in and get him out?"

"We'll have to use helos to get him out. We can get in by helo, or parachute. We could even swim in. We have all our gear."

"Okay, helo in and out would be simplest. We can't land a helo near the base, though."

Issa says, "Drop us in the water a couple of miles out, and we'll swim in."

Mohr gets a big grin on his face, "I know how to do it, KISS."

Klindt, "What?"

"Keep It Simple Stupid – KISS. Swim in, change into sailor uniforms, drive up and knock on the door, simple as that. He has to be used to getting disturbed at all hours. He's in charge."

HANGAR BAY 2, STARBOARD SIDE

1250, 23 December, 1941

Sam and Frank are walking to wardroom 3 for lunch, weaving between parked planes, when Lt. Sandra 'Cargo Britches' Douglas walks up to them. "Hey Spike. Is this guy with you Thud?"

"Why yes, Lieutenant, good to see you again."

Cargo Britches walks up to Thud, wraps her arms around his neck, and lays a serious lip lock on him for several seconds. Pulling back a bit, she says, "Hi, I'm Cargo Britches. Thanks for the steer the other night."

Sam bursts out laughing, as Frank, red, stammers, "Um, uh,

246

um, sure. Un, wow."

She lets him go, smiling, "You really were my hero that night. We were lost and you showed the way."

Smiling, even redder, he says, "I was, um, glad to help, um, wow."

She turns to Sam, "You're right, terminally shy and a damn nice guy. Take care, Thud. You ever want a date, look me up," and she walks away, smiling as she looks back at him.

Sam smiles at him, "You ought to take her up on that. She's a damn nice girl, and one helluva pilot."

"You set me up, didn't you?"

"No, not really. We told her about you when she asked that night."

"And she just happened along here?"

"YES! I haven't talked to her since that night. She said she'd be looking for you. I'm glad she found you. You know, Frank, I will never plot against you or play games. Real friends don't."

He cocks his head, "Why do they call her Cargo Britches?"

"Why don't you ask her? It's not going to kill you to talk to a girl, you know."

"You aren't going to tell everyone, are you?"

Sam looks him in the eyes, and says softly, "No, Frank, never."

Her plane captain, 'Handy' Washington, approaches and salutes, "Ma'am, you need to come look at your plane. We're done. You too, Lieutenant Jackson."

Frank grins, "Are you thinking what I'm thinking, Spike?"

"Oh no. Okay, let's go see."

Handy leads them up to the aft part of the flight deck where their planes are parked. On the right side of Thud's plane, under his and Speedy's names, are painted seventeen little

Japanese flags in two rows. Back of those is a destroyer profile with the Japanese flag, and under it, two hash marks for the three destroyers he sank. Thud says, "Wow! Thanks, guys, this is cool."

Handy says, "Ace three times over first time out. It's beyond cool."

Spike smiles, "Very cool, Thud, very cool." Then they walk to Spike's plane. Hers is painted the same, with two rows of 10 flags, and one row of two, a destroyer symbol with one hash mark, and a cruiser.

Thud says, "Wingman, you rock."

"Damn, thanks Joe. You guys did a good job. I'd no idea."

Handy says, "You should see the island, they painted everyone's kills there."

She says, "Shall we Thud?" and turns to Handy, "Again, thank you, Joe."

Making their way forward, they see Lt. Carleton talking to Lt. JG Lorne 'Jedi' Luke. Someone on vultures' row yells at Spike and Thud, "Hey, get on a float coat if you're gonna wander around. We're about to start a landing cycle." Carleton looks up, sees them, and quickly walks away.

Thud says, "Well, I guess, another time," and they head inside.

03 LEVEL FORWARD, OUTSIDE WARDROOM 3

1345, 23 December, 1941

Sam is just leaving wardroom 3 after lunch when CDR Holtz calls out to her, "Lieutenant Hunt, could I have a word?"

"Yes, sir."

He turns down a thwarts ship passageway leading to the flight deck and stops in an alcove, "I just wanted to say I'm sorry for being such a jackass to you and Lt. Hoolihan. I know

I fed into Carleton's idiocy, instead of stopping it. I know, we can't start over, but I'm sorry."

Sam puts out her hand, smiling, "Commander Holtz." Looking confused, he takes her hand and shakes it. "Commander Holtz, I'm Lt. Hunt and I'm happy to be in your squadron. I look forward to working with you."

Smiling, Jim Holtz gets it, "I'm glad to have you in the most kick ass squadron in the Navy. I know you are a great addition to a solid line up."

"Well, thank you, sir. I'm going to be happy here." She cocks her head, her smile lighting up her eyes, "Now, that wasn't so hard. Oh, and Commander, apology accepted.

Holtz blinks, seeing her as if for the first time, shakes his head, realizes he's still holding her hand and lets go. "By the way, flight rotations just got posted. We'll be alternating with the Tomcatters, two on ready five and two in the air on far Cap from here to Hawaii, including Christmas day. I put you and Thud in for tonight, okay?"

"Yeah, it's fine. I'd have taken Christmas day, sir."

"I know, but it didn't work out that way. I'll see you later."

CHAPTER 24

HANGAR BAY 3, STARBOARD SIDE

1430, 23 December, 1941

The chaplain, Commander Perry Chandler, a small, thin man with blonde hair and sad eyes, finishes his sermon, then reads the names of the fallen sailors of the Benjamin Stoddert, those who were rescued and didn't make it, and those whose bodies were recovered from the sea. As he says each name, the board holding the body is tipped up by sailors in dress uniform, and the body is consigned to the sea.

Frank Jackson is praying, garrison cap in hand, head down. Sam stands with Greg Newburg and Oscar Hammond, who's in a chair at the end of a row of wounded survivors. They can see the Church flag flying above the American flag on the Long Beach. She is also burying fallen from the Stoddert. A radio operator repeats each name from each ship so the survivors can hear both services.

Attending in their working uniforms are the off-duty sailors and airman. Admiral Ren, Captain Johnson, Captain Lee, LCDR Curtis, XO of the Stoddert, the Chaplain and his staff, are all in dress uniforms. After the last Stoddert sailor is named, Chaplain Chandler pauses, "We have one recovered Japanese sailor. Americans have always honored the fallen, regardless of who they fought for. We do not know his name, but may the Lord comfort him. Gentlemen," and they tip a board covered with a Japanese flag.

Then Chaplain Chandler continues, "There are two more we

have lost. Ensign Bolen was a great pilot, and to many here, a good friend. His steadfast valor is plain to see in the success he achieved in the air before being shot down. Ensign Christopher Brandt was a fine Naval aviator and a good friend. They gave their last full measure. Each of these noble dead gave their last full measure so that those who follow may live, so that we the living may re-dedicate our lives to the fight ahead. These are the first we have given in a war we did not expect to fight. They will not be the last. Our enemy is merciless, but let us remember to be merciful. The mission before us is great. Let us dedicate ourselves, not to revenge, but to duty. Let us deliver swift blows in defense of liberty, justice, and freedom, and yes, mercy. May God bless you all. Gentlemen," and the sailors tip the boards of Bo-Bo and Klutz.

HANGAR BAY 3, AFTER THE SERVICE

Walking back to her office, Sam hears voices behind the plane she is next to, "I should bring it up to the Captain, John."

"No fucking way, man. You know, Mike, you know how much shit you could get into."

"I don't care, John. I think it caused us to go back in time. He should be told. I'm kinda responsible for all this."

Going around the plane, Sam says, "Gentlemen." They look up, shocked, and their hands shoot up in a salute. She returns the salute, "Walk with me."

MM2 Mike Reed says, "Ma'am, ma'am, we have stuff we need to do."

"Do you mind telling me what you two were talking about?"

Reed realizes the cat is out of the bag, and relieved, says, "Um, yes, ma'am, I guess so. Ma'am have you ever read the Talon Sword by Philip Cullen?"

"Yes, so?"

"Well, ma'am, do you recall the time machine in the book?"

"Yes. Just say it, Petty Officer, I don't have all day."

"Well, ma'am, I'm getting to it. The author was a Lit major at Oxford. He didn't know a time machine from a plowshare, so I did a little digging. That's what I do, I mean, I'm a nuke."

She smiles, "Point, Petty Officer?"

"Yes, ma'am, anyway, there's no way Cullen would know anything about machines like that. At least, I didn't think so, so I dug into it, and it turns out he got the idea from a paper written by Dr. Heinrich Heinlein."

"You're kidding, right?" then stops, "The paper, when was it written?"

"1934, ma'am, and as I was saying, this Dr. Heinlein helped the British build the machine."

"Build the machine? Sorry, I sound like a parrot. What do you mean?"

"Yes, ma'am, they built it out in the Australian desert and tested it, December 19, 1941."

"This was in the paper?"

"Well, no, ma'am. But I looked up Dr. Heinlein and found a newspaper report that talked about it."

"British? Australian?"

"British, ma'am, it was in the London Times Herald."

"Do you have a copy of the article and the paper? Are they on the boat?"

"Yes, ma'am, but that's the thing, what I'm talking about. Do you remember how the time machine worked in the book?"

"Vaguely, Petty Officer, it was a few years ago."

"Well, ma'am, the power for the machine was back in the 1940's, and they transmitted the power. Then the people in the future who'd built the antenna went back into the past. I got a copy of the paper and I built one of the antennas, ma'am."

"Oh Lordy, and you brought it onto the Carl Vinson?"

"Well, yes, ma'am, I don't live anywhere else."

Sam shakes her head, "Why don't we go to your Chief's office. I need to talk to him."

MM3 John Nolan asks, "Ma'am, I didn't build anything. Can I go?"

"Does he have anything to do with this?"

"No, ma'am, I showed it to him once. We went to power school together."

"I see. Petty Officer Nolan, do not talk to anyone about this, clear?"

"Yes, ma'am, clear."

"Okay, you may go," and he bolts away.

MM2 Reed shows the way to the Reactor Mechanical Division office. Inside are a female lieutenant, two petty officers, and a senior chief. Sam says, "Senior Chief, does this petty officer belong to you?"

Senior Chief Argo says, "Yes, Lieutenant, can I help you?"

Lt. Patricia Sawyer asks, "do we need to clear the office, Lieutenant?"

"Yes, please."

"Okay, guys, clear out. Ruiz, leave your boards here, I want to look them over."

Senior Chief Argo asks, "You want me to stick around?"

Sam nods her head, and the room clears. She turns to Reed, "Well, Petty Officer Reed, spill it." He repeats all he told Sam, the senior chief and the lieutenant silent, not interrupting once.

When he finishes, Sawyer asks, "What's this antenna made of?"

"Well, ma'am, it had a small iron core coated in platinum that was a perfect hollow sphere, sitting on a glass rod. There was an inner sphere of copper plated with cadmium on its outside and silver on its inside. The space between the two spheres had to be evacuated and filled with chlorine gas. They were held inside another sphere of glass. I coated the outside of that with silicone carbide, then three coats of urethane, evacuated the outer sphere and filled that with argon. The whole thing is set on a glass rod and holder."

Senior asks, "Where is it now?"

"What's left of it is down in 2 plant, Senior."

Argo asks, "Lieutenant Sawyer, and ah, Lieutenant Hunt, can you hang out while I take the culprit down to his locker and take a look?"

"Not a problem, Senior," answers Sam.

Lt. Sawyer says, "You do that, Senior. I'm going to brief in the RO. Lieutenant Hunt, would care to join me? The RO doesn't bite."

Sam smiles, "I know. He's great." Sawyer gives her a questioning look.

Outside the RM division office are MM2 Miguel Ruiz and MM1 Hughes. Shawn looks shocked to see Sam walking out of his division office, "What's going on, LT?"

"Not now, Shawn, later." And collects another odd look from Sawyer.

When they get to the RO's office, Lt. Sawyer asks the yeoman, "Is the RO in?"

"Yes, ma'am, but he's talking to the Captain."

Sam says, "Good, he needs to know about this, too. Would please ask if we may interrupt?"

The yeoman looks at Sawyer, who nods her head, so he pokes his head into the RO's office. A moment later Captain Klindt and Captain Johnson step out, Klindt says, "Hi, Lieutenant Hunt. What have you brought us?"

"Sir, this should be private."

"Okay, Petty Officer Cutting, Lieutenant Neyhi, could you please step out."

After they leave, Sam says, "Petty Officer Reed built a time machine based on a science fiction book, which itself was based on a physics paper the author found in the Bodleian Library." She takes a deep breath and tells them everything Reed told her, and where he is now. "We thought it might be a good idea if you were informed, sir."

Captain Johnson says, "A Heinlein device, eh?"

"You've read it, sir?"

"Sure, I read more than reports. But, I don't know much about the device."

Klindt asks, "So, the device is real?"

"Yes, sir."

There's a knock on the door, and Klindt says, "Enter."

Senior Chief Argo and Reed walk in, "Captain, oh, and Captain, we have recovered the time machine." The device Reed is carrying is about a foot and a half tall, the base spread out to six inches, and the top appears to be melted.

Klindt says, "Thank you, Senior. Do you have any idea how this thing works?"

"Not the foggiest, sir."

Sawyer says, "Sir, I was an English lit major. I have no idea. Honestly, maybe you should ask her?"

Sam says, "Sir, we've talked about this. Nobody knows if time travel even works, but it appears it did. Petty Officer Reed seems to have a better idea, seeing as he built the thing."

Reed says, "Sir, it's sort of like a cosmic slinky."

Klindt says, "Keep the nukese to a minimum."

"Yes, sir. As I understand it, basically, when Dr. Heinlein built the original device in the Australian desert and discharged it, he put 1.2 terawatts of energy into motion. The system is elegant. Once he discharged the energy, the receiver or antenna moved forward in time to the point where the energy was to discharge. Like throwing a slinky out, only through time. When it arrived at the right point in time, the receiver acted as a focus of energy, gathering the materials around it and pulling, well, us back to the time of origin, a cosmic slinky."

They all just stare at him, and Sam says, "Well, that really clarified everything."

Klindt asks, "Why didn't it change the world war we know?"

"That's just it. It didn't work. Nothing happened. What really got my attention when I read the news article, is they discharged over a terawatt of energy, and nothing happened. No explosion, no melting, nothing."

Johnson says, "I love science fiction, but this is giving me a headache. If it didn't work, then why are we here?"

"Well, going out, well, further out, on a limb, the discharge created a decision point that could not be resolved until the correct time. When that time came, and there was a device in place, it resolved, and we came back."

Johnson asks, "Okay, then, I bite. How do we get back?"

Sam says, "If this is the same technology used in the book, we don't?"

Argo asks, "1.21 terawatts is an incredible amount of power. How did they generate that much in World War II?"

"Dr. Heinlein built a large number of capacitors and used the power plant to charge them all, one bank at a time. Then, when he was ready to use the machine, he discharged them all at once. The original power plant only generated 800 megawatts, if I read the paper correctly."

Klindt says, "I guess this could make sense. According to string theory, it is possible for multiple flows of time to exist. When we were hauled back, we could have, essentially, started a new path in time, a new time stream. We discussed that in the brain trust meetings."

Johnson says, "Okay, you broke out your inner geek. Can you give it to me in English?"

"Put simply, it has been hypothesized that more than one timeline exists. In fact, some physicists speculate that there could be millions of different timelines. Rather than drawing the military technology back into the timeline we are familiar with, that is, the time line where the device was actuated, the power surge created a separate timeline and drew us into it because of the...thing Petty Officer Reed here made." He pauses, thoughtful, "Sir, if that is the case, there probably isn't any going back, we're stranded in another time line."

Sam says, "I think, perhaps, it would be in everyone's best interests if nobody outside this room found out that Petty Officer Reed did this. It might get bad."

Klindt gives Reed a stern look, "It's crossed my mind to keelhaul him myself. How many other antennas might be out there?"

"It was a popular book in geeky circles, sir. It's a lot of work to make, though. I don't know. The original is probably still around. I think, sir, anyone around that one, well, they're back in 1941, too. At least, that's what I think, sir."

"Do you have a copy of the book and the plans?" asks Johnson."

"Um, yes, sir, I will bring them to you."

"No, son, bring them to Captain Klindt. His brain trust is figuring this all out." He turns to Klindt, "Thank you, Captain. Please let me know what you find in the papers." He then gets up, and everyone else stands as he leaves.

CHAPTER 25

ORDINANCE OFFICE, 3RD DECK FORWARD

1510, 23 December, 1941

Lt. Jackson stands outside the door to the ordinance office, lifts his hand to his ball cap, puts his hand down, puts it back to the cap, and grabs it, "Jesus, man, it isn't the prom." He knocks on the door and walks in. Ensign Severn is sitting at a desk in a fairly large office crowded with more desks that are occupied by chiefs and petty officers. When she sees him, she says a guarded, "May I help you, Lieutenant?"

Crushing his cap, he says, "Um, yes, I owe you an apology. I was a…an, um, my behavior like sucked. Anyway, this is for you," and pulls a bar of Cadbury chocolate out of his pocket, giving it to her.

Startled, she takes it, "Thank you, Lieutenant? Um?"

"Jackson, ma'am, Thud Jackson."

She laughs, "Right, I remember now, like James Bond." He stops crushing his cover and laughs. "Did you come all this way just to give me some chocolate?"

Turning red, "No, I mean, yes. I needed to apologize, ma'am, and ask for your help with something."

She unwraps the chocolate and gestures to the coffee pot in the corner, "Okay, apology accepted. Do you want to share? There's coffee over there?" Thud gets his coffee and sits in front of her desk. She hands him a piece of chocolate on a napkin, "Here you are. You need my help?"

"Yeah, you see I'm a member of the brain trust, and we, well, um…"

"What brain trust."

"Oh, Captain Johnson's. We've been figuring things out for him, like what is going on with the war and how good the Japanese planes are and stuff like that. Did you know the long lance torpedo uses liquid oxygen?"

"Everybody knows that."

Thud smiles, "Exactly, that's what I said, but I guess they didn't know. Anyway, do you know anything about missile propellant?"

"Sure, I mean, I have a degree in chemistry and I work with them here. You have to know what you're handling, right?"

"Yes, I knew you could help."

"Help with what?"

"We need to make new missiles because we're running out of the ones we have."

"No one knows how to make missiles correctly in 1941. They can't do it."

"You know how."

"Yeah, but, um, oh jeeze."

FLIGHT DECK ON ALERT 5

2358, 23 December, 1941

In the cool night air, Spike and Puck, Thud and Speedy sit in their cockpits, canopies up, enjoying the tropical breeze. The ship is steaming on a base line to Hawaii, but as always, there's a CAP up and Alert 5 and Alert 15 on standby. Puck says, "I saw you talking after the service with those two guys. What was that about?"

"Um, we may have found our problem."

"You solved world hunger, which problem."

"The problem concerning how we came back in time."

"I apologize for the snide comments, please continue."

"We know what happened and who the facilitator is, but that's all I'm allowed to say right now."

"Oh, okay. We haven't had a chance to talk about the Book thing. Are you alright?"

"Yeah, I'm fine. Honest."

"I hate it when peoples says 'honest'. Does it mean they lie to you the rest of the time? After the things he said, you're okay?"

Spike laughs, "Puck, in a sense, he set me free. I now know the command trusts me. I actually feel sorry for him. It's really horrible to have lost Bo-Bo and Klutz, but a weight has come off my shoulders. I feel light."

"Okay, how's Gloria?"

"She seems okay. We're both used to dealing with people not liking us, or at least not wanting us around."

"I understand, but it's bull shit that you have to. Indians deal with that attitude, too. You know, it's going to be worse when we get back to the States."

"Yes, I know. I fully expect to be kicked off flight status and thrown out of the Navy. I know Captain Johnson and Admiral Ren will fight it, but I don't think they can win this battle."

"I'm pretty much expecting the same thing. At best, they'll make me a cook or something."

"Yeah, it's going to be tough. I don't know what I'll do. I can't go back home, my dad's just a teenager. It'd mess everyone up."

"I at least have the reservation. You're welcome there. One thing I'm thinking about. I'm going to buy some stock in

IBM, Raytheon, and maybe, GE."

Laughing, "You gotta have a job first. I might take you up on that. I would be the world's first blonde Indian."

"Not hardly, I've a second cousin who's blonde. My tribe is a family and we're happy to adopt."

"Okay, that makes me feel better. How are you with the Book thing? You were right in the middle of it."

He chuckles, "I got away with helping Swede. I think I came out good. Hell, so did Swede."

"Yeah."

"About the money thing, how much cash do you have on board?"

Spike pauses, then, "I brought a few thousand. Everything I had in savings. You never know what you're going to need."

"Me too. I figured to bring cash and save my pay. How much do you suppose an average working stiff makes in 1941?"

"Not much, but the cost of living was really low compared to our time."

Puck, "I looked it up. The average annual income was about five hundred dollars. Now, how far could we go on, say, ten thousand?"

"Damn, handled properly, that's a good stake. Invested properly, we're set for life. That is, if they take our money. Think about it."

"We'll need to get it exchanged, but they have to accept it, it's legal tender."

Spike, "No, they don't. This is all different."

"Way to burst my bubble. You could make a clown cry."

"Sorry."

"You know, it's after midnight. It's Christmas Eve. I don't much feel the spirit."

ALL OFFICERS CALL, WARDROOM 1

0800, 24 December, 1941

Captain Johnson is standing in front of the nearly three hundred officers not on watch in wardroom 1, the formal wardroom, with upholstered chairs and white tablecloths. Spike is with Puck, Hot Pants, GQ, Thud, and Speedy, all in their flight suits, as they could be called at any minute.

"Thank you for coming. It hit me last night, as I wrote a few more reports which I can't send to anyone, tomorrow is Christmas. There will be no care packages from home, no letters from loved ones. This is going to be a hard Christmas for all of us, separated by both distance and time from those we love. We in this wardroom must provide the Christmas our sailors will be missing.

"In that vein, I have ordered the bakery to make 70,000 cookies and other pastries, so everyone can have a care package. I'm also raiding the ships stores to provide each sailor with some toiletries. I want all of you to come up with ideas for small gifts of some sort, be it only a personal card, for each of your people. For those of you with large divisions, you may recruit your chief, but the goat locker is already doing their part. Be creative. Your people deserve it. Thank you. Any questions?"

Lt. Neyhi from RC division asks, "Sir, what is our budget?"

"We're you planning on ordering something from Tiffany's We have what we have. Be creative and work together. I don't mind if you raid the Sup-O for materials, but keep it reasonable."

Ensign Hagworth from S-2 says, "Us supply officers are being doubled nailed. We're already making cookies."

"Be honest, your guys are making the cookies, you're making gifts for your guys. I would also like to decorate the place a bit and make it more festive."

Lt. JG Rick 'Jail Bait' Funk from the Red Cocks asks, "Sir, do we have to make the gifts ourselves?"

"Funk, I'm not going to hold your hand. They are your people and they deserve your best. You're an officer, figure it out."

Lt. Hunt raises her hand, "I have a small division. I have no problem helping some of you guys with large ones."

At first a few guys chuckle, but Lt. Warren jumps at the chance, "I have thirty-five nuke electricians I need to gift. I have some ideas. May I join you?"

"Absolutely."

Pulling up a chair, he settles in, "I have copper wire and electrical doodads in the shop, but no ideas what to do with them. Oh, and do you have any females in your division, Sam?"

"Yeah, I got two, Heidi and Lori."

"Cool, I have a perfume sampler set I bought in Pearl for my wife. You could have two. Um, your friend can have some for the girls in her division, too. It's too weird for a guy Div-O to give perfume."

Before Sam can answer, Gloria says, "Hi, I'm her friend, Gloria Hoolihan," looking at Sam with one eyebrow raised.

Sam says, "Oops, Gloria, sorry. This is Lt. John Warren. I know him from the brain trust." She looks around to introduce the others, "Where did they all go?"

"No idea, maybe Puck went to gather his stock of tomahawks."

Sam says, "Anyway, that copper wire, maybe make it into bracelets."

Warren says, "I don't think bracelets will work, it's too soft. I do have an idea. Electricians have a stock of tape with six different colors. Anything we can do with that?"

Gloria smiles, "Yeah, make supersized candy canes for decorations."

"Good, but we still need gifts."

Sam sighs, "I wish I could think of things like that."

Warren says, "Yeah."

She stares into space, then, "It's hot down in the plant, isn't it?"

"About 130 degrees on feed pump flat."

Gloria says, "I got it. We take some plastic bags for ice water and put them into like, maybe, the sleeves of flight deck shirts. Sew one end shut and have the other tied so it can be refilled. They put it around their neck and stay cool."

Sam points at Gloria, "See, my brilliant friend."

Warren nods, "We have this plastic sheeting stuff that would be better than bags. It's heavier and we can seal one end with duct tape and fold and use one of those heavy paper clips for the other."

Puck walks up carrying a bunch of parachute line, and says, "It won't work unless you use two bags, one on each side, so the paper clips stay up, holding the water in."

Gloria turns to Sam, "Want to help me raid the store room for a box of extra-small shirts?" They never fit anyone anyway."

As they stand up, Sam says, "That's the truth. Why we stock so many is a mystery to me. Um, Eric, what are you doing with all that para cord?"

"Making bracelets, it's handy to have around and a simple gift."

"See, someone else who's creative. It's enough to destroy one's self-esteem," says Sam, laughing.

Warren says, I'll get the plastic, clips, and duct tape. If we have enough materials, we can make some for other divisions and swap."

Captain Johnson surveys the wardroom, officers from all departments working together, hatching plans; airdales, nukes, supply officers, gunners, staff, ordinance, all working together. Quietly smiling, he says to his group, "We have scotch tape coming out our ears. Let's us tape instead of glue on the paper chains, it'll hold better."

That evening on the 1MC, "Good evening, Carl Vinson, this is your Captain. As no doubt everyone knows tomorrow is Christmas. The salty folks among us know that traditionally we would stand down on Christmas day, and for the most part, we will. We are also going to break from the routine a bit, tomorrow. First, after mid-rats, we will start setting up hangar bay 2 for breakfast. The whole crew will have a late breakfast, and dinner, in the hangar bay. That means we will need a working party to set it all up and break it down after. Then, though, we are out of contact with Washington, Santa managed to get a message in and he assured me he will be making a delivery tonight. That means I need lookouts and gunners to be especially careful. We don't want to shoot the jolly guy down after he's gone through all this trouble.

"I want all personnel not on watch in hangar bay 2 after breakfast to meet Santa. Uniform of the day will be relaxed. PJ's are fine with me, as it is Christmas morning. Just keep it appropriate and be sure to have something on your feet to protect from the non-skid.

"After breakfast, Santa and I would like clean up to be all hands. After Christmas dinner, the goat locker and wardroom will be putting on a talent show. After the show, the choir will lead us in carols. I know we are far from home, and I know it is hard. I want this Christmas to be the absolute best we can make it for each other and I know you will all help. Thank you, and Merry Christmas."

CHAPTER 26

GLORIA AND SAM'S STATEROOM, CHRISTMAS MORNING

Gloria gets out of bed as Sam comes back from her shower, "I hope I don't have to fly; my hands are numb from sewing."

"You worked hard. Are you okay?"

Gloria bounces out of bed, puts on her flip-flops and grabs her robe, kit, and towel, "Yeah, I'm good. Don't go down yet. I want to give you your gift first."

Sam grins, reaches into her locker and pulls out a beautifully wrapped package, "Okay, I'll wait."

Gloria smiles, tosses her head, flipping her hair, and leaves. When she returns, combing her wet hair, she asks, "Okay, who goes first?"

"You do," handing her the box.

"Watcha got me?" and opens the box revealing a nightgown and robe of deep emerald green shimmery silk charmeuse. Her breath catches as she slips them through her hands. "Oh, Sam, they're beautiful. Oh my. Thank you," and gives Sam a hug.

Gloria then pulls two boxes out of her locker and hands them to Sam, "The big one first." Sam opens the larger box and finds four bottles each of salon quality shampoo and conditioner, "I thought by now you'd be out. Open the next."

"Yeah, I'm pretty low and this is really nice stuff. I'd never buy it for myself."

"That's what gifts are for, open the other."

Sam does, and takes out a sterling silver chain with a Star Trek IDIC symbol in silver with one diamond inlayed, and a pair of matching earrings. "Wow! They're beautiful. You've definitely captured my inner geek. I'm going to wear them today. Think I'll get away with it?"

"Yeah, no problem. There's no way I'm wearing these beauties to breakfast. I would need a whip and chain to keep the guys away."

"No kidding, but that's the idea. You're the most feminine woman I know. They spoke to me."

"Thank you and Merry Christmas."

"Merry Christmas to you, too, honey." Sam hugs Gloria, who asks, "We wearing PJs to breakfast?"

HANGAR BAY 2, CHRISTMAS MORNING

Gloria and Sam show up for breakfast in jeans and t-shirts. Sam is wearing her new necklace and earrings. Most are in working uniforms, although there is a sprinkling of crew in PJs. The girl ahead of them in line is wearing a pajama top with workout shorts. As they take their trays to a table, Eric waves them over to join him. He's wearing Wranglers and a dark blue and buff double-breasted shirt. Thud's in jeans and a red and white checked western shirt, and Swede's in jeans and a hickory shirt. Gandhi is wearing a Gi, and GQ, as usual, is in pressed khakis. Sam shouts over the noise of a thousand voices all trying to be heard in the vast steel box of the hangar bay, "Merry Christmas, everyone."

Eric says, "You look nice, Sam," then shuts up.

"Thank you, Eric," and looks him up and down, "You're pretty sharp. I like the shirt."

Swede and ALL the other guys in view are looking at Gloria, "It's jeans and a t-shirt, put your eyeballs back in." She looks at Sam, laughing, "Guys."

Frank sees Sam's jewelry and does the Spock hand salute, "Live long and prosper."

She smiles and returns the salute, "And you also."

Speedy dressed in khakis, sets his tray down, and puts up his hand, putting his middle and ring finger together, with the other two apart, "It's more like, 'live long and suffer'."

Sam says, "And Merry Christmas to you to, Jose."

They tuck in for some serious eating as they see Captain Johnson walking up to a microphone, "You still have time to eat. I just wanted to let you know that Santa is on final. Once he makes it to the hangar bay, we'll start calling division officers up to act as elves."

Soon they hear, "North Pole, arriving." An airdale chief walks up to the Captain and whispers into his ear. "I would like all division officers to come up here as soon as they are done eating. I'm told the big guy caught an ok three wire, and is making his way to elevator 2."

Just as they're finishing, Holtz walks up, "I'll take care of your trays so you can line up. A question, though."

Swede says, "Yes, sir?"

"Um, we have a talent show thing. Can you guys lip sync, or something?"

Sam stands up, "I can't, but Gloria can. She has a beautiful voice."

Gloria gives her friend a dirty look, "Thanks, friend."

"You even have some sheet music, Gloria. I saw it on your desk. Did you bring your guitar?"

Papa says, "Great, she plays guitar, too. Does anyone else play an instrument?"

Frank says, "I think Jose plays the maracas."

Jose hits him on the shoulder, "No, mi Amigo, pero puedo tocar tambores en su cabeza." Then, to Papa, "I will, if the lady wishes, play Spanish guitar. My singing, though, is not so good."

"What did you tell Thud?"

"I told him, he was wrong, but I can play the drums on his head."

Papa says, "Okay, the Captain's waiting, you all better get up there. I'll see who else I can find."

As they go up, Gloria says, "Sam, you'll pay for this."

"I know, but the look on your face was worth it, besides, you can really sing."

"In the shower." They line up as the Captain motions them all into place. Then the elevator comes down.

Sam says, "Okay, tell me, you never sang in your church choir."

"Of course, I sang in the church choir, and the school choir, and I soloed some. I had to do something to shut my mom up."

"Exactly, it's not a shower thing." As the elevator clears the overhead, they see a C-2 Greyhound with its cargo door closed, tail facing toward them.

Gloria, "It is now."

"You sing wonderfully, and the kids deserve a show."

"Okay," The C-2s rear hatch opens up.

"What do you know that uses a Spanish guitar?"

"Patsy Cline, if that doesn't tear them up, nothing will."

Away from the mike, Captain Johnson says, "Girls? Quit bickering. Did you get a lump of coal in your stocking?"

They look up at him, "Sorry."

The rear ramp lowers and Santa is revealed. As the ramp hits the elevator surface, Santa says, "Ho. Ho. Ho. Merry Christmas. I bet you all thought I would miss you this year. Not a chance. You showed up on my list as soon as you arrived. There was a bit of turbulence passing over Adak, hmmm, might have been ack-ack, now that I think of it. Oh well, Tojo is already on the naughty list, but I have a warm spot in my heart for sailors, soldiers, airman and jar heads, um Marines. Are these the elves you promised me, Captain?"

"Yes, sir."

"I have a lot of gifts. They seem kinda scrawny. Do you think they can get the job done?"

"I think they can."

"Okie dokie. They aren't dressed like elves, though, so, I'll have to fix that, too. You just call out the divisions, I'll get the right bags."

"Yes, sir, first division."

The 1st division div-o comes up and Santa puts a blue elf hat on his head and gives him a bag. The process repeats until all the division officers are lined up with gift bags and hats on their heads. Santa says, "Spread out some," then, "Okay, without a stampede, all of you come sit or stand by your division officer." It soon becomes very clear that the division officers need to spread out a little more. Then, when everyone has found their place, Santa says, "Okay, elves, deliver your presents."

Sam, grinning and wearing a green elf hat, pulls out a wrapped gift, "Sass, looks like this is for you." Soon, she's handed all the gifts to her people. They each have at least three, including Chief White and Sam. There are bags of cookies, pastries, candy, soap, shampoo, toothbrushes and toothpaste. Sam also gave each one in her division a miniature display F-14 with Black Knight markings that she'd bought before deployment.

Joe says, "Oh my God, boss, these planes are so cool."

"Yes, they are. Santa must have made them in the workshop,

because you can't find them in the ship's store."

When Heidi and Lori find their perfume, they tear up a bit and give Sam a hug. Gellar gets a Louis L'Amour novel, and Chief White gets a poster of the Grand Canyon. Sam has given a personal gift to everyone in her division. When they have finished opening theirs, she opens hers. From 'Santa' is Scott's 'Ivanhoe'; from Eric is 'Bury My Heart at Wounded Knee' with a note: "I don't know if you've ever read this, but I hope you enjoy it." She looks up, catching his gaze, smiling. He grins back, holding up his gift from her, Shelby Foote's 'The Civil War in Tennessee'.

It isn't long before gift wrap is everywhere and all the gifts are opened. The Captain says, "Quit a haul, folks. Before we all go about our day, I would like to thank Santa for coming all this way, and ask that we all pitch in to clean up. Santa, if you can stick around a bit, I can have the crew install some counter measures on your sleigh."

Santa laughs, "Captain Johnson, you surely are a good boy."

CHAPTER 27

TUNNEL FORWARD OF HANGAR BAY 1

0950, 25 December, 1941

Lyle "Packs' Boxter walks forward into the tunnel wearing khakis and carrying his Bible and Book of Mormon. Book runs after him, "Hey, Packs, you got a moment?"

"I'm reading for the Christmas service, Book. Can't it wait?"

"Shit man, I just wanted to say thanks for the Cross pen set. It's cool. You want to join me and some of the guys? It's a stand down day and we're playing Hearts."

"No, man, it's Christmas. I belong in church."

"Okay, but how about later?"

Packs shakes his head, "Thanks, Book, I appreciate the invite, but today is Christmas," and walks away. Book watching his RIO leave, looks at the ceiling, then turns and walks back aft.

VF-154 POWER PLANT OFFICE

1000, 25 December, 1941

Chief White walks in to see Sam in her chair, feet up on the desk, a bag of cookies open, a cup of coffee handy, and reading the book Puck gave her. He shuts the door, gets himself a cup of coffee and sits down, putting his feet up. Lifting his cup in salute, he says, "LT, you're coming along. It was a good thing you did for your division with the gifts. I think you handled Joe pretty well the other day, too."

"Thanks, Chief. I hope so, cookie?"

"I know so. You out of chocolate chip yet?"

Smiling, "No, here you go," shoving the bag in his direction.

"Are you worried about Carleton?"

"I'm more worried for him. He reminds me of my mother, he just doesn't know how to be happy."

"You're a fixer, LT. Did you know that? It's a good thing."

"Okay. I didn't know that. I don't know how to fix Book. Anything I do, he'll just resent me more."

"That's the thing about fixers, they make the world we live in a better place. They try to improve anything they touch. The problem is when they find something they can't fix."

"Yeah, it's painful knowing that whatever I do will just make it worse. It hurts."

"Do you know the Serenity Prayer? It was written for fixers."

"You mean St. Francis, that's my grandmother's prayer."

"No, Reinhold Niebuhr. He's an American theologian who died back in...um, I guess he's still alive. Anyway, he said, 'God, grant me the serenity to accept the things I cannot change; the courage to change the things I can; and the wisdom to know the difference.' It's the fixer's prayer."

"I think I need that one plastered on my forehead."

"Just think about it. Do your best and don't fret too much about the things you can't fix."

"Okay, thanks, another cookie?"

CHRISTMAS DINNER, HANGAR BAY 2

1630, 25 December, 1941

After breakfast, the tables were set up for dinner. Arrangements were made to dog the watch so everyone could eat together. There's a lot of buzz about the talent show after dinner and acts are squirreled away all over the ship perfecting their art.

Good to his word, Santa stuck around for dinner, staying mostly to air-conditioned spaces. He wandered around talking to sailors and doing his best to make the holiday a jolly one. He did make a brief visit to number 2 engine room where there was a problem with his steam driven fire pump.

Hangar bay 2 rapidly fills with crew in the uniform of the day. For Sam, Gloria, Eric, and Byron, it's flight suits. As they get in line, Eric looks over the mess cranks, in their white aprons and hair nets, carving turkeys. "My God, we've driven the species extinct."

Gloria says, "I don't think so, doesn't the President pardon one?"

Eric replies, "Yes, true, but it takes two."

Byron says, "At least, we know there'll be plenty to go around."

The array is staggering: turkey, ham, stuffing, potatoes and gravy, yams, cream corn, peas, biscuits, fruit salad, apple pie, pumpkin pie, and berry pie. They heap their trays, then grab something to drink: milk, coffee, soda, fruit or bug juice are on offer. Going to an empty table, Sam catches Dixie's gaze. He's sitting with enlisted crew. She smiles and he returns the smile, turning back to his conversation. Thud is eating with a pretty blonde officer.

Gloria says, "My thighs are going to wobble for a week."

Sam peers at her tray, "You took one of everything?"

"It was there."

Eric says, "God, this is good, but I think they forgot the sage in the stuffing."

As they eat, a young JG, with a guitar, mounts the stage built on a couple of tractors at the aft end of the hangar bay. He sits down in a chair, strums his guitar, and says, "Good evening, folks, I'm Johnny Cushman from nav. department, and I love Johnny Cash." He goes into a rendition of 'I Walk the Line'.

Gloria leans over to Sam, "I think we're going to surprise some of the guys."

The next act is Ensign Sean 'Irish' Fitzpatrick from the Tom-catters. He sings the 'Rose of Tralee', in his soft Irish tenor, a few folks songs, and closes with 'Danny Boy'.

Gloria says, "Yes, and it's time for me to get ready," as the Eightballers go up on stage for a comedy skit.

Sam says, "Remember, hon, it's for the guys. It's not a competition."

Gloria, "It's ALWAYS a competition."

Next up is Captain Klindt and Commander Tucker. Tucker starts playing his guitar, and they mis-start the song, off time and off key. They stop and look at each other, "Shall we try that again, Tucker?"

"You go first," and strums the guitar.

Klindt begins, "My reactor has a first name."

Tucker, "It's N.A.V.A.L."

"My reactor has a second name."

"It's classified as hell."

Then together, "We love to scram it every day, and if you ask us why, we say, 'cause radiation has a way of screwing up our DNA."

The nukes go nuts, yelling and stomping their feet.

Klindt says, "You'll recognize the tune of this song as well." Together;

'Hello darkness, my old friend. The reactor lost the load again.

The engineers run screaming, as the ship it stops steaming,

And the sound that echoes through my mind, is the sound of

silence.

Then a diesel roars to life. It cuts the silence like a knife.

The RO stands screaming. He wants to know what stopped the ship steaming.

And the sound that comes to every ear, loud and clear, is the sound of silence.

Who's to blame we do not know. The silence like a cancer grows.

We must run and fight and start the ship again, to purge the sin of the sound of silence."

The cheering is deafening, as the crew stomps and whistles.

Next, Ensign Tabatha 'Sweets' Younger on electric guitar, Lt. Mike 'Too Tall' Mohr on bass guitar, and Lt. JG James 'Sugar' Brown on drums from the Wizards, VAQ 133, are up. The do 'The Wall' by Pink Floyd, 'Danger Zone', and close with 'You Lost That Lovin' Feeling', and are also much appreciated.

Then Lt. Neyhi performs Tom Lehrer's 'Nikolai Ivanovich Lobachevsky Is His Name'. By now, everyone is done eating, the trays are put away, the tables are stacked and out, and the crew is standing in front of the stage.

Neyhi bows to tremendous applause and cheers and steps down off the stage, walking toward Gloria, "They're all yours, Lieutenant, knock 'em dead."

"Thank you. Tough act to follow," grinning at him. He gives Gloria a high five and joins the crowd. Gloria's on acoustic guitar, Speedy's on his Spanish guitar, 'Gunner' Harden on electric guitar, and Truman 'Johnny' Walker is on the drums. Gloria steps up to the mike, "Good evening, Carl Vinson."

The return cheers stun her a bit, and off mike, she asks, "Are we ready?" The guys nod, and she starts the beat. One, two, down beat, and she begins to sing 'Walking After Midnight' by Patsy Cline.

The crew begins cheering before she even finishes. She waits for them to settle down and begins, 'Sweet Dreams'. When she's done, the crowd is rocking.

She pauses again, then sings 'Hallelujah'. Gloria feels the words and her voice gathering power, then Gunner starts singing harmony. The power of the song washes out, over them all, lifting them up, giving voice to how they feel. As she finishes, everyone is swaying, some with tears on their cheeks. The music ends and there is silence. Then, 'SING IT AGAIN!"

Startled, she looks to Captain Johnson, who spins his hand in the air. Turning to the band, she nods her head, and begins. Many of the crew join in, filling the hangar bay with the sound of thousands of voices. At the end, there's a deep silence.

Chaplain Chandler comes up on the stage and Gloria hands him the mike, "Hallejulah, hallejulah. Thank you, Lieutenant Hoolihan, Lieutenant Harden, Lieutenant Gonzalez, and Lieutenant Walker. That was amazing. Will you accompany us in a few carols?"

Gloria says, "Yes, of course."

They start with 'What Child Is This', then 'Little Town of Bethlehem', then 'The Little Drummer Boy', ending with 'Silent Night'. The hangar bay, again, filling with the sound of thousands of voices, airdales and nukes, officer and enlisted, side by side, old rivalries forgotten, with this, their first Christmas truly separated from home.

HANGAR BAY 3

0830, 26 December, 1941

Sam walks through the hangar bay hearing sailors singing songs from the night before. Airman Lori 'Sass' Givens comes up, "Ma'am, did you know Lt. Hoolihan could sing like that?"

"Yeah, I knew, Lori. She sings like an angel. What do we have on board today?"

"We're inspecting a crate engine and re-patching some holes on Thud's plane, ma'am."

Sam smiles, "Sounds good. It was a good Christmas, considering, wasn't it?"

"Yes, ma'am, it sure was."

"You haven't said much about who you're missing."

"That's because I'm not missing much. My dad died in a logging accident when I was thirteen, and a few years later, my mom moved in with this, um, herbalist. She and I aren't very close."

"Sorry, yes, sometimes mothers can be difficult."

Sass shrugs, "It's okay. I'm glad to be away from there, really. I also had a thought. I might get to meet my dad again. He and I were close."

Sam looks at Sass in wonder. "Oh."

Lt. Warren joins them, "Lieutenant Hunt, the Captain is calling the brain trust together again."

"I'll be there in a moment, thank you," and turns back to Sass. "Maybe we can...my dad was a marine on Guadalcanal."

"Did you lose him in the war?"

"No, but I might as well have."

Sass looks down, then up at Sam, "They were setting up a yarder and a guy wire let go. It cut him in half."

"Oh, I'm so sorry," and puts a hand on Sass's shoulder. "Tell you what, when we get time later, let's talk. I'm not trying to pry, it's just...let's talk, okay?"

"Okay, ma'am. Oh, and ma'am, the music was beautiful last night. I cried."

"So, did I, Lori, so did I."

OUTSIDE THE BLACK KNIGHT READY ROOM

0842, 26 December, 1941

Lt. Carleton has Lt. JG Hyam 'Joker' Alberts, RIO for 'Bug' Ulster in Knight 101, cornered, "You and I both know she's going to unravel and someone is going to get hurt."

"Book, do you really think so? Any one of us could unravel, not just her."

"I tell you, Joker, she's going to hurt someone. She doesn't much act like an officer with all that crying and all. I saw her crying last night. I tell you, she'll unravel and kill someone."

"You're kidding, right? We were all crying last night. I said any one of us could unravel. I was wrong, Book. You already are. Just drop it, okay. She does her job. The only one causing problems is you."

CHAPTER 28

RT CLASSROOM

0900, 26 December, 1941

Captain Klindt says, "I hope we all had a good Christmas, now it's back to business. Before we get into the technology reports, we need to talk more about time travel. The device that brought us back in time is called the Heinlein device, after its inventor. I've asked John and Scott to go over the materials we have and brief us. So, what have we learned about the Heinlein device?"

Lt. Warren says, "Sir, I've read through the book, papers, and news reports, and all were open source. The good news is there's no indication the novel was ever translated into Japanese. However, it was translated into French and German, so that's a concern. The antenna design is odd, but any competent individual should be able to produce one. Also, there seems to an underground fan base for the book and that makes it likely there may be other locations with transference. There is an editorial in Der Spiegel about the upcoming time travel date. The likelihood that a locale in Germany came back is relatively high. Japan is doubtful."

Klindt says, "Thank you. What do we tell Admiral Ren and Captain Johnson about returning to our own time?"

Richardson replies, "Based on Dr. Heinlein's research, there is no mechanism for returning. It's a one way trip. I've gone over the mechanism and the math myself, we're stuck."

"Thank you, for that good news. Any questions?"

Hughes asks, "Yes, sir, how did the device get on board?"

"Sorry, Shawn, that is being held close to protect the individual involved."

Hughes says, "Oh, yeah, I saw Lt. Hunt leaving the RM office with my div-o. I can pretty much guess. It was that f…"

Klindt interrupts, "Stow it, Shawn. No speculation. No retribution. Just drop it."

After a moment, Mohr asks, "So, is it ASTC like I thought?"

Richardson says, "Yes, basically, you nailed it."

Mohr pumps his fist, "Yeah!"

Sam says, "A pyrrhic victory, isn't it?"

"Yeah, well, all those times I was called lazy for reading science fiction just paid off."

Klindt says, "Right, okay, if there are no more questions, let's move on to the technology reports. John, can you start us off."

Warren answers, "Best I can tell they are already working with most of the metal we will need, except uranium, of course. Biggest problem will be QA. No one made equipment to the tolerances we need. I believe the primary location should be the Puget Sound Naval Shipyard. They were doing a lot of the maintenance on us in '90, so we know it can be done there.

"The Navy is also going to need to build super carriers. I think they ought to be constructed on the flats of Tacoma where they'll have rail access. They can be finished at PSNS. I don't think PSNS has a dry dock large enough to handle us at this time. No one does. That has to be upgraded, too. There is so much that needs to happen, it makes sense to put it all in one place."

"How long until they can handle the Vinson?"

"They'll need to upgrade service power to whichever pier

we're parked at, and they'll need a source of pure water. They may already have a plant, but I doubt it meets our standards. I think, if they are pushed, they can have a pier ready in a month, or so. But for a dry dock, they'll need at least two years.

"Oh, the Long Beach has enough fuel for five or six more years and can be refueled one more time, for a possible life span of twenty more years. They're not nearly in as good of shape as we are, given they were commissioned in 1961. Their needs are much the same as ours, except they shouldn't have problems with shore power or dry dock size."

"Okay, write it up. Be as specific as you can. Include all the QA, maintenance shops, oversight, materials, and dry dock requirements. Give me an organization chart for what nuclear maintenance department should look like. Also, get the blueprints for the Vinson and the Long Beach. See if we can begin planning a fossil fueled super carrier like the Kitty Hawk. Get it back to me in six days. Lt. Mohr?"

Mohr says, "I researched the JP-5 we use and it's based on kerosene, but it has a number of additives, including naphtha, alkanes, and some other stuff. I have the exact mix. A 1941 refinery should have no problem making it. It does take longer to make than avgas or diesel, though. Really, the only challenges are logistical. If a refinery in southern California starts making it, we should be able to get new fuel within a month or so. QA will be a problem, but not unsurmountable."

"Okay, I want a full report in six days, including the exact formula, and how it's to be transported. I, also, need a recommendation for who would manage the QA at the refineries. Lt. Jackson, missiles."

Frank says, "It was way more complex that I thought. Basically, our rockets use a double base propellant; a nitrocellulose and nitroglycerin base propellant, and ammonium perchlorate and powdered aluminum. The trick is the process and the percentages of each ingredient. All of the ingredients are dangerous. Put together, they are extremely dangerous. Ensign Severn says that existing gun powder and chemical plants could make it. With the required safeguards, it should still only take a couple of months to get production going. The airframes, fins, operating mechanisms, and all that are straight forward. Of course, guidance is the issue, but that's Scott."

"Excellent. Ensign Severn, do you think she could supervise the industry?"

"Yes, sir, she's an expert."

"Okay, same as everyone else, report in six days with all the details. I also want you to find or produce blue prints, and break down what it will take to put together new missiles, including flight controls and nozzles. Denton, communications."

Denton says, "In WWII, they used, basically cypher codes. They used layers of letter substitution, as well as filler on the end of messages, which is why Admiral Halsey received that stinging rebuke. Um, well, it hasn't happened yet. Anyway, it was fairly secure as long as the codes didn't fall into enemy hands, like us getting the Enigma machine. All the comms were over short wave and VHF during the war. Short wave is long range, but fickle. It isn't uncommon for atmospheric conditions to cause interference. VHF is line of sight. It would be real nice to get some communications satellites up. GPS, too. We would have to advance rocketry about fifteen years, though, and build computers, so that isn't going to happen."

"Have you researched the satellite designs and rocket systems needed?"

"No, sir, um, I thought them beyond reach."

"See if you can find out how heavy the satellite would have

to be, and what the technology constraints are. It may take some time to put it together, but no sense sitting on our hands. You've the same six day schedule. Put it all in the report."

"Yes, sir, one other thing. If any other modern areas came back, like we did, they may also have our codes."

"Good Point. CT1 Barr, you're supposed to brief us on those issues."

Barr says, "Yes, sir. The problem is, we don't know. I would hate to trash a good system on a worry. Denton is right, though, about the risks to our systems. In some ways, the WWII code is better. Any modern German or Japanese unit may be able to understand our transmissions, but just like we don't know WWII codes, no other modern unit would know them either. To make our comms truly secure, we need a brand new system. I'm working out the details, and will have the basics by deadline."

"Good job, Barr. Hughes, metallurgy?"

"Yes, sir, like Lt. Warren said, QA is the big issue for metals. Also, they were not working much with titanium or stainless steel. They knew how though. It's just a matter of getting the whole thing scaled up to produce the volume of parts we need. There are several processes for making titanium. The Kroll process is the most common. It's a pain to make titanium, though, no matter the method. It will probably take a few months to get the system up and running correctly.

"Stainless is easier. It's a blend of nickel and other metals and is easier to work with. To start making nuclear grade valves and stuff will take at least half a year. They already have suppliers for steam plant valves, the only issue is QA."

"Do you know the exact blend of metals in every alloy we use, so they can be reproduced?"

"Yes, sir. I don't have all of them together, but I'm working on it."

"Okay, six days. Lt. Hunt?"

Sam says, "There are a number of material issues with jet engines. The first, being the titanium used, but there are also graphite linings, precision valves and fuel nozzles. Once those hurdles are jumped, the whole thing has to balance precisely. Not an easy task by itself. Given that none of it can start until we are making good titanium parts, I think jet engines are at least nine to ten months away. Our existing engine supply should probably get us through, depending on our op-tempo. It's way easier, in a way, being we're reverse engineering. Still, about eight to ten months is probably about right."

"Who would you put in charge of building them?"

"For the GE -F110-400 engines used by the F-14, I would recommend ADCS Ronald Cassidy. He's the chief of the Tom-catter engine shop. Chief Cassidy is split service. He spent three years building F-14s for Grumman, before getting back into uniform. He has a degree in mechanical engineering and understands the engines better than anyone. Also he speaks geek. A couple of pilots might make better supervisors in the program, but no one knows more than Chief Cassidy, and we really need the pilots."

"What about the other aircraft? Do they all have the same material issues?"

"Yes, sir, they use similar materials. I have a list of first class and chief volunteers."

"Who will be in overall charge?"

"I'm not sure, sir, probably Senior Chief. He's the expert. I will get them all together and sort that out."

"Right, six days. We need non-pilot experts for each engine and someone in overall charge of that program. I also need someone who can ramrod building new aircraft. He might have to be a pilot. Chief Richardson?"

"I think the integrated circuit is the limiting factor for a lot of war materials we need. If we build new missiles and fuel them, they are still useless without sensors and circuits. It's going to take up to a year to bring the electronics industry to life."

"Why so long?"

"Well, sir, it's a matter of miniaturization. We need the technology to build the technology to build better technology. Also, we use thousands of different processors to run this battle group. I will need to create a production line for all of them. Most critical, though, are missile and torpedo cards, aviation cards, and weapon systems control cards. Things like boiler cards can wait.

"Sir, we'll be building new ships and upgrading existing ships to fire missiles and torpedoes. They'll have to have cards to work. Guided torpedoes and modern sonar will change everything in the battle of the Atlantic. Once we have the technology moving forward, we need an expert in every weapon system to stand up their production line. I know Lt. Jackson's friend can handle the missile designs, but there are other systems. We need a guy for the RIM-7 launcher, Mark 10 missile launcher, Mark 13 missile launcher, Mark 41 missile launcher, torpedo launchers, radar, counter measures, sonar, ASROC, five-inch and three-inch gun systems, and the R2D2 thing. The technology team will outgrow the brain trust quickly."

Klindt asks, "R2D2?" as most of them laugh.

"Yes, sir, the Gatling gun, forgot what they are called."

Frank says, "The Phalanx Close in Weapons System."

"Yeah, that's it. We need all these experts with hard design information ready to hit the beach even before we stand up the electronics industry. We can have missiles and torpedoes waiting for cards. As soon as the card is tested and ready, you finish assembly and ship it."

Klindt asks, "Can we simplify by cutting out construction of older technology like the Mark 10 on Long Beach and Horne?"

Frank says, "Sir, the Mark 41 vertical launcher was being tested for launching a modified standard anti-aircraft missile, but we were not using them yet. There are structural and controls issues involved. Right now, the Mark 10 and Mark 13 are our only platform for launching long range surface to air missiles."

"Is it possible to produce the SM2-ER in a vertical launch configuration?"

Frank replies, "I think so. It's basically strengthening the airframe and adding a guidance step."

Klindt says, "I don't want to leap forward to twenty-year old technology. Let's focus on building the Mark 41. It simplifies the mission and improves capabilities."

"Yes, sir."

Okay, people, you've got six days for all your reports. Scott, Shawn, John, you're all off the watch bill. You know what we need. Set it up."

Richardson says, "But, sir, shouldn't an officer take the lead on this?"

"You know what needs to be done, and you have my confidence."

The enormity of the task sinks in and they all look at each other. Hughes, "Is there anything else we should be doing? I mean, with our spare time?"

Klindt grins, "Get outta here."

CHAPTER 29

KNIGHT FLIGHT 3, 600 MILES NORTH EAST OF THE BATTLE GROUP AT 40,000 FEET

1245, 26 December, 1941

Spike asks, "Puck, is there anything out there?"

"Not a blessed thing. We're 25 minutes to Wake. I can see clouds above it."

"Do you suppose the Japanese have come and gone? The Admiral wants to hit their task force."

"You're thinking like a leader, Spike. I can only see what's there."

"Sorry, I guess it's getting to me."

"Can you talk about the brain trust, or is it all, hush, hush?"

"We're trying to figure out how to bring 1941 into the 90's technology wise. My bit is jet engines."

"Yeah, we'll need those. Can it be done?"

"Yeah, it just takes time. We've a female weapons officer who's going to be in charge of missile production. The '41's are probably not going to like it."

"True. Are they going to drag you off the ship?"

"Not yet, anyway. Of course, once congress gets a whiff of us, all bets are off."

Swede waggles his wings and begins the descent for a TARPS run over Wake Island. Spike waggles her wings to acknowledge and stays at altitude with Thud as high cover, flying under radio silence. Puck says, "It was WWII that really brought women into the work force in numbers. After the war, the men wanted them to stay home and make babies. That ensign may be okay."

"I hope so. It'll be hard."

"Hold on, bogeys, 11 o'clock low, above the clouds. I think they're reacting to Swede."

"Okay, rolling in," and she inverts into a dive with Thud following.

"Okay, Spike, they're Wildcats. We have to still be in control. That, or a carrier group is nearby."

"Friendly or not, we have to keep them off Swede and Hot Pants." She lines up a pass, and as they dive they break the speed of sound. "I'm going to pass right by them." She passes 200 feet from a F4F Wildcat going 780 knots, more than twice the WWII fighter's top speed. The Wildcat's pilot tries to pull into her and fires a burst, but all the rounds fall short.

Thud, above and behind, maneuvers to miss the Wildcat, and Speedy breaks radio silence. "Shit, that was close. Puck, they popped a few your way. Do we engage?"

"Weapons tight, Speedy, they know not what they do."

"Okay, Puck, but those friendlies are being decidedly unfriendly."

"I know, Speedy," and to Spike, "Can we circle around and show our wing markings?"

"Do we have their frequency?"

Puck asks, "Gandhi, do we make radio contact?"

"My man says negative. We're just finishing out pass. RTB. And Puck, as we climb out, illuminate and do a circle looking for shipping."

"Roger, Gandhi."

As they climb, the propeller planes are left far below. They do a lazy turn to the left with the radar on, "See anything, Puck?"

"Nothing. I can see 400 miles. There is nothing." Then, "No shipping, Gandhi."

"Understood, we still control Wake and the reinforcements made it. Let's go home, radio silence."

HANGAR BAY 1

1810, 26 December, 1941

Chief Fronzak stands, in his Gi and black Hakama pants, on the workout mats with AT2 Julie 'Mouse' Mulligan, in her Gi, Hoolihan and Hunt in workout attire. They're working through a kata, one move to the next, fluid and smooth. They go through the kata twice, then he stops, and tells them to repeat it, watching. "Gloria, your wrist needs to be a little higher with the fingers together. Good."

As is pretty normal, they have an audience. As they finish, Lt. JG Kyle 'Gandhi' Jacobs walks onto the mats wearing his Gi. He bows toward Chief Fronzak, "May I join, Sensei?" Fronzak returns the bow and motions him to join in.

Book and Packs walk up, "My God, it's Private Benjamin and her sidekicks practicing, 'who flung dung'." Fronazk looks at him for a moment, then they all continue.

Packs says, "Just let them be."

"Fuck that, Packs, don't wimp out on me," moving closer, "You can't use the Vulcan death grip on a Zero, girls. You're wasting your time."

Fronzak slides his feet together, spins to face Book, and in one smooth sliding motion, they are nose to nose. "Sir, I believe, you have someplace important to be."

"Why, are you planning to assault an officer, if I don't?"

"I understand it wouldn't be the first time, sir, and now I see why. I'm a SEAL, sir, do you really want to piss me off?"

Sam steps up, "Lieutenant, we are simply exercising. Something we have to do. You know, you could always join us."

Book sneers, "I don't need 'who flung dung', it's a waste of time."

Fronzak quietly says, "Are you willing to spar with me, Lieutenant, so I may demonstrate Aikido's value?"
"Hell no! Once you're done, send them back into the kitchen. I need some dinner." Book turns and walks away, and sees that Packs has already left.

Fronzak watches him go, then turns back to his pupils, "Another good reason to master martial arts, shall we continue?"

BLACK KNIGHTS READY ROOM

0815, 27 December, 1941

Sam walks in with a stack of technical manuals. Most of the guys are kicking back watching Star Wars and talking. Swede and Gloria are on far CAP. Holtz motions to her to come into his office. She sets the books down on a table and goes in. Leaving the door open, he hands her a cup of coffee, "How are you doing, any problem?"

"No, everything's great. I've a lot of work to do, but it's good to stay busy."

"I want you to know, I appreciate what you did the other day, twenty-two kills in one day, beyond amazing."

"Sir, you are welcome, sir."

"Well, I guess, I ought not to beat around the bush. How do you feel about taking the XO position? I was thinking of Swede, but after he thrashed Book, we both know he can't be XO."

"Yeah, it's too bad, too. He'd be good." She pauses and smiles,

"I've noticed you've been buried in your office a lot lately. I can help you catch up on paperwork."

"In truth, you've earned the position. Had you not transitioned to fighters, you would already be an XO, and it's nothing less than what you deserve."

"Thank you, sir. Is this acting or permanent, so I know where I stand?"

"It's permanent. You're first duties will be writing up promotions and awards for the squadron officers. Pass down to the div-o's that they need to do the same for their people. I'm giving your division to Walker. I think you should write up their recommendations, seeing as he'll be new."

"Yes, sir, not a problem. By the way, all the books are about the brain trust. Thud and I are putting together aviation technology development plans. The RO wants a recommendation as to who should be in overall charge of building new aircraft. I think it needs to be a senior pilot. Any recommendations?"

"Do you want to do it? You're the leading ace. Most of us want to fly."

"No, I can't do it. I'm a woman. I doubt the leadership from 1941 will take me seriously. It has to be someone with gravitas. Do you want it, sir?"

"Me? No way, I want to fly. Maybe Groovy, the skipper of the Tomcatters. He's a Commander and I heard he did well. Or maybe, Dixie, he's the most senior. For that matter, maybe one of the other squadron skippers. Anyway, let's tell the guys there is a new sheriff in town."

They walk out together, and Holtz says, "Listen up, you goofs. Lt. Hunt is now the squadron XO. Give her all the respect you would me, especially the paper work. Carry on."

ON CAP 50 MILES FROM THE BATTLE GROUP

0820, 27 December, 1941

Swede and Hot Pants do slow laps ahead of the battle group, using their cameras to watch for any ships or aircraft, and enjoying the beautiful clear skies. They're doing 400 knots, with their radar off. GQ says, "You really rocked the show the other night."

"Thanks. At first, I didn't want to do it, but it was fun."

"I didn't know you could sing."

"Yep, GQ, there's a lot you don't know about me. Tons, I don't know about you, either."

"Okay, what do you want to know?"

"I like the fact that you're about the only guy who's never hit on me, but it intrigues me, as well."

"Oh, man, you would ask that. Okay, I knew going in that if I thought of you that way, it would mess me up."

"I can see that. Please understand, I don't think I'm all that pretty, but since high school I've had to beat guys off with a stick. It's maddening."

"I'm kind of surprised you aren't married. A ring would keep guys away."

"My mom married at eighteen and spent the rest of her life changing diapers, cooking meals, and doing laundry. I want to fly, not fry. Besides, you underestimate the libido of the American male, rings don't deter them. I've seen it."

"He laughs, "True. There are no shortage of cads and scoundrels. How do you suppose Spike and Puck do it?"

"Do what?"

"Avoid emotional issues in the air."

"I suppose the same way you do. Puck probably just doesn't see her like that. Indians are so stoic."

"No, if I'm not wrong, he likes her."

"You think so? I can't read him. You know everyone reads Sam wrong, though. They think she's cold and she isn't. She tries so hard to get it right, to earn respect. She doesn't know how to flirt, so she seems like a bitch."

"Eric isn't all that cold and stoic, either. Listen to him on the radio, he comes alive in the air. He just puts the Kalija face on in public."

"Kalija?"

He sings the Hank Williams Sr. song, "Kalija."

She laughs, "Oh, that. Yeah, he does that. So, you think he likes her? That would be a kind of hell, you know. It circles back then to how can you lock down your feelings."

"Okay, in truth, you're really not my kind of girl. I think you're pretty, and all that, but well, not for me. I would rather be friends."

"I like that. I can live with that just fine."

"HP, I see something, straighten us out." She waggles her wings to get Swede's attention, and straightens out. "Okay, it's a submarine on the surface. Come right 20 degrees." She follows his steer, watching Swede, making sure he's adjusting. Then he's flying next to them, thumbs up. They see it, too. Even though, the sub is 40 miles away, they can see it clearly.

Gandhi makes the call, "Gold Eagle, Knight Flight 3. We've spotted a submarine on the surface bearing 350, range 40 miles. It's closing the fleet."

"Knight Flight 3, Gold Eagle, can you identify the nationality?"

"Not yet, permission for a fly by?"

"Permission granted."

Swede motions to Hot Pants, then inverts and leads them down in a three G pull, lining up for a pass. "Let's rattle their cage." Their wings sweep back, as the fighters gain speed in the dive. At 15,000 feet they exceed the speed of sound and the distance closes quickly.

CHAPTER 30

USS DOLPHIN, SS-169

0850, 27 December, 1941

Ensign Rector and BM3 Pilton are on the sail, binoculars to their eyes, heading out on their first war time patrol. Their skipper, Lt. Gordon B. Rainer, calls up on the sound powered phone, "You two staying awake up there?"

Rector says, "Yes, sir, it's a beautiful day. Not a ship in sight, sir."

Rainer says, "Look for aircraft, too. The boys at Hickam are pretty jumpy. I don't want to be hit by a friendly."

Pilton asks, "Sir, what's that at 10 o'clock high?"

Rector looks and sees two triangles falling from the sky. They are far enough away and moving so fast, markings can't be seen. Then he sees a glint from the canopies, "Aircraft, 10 o'clock, diving on us. Clear the bridge."

Submariners practice crash dives to avoid aircraft. The two men pull the phones from their jacks, put the cap on the circuit, and practically jump down the ladder. The boatswain mate first, then the ensign. As he starts down, Rector looks up and sees the two aircraft flash by and the whole sail shakes. He feels a compression on his chest. He slides down the ladder, dogs the hatch, and reports, "Last man down. Bridge is rigged for dive, sir."

The Chief of the Watch says, "Green board. Boat is rigged for dive."

Lt. Rainer orders, "Call dive, dive. Sound three times on the dive alarm. Then dive, dive. Diving officer, make our depth 100 feet."

The boatswain mate of the watch sounds the a-ooga horn, then says on the 1MC, "Dive. Dive," then sounds the horn twice more.

Rainer asks, "What kind of plane, John?"

"I've no idea, sir. They were a type I've never seen before. They were extremely fast."

From the squawk box comes, "Engine secured, green light in engine room. 90% on batteries."

Rainer pushes a button, "Okay, Clyde."

The dive officer, Lt. JG Karl Helmstein says, "Dive planes down 15 degrees, flooding tanks to 6 degree down bubble. We are ahead standard on batteries."

Rainer says, "Very well," then to sonar, "Do you have anything?"

ST2 Bagley says, "Sir, there are faint noises down south, but they are far away. The blast from the aircraft nearly broke my ears, sir. I think they dropped depth charges on us."

"Okay, let's get this thing underwater and start maneuvering."

The dive officer says, "50 feet, 5 degree down bubble. Helm ease to 10 degrees down angle."

"10 degrees, aye."

Rainer says, "Left full rudder, let's see if we can wiggle away."

IN THE AIR ABOVE THE DOLPHIN

GQ says, "Well, we rattled their cage. The bridge watch cleared out in a hurry. I saw the number 169 on the sail."

Hot Pants says, "Okay, call it in."

GQ, "Gold Eagle, Knight 894, the submarine is submerging. Not sure of nationality, but the number on the superstructure was 169."

"Understood, Knight 894, orbit and standby. We are sending an S-3 to prosecute."

Captain Tenzar on the Long Beach says, "Gold Eagle, this is Long Beach actual, we are surging out to identify and support. Our small boys haven't the fuel to be sprinting around."

Captain Johnson replies, "Long Beach, Gold Eagle actual, we can't afford to lose you."

Tenzar says, "Thank you, sir. It's good to be appreciated. The S-3 cannot talk to the submarine, we can."

"Understood, we'll send out a couple of helos to help you, standby to receive."

LONG BEACH, #1 ENGINE ROOM, UPPER LEVEL

On the 2MC, "Set maneuvering, ahead full." Watch standers scramble, starting a second condensate pump and securing the steam driven sea water pump. A few minutes later, the engineering officer of the watch announces, "Ahead flank power limiting."

The main engine throttle opens further, and MM1 Cullen walks out of the auxiliary throttle station to check on his watch standers. The main engine watch, Walters, is leaning over the lube oil strainer checking the DP. MM3 Hall pokes his head up the lower level ladder in the center of the engine room, "What's going on, Carl?"

Cullen says, "Beats me. Are both condensate pumps running?"

Smiling, Hall says, "Yep, and level is good."

"Well, quit grinning at me and keep an eye on your watch."

Walters walks up to him, "Engine temperatures are fine. Vacuum is a little low."

Cullen says, "Watch it. Call if it reaches the limit."

Captain Tenzar, on the 1MC, says, "Good afternoon Long Beach, patrol aircraft have identified a submarine 50 miles away. We're going to intercept and identify the sub before it can get within torpedo range of the carrier. We do not yet know if it is a hostile, but we are going to operate that way until we do. I will be calling General Quarters in a bit, but for now, keep on your toes."

Walters looks at Hall, "Damn."

LONG BEACH, #1 ENCLOSED OPERATING STATION

A power limiting bell is stressful. It takes a 28 year old plant and wrings every available ounce of steam from it. The reactor operator, ET2 Mike Simmons, watches his control panel intently. The watch officer, LCDR Buckman says, "Watch your power, RO." Buckman is standing at his desk and can see the reactor power panel as well as Simmons. Simmons, his hand on the shim switch, is ready to react if power gets too high. Per procedure, he calls out reactor power every few seconds, "Ninety six percent, ninety seven percent. Hold throttle." The man besides him stops moving the throttles.

IN THE AIR APPROACHING THE DOLPHIN

Lt. JG Vance "Splash' Bunton, flying Bird 621, a S-3 Viking from the World Famous Screw Birds, is approaching the contact, designated Sierra 2. He says, "Knight 309, Bird 621 approaching at angels 1. Can you give me a starting point?"

Gandhi says, "Good morning, Bird 621. Come right 10 degrees and you should be 6 miles out."

As the S-3 comes in, it extends its magnetic anomaly detector. Submarines are made of steel, a ferrous material, and are magnetically active. Modern subs go to great pains to hide their magnetic signature, but in WWII the technology was brand new. On the second pass, the sensor operator, AW3 Lewis 'Knucklehead' Baker, says, "I have it. Float dropped."

Splash says, "Okay, circling for another pass." A couple of minutes later, Knucklehead says, "Another hit, float dropped."

They make another pass, drop a third float, and tactical controller, Ensign Mike 'Guppy' Tucker, says, "Course is 190, speed is 5 knots."

Splash calls it in, "Gold Eagle, Bird 621, confirmed submarine contact bearing 030, range 45 miles, speed 5 knots, standing by."

"Bird 621, Gold Eagle, track and monitor, weapons tight. Long Beach is inbound to prosecute."

"Gold Eagle, Bird 621, roger," then to his crew, "Damn, we find it and the surface squids get to kill it. It's bullshit. Guppy, what's the status of our fish?"

Guppy says, "Both fish check fine."

"Well, maybe they'll miss."

From the Vinson, "Knight Flight 3, continue mission."

USS LONG BEACH COMBAT INFORMATION CENTER, 4TH DECK

The Long Beach cuts through the waves, leaving a long frothy wake. At 721 feet, it's the largest cruiser in the US fleet. It's two nuclear reactors, though old, can still drive her up to her top speed of over 30 knots. Her weapons suite includes standard missiles, Tomahawk cruise missiles, two Phalanx Gatling guns, two Harpoon anti-ship missile launchers, ASROC rocket propelled torpedoes, and five inch guns. She's easily identified by the huge boxy forward super-structure.

Within an hour of starting the sprint, the target submarine is within ASROC range. At high speed, the sonar, located inside the bow, is worthless because of the flow noise of water passing over the ship. At 15 nautical miles, Captain Tenzar orders, "Ahead standard, sound general quarters."

The throttles are slowly closed on the main engines to prevent over-torqueing the shafts. A ship of 15,500 tons takes a long time to slow. ST1 Todd Calvin says, "Combat, sonar, submerged target bearing 349, range 13 miles, depth 200 feet."

Tenzar calls the bridge, "Bridge, Captain, make our course 320, slow to two thirds."

The OOD says, "320, at two thirds, aye."

Tenzar then tells the tactical action officer (TAO) running the CIC, "Weapons tight, George. No mistakes."

LCDR George Sulu says, "Yes, sir. Weapons tight."

Then, over radio, "Long Beach, Eightballer 1 approaching Sierra 2 with Eightballer 416, ready to assist."

Tenzar picks up the radio, "Roger, Eightballer 1, weapons tight at this time. Acknowledge."

"Eightballer 148 acknowledges weapons tight," says CDR David 'Yankee' Crocker.

"Eightballer 416 acknowledges weapons tight," says Lt. Sandra 'Cargo Britches' Douglas.

A moment later, Tenzar says, "Bird 621, acknowledge weapons tight."

"Bird 621 acknowledges weapons tight."

Tenzar says, "Eightballer 1, do you have dipping sonar?"

"Negative, Long Beach."

"Okay, Bird 621, can you drop a passive sono-buoy near the

subs track and attempt to identify?"

"Long Beach, Bird 621, will do."

USS DOLPHIN, SS-169, CONTROL ROOM

The air in the sub is already feeling close. The smell of sweaty men permeates everything. Lt. Rainer says, "Right full rudder, come to periscope depth, ahead slow." The OOD repeats the order, and the deck of the sub tilts in a tight right turn. Then, "Sonar, range to target."

ST2 Bagley says, "12 miles, sir, they are slowing."

"Any idea what it is?"

"I don't know, sir. Two screws, propulsion noises I don't understand, and one of the engines is louder than the other. I've never heard it before, Skipper. Something just dropped in the water ahead, portside."

"Torpedo?"

"No, sir. No screws. Surface contact is 10 miles, bearing 010 and changing as we turn."

The OOD says, "Sir, we are at periscope depth."

"Okay, up scope."

The periscope slides up, Rainer flips down the handles and starts a quick circle, "Mark."

Rector says, "112."

Continuing the circle, he stops, "Mark."

"225."

Then, "Mark."

"002."

Rainer stays a moment, studying the superstructure of the approaching ship. The huge box is baffling. "It must be Japanese, we have nothing like it. The other two bearings are aircraft, down scope. Left full rudder."

EIGHTBALLER 416

Lt. JG James 'Smooth' Lowandowski, Cargo Britches co-pilot says, "Periscope. I saw a periscope. The sub is turning left."

CB says, "Okay, Smooth." Then on radio, "Long Beach, Eightballer 416, we have a periscope sighting. Sierra 2 is turning left."

Tenzar answers, "Thank you, Eightballer 416."

LONG BEACH CIC

Tenzar hooks the mike into its holder and goes to the anti-submarine warfare data plotter. The ASW plot is a large glass screen on a table that projects data from below, allowing the sonar technicians to keep the plot up to date. He says to himself, "Oh no, you don't." Pushing the squawk button, "Bridge, right full rudder, back full on number one engine, ahead full on two."

LONG BEACH ENGINE ROOM

Number one engine slows to a stop, as MM1 Parker, the GQ main engine watch, runs to the reduction gear to monitor thrust. The engine starts spinning backwards, and as the rotation speeds up, the whole engine room starts to shake. The distilling watch, MM3 Joh Hart, runs over as the whole room starts moving, the steam pipes shaking the hardest. Hart says, "Oh shit. Oh shit. The whole thing is gonna blow."

Parker looks up, "This is normal, John. If it don't move, then get scared."

USS DOLPHIN, CONTROL ROOM

ST2 Bagley says, "Skipper, the target is making a lot of noise." The sound of the thrashing screws can be faintly heard through the hull.

Rainer says, "Rudder amidships, up periscope." He walks the scope around, "Mark."

Rector says, "112."

"Mark."

"209."

"Mark."

"347."

Rainer lingers on the scope, "The bastard is turning." He spins the scope to 112, "How is it possible? The plane is pacing us? No airplane can go four knots and fly. Down scope, make our depth 250 feet. What's the range to target?"

"Sir, she is 9 miles."

"Left full rudder, ahead full."

LONG BEACH, PORT BRIDGE WING

BMSN Guiles feels his heart race. His mouth is dry. His eyes to the binoculars, he sees the periscope. He pushes the sound powered phone without wiggling his binocs. Voice cracking, "Bridge, port lookout, periscope at 290, range nine miles."

The XO, CDR Arron Grey, trains his binoculars on the bearing as the OOD acknowledges the lookout. Seeing the periscope retract, "Captain, periscope sighting 290 at nine miles."

"Understood, left full rudder. Ahead full on number one engine. Back one third on number two."

CHAPTER 31

BIRD 621 ORBITING BEHIND THE CONTACT

"Bird 621, Long Beach, you have a buoy in the water. What's he doin?"

"Long Beach, Bird 621, he appears to be maneuvering toward you. It's hard to tell with all the racket you're making."

"Bird 621, Long Beach, understood. Stand by."

Splash says, "What the fuck does that hot dog think he's doing? He's playing cat and mouse with a Jap and he's gonna regret it."

Knucklhead asks, "Sir, how do you know it's a Jap?"

"Because it's moving in to attack. If it wasn't a Jap, it wouldn't do that."

LONG BEACH, CIC

Tenzar looks at the ASW plot table, "Okay, it's time, sonar. Yankee search."

ST1 Todd Calvin says, "Aye, sir," and activates the search function of the hull mounted sonar. A loud pulse sounds through the boat and the water. It's a directed pulse, rather than the ping of earlier sonar. The AN/SQS-23 makes a boo-waa sound. In a few seconds, sonar says, "Sir, sierra 2 is 345 at 8 miles. She's turning left and diving."

Tenzar pushes the squawk button, "Bridge, steady as she goes. Ahead two thirds." Then to sonar, "Let me know when his bearing is reciprocal. I want to keep him on my port beam."

"Aye, sir."

Tenzar asks, "Does anybody know the submerged endurance and design depth of a WWII sub?"

All he gets is blank stares. The intelligence officer says, "I might find it in the library."

"Don't worry, I know someone who will know." He keys the radio, "Gold Eagle, Long Beach actual, is Gold Eagle actual available?"

"Hello, Long Beach, this is Gold Eagle actual, go ahead."

"Has your brain trust given you the performance stats for old subs?"

Johnson says, "Stand by."

Sonar says, "Sir, she's coming abeam."

"Bridge, back one third, maintain heading," and to sonar, "How far?"

"About one mile, she's starting to turn toward us."

"Bridge, left full rudder, ahead full one engine, back one third two engine."

"Long Beach, Gold Eagle actual, Lt. Jackson is coming on line."

Tenzar says, "Standing by." Then to the bridge, "All stop, steady as she goes."

Thud Jackson comes up on the radio, "Sir, it depends on whose boat and how new the batteries. All of them are pretty shallow, about 250 feet. The endur..."

"Hold on," Tenzar cuts him off as sonar says, "Sir, she's trying to back up."

"Bridge, left full rudder, ahead two thirds," and on radio, "Okay, son, continue."

Thud says, "The endurance is no more that sixteen hours or

so. Less if they do a lot of maneuvering. I heard it was on the surface. Did we get the hull number?"

"Yes, we did, 169. Mean anything to you?" To the bridge, "All stop, hold the rudder over."

Thud says, "I'll have to look it up, sir. I'll get back to you in a minute."

"Okay, thank you, Lieutenant Jackson." Then to the TAO, "I'm hoping he has noticed that we are not attacking." Then to sonar, "ST1, do you think he's done yet?"

Calvin says, "Sir, he's still trying to back up."

Tenzar asks, "Okay, where do we keep the Gertrude."

The TAO says, "Above the ASW plotter, right side, sir."

"Thanks," and picks up the underwater phone, "Unidentified submarine beneath this vessel, I can play cat and mouse all day. Why don't we talk."

Sulu says, "Sir, I doubt a Japanese sub will respond."

"I agree, but an American one will."

"Long Beach, this is Lt. Jackson."

"Go ahead, Jackson."

"Sir, if it is an American boat, it is the Dolphin, a 'V' class sub; 319 feet, test depth of 250 feet."

"Stay on the line, Jackson. I'm talking to her now."

A garbled message comes back over the phones, "Vessel authentication bravo, bravo, delta one."

"Excellent, a forty-nine year old pass word." He answers, "USS Dolphin, we're new in this theater and haven't received the codes yet. I'm willing to offer ice cream and coffee as a bribe, though."

"What vessel?"

"We are the USS Long Beach, CGN 9. By the number on your conning tower, you are the USS Dolphin, V class boat. Oh, another thing, if it makes you feel better, you're welcome to take a pot shot at us, if you must. Your torpedoes won't work."

CONTROL ROOM, USS DOLPHIN

Rainer sets down the phone, "What the hell is happening? They know who we are. Have you even heard of the Long Beach?" To the OOD, "All stop. No sense wasting battery. We'll need it later."

The XO, Lt. JG Brian Porter, says, "No, sir. It beats the hell out of me. Ask him what's wrong with our torpedoes."

"Right," and on the Gertrude, "USS Long Beach, what's wrong with our torpedoes?"

"Dolphin, Long Beach, the mark 14 torpedoes you carry have faulty magnetic detonators. Why don't you come up for a chat?"

Rainer slams down the phone and shouts, "You bastard! My first damn patrol and I run into this son of a bitch. He seems so sure of himself." Putting both hands on the chart table, he steadies himself, "Ready torpedoes 1 and 2."

Porter asks, "What if he is American."

"Then we won't blast the bastard to hell."

"Will we have coffee with him?"

"No, it has to be a trick." To the OOD, "Ahead two thirds on starboard shaft, back one third on port shaft, left full rudder, blow ballast, 10 degree up angle. Are the torpedoes ready?"

TM1 Dundale says, "Yes, sir."

"Okay, flood and open doors."

Bagley says, "They're on our port side, about one half mile."

The OOD says, "180 feet."

"Very well."

"150 feet."

The Gertrude message is garbled, and all they hear is, "Thank you."

Rainer says, "You're going to get welcomed."

"125 feet."

"Very well, all stop."

Bagley says, "Captain, our bow is coming around. They are staying in place."

"Very well."

"100 feet......75 feet."

"Up scope." He orients the scope toward the Long Beach and waits for it to break the water. "Set the torpedoes for 25 feet, 5 degree spread."

EIGHTBALLER 416 ABOVE THE DOLPHIN

Cargo Britches says, "Shit, the bastard is lining up a shot." On radio, "Long Beach, kick it in the ass. He's tricked you."

LONG BEACH, CIC

Tenzar says, "Emergency ahead flank, left full rudder." On radio, "Eightballer 416, what's he doing?"

CB replies, "He used his bubbles to hide a turn. He's oriented toward the rear quarter of your boat."

"Understood," the Long Beach shaking as she picks up speed.

"Bridge, port lookout, periscope in the water one half mile abaft the port beam."

Tenzar says, "Orient torpedo tubes out. Weapons tight, again weapons tight, people. He's a confused American."

Sulu says, "More like an angry American, sir."

Tenzar picks up the Gertrude, "Knock it off, knock it off, we're friendly."

USS DOLPHIN, CONTROL ROOM

Lt. Rainer gets a good look at the huge vessel, it's stern digging down as it accelerates. Then, he sees the main mast sticking up from the large box, and there's the American flag. The ships movement and wind open up the stars and stripes, and there is no doubt. "Shut the tube doors. Safe the fish."

TM1 Dundale says, "Yes, sir," then the sub surfaces, rolling in the choppy seas.

Rainer says to Porter, "Want to join me topside to take a look at the Long Beach?" On the sail, they look up at the strange cruiser, and Rainer says, "Where are the stacks?"

Porters answer is drowned out by the rhythmic thumping of an approaching helicopter. They shield their eyes from the spray as the aircraft settles lower and closer to the sail. They can clearly see the pilot at the controls maneuvering closer to their side. The wind and spray are nearly painful. Then the side door slides open and a crewman throws a rope in the water. The helicopter moves closer and closer, adjusting to the motion of the sub. The crewman shouts, "You want a ride to the Long Beach?"

"How?"

AW2 Paul 'Yogi' Chatman pushes out the winch and lowers the harness to the sail. When Rainer grabs it, Chatman pantomimes putting it on, and Rainer struggles into the harness. As he gets squared away, Porter points away from the cruiser; the battle group is approaching. The carrier catches Rainer's gaze, it's huge, and before he can take it all in, he feels the harness tighten and he's lifted up and away from his boat. Disoriented as he spins, all of a sudden someone grabs him and he's pulled into the helicopter.

EIGHTBALLER 416

Yogi removes the harness, "Welcome to Eightballer 416, sir," then on intercom, "He's inside, ma'am."

"Ma'am?" asks Rainer. Looking into the cockpit he's two pilots, but they are in helmets. Yogi folds open a jump seat and sits Rainer down, strapping him in.

In the cockpit, Smooth points at a light, "High transmission temp, it's time to find a home." With only one transmission to translate the engine power and control inputs to the main rotor, they can't even auto-gyro if it goes out.

Cargo Britches says, "Long Beach, I'm declaring an emergency. I have high transmission temp, approaching now." To the crew, "Coming in fast, guys."

"Roger, Eightballer 416, the flight deck is clear for your approach."

She makes the approach from the port side so she has to crab right to get a clear view of the boat. Because of her speed, she has to apply the collective and flare at just the right moment to allow her bird to come to a hover over the deck. Once in hover, she quickly settles her bird to the deck and yells, "Chock and chain, Yogi."

Yogi shoves open the door and jumps out, holding his arms forward, palms down in fists with thumbs pointed together, moving them back and forth in the signal to chock. Sailors run out with orange chocks, ducking their heads as they pass under the rotor. Then, others run out and chain her to the deck. Yogi runs around the bird, checking the tie downs, then stands in front, right hand at chest height, index finger pointing down and turning in a circle, only then does Cargo Britches shut down the engines.

Yogi returns to help Rainer out of the bird and finds him struggling with his seatbelt. He helps him out and holding his head down, they run out from under the still spinning rotor. As they run, the ship tilts, bringing the rotors close to them, then it tilts back.

On the outboard side of the Tomahawk launcher are two men in khakis. Yogi takes Rainer to them, past the fire crew in exposure suits standing with their hoses. A tall thin, black-haired man steps forward, "Hello, Lieutenant. I'm Captain Tenzar and this is my XO, CDR Arron Grey. Welcome to the USS Long Beach, CGN 9. Lieutenant, you didn't fall down the rabbit hole, we did."

Rainer salutes, "Thank you, sir. What is this vessel?"

"She's a light cruiser, armed with missiles, and powered by the atom."

"Atom, sir? But from where? How? I've never heard of it?"

"I promised you a cup of coffee and goodies for your crew. Let's retire to the wardroom to talk. By the way, Lieutenant, what's your name?"

"Lt. Rainer, sir, Gordon Rainer."

Lt. Sandra Douglas runs over to them as the rotors slow to a stop and removes her helmet. She salutes, "Captain, could we get some help pushing our bird closer to the Tomahawk launchers so we can land another helicopter with techs and parts?"

"Of course, please see to it, Arron." He grins, "Welcome aboard, Lieutenant. That was some nice flying."

"Thank you, sir, and sir, you absolutely kicked ass maneuvering your boat into position." Rainer blatantly stares at her. She turns to him, "That was a smart maneuver using your bubbles to mask a turn. I'll remember that."

"Yet, you figured it out, how?"

"The orientation of your bubbles changed, and when you hit about 80 feet, I could see you because the water was fairly calm. Fixed wing might have missed it, but I can linger and really look."

Rainer points to the helo, "What kind of aircraft is that? It looks like a gyrocopter."

ML Maki

"Close, a helicopter, it can hover, making it a great ASW platform." She turns and salutes Tenzar, "By your leave, sir?"

"Of course, Lieutenant. Now, Lieutenant, how about a brief tour on your way to that cup of coffee?"

CHAPTER 32

USS CARL VINSON, AIRCRAFT ENGINE SHOP

1100, 27 December, 1941

Lt. John 'Book' Carleton walks into the shop and spots Joe 'Mouth' Cervella, "Get your people together, I want to talk to them."

"What about, you're not even in the squadron anymore."

"Just do it. We need to talk about Hunt," looking around the enlisted crewmen working on engines. "I know how hard it must be taking orders from a woman."

Joe looks startled, "Excuse me, sir? What's this about?"

"I just know you've had a tough time having to deal with a woman boss. It's bound to be better, now."

"Sir, did you ever have a mama?"

"Sure, what does that have to do with anything?"

"Well, sir, when she told you to take out the trash, or clean your room, did you tell her to fuck herself?"

"Petty Officer Cervella, you're out of line."

Joe steps forward, "No, sir, you're out of line, and you see my point. All of us obeyed orders from a woman, so what's the big diff?"

"She ain't your mama, and sure as hell, she ain't mine."

Lori 'Sass' Givens asks, "Didn't your mom hug you enough?"

Book glares at her, "Shut up, airman."

AD1 Gellar says, "She has a point, what's your issue with women?"

Chief White opens the office door and stops, listening.

Book says, "Look, women have a place in our society. They make meals and they make babies. On a ship they're little more than a distraction. Hunt is impossible. She was bad enough as a division officer, she'll be horrible as XO."

Gellar, his back to the officer door, says, "Sir, you're way out of line, and you need to go."

Sam walks in from hangar bay 3, carrying an empty duffel bag, and stops.

Givens says, "Sir, why can't you just leave it alone? You've been riding our Lieutenant since she came on board. She's alright, and she's a kick ass pilot. It's you that has a problem, sir, not her."

Book, face red, tenses up and raises a hand, and Gellar grabs it. White steps out from behind Gellar, "Let him go, Bobby." Then steps close to Book, "Sir, Get. Out. Of. My. Space," pushing him toward the door.

Book sees Hunt and stops. Behind him Gellar says, "Sir, don't make me finish what Swede started."

Sam, looking Book in the eyes, "That won't be necessary, AD1. Lieutenant Carleton, what are you doing here?"

Seeing Hunt, Gellar tips his ball cap way back on his head, and grins, "Don't mind him, ma'am, he was just leaving. And Carleton, don't go away mad, just go away."

Book stares at Hunt, his mouth and hands clenched tight, and walks past her as Gellar and Cervella high five.

Sam turns to White, "What was that all about, Chief?"

"Something has to be done about Carleton. He was down here trying to stir up trouble. Bobby and I sent him packing."

"I see."

Gellar says, "Joe asked him if he had mommy problems, and Sass asked him if he needed a hug."

She presses her lips together, suppressing a smile, "Okay."

White asks, "You down here to clear out your desk?"

"Yes, I am. Could I have some help, Chief? I'd appreciate it. Oh, and all you miscreants, thank you." White follows her into the office. She sits down and looks up at him.

White, leaning against the door jamb says, "A lot to take in, huh?"

"Yes, yes, it's a shocker. You know, Chief, I've been working with Captain Klindt, right?"

"Yeah sure, why?"

"We're going to need equipment built as soon as possible. I've recommended Senior Chief Cassidy to set up the manufacture of new F-14s and engines."

"A good choice, he helped build them before. No need to apologize to me about it. I'm where I want to be."

"Thank you, Chief."

"So, when is he going to leave?"

"Don't know yet. First, we have to make contact with Admiral Nimitz. I guess, he'll decide."

"You know, his LPO is pretty green. Should we send him Gellar? He's ready for an anchor."

"I'll think on it. Bobby handles the girls well. The Tomcatters are still all male." She begins clearing her stuff off the desk and putting it the duffle.

"Okay, ma'am, but I whip their guy into shape or move 'Socks' into the LPO spot. Besides, I need to stick around to train Ensign Walker. You know, for some reason, he thinks he's in charge."

She grins, "If we give them Bobby, I want one of their stars in exchange."

"Thatta girl, already thinking like your managing the Yankees."

CHITOSE AIR BASE, JAPAN

1232, 27 December, 1941

Lt. Kenzo Koizumi climbs stiffly from the staff car. Only the last few miles of the roads on north Honshu were improved. A staff lieutenant salutes, "Your belongings remain in the car. Please, come with me. I am Lt. Nishimura, Colonel Nagasawa's staff adjutant." He take Koizumi through the side door of a large concrete hangar, "He wishes for you to see this first." Nishimura turns a switch and the hangar blazes with light from strange rectangular fixtures. In the center of the hangar is a huge aircraft. It's angular in design, with two vertical stabilizers and a cavernous engine intake on each side of the cockpit. Beneath the wings hang rockets bigger than any he's ever seen.

Koizumi asks, "What is this? It is different from the American planes I fought, but obviously of the same general type?"

"It is a F-15 Eagle, a jet fighter plane."

"With these, we can crush the Americans and destroy their navy. How many do we have?"

"Forty-two of this type and some of another type, unfortunately, we have few pilots to fly them. It is why you are here."

Koizumi bows, "I will bring honor to the Emperor and my family."

USS DOLPHIN CONTROL ROOM

1410, 27 December, 1941

Lt. Rainer and Lt. JG Porter look over a chart. The rhythmic thump of the diesel sounds through the ship as they run on the surface. Porter says, "Sir, I'm not sure the ice cream they sent over is any good. It says it expires July, 1991."

"It's fine, Brian. Those ships are from the future."

"Sir, isn't that impossible?"

"It used to be impossible for men to sail beneath the sea, but here we are."

ADMIRAL'S CONFERENCE ROOM

1430, 27 December, 1941

Admiral Ren greets Captain Johnson and Captain Tenzar with a handshake, "That was fine work with the submarine, Captain. Damn fine work. Please, have a seat." He pushes a call button, "Will, coffee and cookies, please." The steward comes in with a tray, serves them, and leaves, closing the door. "The brain trust William set up has done very well, however, there's another situation I feel should not leave this room."

Both captains say, "Yes, sir."

"We need to discuss the special devices which must not be confirmed or denied."

Johnson looks at Tenzar and back to Ren, "We can't use them without presidential authority, sir. That hasn't changed."

Ren rocks back in his chair, waving his hand, "Of course not. I'm of half of mind to toss them over the side."

Johnson says, "If the president found out we did that, there would be hell to pay."

"I know, Will. But, if we let everyone know they are available, Tokyo may be ashes. We can't go down that path again."

Tenzar asks, "Who has to know?"

The three men look at each other, and Ren replies, "We'll have to tell Roosevelt, anything else would be treason."

Johnson says, "I agree. Only him, and brief him in completely on the consequences. Do we have any video or still photography of Hiroshima and Nagasaki?"

Tenzar answers, "I do. I use them for training."

Ren says, "Okay, I'll have my staff put something together." He lowers his head for a moment, then looks up, "We could probably end the war in a few minutes over Tokyo, but…" He looks each of them in the eye, "but we have an opportunity do things better than we did in our own history. I'll not waste this opportunity, gentlemen. I won't."

CHAPTER 33

BLACK KNIGHT READY ROOM

1442, 27 December, 1941

Sam is at the ready room door when Thud walks up, "Hey, Spike, did you talk to all the people you were supposed to?"

"Yeah, just finished with Chief Dobson. He was my last one, you?"

"Yeah, who's Chief Dobson?"

"Power plant chief for the Eightballers. Anyway, I have to set up my office."

"Oh yeah, congratulations."

Sam rolls her eyes and walks in, Thud following.

Lt. JG John 'Gunner" Harden, a black pilot from Chicago says, "Hey, Spike, you're almost on. Why don't you sit a bit and watch your gun footage?"

"What?"

"They put together a video of all gun camera footage from PI. It's Swede right now. See his name at the bottom of the screen? They're doing it by flight rank, so you should be next."

"Oh," she drops her duffle in her new office and comes out to join the others. 'Johnny' Walker tosses her a bag of popcorn.

Gandhi says, "See that maneuver Swede, my back aches just watching it." The others laugh as they watch Swede roll his F-14 and pull violently out to line up a shot. Then, it shows them rolling and diving to avoid SM-1s.

Holtz asks, "Was that the Horne?"

Swede answers, "Yes, sir, nearly a boo-boo." The film pauses and white letters on a black background say:

Friendly fire is not friendly and is not okay.

It will not be tolerated.

Ad-miral Ren

The last footage shows him shooting down a Kate. Then the screen comes up with the Black Knight logo showing Swede and Gandhi's kills: 17 air to air, and two destroyers. Sam sitting with Puck thinks, "This is a performance review. Oh God, did I fuck anything up? It will all be up there."

The next screen shows the Black Knight logo and Spike's and Puck's names and flight number. The tape shows the few seconds before and after each kill. Where other pilots were often jerky, wobbling onto their target, the footage from Spike's plane shows her smoothly pulling into each sight picture, shooting, then pulling through to avoid debris. The room gets quiet. As she fires each missile, they see her rotate and follow each missile in to make sure it hits. After a bit, Johnny says, "This is almost boring. Anyone need more popcorn?" A couple of guys raise their hands and Johnny tosses each a bag.

Swede leans over to Gandhi, "Damn, she's good."

Hearing him, Sam turns red, thinking, "Am I that good? I so look up to Swede."

Then the footage of her diving on the cruiser comes up. They see the tracers reach out and hit the center of the ship. First, there is a small explosion, then a huge one as she pulls out of the dive. The screen pauses as the ship explodes and text appears, "26 rounds of 20mm and bye, bye cruiser."

ENS Tyler 'Stinky' Lewis, RIO for Lt. JG Lorne 'Jedi' Luke of Knight 916, says loudly, "No fucking way! How the hell did you do that?"

Puck calmly says, "Know your enemy, or better yet, make friends with Thud."

Sam laughs, and Thud turns red. Speedy says, "Thud figured out they use liquid oxygen in their torpedoes."

Lewis says, "Damn. Well, next time, let us in on the secrets, okay?"

There's a pause, then, "Third Flight and fleet attack." It shows her shooting two destroyers in a row with AIM-7 missiles and guns. Next is the attack by the bombers. After a few scenes, it shows her pull up into a tight barrel roll, the gun camera passes Swede's plane and briefly lines up on a Zero, and a handful of rounds disintegrates the Japanese fighter. Gunner says, "Holy shit, that has to be a sustained nine g's."

Puck says, "My eye balls fell out my asshole."

The footage shows her slewing around to miss the debris. Then, the scene repeats in slow motion, pausing as the rounds impact the Zero. Text comes up, "Let's see this again from another view." The footage is repeated from the vantage point of a F/A-18 gun camera. It shows clearly the Zero's attempt to fire on the belly of Swede's plane and her aggressive maneuver to shoot it down. Swede turns around and looks at her, "Thank you, Sam, for saving my sorry ass."

Gandhi says, "Um, our sorry asses."

Sam says, "You're welcome," thinking, "I like these guys. They're my brothers."

The footage continues, showing her attacks on the bombers. Then it shows a clear image of the two missiles launched from the USS Horne. Again:

> Friendly fire is not friendly and is not okay.
>
> It will not be tolerated.
>
> Admiral Ren

The footage shows the destruction of the final Kate bomber. Then the Black Knight logo comes up, "Lt. Samantha 'Spike' Hunt/Lt. JG Eric 'Puck' Hawke – 22 air to air kills, 1 light cruiser, and 2 destroyers; the squadron, air group, and national ace of aces."

Sam's face turns a deep red and she lowers her face into her hands as the squadron erupts in cheers. Puck leans down, "You okay?"

"Yeah, but did they have to do that?"

"You are that good."

"You are that good, too."

Packs says, "XO, you're making me a believer. That was outstanding."

CAG OFFICE

'Book' Carleton and 'Dixie' Lee are watching the same video with the air group staff. Dixie says, "My God, that's flying."

Book says, "She's just showing off."

Dixie turns and looks at him, "You still don't get it, do you?"

Book sits up straight, "Yes, sir, I do. I just don't like it."

"You best learn to like it."

USS LONG BEACH, CAPTAIN'S CONFERENCE ROOM
1510, 29 December, 1941

Captain Tenzar and Captain Klindt are going over paperwork and sipping coffee. Tenzar says, "This is going to leave us shorthanded."

"I agree, but there just isn't any other way. Have you found a submariner?"

"Yes, MMC Keven Holloway He served eleven years in fast attacks, then courtesy of a kidney stone, he came to Long Beach."

Klindt says, "Lt. Warren can handle a lot of the organizing, but he isn't a NAVSEA 08."

"I know, it has to be one of us. You want it?"

"No, not really, you're welcome to it."

Tenzar asks, "If I take it, who will take command here?"

"Is your XO ready for command?"

"I don't want to give it up. You take the Godfather Nuke job."

"Klindt says, "What about Rickover?"

"He's only a lieutenant commander right now, and besides, do you really want to work for him?"

"I don't want to deny you your chance at command, so I guess it's me," Klindt sighs.

Tenzar says, "Rock, paper, scissors?" Loser is NAVSEA-08."

"Nah, I got it. Just remember, when you're out having fun, I'll be stuck in Washington arguing with congressmen."

FLIGHT DECK, CARL VINSON, 300 MILES SOUTH OF HAWAII

2200, 2 January, 1942

The SH-3 Sea Knights are already spooling up as the sixteen SEALS cross the flight deck with their gear. Chris 'Broke Dick' Langley says, "Damn, this is the craziest, swimming in with our dress whites in a bag."

HM1 Larry 'Munchkin' Shockley, the platoon corpsman, says, "Not as crazy as Korea."

ET3 Gerry 'Meat' Monahan asks, "What happened in Korea?"

RM2 Lawrence 'BJ' Carbone says, "Our last LT swam us into North Korea by accident. Abdul is a god in comparison."

Meat asks, "So, what happened?"

Larry leans toward him, shouting over the engine and rotor noise, as they take off, "We died, of course."

FIVE MILES FROM KAENA POINT, NORTWHEST OF OAHU

0030, 3 January, 1942

The blacked out helos fly a few feet over the dark ocean. The pilot of the lead chopper, CDR David 'Yankee' Crocker, watches his altitude closely as his co-pilot, Lt. JG Aron 'Egg" Eagan, navigates and watches the other instruments. Egg says, "One mile out, open doors." The flight engineer, AW3 Harry 'Nuts' Rodney, begins slapping SEALS on the back. First, they push out a deflated boat from each side, then drop out of the chopper, falling five feet to the ocean below. As the helicopters bank and fly away, the SEAL team inflates their boats, test the engines, then, using hand signals, navigate their way around to the west shore of the island.

THREE MILES NORTHWEST OF OAHU

The black rubber boats ride very low in the water, each with eight men lying down to keep a low profile. The electric motors make a quiet buzz as they cut through the water. Coming around Ka'ena point, Lt. Issa sees a destroyer escort only a few miles away. Looking through his NOGs, he can see look outs on the deck of the DE, and motions the boats to stop. Moving through tropical water stirs up bioluminescent plankton, and when the motors stop, the glowing green water slowly turns black again.

Once the patrol vessel passes and it's clear, Issa gives the hand signal to continue. When they reach the surf zone west of Makakilo Ridge, they stop the motors and drift, watching for movement on the rocky shore. Off to the south, the beacon light of EWA Marine Corps Air Station is only a few miles away. Not seeing any movement, they work the boats through the surf onto Kahe beach, and as the boats hit the sand, the SEALS leap out, lifting the boats and carrying them ashore. A short distance in, using trees for cover, they deflate and pack the boats. The only interruption a passing truck on the nearby road.

Then they cross the road in bounds, and start up Makakilo Ridge. On its flank, the team splits up, ENS Russell 'Triage' Jeremy taking his team up into the hills to set up a landing zone further north. Lt. Issa leads his team east along the hill. Voices travel at night, so all communication is done by touch and hand signals. No one needs to be told what to do, as this maneuver is straight out of the SEAL playbook.

After an hour, Issa raises his hand, signaling everyone to stop. He kneels and pulls out a map. BM1 Paul 'Grunt' Bruce lays a poncho over himself and Issa, and using a red pin light and compass, they check their position. Light, map, and poncho are put away in under ten seconds. Issa stands, points out their direction, motioning the point man to continue. A bit over an hour later, they leave the hills and enter the Dole plantation on the flats. Here there is very little cover, but it can't be helped, so they move at a fast pace, walking on field access roads.

In another hour, they've made it to the road connecting Wheeler Army Air Field with Pearl Harbor. A few hundred yards from the road, they kneel and study the situation. It's still only 0330, but the road is busy. Issa times the traffic, smiling as he sees his guys spread out in a tactical watch position, then he motions them back together. "To much traffic to cross the road and we're wasting time. Grunt,

Munchkin, Broke Dick, and Meat, get changed."

Broke Dick asks, "This soon, sir?"

"Yeah, Broke Dick, we're going to hitch a ride."

The four men strip nude and wash down with the water from their canteens. Broke Dick says quietly, "Hey, Meat, will you wash my back?"

Issa sighs, "Stow it."

Soon the four are in their dress whites. Issa, Zoo, BJ, and Mac change next. When they're done, Issa says, "Stow the rifles. No one here has ever seen and M-16." Grumbling, they put their long arms in their duffle bags with their BDU's and gear.

Grunt asks, "Sir, what about the sidearms?"

"They look close enough to 1911s."

"Sir, no one used ballistic nylon, though."

"True, but it's close enough to the cotton they did use." Issa signals for a line march ahead and they walk out, fully exposed, to the road. Issa tells the point man, "Pearl Harbor, and walk casual. Remember, we are among friends."

Broke Dick says, "Isn't that what Tonto told the Lone Ranger?"

Grunt says, "Sure, and Tonto was."

A truck comes up behind them and rolls to a stop. The driver looks out at them from a vintage 1930s Ford truck, stake bed. "You boys are a long way from Pearl. Where're you headed?"

Issa answers, "Our first day on the island, we're supposed to drive a truck to Wheeler, but I took a wrong turn and ended up stuck. Could you give us a lift to the motor pool at Pearl?"

"Sure, I'm headed that way. Hop in. Where'd you get stuck? I have a bit of time. Maybe I can yank it out and save you some embarrassment." The team climbs in the back and Issa gets into the cab.

"It's an idea. Thing is, I'm not sure where we left it. It ought to be easy enough to find in the daylight. Guess, I should just bite the bullet."

They hear a slap on the cab and the driver says, "Okey dokey," puts the truck I gear and moves out. "My name is Oliver Smith."

"I'm Rob Issa. Lt. Issa."

"Pleased to meet you, all kinds of new folks arriving since the Japs bombed us. More work for me, though, and the money is good. Has Halsey found those bastards yet?"

"I would read it in the papers same as you."

"Now, I doubt that, son. I doubt that. What's that gold thing on your chest?"

"Oh, this?" fingering his Budweiser, "This is a Navy Special Forces pin."

"What does it mean?"

"It means I'm really good at keeping my shoes polished."

"Okay, here we are at the gate. The motor pool is just a bit further on Russell Street."

"Thank you, sir."

A gate guard pops up onto the running board, "Good morning, Oliver, morning Lieutenant."

Oliver says, "I picked me up some strays down the road apiece. Seems they got themselves stuck."

The guard looks at Issa, "Master Chief Oakley is gonna love you." Issa gives him the officer stink eye, and "Um, sorry sir, go on through."

In a couple of minutes, they are unloading at the motor pool, the sun just coming up as Oliver drives off. Broke Dick, says, "Damn, I thought we were screwed at the gate."

Grunt says, "Trust your elders, Broke Dick. Shall we, Abdul?"

Issa nods and walks into the office and a second class, with a cast on his right leg, says, "Can I help you, Lieutenant?"

"Yes, I need a truck with a canvas cover and a sedan."

"Sir, what command are you with?"

"Admiral Ren's staff."

"Admiral Ren, who's he?"

Issa leans toward him, "You don't know him? Well, you will soon enough. We sank a Jap flat top a few days ago. Anyway, I need those vehicles."

"Yes, sir, if you sign these two forms, I will get the keys. I'll give you 262, it's a nice Ford, and the truck is a Dodge. That work?"

"That will be fine, thank you," signing the papers. He accepts the keys, and in a few minutes, they are loaded up and leaving the motor pool. As they drive off, a stout master chief shows up in a jeep. He gets out and stands looking after them, scratching his head, as Broke Dick waves out of the back of the truck.

Issa riding in the back of the sedan, studies the map, "Shit, Grunt, the bridge isn't built yet. Go straight, okay, first, um, no second right."

PEARL HARBOR NAVAL BASE, NIMITZ HOUSE

The sun is up as Issa climbs out of the sedan, "Stay casual." Straightening his jacket, he walks up the stair of the porch carrying a briefcase. Looking for a doorbell, he shrugs his shoulders, and knocks. A Philippine steward answers the door, "Yes?"

"I need to see Admiral Nimitz."

"The Admiral is busy, come back later."

"No, Hindai. I need to see him now. Just open the door, please."

The steward looks out the door, "Is the Japanese attacking us?"

A lieutenant comes up behind the steward, "What is it, Billy?"

"This lieutenant wishes to see the Admiral. I say he is busy."

"Thanks, Billy, I'll take care of this. Lieutenant, please, enter."

CHAPTER 34

PEARL HARBOR NAVAL BASE, NIMITZ HOUSE

0541, 3 January, 1942

Issa walks into the foyer and the lieutenant puts out his hand, "Emerson David Grant, sir."

Issa shakes, "Robert Issa with Admiral Ren's staff. I do need to talk to Admiral Nimitz."

"I'm sorry, but the Admiral really is busy, and is not to be disturbed. Who is Admiral Ren?"

"I would rather explain it once and to the admiral. Would you be so good as to tell Admiral Nimitz that I have a message from Admiral Ren on the Gold Eagle. If I'm not mistaken, General McArthur has already contacted him."

Emerson gives him a measuring look, "I see, the mystery unit. I'll ask him, but no guarantees."

Issa paces the living room, looking it over, and under his breath, says, "He's an admiral, the big screen tv should go right there."

"Lieutenant, you wanted to see me?" Issa stiffens and turns. In front of him is the legend, Admiral Chester Nimitz, CINC-PAC, wearing khaki pants, slippers, and an undershirt, and there's still shaving cream on his face. Nimitz holds out his hand.

Issa takes it, "Lt. Issa, sir. It's fantastic to meet you, sir."

"Yes, well, can you tell me what this is about?"

"Yes, sir. Admiral Ren sent me to ask you to come out to the carrier group and see it for yourself. You see, sir, we, I mean the whole group, sir, we're from the future."

"Now, son, that's the last thing I thought I would hear. How is it possible?"

"Sir, honest truth, I've no idea. I'm not a technical person. I know the Admiral's people figured it out a few days ago."

Grant hands Nimitz a towel and Nimitz wipes his face, "Thank you, Emerson. You mean you didn't come back on purpose?"

"No, sir, for us, it just happened. But we figured it out, and when we did, Admiral Ren decided to hit the Japanese at PI, because we knew from our history books they would be there."

Nimitz slowly lowers the towel, "Do we win?"

"Yes, sir, but they tell me everything has changed now that we are here. With our technology, we ought to do better, sir."

"What's that gold pin on your uniform?"

"It's the SEAL trident. It means I'm a SEAL, a navy frogman, or commando."

"How did you get here?"

"We were dropped off by Sea Knight Helicopters about five miles out and we came in by small boat."

Grant says, "Preposterous. We have patrols. This whole thing is an elaborate practical joke of some sort."

Issay says, "We saw one of your patrols. I wasn't impressed." Then to Nimitz, "Sir, we are very good at what we do."

Grant says, "You believe this, sir?"

Ignoring him, Nimitz asks, "What's in the case?"

Issa opens the briefcase and pulls out 'Admiral 'Bull' Halsey, The Life and Wars of America's most controversial commander' by John Wukovitz and hands it to Nimitz. "I would have brought your memoir, but it seems you never wrote one."

"I haven't done nearly enough, son."

Issa says, "Perhaps not yet, but after you lead the Pacific fleet to victory..."

Grant cuts him off, "This is ridiculous."

Issa pulls out gun camera photos of the sinking of the carrier Ryujo, and then a glossy color photograph of the Carl Vinson battle group. "Did all these ships come back?"

"No, sir, one destroyer, the Hewitt failed to come back, and we lost the Stoddert to a torpedo attack before we realized what had happened."

"So, your ships are not invulnerable?"

"No, sir, but they are capable. I would like to fly you out this morning, so you can see for yourself."

Grant says, "Why don't you just sail on in to Pearl Harbor? Why all this intrigue?"

Nimitz says, "They didn't sail into Pearl because the harbor defense would take them under fire. You're not thinking, Lieutenant Grant. Seeing as your faculties seem rather unlike your normal self, please refrain from further outbursts and do something constructive, like cancelling the meeting and calling John, Lewis, and Phil. They need to get here as soon as possible. Tell them to pack an overnight bag. You should pack one as well, and tell Billy to pack mine."

"Me, sir?"

"Yes, the apostle Thomas needed to put his finger in the wounds. You ought to have the same opportunity."

"You mean, you believe this, sir? Time travel is impossible."

"Lieutenant, General McArthur is a horse's ass, but he is not insane. He saw the aircraft from the Gold Eagle and attested to the damage they caused the Japanese."

"But, sir?"

"Look, Emerson, do you see his uniform?"

"Yes, sir."

"What material is it made of?"

"I don't know fabrics, sir."

Issa says, "It's polyester, a material derivative of the petroleum industry, and I don't recommend it for anything, but, maybe 70's leisure suits."

"It has problems, Lieutenant?"

"Yes, sir, it melts on contact with fire, leaving the wearer with burning plastic on his skin. Wool and cotton are better, even if they are a pain to maintain. Sir, how many people, and when will they be here?

Nimitz looks over at Grant, "Five, and about a half hour, after Emerson makes the calls."

Grant says, "Yes, sir," and leaves.

Nimitz turns back to Issa, "How long have you been in the Navy, Lieutenant?"

"I graduated from the Academy in 1984,sir. Six years, sir."

"Tell me about your navy commandos."

"Sir, we are specialized troops. We are all expert divers, swimming underwater with a breathing device. We're expert in small arms, and a variety of aerial insertions. The missions we excel at are intelligence gathering, precision demolition or removal of high value targets, beach clearing, attacks on moored vessels, and extraction of important personnel. What we are not is normal combat troops. Marines are suited to that mission, we are not."

"Have you ever seen combat?"

"I've patrolled to suppress insurgencies in Thailand and Cambodia. I've never seen any real action, though. Some of my men were in the invasion of Grenada. It was a one-sided fight, but they were involved."

"I see. What kind of aircraft will we be riding in?"

"Helicopters, sir. Vertical take-off and landing craft. Half of my team is setting up the LZ and the other is standing by outside."

"Bring them up to the house. I want to meet them."

"Yes, sir," and Issa heads out.

In a few minutes, the team walk up to the house, just as Nimitz walks out. Fully dressed in his khakis, he says, "Good morning, gentlemen, what are your names?" They all salute.

"I am BM1 Paul Bruce, sir. They call me Grunt," and Nimitz shakes his hand.

"I'm HM1 Larry Shockley, sir. They call me Munchkin."

Nimitz smiles, "Of course, they do," shaking his hand.

"I'm RM2 Lawrence Carbone. They call me BJ."

As Nimitz shakes his hand, "Why is that?"

BJ turns red, "It's a Guamanian thing."

"I'm HT2 Chris Langley. They call me Broke Dick."

Nimitz smiles, "Why?" and the others laugh.

"It was a parachuting accident, sir."

"I see."

"I'm EN2 John Zukowski, sir. They call me Zoo."

"I'm BM3 Steven Cook, sir, and they call me Mac." I break things."

"I bet you do."

"I'm ET3 Gerry Monahan. I'm called Meat, because I'm new."

"Why don't you have the trident, son?"

Issa answers, "Because he's too new sir. He'll earn it soon."

A short balding man in khakis, carrying a bag, walks up the steps, "Someone parked a truck in my way. What's going on,

Admiral?"

"Lieutenant Issa, gentlemen, this disreputable looking fella in commanders wear is my intelligence officer, Phil Morton. Phil, this sharp looking lieutenant is a navy commando."

"Admiral, what are you talking about? We don't have navy commandos."

Nimitz raises his hand to two other men coming up the steps, "I know. I know, but we do now." To Lt. Issa, "Let me introduce Captain John Duncan, my chief of staff, and Captain Lewis Burbank, my logistics officer."

Duncan asks, "What is this, Admiral?"

Nimitz smiles, "Gentlemen, we are about to go out to the Gold Eagle. Emerson, are we packed?"

Lt. Grant says, "Yes, sir."

"Lieutenant Issa, how do we do this?"

"We go for a drive to the LZ, sir. You might want to tell someone to bring the cars back. Oh, and sir, could you inform your radar station to disregard a few incoming contacts. We set up the LZ on the west shore."

"John, see to it. I'll bring my driver, he'll take care of the vehicles."

Issa pushes a button the radio on his belt, "5 Bravo 2, Five Bravo actual, I have the package in hand and we are inbound LZ Alpha. It will be the package plus 4. Time out, 70 mikes."

"Morton asks, "What are you doing, Lieutenant?"

"Letting my other team know we are coming. They will call for the helicopters."

"Where is your radio?"

"Oh, it's on my belt, sir. I'm using a throat mike."

Nimitz says, "Let's get moving, gentlemen. He'll explain later."

SOUTH SLOPE OF WAIANAE RANGE

0900, 3 January, 1942

Lt. Issa stops the caravan of vehicles and everyone gratefully gets out. The last mile was on a kidney punishing gravel road. During the ride, the SEALS changed back into their tactical gear in the truck, but Issa, riding with Nimitz, is still in his whites. "Excuse me, Admiral," and he grabs his bag and goes into the brush. A few minutes later, he's out in forest camouflage BDUs and geared up. "This way, sirs, tactical approach, guys." The SEALS disappear into the brush by the road and Issa starts walking up a trail, then stops when he realizes no one is moving, "This way, sir, it isn't far."

Duncan says, "Chester, this is nuts."

Nimitz starts up the trail, "Patience, John. Son, what is your rifle?"

"M-4 carbine, sir, a shorter version of the standard M-16 rifle. It has 2.23 high velocity rounds and a 30 round magazine. It's capable of full automatic fire, but we rarely use full auto. It's fun, but it's inaccurate and a waste of ammo."

After about 100 yards, Issa raises a hand. They can see a clearing ahead where the brush has been cut back and square orange panels set on the ground in a 'T' shape. There's a faint whooping sound, slowly getting louder, and the SEALS materialize around the Admiral and his staff. "Five minutes out. Hold onto your hats and squint your eyes when it gets close. The bird will kick up a lot of dust. Once it lands, my team will escort all of you onto the bird, and we will extract. This'll happen fast, so make sure you have everything, and hold onto your hats."

The SH-3 Sea Knight makes the approach fast, flaring at the last second, and settling into a hover just above the ground. The noise is tremendous. As it settles to the ground, The SEALs, one arm around the back, the other pushing their heads down, run the officers onto the bird. As they run, Grant loses his hat and it sails up and away from the helicopter. Issa does a quick head count, taps the crew chief on the shoulder, and gives the thumbs up that everyone is aboard. A second later they are forced down in their seats as the helicopter climbs, spins in the air, and flies out over the ocean. Another helo comes in for the other rest of the team, who are already picking up their gear. As they climb away, Lt. Grant shouts, "I lost my hat."

Issa, strapping Nimitz into the jump seat by the door, shouts back, "I know, dumb ass. You could have killed us all if it ended up in an engine. I told you to hang on to it."

"You could have warned me!"

Issa gets nose to nose with him, "I told you twice. I assumed you weren't a dumb ass, dumb ass. Now I know better."

Issa takes a cranial off its rack, "Sir, if I can put this on you, you will hear everything." Nimitz smiles and nods, and Issa, already wearing his, puts the cranial on Nimitz's head and plugs it in, "Can you hear me, sir?"

"Yes, yes I can. Why was it necessary to board so quickly?"

"The helicopters kick up a lot of dust, grit, and debris, which can damage the engines if we stay in ground hover too long."

"Oh, what kind of aircraft is this?" On his cranial Nimitz hears, "Sir, I am your pilot, Lt. Sandra Douglas. This is a SH-3 Sea Knight, anti-submarine and transport helicopter. Welcome aboard Eightballer 416."

Nimitz is silent for a moment, "You mean this aircraft is being operated by a woman?"

"Yes, sir."

"How long have you been in the Navy, Lieutenant?"

"Five years, sir. I've been flying since completing training. This is my third deployment."

"You know we are fighting a war?"

"Yes, sir. I'll do my part, sir. We hunt subs and rescue people from the water. And, sir, I'm not the only female pilot."

Nimitz shakes his head, "Congress is going to have a cow."

"I understand, sir, but we only have so many pilots, and these aircraft are not easy to learn. When we get close to the fleet we're going to open the door so you can see out. We'll orbit the fleet so you can see what we bring to the fight. We also have a little air show lined up."

USS CARL VINSON BATTLE GROUP SOUTHWEST OF OAHU

1125, 3 January, 1942

They approach the fleet at 1000 feet and slow to 20 knots as Yogi pulls open the door. Soon the Long Beach in the plane guard position can be seen with its distinctive box. Nimitz asks, "What the hell is that, and where are the guns?"

Issa answers, "That, sir, is the cruiser Long Beach. Its main battery is guided missiles, rather than guns. I've heard it's the first ship to down aircraft in combat using missiles."

"So, it's new?"

"No, sir, it's nearly thirty years old. I don't know the story of the box, I think it had something to do with a radar."

Then the Carl Vinson comes into view, and Nimitz says, "Mother of God, she's huge!"

Lt. Douglas on radio, "Yes, sir, you see the aircraft, two near the bow, and two toward us?"

"Yes, I see them."

"The ones toward us are F/A-18s, all weather attack and fighter aircraft. The bigger planes on the bow are F-14s, air superiority and fleet defense fighters."

"They look too big to be fighters."

Issa says, "I know, but that's what they are."

Lt. Douglas cuts in, "They are about to launch, the Tomcats are cleared for unlimited climb." The Hornets launch first. As they clear the waist cats, they roll off the afterburner and climb to 15,000 feet. The Tomcats launch next and fly level for a moment, picking up airspeed, then roll back into a vertical climb, continuing to accelerate as the climb to 20,000 feet.

Nimitz says, "Oh, my Lord!"

Douglas says, "You haven't seen the half of it. I've been ordered to set down so you can watch the show."

CHAPTER 35

USS CARL VINSON BATTLE GROUP

1145, 3 January, 1942

Eightballer 416 circles around parallel to the carrier on its port side, side slips to line up over a circle painted on the deck. Matching her speed with that of the carrier, Lt. Douglas sets it down. Deck crew scramble to chock and chain, and Yogi steps out to check. He signals all clear and Douglas secures the engines.

When the rotor is spun down, the rainbow side boys run out and form two lines facing each other. Admiral Ren, his chief of staff, Captain Van Zandt, Captain Johnson, his XO, Captain Nathan Patterson, Captain Klindt, and Captain Lee walk out to meet Nimitz as the 1MC announces, "Pacific Fleet, arriving." The rainbow side boys, male and female, in clean, sharp-pressed flight deck uniforms of red, brown, yellow, green, blue, white, and purple, salute as Admiral Nimitz and his staff are helped down from the helicopter. "My God, it's like I fell down a rabbit hole."

Issa replies, "I understand, sir."

Nimitz walks through the side boys as a boatswain mate pipes him aboard. Admiral Ren salutes then offers a hand, "Welcome aboard the USS Carl Vinson, CVN 70, Admiral. We call her the Gold Eagle. I'm Admiral Ren. This is my chief of staff, Captain Van Zandt. This is Captain Johnson, commanding officer of the Carl Vinson, his executive officer, Captain Patterson, the Reactor Officer, Captain Klindt, and Commander Air Group, Captain Lee."

Nimitz returns the salute, taking the offered hand, "I'm very pleased to finally meet you. General McArthur was, emm, rather expressive. The gentlemen with me are Commander Morton, my intelligence officer, Captain Duncan, my operations officer, Captain Burbank, my logistics officer, and Lt. Grant, my aide." They all shake hands.

Duncan asks, "Isn't Carl Vinson a senator?"

Captain Johnson replies, "Yes, sir, this ship was commissioned in 1982, long after he retired. Please, this way, we have seats set up to watch the show. It's brief, as we need to conserve fuel, but we felt it necessary so you can see what we can do." He leads them to seating on the port side just aft of the bow cats.

Admiral Nimitz stays standing, "How big is she?"

Johnson replies, "One thousand ninety-one feet and ninety-one thousand tons of diplomacy."

Nimitz nods his head and sits down. Admiral Ren signals PRI-FLY and the Air Boss, Commander Forrester, begins, "Good morning, Carl Vinson and Air Wing 9. Greetings distinguished guests. I would like to bring your attention to the area forward of the ship, where you will see two F/A-18s of the Fighting Red Cocks performing a high-speed pass." The aircraft dive, vapor flashing over their leading edges, as they break the speed of sound. It's silent until the plane passes, then the ship is hit with a sonic boom. Each person on the flight deck feels the thud on their chest caused by the compressed air. The Hornets pull vertical, zooming up as they do a cork screw roll, then break over the top, rolling upright at 10,000 feet.

Forrester continues, "If I could move your attention forward, a two-plane element of the Black Knight squadron is approaching at an altitude of 50 feet, doing a high speed pass." Two F-14s, their wings swept back, approach silent, vapor on the leading edge of their wings. They pass portside, hitting everyone with a sonic boom. Instead of climbing out, they continue level for a couple of miles, roll on their side, pulling into an 8 G turn, and circle back to the carrier. Turning, they lose air speed, dropping to subsonic, then straighten back out, and stern to bow, pass over the flight deck at 300 feet and 500 knots, the roar of their engines deafening. Then, they go vertical, climbing to 15,000 feet.

Nimitz asks, "The planes are silent until they pass the ship, why? And what is that boom?"

Ren replies, "Sound travels in the air at about 600 knots, when the planes are flying faster than the speed of sound, they arrive before their own noise."

Forrester continues, "The Fighting Red Cocks will now demonstrate the accuracy of precision laser guided ordinance. The plane guard helicopter has dropped a float off the port side at five miles. Beefeater 2 will laze the target, and Beefeater 1 will drop two practice bombs." One F/A-18 orbits at 10,000 feet and the other approaches the target. They can see two bombs detach from the second bird, falling side by side. They both hit within six feet of the target.

Nimitz says, "Mother of God," as Forrester says "Bulls eye! Now Beefeater 2 will drop a flare and Knight 211 will shoot it with a guided missile from two miles away." As he speaks, the flare is dropped and the F/A-18 flies clear. Spike is flying 2000 feet above where the flare was dropped, she continues for two miles, inverts in a reverse Immelmann, and dives toward the flare. At two miles, a sidewinder drops away, fires its engine, and rockets toward the flare, correcting its path to fly within a couple of feet of the flare.

Captain Duncan asks, "Was it supposed to explode?"

Johnson replies, "No, Captain, it was a training round. We didn't want to risk debris falling on the ship."

Forrester says, "The two aircraft of the Red Cocks and the

two Black Knights are now going to perform a mock dog fight, illustrating the strengths of the two fighter types. They will meet in the merge off the port bow, and then, it's game on."

They fly toward each other, supersonic. When they pass in the merge, the Hornets roll on their side, beginning a tight climbing turn, and the Tomcats go vertical, rolling over the top. Then, the two elements meet again with the Tomcats diving on the climbing Hornets. After the second merge, The Tomcats pull back into a vertical scissors. They cross a third time, both climbing to altitude, then again, and again.

At 30,000 feet, the Hornets reverse into a dive, with the Tomcats in pursuit. The Tomcats seem to twist in the air, staying on the smaller Hornets. Then one Tomcat gets right on the tail of one of the Hornets. The Hornet jinks and turns, trying to lose its pursuer, but he can't shake it off his tail, and it holds that advantage for several seconds. Then the Hornet pulls out, flying straight and level, and Forrester says, "That is a kill for the F-14. The Tomcat is the best fleet defense fighter in the world. The Hornet, though, is no slouch. The pilots of the Fighting Red Cocks gave the Black Knights a run for their money. Now, would the viewing group now walk aft, following the directions of the flight deck crew, to watch the recovery of the aircraft."

As they walk, Nimitz asks Ren, "Where did all this come from?"

"We are from the future. 1990, to be exact. Our coming back was an accident due to a British experiment in the Australian desert." He then explains everything they have learned. When he's finished, Nimitz says, "I would have thought it impossible."

"I, as well, but here we are. We can safely watch the planes land from here."

Nimitz asks, "Why does the flight deck stick out of the port side of the ship?"

Ren answers, "It allows a pilot to apply power and go around if they miss the wire. It also lets us launch and recover at the same time."

The Hornets trap first, coming in at 140 knots, with tail hook and landing gear down. As they catch the wire they go to full afterburner. Then are pulled to a stop and they throttle back to idle. Next, the Tomcats land, wings forward, and Nimitz asks, "Why do the engines get so loud, then so quiet?"

"Thy go full power to have the energy to keep flying should they miss a wire. Now, I would like you to meet the pilots." The Hornet pilots are just climbing out of their planes. Seeing the Admiral, they walk over and salute. "Let me introduce Commander Jeremy Winters and LCDR John Dillon, CO and XO of the Fighting Red Cocks."

Returning the salute, Nimitz shakes their hands, "That was good flying, gentlemen."

Winters say, "Not good enough."

"Which one of you got in their cross hairs?"

Dillon raises his hand and points behind him, "Spike got me. She's over there."

They all turn to look as, first Hot Pants and GQ, then Spike and Puck unass their planes. When they hit the deck, they all remove their helmets. On Ren's orders, Hot Pants did not braid her hair tight to her skull as normal, so when the helmet comes off her flame red hair flies in the wind. With a rueful grin, Spike just finger combs her short blonde hair.

Admiral Ren smiles, "I would like to introduce the F-14 Tomcat pilots and radar intercept officers who were flying today. The XO of the Black Knights, Lt. Samantha Hunt and her RIO, Lt. JG Eric Hawke, and Lt. JG Gloria Hoolihan and her RIO, Lt. JG Standley." They salute the admirals and shake hands.

Nimitz says, "So, you ladies outflew the men flying the other planes?"

Spike answers, "This time, sir. Frosty and Marshal are really good."

"How many female pilots do you have?"

Ren answers, "Right now, nine, and about twenty-five air crew. Also, we have over five hundred women on board. That's about nine percent of the crew and air wing."

Nimitz says, "Could you excuse us for a moment?" taking Ren aside.

Commander Morton shakes Hoolihan's hand, "Incredible flying."

She smiles, "Thank you, Commander."

Captain Burbank shakes Spike's hand, "How long have you been flying?"

"Since I was thirteen, sir."

"They didn't commission you that early, I hope?"

She laughs, "No, sir, my brother and I paid for my flying lessons as a kid. I was commissioned an ensign at twenty-two, sir."

"You fly very well."

"Thank you, sir."

Lt. Grant steps up, "That was all staged. The aircraft are amazing, but I don't believe any woman can outfly a man."

Spike looks him in the eyes, "Who are you, Lieutenant?"

"I'm Lt. Emerson Grant, aide to Admiral Nimitz. If you're really from the future, you've no doubt heard of me."

Burbank snorts.

She says, "Grant?" and pauses a moment, "No, I don't think so. What exactly are you saying, Lieutenant Grant?"

"I'm saying, you were up in the front seat, and your co-pilot flew the plane. I think the whole woman in uniform thing is some strange act."

Puck says, "Just show them the plane," turning to Grant, "I'm a RIO, not a pilot."

"Right this way, gentlemen," leading them to her plane where the twenty-two Japanese flags can clearly be seen."

Burbank says, "Twenty-two kills? How does that compare to your fellows?"

Puck replies, "A couple have seventeen, but she's the best pilot in the air wing."

Lt. Grant stares at the flags, "I see, perhaps, I spoke in error."

Nimitz and Ren walk up behind them, and Nimitz says, "My God, that's a lot of kills. Lewis, Emerson, Admiral Ren and I will be unavailable for some time. Please keep yourselves busy learning about this incredible vessel."

Ren says, "Lt. Hunt, Lt. Hawke, why don't you show them to wardroom 3. I have posted watches over any forbidden areas, but otherwise, they're free to roam the ship."

Burbank says, "Forbidden areas, sir?"

"Yes, I can't have visitors down in the reactor spaces. It's not safe for you down there and it's just not allowed. Perhaps Captain Klindt can arrange a tour later."

As the Admirals walk away, Grant asks, "What's so special about wardroom 3?"

Spike asks, "Have you had lunch?"

Burbank says, "No, we missed breakfast, too, now that you mention it."

"Well, wardroom 1 is closed until dinner, but wardroom 3 is open."

HANGAR BAY 3

1400, 3 January, 1942

Sam walks through hangar bay 3 after taking the officers to wardroom 3 and hears Greg 'Duck' Newburg talking, "The squadron is great guys, really. They let me take the time to look after Ham, and everything."

MM3 Peter Gant, another survivor of the engine room 1 on the Stoddert says, "Yeah, Newburg, but you're a fireman, not an airman. What do you know about airplanes?"

"Yesterday I helped swap out an engine. The turbines ain't much different, really, just smaller. Really, Pete, ya ought to ask for a transfer if you don't like the engine room here. You, too, Donny," speaking to BT3 Donny Petrakis, the only survivor of fire room 1 on the lost ship.

Sam comes around a plane and joins them, "What are you doing, Duck, recruiting?" Newburg and the two petty officers snap to attention and salute. Newburg says, "Pete is complaining that they won't let him qualify any good watches down in the engine rooms here. Ah, and Donny is a BT, ma'am, a boiler technician. They ain't got boilers here. I thought, well, ma'am, I thought if they wanted..."

Petrakis asks, "Ma'am, are you the pilot who pulled Greg and guys off the fantail that night? Greg won't stop talking about you."

"Well, yes, but it was Lt. Hoolihan, too. I wasn't alone."

"It was a good thing you did, ma'am, you being a pilot and all."

Sam grins, "Thank you."

Gant says, "No, ma'am, thank you. I hope you don't mind, though, that I don't want to become a wing wiper. Um, begging your pardon, ma'am," turning pink.

She laughs, "No, I understand. What's the problem in the engine rooms?"

"Only the nukes are allowed to stand important watches. I was main engine watch on the Stoddert, ma'am. I don't really want to get stuck on DU watch."

"DU watch?"

"Yes, ma'am, distilling unit, it's the machine we run to make all the water you airdales waste."

"I'll let that one slide, but on this boat, we at least try to get along."

Petrakis elbows his friend, but Gant continues, "My apologies, ma'am, no offense was meant. It's just the truth. A few days ago, some airdales were washing planes and just let the hose run. We damn...darn near ended up on water hours."

"Do you know who they were?"

Gant says, "No, ma'am, only they were washing F-14s with markings like this one here," pointing to a Black Knight bird.

"Thank you, I'll take care of it. I'll look into the issues in the engine rooms, too."

"Yes, ma'am."

CHAPTER 36

BLACK KNIGHT ORDINANCE OFFICE, HANGAR BAY 2

1425 3 January, 1942

Sam walks through the hatch, "Hey, Fluffy, got a minute?"

AOCS Bruce 'Fluffy' Bond, the squadron senior enlisted adviser says, "Sure, Spike, what's up?"

"I just got a complaint from reactor department. They said our guys let a water hose run when we were washing planes yesterday."

"Fucking nukes, they're always bitching about something."

"Senior, when our people waste water, the whole ship could end up on water hours. That's almost what happened. It isn't the nukes fault. They're doing their job trying to keep us in water."

"Yeah, you're right. I'll talk to the guys. It just irks me when the nukes come whining. They act like they're all Einstein prima donna's."

She grins, "They are Einstein's, Senior. This command wants airdales and nukes to get along as best as possible. I've made good friends among the nukes and this animosity needs to end."

"I didn't know you were slumming amongst the glow worms."

"Senior."

"Just kidding, boss. Okay, I'll try."

WARDROOM 3

0700, 4 January, 1942

Sam is eating breakfast when Thud joins her with a tray mounded with an omelet, hash browns, bacon, sausage, biscuits, and two glasses of milk, "Mind of I join you?"

"I see you decided to eat like a linebacker today."

Thud says a brief prayer under his breath, then tucks in. Between bites, "Admiral Nimitz has been on board for nearly a day, and we've heard nothing."

"Patience, Thud, he has a lot to take in. Anyway, their admirals, Thud, their ways are not our ways."

"They're human beings, aren't they?"

"No, Thud, they're admirals."

"What, are they aliens now?"

"When they want us to know something, they'll say."

On the 1MC, "Now muster the Captain's brain trust in the admiral's conference room."

"Finish eating, Thud. They're playing our song."

"Hang on, just a few more bites," and stuffs omelet into his mouth. Then he walks the tray to the scullery and pulls the biscuits off, as he sets it down. "Spike, I have to get some books. Meet you there."

ADMIRAL'S PASSAGEWAY

They meet Hughes and Richardson outside the conference room. Hughes pauses before knocking, and Richardson says, "Come on, Hughes, the altitude doesn't have you light-headed, does it?"

"Nope, the brass. I feel like I'm going to the principal's office."

As the other members of the trust show up, Richardson

opens the door, "You haven't been throwing spit wads again, I have you?"

Sam says, "Shawn, you'll be fine."

Walking in, Hughes says, "Admirals eat petty officers for lunch." Sam grins.

Admiral Nimitz, at the conference table with his staff, Admiral Ren, Captain Klindt, and Captain Johnson, says, "You're wrong, petty officer, my diet goes more to beef and beans."

Hughes face goes red, "Um, un, yes, sir," and Sam lightly touches his arm. They gather on one side of the room, and Nimitz says, "Please, get a cup of joe and sit down." When they've settled down at the table, Nimitz continues, "I've had an opportunity to review your work, so I have some questions. First, do I have secure communications?"

CT 1 Barr answers, "In a way, sir, yours are more secure than ours. Books and records discuss the principles used in WWII, but not the actual codes. Any German or Japanese that came back, if they did, might be able to steal our codes from co-located American units. I can make our current system more secure, though, without too much disruption once we are making circuit boards."

"Thank you. I know jet fuel is your most pressing need. Beyond that, what is most urgent?"

ETCS Richardson says, "A thousand things at once. Most of it hinges on creating the electronic industry. However, many items can be built concurrently."

"What do you mean?"

Lt. Hunt says, "What he is saying, Admiral, is nearly every system on this boat; weapons, planes, communications, radar, and propulsion uses electronics and computers. Even the missiles carried by the planes."

Richardson adds, "Exactly. What I meant about concurrent manufacture is, what we will be doing is reverse engineering. We already know what will work and how it is designed. We could build parts and have them waiting for the circuit boards to be made."

Nimitz nods, "I see, but how can you know that everything will fit?"

Richardson smiles, "It isn't really hard to do, a card is shaped how we want it to be."

"So, how many cards are we talking about?"

"I've been working on that. There are three thousand six hundred and seventy-two cards used by the battle group. Of them, about two thousand are critical to war fighting tasks. Some are irrelevant now."

"Irrelevant?"

"Yes, sir, global positioning system cards make no sense when we do not have the geosynchronous satellites we need to make the system work."

Ren asks, "Is there any way we could cut down that number?"

Richardson replies, "Yes, we've been looking at that. We could reduce the number of different platforms. If we don't replace the A-6 and the EA-6B, we could replace them with F-14 platforms capable of performing their functions. That would cut about two hundred. There are other weapon and radar systems that could be designed with commonality. By using the same card for different functions, all that would be necessary is to build the card with multiple functions and arrange pin connectors to make them work in each system. It would make each card a little more complicated and expensive, but would cut the number to, maybe, one thousand, or so. We couldn't do that with aviation cards, though, weight and size are too critical."

Nimitz asks, "You're talking about manufacturing new aircraft. I understand the F/A-18 is the newest, why not copy it instead of the F-14?"

Lt. Jackson answers, "The problem with building new F/A-18s is the carbon fiber wings. To build them, we would need to create quality carbon fiber and binders, as well as the software and computers to design and build the wings. Each wing has the fiber mesh laid down precisely. It's what makes it strong. The F-14 is aluminum and titanium, and you're already working with these materials in 1942."

"I see. Which of your aircraft should be produced?"

Lt. Mohr says, "F/A-14, E/A-14, S-3, K-3, C-2, E-2, and the SH-60. That's three airframes and one helicopter. We could also use a dedicated ground support aircraft that can fly low and slow. Even the A-6 is a little fast for the job. The A-6 is a good aircraft, but it's subsonic and an attack 14 could carry as much ordinance and defend itself."

Jackson adds, "We could build a navalized A-10 using S-3 engines."

Hunt looks at Jackson, "Yes, the A-10 is the best ground support aircraft made. Marines love it."

Ren asks, "How fast could we get all this going?"

Richardson replies, "Like I said earlier, the integrated circuit is the limiting technology. At a guess, in the neighborhood of a year before we are making the types and numbers of circuit cards we need. In a year, everything else should be ready."

Jackson says, "We will also need to upgrade the Army. The Sherman tank was worse than worthless, they need the M-60's or the new M-1 Abrams."

Johnson says, "We could find a smart marine to help there."

Mohr says, "Now there's a contradiction in terms."

Klindt sighs, "Behave, Mohr," and they all chuckle.

Nimitz asks, "What is this A-10?"

Jackson pulls out a picture, "Sir, it's a tank killer designed during the cold war. The whole plane is armored and it uses a 30mm Gatling gun that fires depleted uranium rounds. It eats armor like a fire breathing dragon."

"Do we have any plans or schematics?"

Jackson replies, "I found a couple of books on the A-10. We don't have exact schematics, but it should be producible. The 30mm gun is basically an upsized 20mm, and we have the plans for that. The engines we use for the S-3 are basically the same. They are both GE TF-34s. The books have the wing loading, shape, and size."

"Yes, I want it. Rick, I see why you value these people. You know I will be taking most of them with me to Washington?"

Ren answers, "Yes, sir, I only ask to keep the pilots. We really need them."

"We'll talk about that in a bit. First, though, we have the matter of enlisted experts."

Ren says, "I had considered field commissions, but I felt it would be pushing my luck."

"I understand, let's push our luck, shall we? Captain Klindt, please, they are your people."

Lt. Grant says, "Field promotions, sir? Won't congress have your hide?"

"The first thing the congress will know is their promoted rank. By the time this detail is sorted out, these folks will be indispensable. Besides, Emerson, we're fighting a war, field promotions happen. Go ahead, Captain Klindt."

Klindt stands and says, "Attention to promotion." They all stand and he continues, "RM1 Denton, CT1 Barr, MM1 Hughes, ETCS Richardson, please raise your right hand and repeat after me:

I, state your name, having been appointed an Ensign in the Navy of the United States, do solemnly swear that I will support and defend the Constitution of the United States against all enemies, foreign and domestic, and that I will bear true faith and allegiance to same. That I take this obligation freely, without any mental reservations or purpose of evasion, and that I will well and faithfully discharge the duties of the office upon which I am about to enter, so help me God."

The men repeat the oath, Richardson choking a bit over the line about it being freely. Klindt steps up to them, "We'll sort out the uniforms later. Congratulations, Ensign Barr."

"Thank you sir," and they shake hands.

He shakes Denton's hand, "Ensign Denton, congratulations, we're expecting great things from you."

"Thank you, I'll do my best."

Klindt shakes Hughes hand, "Ensign Hughes, congratulations. We will have your EOOW boards this afternoon. You will be a nuclear officer."

"Sir, is this really necessary? I've never even been to college."

"You know things books can't teach, and you don't take crap off anyone. We need you out there."

"Yes, sir."

Klindt shakes Richardson's hand, "Ensign Richardson, congratulations, you have a lot of work ahead of you."

"Thank you, sir, but I didn't want to be an officer."

"I know, but we need you. You're the only one who can do this."

"Yes, sir."

Klindt turns to Admiral Ren, "Can I send someone for ensign bars?"

Nimitz and Ren had been quietly talking during the commissioning ceremony, and Nimitz says, "Let's hold off on that a bit, we have a new problem. No one really listens to ensigns. Everyone knows they're brand new. I need all the first classes to be lieutenants."

Grants eyes about bug out, "Sir?"

"Now, Emerson, would you be so good as to ask Admiral Ren's staff for three sets of lieutenant's bars, and," he looks at Richardson and the rest of the brain trust, and whispers in the Grant's ear.

Grant stands stiffly, "Yes, sir," and leaves the room.

Nimitz turns to Johnson, "Now, is it going to be a difficulty to outfit these three blue jackets with the correct uniforms?"

"We can set them up with a few uniforms, but we can't get them a full sea bag. Most of those items are not carried on board."

"I just need them to arrive in Pearl in proper uniform."

Hunt raises her hand, "Sir? That brings up another problem we've been talking about, inflation of the dollar."

Nimitz looks at her, "What do you mean?"

She continues, "Well, in 1942 a seaman makes about $40.00 per month. In 1990, the same seaman makes $800.00 per month base pay. That's worth about the same in buying power as the $40.00 paid now. The thing is, some on the ship are carrying a great deal of money in 1941 terms, just to have spending money during the deployment. All the currency minted after 1942 isn't legal."

Ren says, "Her figures are about correct across the board."

"How are they paid? Is it in cash?"

Johnson says, "No, sir, their checks were directly deposited into their banks back home, minus an amount of hold back that is sent to the ship. The ship maintains accounts for all sailors that they can draw upon like a bank. We have about forty million in cash aboard to support the system and about one hundred eighty-five million for the other ships functions, paying for food, and such."

Burbank asks, "In cash? Incredible!"

Johnson smiles, "In 1990 terms, it costs about one million dollars a day to operate this ship, nearly two million for the whole battle group."

Hunt says a soft, "Wow."

Nimitz turns to Burbank, "Lewis, let's get some cash out here. We'll set up an exchange at twenty 1990 dollars for one of ours, and give these folks some money. Oh, and also, pay them for the work they've done for the past few weeks."

Burbank asks, "Do we withhold like Captain Johnson described, or pay them in full?"

Klindt says, "Withhold for whom? We all lost our families when we came back in time."

Nimitz and his officers go very quiet, and Burbank says, "I'm sorry, Captain, I meant no offense."

Nimitz says, "That's something that had not crossed my mind. It isn't unusual for the occasional sailor to lose someone back home, but you've lost everyone and everything. You don't even have friends or a home town to go to. We need to attach all of you to your families, if they can be found. Admiral Ren, do you have a home of record and next of kin for everyone?"

Ren replies, "Yes, of course, it's all part of their jackets. I can have the personnel department compile a list."

"Good, I want it as soon as possible. American fighting men, fight for their country, but more than that, they fight for the folks back home. They fight for mom and dad and sister Sally. As long as this group is disconnected from home, they are disconnected from the community that needs them. We need to fix that."

Grant comes back in with a box and hands it to Nimitz, and he opens it, "Good, let us get back to the promotions." He stands, and the rest stand as well. He walks over to the brain trust, "Lieutenant Denton, congratulations," and hands him his lieutenant bars, shaking his hand. "Lieutenant Barr, congratulations," and hands him his bars and shakes his hand. "Lieutenant Hughes, congratulations," handing him his bars and shaking his hand. Then he stops in front of Richardson, "Commander Richardson, congratulations," handing him commander silver oak leaves, and shakes his hand.

Richardson croaks out, "Full commander, sir?"

Nimitz smiles, "Sorry, Commander, I just don't think you're ready for captain."

"I don't think so, either, sir."

Nimitz moves on to each of the members of the brain trust, "Lieutenant Jackson, congratulations," handing him his bars, and shaking his hand.

"Thank you, sir."

"Lieutenant Commander Severn, congratulations," handing her LCDR gold oak leaves and shaking her hand.

She squeaks, "Thank you, sir."

"Commander Warren, congratulations," handing him silver oak leaves and shaking his hand.

"Thank you, sir."

"Lieutenant Commander Mohr, congratulations," handing him gold oak leaves and shaking his hand.

"Thank you, sir," with a twinkle in his eye.

"Lieutenant Commander Hunt, congratulations," handing her gold oak leaves and shaking her hand.

"Thank you, sir."

Then the officers get in line to shake hands and offer congratulations. Nimitz says, "I like doing this, but we need to get back to business. But one more item, we need someone to lead this technical team. It makes sense that Captain

Klindt, who has ably led them so far, should continue to do so. A captain can do so, but an admiral can do it better." He turns to Klindt, "Congratulations, Rear Admiral. Now Admiral, you will have to wait until you turn over your department before we pin you. Admirals can't be department heads."

Klindt says, "Of course, sir. Thank you."

Hunt says, "All of us?"

Nimitz says, "All of you. Now back to business. I'm going to bring this team back with me to Hawaii, then on to Washington. The President, his staff, and Admiral King need to hear the story from the horse's mouth, so to speak, Also, we need to order you some fuel, immediately."

Ren says, "Sir, I need my pilots here. I only have what I have, and until we can put together a training pipeline, sir, they are it."

Captain Duncan asks, "How long does it take to train jet pilots?"

Ren says, "Two years, sir, and even in war time not much can be shaved off that time. They have to be able to land on a moving deck in foul weather, at night, flying 140 knots. It takes time to learn how. Also, all of our jet pilots have engineering or mathematics degrees.

Nimitz says, "I need one pilot. I need someone smart, with experience in command, and high enough rank that he can get the job done. I like what your team has done, but I don't see that pilot here. I met your CAG, Captain Lee, earlier, I want him. Can I have your air group commander, Admiral?"

Ren says, Yes, sir, I'll need to assign someone else to his spot."

"Who is your highest ranking commander?"

"Commander Holtz, commander of the Black Knights, is the senior squadron commander. He's Jackson and Hunt's skipper."

"Good, you already have a lieutenant commander in the squadron to take his place. Having a woman commander will cool some of the objections in congress. Well, that's settled."

Hunt listens to the admirals in shock, the room dimming around her. Hughes touches her elbow, "You okay?" Not trusting her voice, she just nods.

Nimitz says, "That done, I need to talk with my staff. Thank you all."

Klindt says, "Okay, guys, I think a celebration is in order. Meet you all in the RT classroom at 0900."

CHAPTER 37

15 MILES SOUTH OF DIAMOND HEAD HAWAII

FLAG BRIDGE, USS ENTERPRISE, CV-6,

4 January, 1942

Captain Murray walks into the bridge, "So, Admiral, are you going to let me in on the secret? Why did we sortie this task force?" Admiral William 'Bull' Halsey grabs a message envelope and hands it to the Enterprise's captain: To Commander Carrier Group 2/Task Force 8. From Commander Pacific Fleet: Sortie Enterprise Task Force as soon as able. Meet with Carrier Group 72, USS Carl Vinson 'Gold Eagle' group at north 27 degrees 37 minutes 30 seconds by west 156 degrees 7 minutes 30 seconds. Provision for two months."

Murray says, "USS Carl Vinson? What the hell is the Carl Vinson?"

Halsey looks at him with a grim smile, "Do you remember the ruckus about two weeks ago down in the Philippines?"

"Oh, the phantom group. So McArthur isn't touched in the head?"

"Well, I won't say he isn't, but Admiral Nimitz disappeared yesterday morning. He didn't fly out of any field and no ships got underway. Early this morning this comes in with his code. Don't know what is going on, George, but I do know we will find out this afternoon. You might want to get your command squared away. You may be hosting the fleet commander soon. By the way, George, he likes his steak medium."

"Yes, sir, isn't Carl Vinson a congressman?"

"Yep, get with it, George."

CARL VINSON RT CLASSROOM

0900 4 January, 1942

Knowing his people were going to be promoted, Klindt arranged cake and ice cream. It was the first thing they all see when they entered the now familiar room. Klindt says, "Commander Severn, would you do the honors of cutting the cake? I brought my cake slicer down," and hands her his dress uniform sword. "You know all of you are going to need one of these."

Jackson asks, "Why?"

With a rueful sigh Hunt says, "So, we can clank when we walk."

Klindt says, "I think most of you are missing the opportunity we now have before us. This group, all of you right here, are going to decide the future of our great nation. Lieutenant Jackson, what was the biggest mistake our country made during WWII."

"Dropping the bomb on Japan, sir. It may have ended the war sooner, but we've been dealing with the fallout ever since. Plus, I don't take kindly to killing civilians by the hundreds of thousands."

"I agree, we can prevent that mistake. Commander Hunt, what was the biggest mistake we made in Europe?"

"The so-called strategic bombing over Europe. It destroyed cultural icons like Dresden, and it didn't accomplish much except to drive production underground and increase the use of slave labor."

"True, I would have said that we needed to do more to liberate the death camps, but you are right."

"It actually did more to continue the camps because they moved them into the sticks."

Klindt says, "I agree. With our technology, we can precision bomb headquarters, factories, and bridges, without the massive collateral damage. My point is, we can give our country a better future. We can end the war faster, saving untold lives, and minimize unnecessary destruction. What about after the war? Lieutenant Hughes, what was the biggest mistake we made after WWII?"

Hughes says, "Sir, I thought this was a celebration, not an oral board. We should never let Russia hang onto North Korea, Poland, and Eastern Europe. The invasion of Poland started the whole thing, and we hung those people out to dry."

"I'm sorry, Shawn, my enthusiasm gets the best of me, but you are exactly right. We can change that. Anyway, I hope you all get my point. We have a lot of work to do, and it is we few that must do it. Congratulations to you all."

Sam turns to Scott Richardson, "Congratulations, Commander. It's about time. You can't hide your light under a bushel your entire life."

"You knew about this?"

"No, I've just been watching you in these meetings. You're brilliant."

"Congratulations back at you, commander of the Black Knights."

"I think condolences are more in order."

"What did you say about hiding your light?"

"It's not quite the same thing."

Warren joins them, sticking out his hand, "Congratulations Scott, Samantha."

Sam says, "Thank you," and someone sticks a glass of punch in her hand. She turn and sees Klindt handing one to Warren. "Thank you, Admiral." He just smiles.

With a chuckle, Jackson says to Richardson, "What a way to jump the line, Commander."

Sam says, "I don't think it was on his 'To Do' list, Thud."

Warren shakes Hughes hand, "Congratulations, Lieutenant, you're off the watch bill."

Shawn grimaces, "Didn't you hear the Captain and Admiral? My board is this evening."

Scott says, "Better you than me."

Klindt overhearing, "What do you mean, Commander? You're standing your board with him."

"Why, sir?"

"Because, I'm not giving up on anyone who is nuclear qualified."

Sam and Shawn sit down, "Shawn, you'll be fine. You know this stuff backward and forward. You just hate tests."

"You're not pissed that I went straight to lieutenant, Sam?"

"No, no, I think it's wonderful. I'm always happy when a friend does well and gets the recognition they deserve."

"Friends. That's allowed now, I guess. I just feel this huge divide between what I am and what he wants me to be."

"Oh, I totally understand."

Klindt hands them each a paper plate with cake and ice cream, "I don't want to change you. I simply want you to have the authority to change everything else. Don't let anyone change who you are. Not ever. Not even me. Be the amazing people you are and the world will change to accommodate you."

Sam and Shawn look at each other in wonder, and he looks at a smiling Klindt, "Sir, I know I can be an asshole. You want that in khakis?"

Sam starts laughing, and Klindt's grin gets wider, "Absolutely, sometimes you have to be an asshole to get things done. The thing about you, Shawn, is you call it straight, and will do so even if the President is asking. I don't think you understand how valuable that really is." Turning, "Sam, I know you're a bit overwhelmed right now. I value your insight. You can look at the big picture and still see the little details in context and figure out how it all connects. You also kick ass. The Navy needs people like you."

"Sir, is this all because I'm a woman? Nimitz said he wanted me to have the squadron so he could tell congress about me. Is this all some affirmative action garbage?"

Klindt replies, "Half the population is female. That means half the potential great pilots, great scientists, great doctors, great leaders are all female. I know some believe women can't do it. I know many women believe they can't. You can do it. I recognize the weight it puts on you, and I'm sorry, but it's yours to bear. It has been since you volunteered for jets. It's just heavier now."

"Yes, sir, I understand. I don't like it, but I understand. By the way, sir, I was talking to one of the survivors of the Stoddert. He's in one of your engine rooms. He was grumbling that he couldn't qualify some watches because only nukes were allowed to stand them. What is that about?"

Warren interrupts, "We don't allow anyone who doesn't understand the reactor to stand a watch that could impact reactor power. It's too dangerous."

"Oh, I understand," replies Sam, "But, where are you going to get new nukes?"

Klindt looks and Warren and Hughes, "See what I mean, insight. I'll talk to the RTA. We need to stand up a nuke school right here, until we can set one up on shore."

CAPTAIN JOHNSON'S OFFICE

0914, 4 January, 1942

CDR Holtz walks in, "You wanted to see me, sir?"

"Yes, sit down." Johnson hands him a cup of coffee, "Captain Lee will be leaving with Admiral Nimitz and on his way to Washington. The admirals decided to give you his spot, and give your squadron to Hunt. We've had some issues with you. Do you understand what we expect as far as female sailors go?"

"Yes, sir. I know I was an ass, and it took me some time to get with the program, but Lt. Hunt and Lt. Hoolihan are okay. I will toe the line where females are concerned, sir. Is Hunt getting promoted, sir? So, she is at command rank?"

"Of course. Truth is, she was due for lieutenant commander, anyway."

"Yes, sir."

CAG'S OFFICE

1105, 4 January, 1942

Sam walks into Lee's office and his yeoman, YN3 Silverman, says, "He's in, ma'am, and expecting you. Go on in."

"Thank you."

When she walks into Lee's small inner office, he's packing, "I take it you heard."

"I was there when they made the decision, Rick. And, of course, you know what they did to me."

"Yeah, moving Holtz to CAG, and giving you the Knights."

"What do you think about that?"

"Sit down. You want a Coke?"

"Yeah, that would be nice."

He pulls two Cokes out of the fridge, opens them, and slides one across the desk to her, "I know how hard this will be on you, Sam. Command is never easy. You don't think you're ready, right?"

"Yes. I've only just been promoted to lieutenant commander. Most squadron skippers are full commanders."

"A lieutenant commander can take a squadron. It does mean you will promote to commander at the first slot, but it has been done before."

"But...but, Rick, am I ready?"

"Sam, no one is ever ready, not really. When we look up at the wise leaders above us, we all count on their experience, wisdom, and noble purpose. Truth, they're a bunch of terrified old guys, hoping and praying they don't screw things up. It's how it always is. It's why the Navy can rebound from horrible leadership and thrive under great leadership. Whatever the category, no one is ready. What counts in the end is character, and you have that."

"I appreciate your faith in me, Rick. I just hope I can do as well as you have."

He looks her straight on, "I don't have faith in you, Sam. Faith is believing without seeing, I've seen you and I know you can do it. Seeing you agonize over it is even more proof. If you took the position as yours by right, then it would be about your ego, and not about the people you need to lead. You just need to wrap your brain around the fact that you can do this. You really can."

"I never looked at it that way."

"Well, it's time to start. I'm off to Washington, so your free leadership lessons are going to stop for a time."

She smiles, "Yeah, you know you're not the only one I've been learning from."

He gives her a mock stern look, "You mean you're two-timing with other teachers?" He smiles, "Good, it's good to learn the leadership styles of several leaders and figure out which tools work for you. There are good ones and bad ones, take care to recognize the difference."

"Are you going to be okay?"

"Me? Yeah. I'm going to miss flying, though. I'm going to miss these talks, too."

"You've come out of it pretty well. You know, I've been worried for you."

"In this time line, Melanie hasn't died. I know she isn't born, either, but somehow, it's better."

"I see that. So, you have my address Admiral Dixie Lee. Write me."

"I will, promise. I see you haven't put our oak leaves on, need a hand?"

"No, I'll take care of it, thanks." Standing, she puts out her hand. He stands as well, takes her hand, and pulls her into a hug, "Take care, Samantha."

"You too, Rick, be careful."

"I'm the very soul of caution, and I've stopped drinking."

"I can live with that," kissing him on the cheek. She gazes into his eyes for a moment, then steps back.

CHAPTER 38

HANGAR BAY 3, STARBOARD SIDE

1155, January, 1942

Sam walks past her aircraft, clutching her oak leaves in her hand. Her eyes blinded by tears, she stumbles into Lt. Grant and Lt. Carleton. Grant says, "Shouldn't you be making some guy happy back behind a barn somewhere, instead of playing pilot? How could American manhood sink so low as to draft women into fighting their battles? You don't belong here. Congress will never countenance an aberration like you, so pack your bags, lady."

Carleton smiles and walks away. Wiping away her tears, she cocks her head and takes a step toward Lt. Grant. He smiles, "What? I've made the girl cry? Go ahead and cry yourself to your cabin and pack your bags and go home."

Sam smiles, looking him in the eye, "Lieutenant Grant, you have taken advice from the wrong person. You forget, none of us on this ship have anyone to go home to." She steps closer, but he stands his ground.

"I don't care, just go away, you don't belong here."

Sam's smile broadens and she steps into his space, holding eye contact. Her east Tennessee drawl deepening, "Bold words for a staff flunky who has never placed his ass on the line in combat."

"Officers should be gentlemen and you are not appropriately equipped."

"And you, sir, are no gentlemen at all. No gentlemen would treat a lady as you have treated me. Your mother would be ashamed of you. Now, please excuse me, Lieutenant, I have a war to fight. Don't you have a memo to write, or something?" Sam turns and walks away.

Sam walks to the edge of elevator 4 and looks out to sea. The waves slapping against the hull shatter the sun's rays into a million sparkling crystal shards. She stares out at nothing. Then there's a smudge on the horizon. Knowing no enemy could get this close, she watches as more ships rise above the horizon. She doesn't recognize the class of destroyers, but sees a larger ship whose guns give it away as a heavy cruiser from the '40s. No current ship, save the Iowa class, carries the big guns. Then, she recognizes the profile of the USS Enterprise, CV-6.

She looks down at the oak leaves in her hand. She clenches her fist, as the ships move closer. Then, she puts them in her pocket, reaches up, removes her lieutenants bars and pockets them. Pausing for a moment, she smiles, then she puts on the gold oak leaves of a lieutenant commander. She watches the Long Beach approach the new task force, as blinker lights flash on the Enterprise. Smiling sadly, she turns and walks back into the hangar bay.

BLACK KNIGHT READY ROOM

1215, 4 January, 1942

Sam walks in and Thud is the first to see her. He rushes over, then stops and puts out is hand, "Congratulations, Lieutenant Commander. This...this is so cool." His new bars are already sewn on his flight suit.

Gloria comes up behind him, "Hey, Thud, don't hog her to yourself. You went to a party with her already." She hugs Sam, "Congrats, honey."

The rest of the squadron is gathering around them, "Thank

you, Thud. Thank you, Gloria, a bit of a shocker."

Holtz walks out of his office, "Hey!" and they all turn to look at him. "Stop sucking up to your new boss, I need to talk to her." They all turn back to look at Sam, "Yes, that's right. The CAG is leaving for Washington, so they're moving me up to CAG, and putting you misfits in her hands. May God have mercy on her soul. Come into the office, Spike, we need to talk." To the rest of the squadron, "There'll be a change of command ceremony on the flight deck in an hour. Gather your people for it. Working uniforms."

The two of them walk into Holtz's office, "Have a seat, we have a lot to discuss. First things first, I know we've had our differences. Truth be told, I'd prefer they move the Tom-catters XO, Lt. Commander Osterman, over because he has more time in the XO position, but the brass have spoken and you have the job. I think they're pushing you too fast for your own good. I'll still be around, though, to look out for the squadron and help you avoid any big mistakes. I don't want any major changes to how things work here unless your clear them with me. Clear?"

"Not a problem."

"Next, I know this is a big shock, as you've only been XO a week or so. I expect some of the folks to have issues. If they get out of hand, I want to know about it."

"Yes, sir."

"Good, okay, we have a pretty good handle on the supply situation, as we have none coming in. I have the electronics division working with AIMD refurbishing control cards instead of pitching them. We need to work with what we have."

"You're right, good move, sir."

"It just makes sense, and in truth, it was Thud's idea. Now, we don't currently have any discipline cases, as you know, but we do have five guys mess cranking. If the ship gets new people in, we will want to get those guys back. Trained airdales are going to be at a premium. Now, for XO, Thud just got his bars and I don't think he's ready. Who do you think, Hot Pants?"

"No, Swede."

"Really. After the fight with Carleton, you don't think that will cause a problem?"

"If Carleton had not said and done what he did, Swede wouldn't have lost it, sir. I think Swede can handle it."

"Okay, call him in. He should be down in weapons," and hands her the phone.

"Black Knights weapons, killing things and loving it, Senior Chief Bond speaking. How my I help you?"

Sam laughs, "Hey, Chief, this is Spike. Is Swede there?"

"Sure thing, ma'am, he's here, just a second. By the way, did I hear right? Is it Lt. Commander Hunt, now?"

"Yes, Fluffy, it is."

"Okay, then congratulations are due. Here's Swede."

"Thanks, Fluffy," then "This is Swede, can I help you?"

"Swede, this is Spike. Could you come up to the squadron office, please?"

"Yeah, sure, XO, be there in a few minutes."

"Okay, good."

Holtz says, "Our roster and binnacle list." She skims them briefly, already familiar with the squadron personnel, and who is sick and injured, and sets them down, "Commander, you don't think I can do this, do you?"

"I don't know. It is what it is, so let's get you off to a good start."

On the 1MC, "Carrier Group 2, arriving. Enterprise, arriving."

Swede walks in, "You want something?"

Sam grins, "Lieutenant Swedenborg, how would you like to be the XO of the Black Knights?"

Swede then notices her gold oak leaves, "You got promoted and no one said anything?"

On the 1MC, "Long Beach, arriving. Salt Lake City arriving. San Francisco, arriving. Horne, arriving."

"It just happened."

"Okay, where are you going?"

Sam sighs, "Swede, I'm not going anywhere. Captain Lee is going to Washington, and CDR Holtz is moving up to CAG. They asked me to be the CO. Do you want it?"

Swede looks back and forth at the two of the, shakes his head in wonder, then, nodding, "Yeah, sure, I'd be honored."

Holtz lets out his breath, "Good, then, all the paperwork goes to you. The squadron is mustering on the flight deck for the turn over. Meanwhile, I need to change offices. Oh, and Commander, Lieutenant, undress blues, please."

Sam asks, "May I wear slacks?"

"Sure, I don't care."

SPIKE'S STATEROOM

Gloria walks in as Sam is changing. She has on the dress blue pants and white button up shirt. The jacket's hanging on the open locker door as she tries to square away her tie. "Here, let me help, commanding officer." She flips up the collar and tightens the tie.

Sam says, "God, I hate these things."

"Yeah, I know, and the hat is hideous."

Over the 1MC, "Jarret, arriving. Fife, arriving."

"God, yes, a misogynist designed it, for sure."

"I know. So, are you moving to Holtz's stateroom?"

"No, I'm staying right here for now. I wouldn't feel comfortable there. Do you mind?"

"Oh, Sam, if you move out, there goes most of my entertainment. Besides, I get to have a private chat with the boss every night. I think I can hack it for a while."

Sam laughs, "I'm your entertainment?"

Gloria feigns offense, "Of course, you are. I can't gossip with the boys, they haven't the knack. Besides, you're about the only one around here not trying to get into my knickers. Well, besides, and maybe Thud, who's too shy to try."

"There's that."

"Are you going to be okay, Sam? I mean, really, okay?"

"Yeah, I guess. I guess I have to be. It's been a hell of a roller coaster ride."

"Let's get your jacket on," and Gloria grabs the dress blue jacket. "Shit, Sam, you've got a lot of medals. What's this one?"

"The Navy Expeditionary Medal, got that in the Gulf during Praying Mantis."

"You got the NAM there, too?"

"Yeah, and another one for end of tour."

"I see the sea service and expert pistol, but where did you get the expert rifle?"

"NROTC, Gloria, I grew up hunting."

"I know, skinning squirrels for dinner and making coon skin hats. You look sharp, Danielle Boone. Now, go knock 'em dead. I'll be hooting from the crowd."

Sam realizes she feels calm and alright, "I love you, too, baby," and gives Gloria a big hug.

CARL VINSON FLIGHT DECK

1400, 4 January, 1942

Except for the watch standers, the entire crew is gathered on the flight deck. When Hunt and Hoolihan arrive, the captains and XOs of the battle group are walking to a stage through the center aisle and being announced by Master Chief Benjamin. When they get to the back of their squadron, Holtz intercepts them, "Admiral Nimitz, Admiral Ren, and Admiral Halsey are on their way up. It seems like a lot of brass just to turn over a squadron and CAG. Know anything, Spike?"

"No, sir. Maybe it's about the brain trust people leaving. Thanks for the heads up, sir." As they move to the back of the formation, the admirals walk out of a water tight door on the island, followed by Captain Johnson, Captain Klindt, Captain Murray, and Captain Lee. Instead of walking up the aisle, Ren leads them to Holtz, Hunt, and Hoolihan, who salute.

Lee says, "Admiral Halsey, Captain Murray, I would like to introduce Commander Holtz, commander of the Black Knights, and my relief. This is Lieutenant Commander Hunt. She'll be relieving Holtz, and Lieutenant Hoolihan. Commander Holtz, Commander Hunt, Lieutenant Hoolihan, this is Admiral Halsey, commander of Carrier Group 2, and Captain Murray, commanding officer of the Enterprise." As Spike takes her turn shaking Captain Murray's hand, she struggles to keep a stupid grin off her face.

Captain Murray, a stern-faced man, asks, "Is something funny, Commander?"

"Sorry, sir, it's just that you're a legend. I studied your tactics during the island-hopping campaign. It's such a pleasure to meet you."

Murray says, "I'm still attempting to understand this whole

thing."

"Us, too, sir." She turns to shake Halsey's hand and freezes.

Halsey askes, "Are you alright, Commander?" He shakes her hand.

"Ub, um, yes, sir. Sorry, sir, it's just…this is amazing, sir."

Halsey smiles, "Why? I don't see why I'm so special, Commander."

"I know my history, sir, and you are…"

Still holding her hand, he says, "Not yet, I'm not. Please keep that in mind."

Nimitz laughs, "Well, I'll be, Will. She seems more taken with you than she was with me. I'm almost jealous. We have folks waiting. Shall we begin?"

Spike says, "Yes, sir. Sorry, sir." She can't stop smiling, feeling like she's in a Ford movie.

The admirals walk up the aisle as Command Master Chief Benjamin announces them from the corner of an ad hoc stage made on several tow tractors. Next, each captain goes up, followed by the commanders, Holtz, Hunt, and the reactor electrical assistant, Commander Tucker. As Holtz walks up the aisle, the CMC announces, "Black Knight Squadron, arriving," then for Hunt, "Lieutenant Commander, United States Navy, arriving." When the get on the stage, they all sit.

Admiral Ren steps up to the mic, "I don't have quite the Master Chief's volume," and the crew laughs. "I gathered all of you here for a series of changes of command, and I would like you to meet your new boss, Commander Pacific Fleet, Admiral Chester Nimitz." He pauses for the murmuring to die down, "We'll start with the Black Knights. Commander Holtz has served the Black Knights well. He's prepared you all for a routine deployment that has become anything but routine. He's adjusted to a world at war, and helped you all adjust. It is because of this leadership and our confidence in him that we are asking him to step up and assume the duties of Commander Air Wing 9. Captain Lee will be leaving us, putting on stars, and representing the jet community in Washington, D.C.; explaining our presence and capabilities. He will lead the new jet aviation branch. He will be sorely missed, but what he will be doing is vital if we are to succeed.

"As Commander Holtz leaves the Black Knights, it gives us an historic opportunity. Lieutenant Commander Hunt will be the first female commander of a combat squadron. An opportunity she has earned. Her outstanding performance, in and out of the cockpit, has prepared her for the trials ahead. I ask that you all give her the same support and respect you have given Commander Holtz, and I know you will.

"Captain Klindt will also be leaving us, putting on stars and leading the effort to bring 1990 technology to our country and our military. Captain Klindt, your wisdom, expertise, and knowledge will be sorely missed. He will be relieved by Commander Tucker, the reactor electrical assistant." He pauses and looks over the crew. "Lastly, I will be leaving as well." Again, he pauses for the murmuring to subside, "I must report to Washington with the others. The Navy Department needs to know what all of you are capable of, and also, what each of you warfighters need in order to do your jobs. I will be relieved by Admiral William Halsey, Commander Carrier Group 2. I am thankful to have had the opportunity to serve with each of you. I will remember fondly my experiences with the Gold Eagle, and the battle group as a whole. To all of you, I say, thank you. Admiral Nimitz, did you want to say a few words before we begin?"

Nimitz steps up to the microphone, "I just want to say that I am, frankly, impressed by the dedication, discipline, and commitment I see here before me. I am more than pleased that the legacy we, of my generation, created has borne fine fruit in each of you. I have much to get used to. Female sailors, it cuts against the grain, but I see in front of me how well it works. This old dog can learn new tricks, and I know I have much to learn from all of you.

"Many of your fathers and grandfathers are fighting alongside us. I know CDR Hunt's father is a marine. Now, she'll be fighting her father's war, as will all of you. The technology you brought to us from the future changes everything. I believe, however, that it is your presence here, with that technology, and your expertise in how to use it, that is even more important. This is why we need a group of your best and brightest to give our industry an enormous leap forward. I'm looking forward to your success, CDR Hunt, as I am looking forward to the success of everyone here. We all are."

Spike flushes, looking over the crowd. In a corner, she sees Lt. Carleton and he meets her gaze, drawing a finger across his throat.

Admiral Ren reads his orders, "From Commander Pacific Fleet, to Richard Ren, Commander Carrier Group 3. Admiral Ren is to detach, when relieved, from the USS Carl Vinson task force to report to the staff of Commander Pacific Fleet."

Admiral Halsey reads his orders, "From Commander Pacific Fleet, to William Halsey, Commander Carrier Group 2. Vice Admiral Halsey is to assume command of Carrier Group 72, incorporating it into Carrier Group 2. He is to shift his flag to USS Carl Vinson and continue carrying out missions as assigned."

Halsey turns and salutes Ren, "I relieve you."

Ren returns the salute, "I stand relieved." At that point, Ren's blue flag with two white stars is hauled down from the signal yard, and Halsey's three-star flag is hoisted up.

Captain Klindt steps up and reads his orders, "From Commander Pacific Fleet to Craig Klindt, Reactor Officer, USS Carl Vinson. Captain Klindt is to detach, when relieved, from USS Carl Vinson to report to the staff of Commander Pacific

Fleet. With this assignment, Captain Klindt is to receive promotion to the rank of Rear Admiral."

Commander Tucker reads his orders, "From Commander Pacific Fleet to Dwight Tucker, Reactor Electrical Assistant, USS Carl Vinson. Commander Tucker is to relieve Captain Klindt as Reactor Officer USS Carl Vinson. With this assignment, Commander Tucker is to receive promotion to the rank of Captain."

Commander Tucker salutes Captain Klindt, "I relieve you."

Captain Klindt returns the salute, "I stand relieved."

Captain Lee steps forward and reads his orders, "From Commander Pacific Fleet to Richard Lee, Commander Carrier Air Wing 9. Captain Lee is to detach, when relieved, from Carrier Air Wing 9 to report to the staff of Commander Pacific Fleet. With this transfer comes a promotion to Rear Admiral."

Commander Holtz steps forward, "From Commander Pacific Fleet to James Holtz, Commander VF-154. Commander Holtz is to relieve Captain Lee as Commander of Carrier Air Wing 9. With this transfer comes a promotion to Captain."

LCDR Hunt steps forward, "From Commander Pacific Fleet to Samantha Hunt. Lieutenant Commander Hunt is to relieve Commander Holtz as Commander VF-154." She turns to Holtz and salutes, "I relieve you, sir."

Holtz returns the salute, "I stand relieved." Then he does an about face and salutes Lee, "I relieve you, sir."

Lee returns the salute, "I stand relieved."

Nimitz steps back to the microphone, "We now have some promotions to attend to. Commander Tucker, Commander Holtz, Captain Lee, and Captain Klindt, would you please step forward. It's customary in naval service for an officer's wife to pin on his promotion rank. The Navy recognizes the importance a spouse will play in their career. Unfortunately, these four officers are separated by both time and distance from their loved ones. Captain Klindt, I understand Commander Tucker has asked you to pin on his eagles. Captain Lee, Commander Holtz would like you to pin his on. Commander Hunt, could you step forward, please?" Spike steps forward and Nimitz hands her two pairs of stars, "Captain Lee and Captain Klindt have asked that you pin these on."

Captain Klindt takes off his eagles and pins them on Tucker, "These brought me good fortune. I hope they do as well for you."

Captain Lee removes his eagles, and pins them on Holtz, "Congratulations, Captain. You've wanted these for a long time. See that they don't weigh you down."

Sam steps in front of Lee, and pins on his stars, smiling through her tears, "Congratulations, Admiral."

"Hey, bright smiles, dear. I'm not dying."

Then she steps in front of Klindt, and pins his stars on, still fighting tears, "Congratulations, Admiral."

"I'll miss you, too. I learned a lot from you."

"Thank you, sir," and returns to her seat.

Admiral Halsey steps up to the microphone, "Thank you," his booming voice startling all. "Sorry about that. They said to talk normally into this thing. I'm normally loud. Thank you for what you've already done in the Philippines. One Jap carrier sunk and almost three hundred aircraft destroyed. I know from that alone, I am assuming command of some serious warfighters. Most of Admiral Ren's staff will be sticking around to help me adjust to this new technology. I'll be doing a walk around the Carl Vinson, and the other ships in the battle group to learn your capabilities. I have much to learn and must learn it quickly. The enemy is out there, and will not wait. I am calling an all captains meeting to determine how the fleet will be organized. Meanwhile, the new ships will fold into Carrier Group 2. I want every man...and woman here to keep sharp. Tojo has forces out here somewhere. I want to find them first and send them to hell. Thank you." He looks startled as the crew in front of him stomp their feet, clapping, and cheering.

Nimitz walks up to the mike, smiling, "Thank you for your attention. Perhaps a brief word as to your orders, once my new staff and I leave, you are to head west. I want you to let Tojo know what Pearl Harbor felt like by bombing strategic targets around Tokyo, destroying fuel storage sights, dry docks, and shipping. If you find their carriers, sink 'em. Make Japan's war machine bleed." He has to stop for the cheering to die down. "I will get you the fuel you need as soon as I can. Thank you. Commanders, take charge and carry out the plan of the day."

CHAPTER 39

03 LEVEL, PORT SIDE AFT

1558, 4 January, 1942

As the crowd streams down off the flight deck, Lt. Hughes walks up behind Hunt, "Hey, Samantha."

She looks back, "Hey, Shawn, just a sec." She keeps walking with the crowd until she steps into a dead-end passageway leading toward her stateroom and turns around, "That's better."

Shawn says, "We're leaving in a bit. I couldn't go without saying...well, without telling you goodbye."

"It's hard. I get it. You know my address, Shawn."

"Yeah, sure, but it ain't the same. I'm gonna miss you. Hell, never thought I'd ever feel like that about an airdale, but there it is."

She smiles, "I'll miss you, too, Shawn."

"I got something that might bring you some luck," and pulls a cream silk scarf out of his pocket. "I know pilots used to wear these things."

She looks at the scarf, then looks into his eyes.

With a rueful smile, Shawn gently puts the scarf around her neck, holding onto both ends and holding her gaze.

"Thank you, Shawn. It's beautiful. I wasn't joking about you writing. You better, or I'm going to pretend I'm mad at you."

He lets go of the scarf and smiles, "I will. I don't hardly write my own mom, but I promise I will. Take care, Samantha."

"Be careful, Shawn." She puts her hand up to wipe away her tears; too many goodbyes today.

"I will." He smiles and touches her hand. He turns and joins the crowd streaming by.

BLACK KNIGHTS CO'S OFFICE

Sam stands in the middle of the empty office, fidgeting, adjusting her uniform. Noticing coffee in the pot, she pours herself a cup, lifts it, and stops. It's a heavy mug with the Black Knights insignia, a black shield with a medieval knight, helmet on, outlined in grey. His drawn sword is tip down in his left hand, his shield grounded on his right. The Black Knight slash is across the shield, and behind him are two finger-four formations passing head to head. Above the insignia is painted her name, LCDR Samantha Hunt, and below it is 'Spike'.

She smiles and takes a sip of coffee and sits in her chair. As she's adjusting it, Admiral Lee walks in and shuts the door, leaning against it. "We're flying out in a few minutes. Are you going to be alright?"

She gets up, and steps into his arms. As he embraces her, she tears up again. After a long moment, she steps back, and wipes her eyes, "I'm going to miss you, Rick."

"I'm going to miss you, too, darlin'. I hate to go, but we both know I need to."

Grabbing a tissue off the desk, she blows her nose, "I'm a mess. I don't think I can do this."

Lee takes her shoulders in his hands, looking her in the eyes, "You can, hon, you can and you will. I need you out here kicking ass, so I can brag to the boys in Washington."

"Is that all I am, bragging rights?"

Lee chuckles, "You know better than that. You're a shooting star. You're going to blaze across the sky, making people everywhere wonder who and what you are. I'm just the lucky old fart who knows some of the answers. I'm proud of you, Sam. I'm proud of who you've become, but more importantly, I'm proud of who I know you can be. You can do this."

She rubs her eyes, "Now, you've got me crying, again."

He hugs her and kisses her on the forehead, "I have to go, darling." He turns and leaves the office. As the door closes, she wipes her eyes again and blows her nose. Tossing the tissue in the trash, she squares away her jacket and sits back down, picking up some paperwork. The 1MC announces, "Flight quarters. Flight quarters..."

CAG OFFICE

Carleton sits across from Holtz sipping coffee, "You and I both know she has my spot. Why did you let them promote her?"

"Just drop it, John. If you would have shut up about her when I told you to, none of this would have happened. You let that chip on your shoulder destroy your career, not me."

"You know she's going to screw it all up. I've been warning everyone that she's going to get someone killed and now we're really going to see it. CO, it's nuts. And why did they have to make a big production out of it?" He mimics Ren's voice, "An historic opportunity...bull shit."

"It is historic. I'm not sure she's ready, but neither are you, and it is what it is."

"The whole thing is just going to blow her blonde bimbo head up even further."

"Why can't you let it go? You're only hurting yourself, and she's doing just fine. She's a solid pilot and a decent officer. Just drop it."

"I thought Nimitz and Halsey would throw all the women out on their ears. There's no way congress is going to let them fight."

"That's up to congress. Meanwhile, we have a job to do."

"She's in my position, Jim. All these senior officers bowing down to her like she's special. It's a shame none of them were fucking her. I bet they'd kick her out if she was pregnant."

"Damn it, John, you know she isn't doing anything inappropriate. You just shut up about all that. Flapping your jaws like that is only going to get you in trouble. She's a good officer and like her or not, she's not stupid, thus, she's not pregnant."

"Probably not pregnant, you know, someone ought to put her in her place. Remind her that she's just a life support system for a vagina."

"Carleton, you're a fucking idiot. Shut up, just shut the fuck up about shit like that. You keep mouthing off like this, I will not even try to protect you."

"No one will do anything to me. We need pilots. When I kick some more ass over Japan, everyone will know I'm a better pilot. She needs to put on an apron and work at some truck stop."

"Just be quiet. Congress may very well pass legislation mandating that she take off her uniform, but you're not helping yourself now."

"Do you think she can lead the squadron? I mean really?"

"I don't know. She's new to it, but she has a level head."

"She'll fail. I'll see to that."

Holtz looks Carleton straight in the eyes, "You listen to me, John. Do not meddle. She will succeed or fail all on her own. Do you hear me? You do anything and your wings will not protect you. I'll throw your ass in the brig. Am I clear?"

"Yes, sir, I'm just saying, I expect she'll fail. I mean, we have 'Bull' Halsey running the show. There's no way he's going to put up with female aviators."

HICKHAM FIELD HAWAII

1848, 4 January, 1942

PFC Walter Duggery stops sweeping the end of the taxiway and leans on his broom. His buddy, Larry, walks up," Hey, Dug, can I bum a smoke?" Walt digs out a pack and shakes one out, "We better smoke off the field or they'll chew our asses and make us sweep the damn thing again."

"What's all this about? Who cares about a bit of sand or junk on a runway? It's just cement, fer Christ's sake." Then they hear a deep rumble out of the south. Looking up they see two large aircraft flying toward the field at low altitude. The grey aircraft fly overhead at about 500 feet with a deafening roar. The friends look at each other as the two planes roll to the right and turn.

Duggery says, "Damn it Larry. That was loud."

"Dug, those planes didn't have no props on them. What the hell?"

Then they hear a higher pitched whine coming from the south. A large twin engine plane, about the size of a B-25, comes in and lands, followed by another. The two planes taxi off the runway, turning toward the tower with a loud roar, the large props beating the air. Then the first two aircraft come in, landing side by side.

Larry says, "Holy cow, Walt, I ain't seen nuthin' like them, ever." The fighters follow the larger planes and open their canopies. One of the pilots waves at them and they wave back. After the planes are parked, the pilots remove their helmets, and the pilot that waved at them reveals tightly braided red hair in a bun at the nap of her neck. "Shoot me dead, buddy, it's a girl pilot. This war just started looking up."

USS CARL VINSON, WARDROOM 1, ALL COMMANDERS CALL

0900, 5 January, 1942

Spike is the only woman in the room and is sitting in the back with Swede. The Enterprise Task Force now comprises sixteen ships, and the captains and XOs of every command are in this room. Admiral Halsey, Captain Johnson, and Captain Murray enter, "Attention on deck!" and all stand.

Admiral Halsey walks up to the mic and says loudly, "Carry on," blasting everyone's ears. "Sorry, about that. Can everyone hear me?" They all chuckle and nod their heads. He continues, "Before we lay out the plan, I would like each command to stand, introduce themselves, their unit, and their XO. I'm sure you all know who I am. Standing to my right is my chief of staff, CDR Miles Browning. Next to him is Captain Chris Van Zandt, who served as Admiral Ren's chief of staff before I nabbed him."

Captain Johnson introduces himself and Captain Patterson, and Captain Murray introduces himself and his XO, and so on around the room. When it's her turn, Spike stands, "I'm Lieutenant Commander Samantha Hunt, CO of VF-154, the Black Knights, and this is my XO, Lieutenant Stephan Swedenborg."

When they've all finished introducing themselves, Halsey continues, "Right. The Carl Vinson task force brings a number of new weapons to the fight. We need to update our formations and our battle plans to incorporate the new systems. First, as most of you have noticed, the new ships are rather short on guns. That's because they use guided missiles instead. It's a rocket that can be aimed in flight. They are extremely effective against aircraft, but they need clear lanes of fire. We'll but putting the Long Beach and Horne outside the inner ring around the two carriers; Long Beach to port, Horne to starboard. In an aerial threat, the missile ships will orient toward the threat. The Fife and Jarrett will be out front and Commander Lamoure of the Fife will be ASW commander. The Vinson also has a number of ASW assets and Commander Lamoure knows how to use them. The supply ships will stay on the starboard side of the carriers and the rest of the destroyers will ring around the group. Questions?"

Captain Ellis M. Zacharias of the Salt Lake City asks, "Who is the AAW commander?"

"Ellis, I know that was your job, but it now falls to Captain Tenzar of the Long Beach. His radar and control systems far outstrip what our older ships can do."

Captain Cassin Young of the San Francisco adds, "Yes, sir, but do the contraptions really work?"

Captain Tenzar says, "My missiles have a range of 85 nautical miles and can engage eight aircraft a minute with a 90% hit rate. Horne, with half the systems, can engage four more. We will not be able, completely, to eliminate a persistent swarm attack, but we can attrite them long before they are in your range. Should we encounter Japanese jets, we are the only platform capable of engaging them."

Captain Young says, "Our gunners are good."

Tenzar replies, "I have no doubt they are. This isn't a question of skill. No gunner can hit an aircraft flying 1200 miles per hour at 40,000 feet. Jets operate in an envelope unlike anything you have ever seen."

Halsey interjects, "Gentlemen, we are all on the same team." He motions to Browning, who uncovers a map of the Pacific Ocean. "We will approach from here. During the approach, the Enterprise will do all the patrols and the cap, preserving fuel on the Vinson, who will maintain four fighters on ready

5 and continue ASW patrols. Once we are at our initial point, the Vinson strike group will focus attacks in the Tokyo area here and here and here. Upon the completion of the strike, we are authorized additional attacks, if it seems advisable. We will retreat in this direction. Vinson will maintain enough jet fuel reserves to fight for two days. I want all ships to keep fuel reserves at 80%. Questions?"

LCDR Sherman of the USS Dunlap, DD-384, asks, "Why 80%, Admiral?"

"If we kick over a hornets' nest, I want to maintain the option to make a hasty strategic advance to the rear."

Spike strives not to chuckle, and Swede quietly asks, "What's so funny?"

"He's quoting Wellington."

"So?"

"Those who know, understand. Those who don't, need to look it up."

Halsey says, "Let's break for supper. I want COs and XOs to split up. I want '41s and '90s at every table. You need to get a chance to know each other."

Spike looks at Swede, "Rock, paper, scissor?"

"Nah, I'll go," and he gets up.

She sits for a moment and realizes she should get up as well. As she's walking between the tables, a lieutenant commander says, "Steward, steward, I need some coffee."

She looks down at him and touches the gold oak leaf sewn on her right collar, sits down at his table, and sticks out her hand, "I'm 'Spike' Hunt, CO of the Black Knights fighter squadron."

He looks at her hand for a moment, then takes it, "I'm Joseph Callahan of the destroyer Ralph Talbot. How is it women are allowed to be officers?"

"The US military finally came to its senses."

"I don't see it, but what do I know."

A '90s lieutenant commander joins them, "Not much, if you're disparaging her. I'm David Crocket, CO of the Eight-ballers. My helicopters flew you over here. CDR Hunt is, right now, one of the leading aces in the United States. She has over twenty kills, and, she sank three Japanese ships. How many have you sunk?"

Callahan says, "Damn, my apologies, ma'am. It's just going to take some getting used to."

"That's alright, Commander. I get it. I do."

Callahan asks, "So, what do you fly?" as a lieutenant commander in khakis joins them.

"The F-14 Tomcat."

"Any relation to the Wildcat I fly?" and the lieutenant commander sticks out his hand, "I'm Wade McClusky, CO of the Fighting 6th."

She shakes his hand, "An absolute pleasure. You're right, my Tomcat is a direct descendant."

"Tell me about it."

Spike glows, "She's a supersonic, twin engine, two seat air superiority fighter. Her wings are variable geometry, meaning they sweep forward for slow speed maneuverability, and back, to go fast. And she is fast. She flies over twice the speed of sound and can climb to 45,000 feet in a minute. She's the best fighter built in my day, no matter what the Air Force tries to say, and she's a dream to fly."

"You sound like a proud parent. Maybe we can finagle a seat swap on our way to Japan."

Spike grins, "Let's see what we can do. I would love to give you a check ride."

"Hey," Crocker says, looking offended," I've been in the Navy twelve years, and I've never been offered a ride."

Spike laughs, "Well, you never asked. When we have enough fuel, and Halsey approves, I would love to give everyone a ride. It gets me in the air."

The stewards begin serving lunch. Crocker grins, "If I didn't know what you were talking about, that comment could get you into trouble."

She looks at him, "David, stuff it," then pauses, turning pink. "I guess that doesn't work, either."

The men at the table laugh, and Callahan asks, "With girls on the ship, don't you have trouble with...well, you understand, with inappropriate conduct?"

Spike answers, "It's not tolerated. Every person on board signs a page 13 order not to, um, comingle. Violating the order is career suicide. And anyway, try it and I'll break your arm." She smiles. The '41s at the table look at her surprised, and Crocker cracks up.

CHAPTER 40

BLACK KNIGHT SQUADRON CO'S OFFICE

1200, 6 January, 1942

Sam sits at her desk with stacks of squadron enlisted personnel service jackets on her desk, on the floor, and on a chair. She's reading one and taking notes when ADC(AW) Paul 'Mosey' White walks in and grabs a cup of coffee, then leans against the door jamb. Without looking up, she asks, "Hi, Chief. What's up?"

"What are you doing?"

"Reading jackets?"

"Why?"

"So, I know my people. So, I understand them." She looks up at him.

"They're all out there. If you want to know your people, why aren't you talking to them?"

"Chief, I need to know where they're from, and stuff. It's all in these."

"They know where they're from. All this reading jackets makes people nervous. Spike, don't go crawling back into your shell."

Sam looks down, "Chief, I don't want to mess this up."

"Look at me, Spike. You manage from a desk, but you can't lead from one. It's more important to know that Joe hates the rain in Oregon, but loves his mama, then it is to know his home of record is in Garibaldi, Oregon."

"I'm screwing up, aren't I?"

"Just like before, you're trying too hard. You're a good student, so when you feel overwhelmed your habit is to hit the books. You need to walk around and be seen. Talk to the guys, but mostly, listen. They want you to succeed, but more importantly, they want to see you in charge. Never second guess yourself or seem tentative in front of the guys. Doubt is a virus that can destroy a squadron."

"Thank you, Chief." She smiles, "How did you get so smart?"

"Chief Patterson, my first chief, he took a dumb assed Okie straight off the farm and tried to make a sailor out of him. I'm just recycling the lesson plan."

"Okay, teacher, I'll close the books and get out there."

CARL VINSON FLIGHT DECK, READY 5

1500, 6 January, 1942

Spike and Puck sit in their bird on ready 5, "Are you okay, Spike?"

"Yeah, I've been crazy busy, but I'm okay."

"Since you've become CO, I hardly see you."

"I'm just trying to get a handle on all the paperwork, and, oh my God, is there paperwork."

"You know, I have your back, right? I mean, outside the cockpit, too. It dawned on me that you have to keep some distance or people will talk. Still, I want you to succeed. I want to help."

"Thank you, Puck. I know and trust that. I have all these official things I have to do that eat up my time. I'm trying to get out and walk around the work areas, too. It's hard to find any break time. About the only time I have is when I eat. You know, let's eat together once in a while, that would work.

That's about as public as you can get, and I don't take work to the wardroom."

"I would like that. Should we arrange a chaperone?"

Spike laughs, "No, we need to be able to talk."

"I agree. I know you're missing the guys on the brain trust… and Dixie. How did you and Dixie get to be friends?"

"It's not my story to tell. He's just a really great guy."

"Yeah, he is. He was a good CAG. Holtz is trying, but he isn't of the same mold. I think you're changing some, too, now that you're skipper."

She braces herself, "Good or bad?"

"It isn't always black or white. You're doing okay, but it's like you're trying too hard."

"I'm not always good at the people skills. I'm always afraid I'm screwing up."

"I get that. The plain truth is, you do your best when you relax and be yourself."

"I've always been told my 'self' is a bitch."

"Whoever said that didn't' know you at all. You're reserved, sure. I get that, I mean, I'm Sioux. You've never been cruel and bitches are cruel. If anything, you care too much."

"Thank you, Puck. I'll try. I want so much to get this right. You know, we have come a long way since you gave me hell over not talking to you. I think, in the air anyway, we jell pretty well."

"I think so, too, can be better, but still pretty good."

"Let's be honest, this is all pretty new to both of us."

"Yeah, but we need to get all of it right. We only have one shot, like sky divers. If you can't get it right the first time, it's a bad hobby to choose." Spike chuckles, as Puck continues, "If you blow it as a squadron commander, there won't be a second female in the position for decades."

She shakes her head, "No pressure there."

"Spike, it's how it is. It's the truth. We have to get it right."

After a moment, she says, "Wow."

"We both know Carleton is out there campaigning against you. Most people just take him to be a malcontent, or a jack ass, but some people are listening. You have to show them you can do it all so well, even the doubters believe."

"That has been made extremely clear to me by several people already."

"While I'm not telling you what to do, I don't know either, I'm asking you if you will let me help."

"Thank you, Eric. I need your help."

"Another thing, I'm worried the Jap's may have jets, too. None of the fields in Taiwan or PI can handle jets yet, so if an airfield came back, they may have limited range. When we approach Tokyo, though, we could walk into trouble."

"If we aren't ready to face jets, we could be in trouble. Do you have any intelligence on this, Puck, or is it a hunch?"

"It's just a hunch, Spike. I don't want to play chicken little because I could be way off base."

There is a knock on the side of their plane. They startle, look at each other, then look over the side. They see Admiral Halsey in a flight suit, "Commander, I want to fly."

She turns to Puck, "Oh dear. We'll talk later. Thanks, Puck." To Halsey, "Have you completed the safety training, sir?"

Halsey replies, as Puck exits the plane, "Yes, I think the ejection seat idea is a fantastic one, but we're not going to play with them today."

Spike laughs, puts on her helmet, and keys the radio, "Gold Eagle, Knight 1. Admiral Halsey is standing by for a check ride. Could you inquire the flight surgeon as to my parameters?"

"Roger, Knight 1. He is cleared, stand by."

When Puck gets to the deck, he offers a hand to Halsey, who shrugs it off and climbs unassisted into the cockpit. Once he's in, the plane captain climbs up to strap him in, "Son, I can do my own harness."

'Handy' Washington says, "Sir, its policy. I'm supposed to check the straps. It's part of the preflight."

"All right, I just don't want to be mollycoddled." Washington finishes strapping him in, checks his helmet, and plugs him into the radio and G-suit systems.

On the radio, Spike hears, "Knight 1, Carrier Group 2 is cleared to 6g's."

Halsey, on the intercom, asks, "Are you checking up on me?"

"Yes, sir. I sure am," then on radio, "Are you ready, Speedy?"

"Standing by, Spike."

Washington checks her straps and kissing his fingers, touches them to the crown of her helmet.

She calls on radio, "Knight Flight requests startup."

"Knight Flight, clear for startup."

She completes the pre-startup check list, talking to herself, then starts the huge GE F110-400 turbofans. They rumble, then begin to whistle as they idle. She watches as the needles settle into the green, then "Gold Eagle, Knight 1, standing by for launch."

Speedy, says, "Gold Eagle, Knight 212, standing by for launch."

"Knight Flight, you are cleared for launch and unlimited climb."

"Roger, Gold Eagle. Speedy, we will keep it at 200 feet at military until we have 500 knots, then light up and go ballistic."

"200 feet until 500 knots, then light and zoom. Acknowledge."

They line up on cats 1 and 2, "Admiral, either cross your arms and hold onto your harness, or keep them on your knees. Don't touch anything. I know you're a pilot, but this is unlike anything you've ever known. Once we're in the air, I'll answer any questions. Are you good, sir?"

"Yes, I'm good, Commander."

The deck crew complete their chores under the bird, give the shooter the thumbs up and he puts his right hand to his chest. Spike applies full military power and checks her instruments, then hand salutes, and grabs the throttle, "Hang onto your lunch, sir." The shooter bends at the waist, touches the deck, and points to the bow, and the catapult is fired, accelerating the '14 down the deck. In two hundred and fifty feet, the aircraft is going 175 knots.

Halsey says, "Oh, my God!" The craft settles, and Spike climbs to 200 feet and slows, letting Thud catch up. His cat strokes a few seconds later, and in a moment Spike hears, "Spike, we're in the slot."

"Roger, Speedy." The F-14s pull vertical, climbing now on full after burner, and accelerate quickly past 5000 feet.

Halsey yells, "Oh, my Lord, this thing goes!"

They hold the vertical climb through 20,000 feet, where based on missile and fuel load, they start slowing. At angels 25, "Speedy, roll on our back, flame off. Let's show the Admiral the view," and they roll over.

"This high, this fast, Commander Hunt, I see what Nimitz means."

"Yes, sir, we'll be doing some acrobatics, so when I say grunt, it's important that you do what you were taught, so you don't pass out."

"I understand."

"Okay, sir, and in the air, it's easier to call me Spike."

"Alright, Spike, I'm ready."

"Wings level," and they come upright, "Okay, Speedy, we'll be keeping to no more than 5 g's. We'll do an Immelman up to 30, then a split S and a Cuban 8. You'll play follow the leader, okay?"

"Roger, Spike, you lead, I follow, 5 g limit."

She says, "Grunt, sir," pulling the stick back and they quickly climb to 30,000 feet. She spins the plane upright and level, then quickly snap turns to 45 degrees right and pulls again to start the split S. "Grunt, sir." Completing the first turn, she spins the plane 90 degrees left and continues the turn. "Grunt, sir." Completing the S, she goes wing level and starts pulling for the Cuban 8. "Grunt, sir." After 5/8th of a loop, she does a half snap into a 45 degree dive. "You okay, sir?"

"Yeah, I'm fine. Oh, my call sign is Bull. Hate it, but there it is."

"Okay, sir." On radio, "Speedy, let's head west about 10 miles, level flight." Then to Halsey, "Bull, is it okay for me to get permission for a supersonic flyby?"

"Will it damage the fleet, Spike?"

"No, sir."

"Sure, go ahead. Everyone is out watching the show, anyway."

She grins, "Gold Eagle, Knight Flight, request permission for a low level supersonic flyby."

"Roger, Knight 1, you are cleared supersonic west to east. Please fly between the Vinson and the Enterprise."

"Thank you, Gold Eagle, acknowledge between Vinson and Enterprise. Okay, Speedy, loose deuce, reverse Immelman to angels one and descend to 200 feet."

"Roger, Spike, reverse Immelman to one grand and descend to 200 and rattle their cage. Five g limit."

"Grunt, sir," and they snap roll and pull downward using

Fighting Her Father's War

their altitude to smoothly break the sound barrier.

Halsey asks, "How fast?"

"Right now, 850 knots and accelerating."

"Oh, my God!"

They pull out at 1000 feet, coming level and upright, then slowly descend, "One thousand knots, sir, about our top speed this low." Then, "Burners on, Speedy, I'm lining up close to the Vinson, you shy to the Enterprise. Let's pass between them at about 100 feet AGL."

"Okay, Spike, looks like a small hole."

They flash by the carriers only 100 feet off the water, "Burners off, Speedy, do a half Cuban to a horizontal minimum distance turn authorized up to 8 g's. Keep it at 1000 feet. We'll circle around so you can pounce on us." Thud pulls up hard, falling behind as she makes a gentle reversal. Thud peaks out at 3000 feet and dives toward the ships at 600 knots. Over the Enterprise, Thud rolls on his side, pulling the stick back in a tight horizontal turn. As he straightens out, Spike flashes by at 600 knots, and he has her, "Guns. Guns. Guns."

"Okay, vertical scissors to angels 10. Grunt, sir," and pull the stick back, climbing past vertical. At 45 degrees, she does a half snap roll upright and repeats. Thud is performing the inverse of the maneuver below her, making sure they do not collide. At 10,000 feet, she says, "Rolling out west. Okay, Speedy, let's give them a 350 knot pass at 500 feet. I'll close my wings, and you open yours."

"Roger, Spike, in and out pass."

"Bull, things might get a little wobbly. She doesn't like flying too slow wings closed."

"No problem, Spike."

They pass west to east, Spike above and right of Thud, his wings full forward and hers full aft. The cobra wobble is manageable at this speed. Speedy asks, "Thud wants to do a mirror pass. You level, and us inverted?"

"Speedy, there's a three star in my back seat, 100 feet minimum separation."

"Okay, let's make the separation horizontal and vertical to make it look closer."

"Okay, Speedy, coming around," and they line up for a mirror pass. "Alright, Speedy, on course, straight and level, 300 feet AGL."

"Roger, Spike, inverting now," and they fly 300 feet above the fleet in a mirror pass.

"Okay, Speedy, call the break."

"Okay, coming upright. Break. Break," and Thud pulls up and clear of Spike.

"Speedy, slow left turn and climb to angels 5."

"Roger."

"Okay, Admiral, I think we've done pretty well. How are you doing back there?"

"Frankly, amazed. Did you two rehearse this?"

"No, sir, he's my wingman. I love flying with him. Remember, sir, I didn't even know I was going to fly before you showed up."

"You both fly very well. You said both Speedy and Thud on the radio. Which is the pilot?"

"Thud is the pilot and Speedy is his RIO. Normally, the RIO is the voice of the plane."

"Okay. How are you finding life in the Navy?"

"I love it."

"It can't be all a bed of roses, a woman in a man's world."

"It's not, but I do love it, and I love the fact that I can make a difference. My dad taught me that it is never easy to do something worthwhile."

"Very true. Thank you for indulging an old man with a ride."

"You're not an old man, sir. Frankly, I'm glad I got to fly today. Thank you for letting me show you what this bird can do."

"I know you need to land in a bit, any requests for your Admiral? You need anything I can give?"

"Yes, sir, there's something you can give. I would like authorization to hold a contest to put a new insignia on our tails. It would be good for morale. My people are coping damn well, but it's not easy."

"Granted, that one's easy. Anything else?"

"Sir, one of my guys came to me with a legitimate worry. We have no intel that indicates Japan may have had a time travel event, but if they did, they may have jets. We should develop a contingency to deal with jets."

"Okay, I'll pass it on. Anything else?"

"No, sir. We're pretty much good to go."

"Okay, let's go home."

"Yes, sir, are you okay?"

"Oh yes, just tired of grunting."

"Alright, Speedy, let's go home. Gold Eagle, Knight Flight requests to marshal."

"Knight Flight, we are ready to receive." Flying loose deuce, Spike makes the cut first, "Knight 1, call the ball."

"Roger ball, 53."

They come in, wings spread, wiggling as she makes adjustments, and she hits the deck, catching the coveted 3 wire. The engines roar, then idle, as she comes to a stop and raises the hook. They park and Thud rolls to a stop beside her. She says, "Well, sir, enjoy yourself?" She opens the canopy.

"I see why all of you are nuts about staying in shape. It was fun."

"I love to fly, sir."

CHAPTER 41

1700, 6 January, 1942

After taking a shower and changing her flight suit, Sam is humming as she makes her way down to the hangar bay. As she swings around to go down the next ladder, she sees Carleton coming up. He stops, a look of anger and disdain on his face, "So, hanging out with admirals, now. Are you going to fuck your way to the top?"

"Excuse me," waiting for him to come up past her.

"There is no excuse for you," He stands his ground, blocking the stairs. A Black Knight sailor starts up the stairs behind him, sees Hunt and Carleton, and rushes back down.

"John, you don't want to do this, it isn't worth it."

"What? Now you care about MY career. The career you destroyed?" A door opens below them, and up the stairs comes Chief 'Fluffy' Bond. He sizes up the situation, "Hey, Skipper, I need to talk to you. Excuse me, Book." He places one hand on Carleton's shoulder and moves him to the side of the ladder. "Skipper, why don't you come down to my office?"

"Yes, Chief, I need to talk to you, too," and goes down past Carleton and the senior chief.

She pauses at the foot of the ladder, and watches as Fluffy leans in close to Carleton, "Mister Carleton, you don't want to get on my bad side. Be a good fella and behave." She continues on to the senior chief's office, Fluffy following. He pours them each a cup of coffee, "Trevor Gonzalez saw you two and came shagging for me. Bright boy, he'll go far. You okay, ma'am?"

"I'm fine. I'm worried about Book. He just can't let go. And he's such a good pilot. It's frustrating."

He gives her a measuring look, "Well, I'll be watching. You need to look out for yourself, too. I think he's getting a bit squirrely, ma'am."

"Yeah, that's what I'm afraid of, too. But it's not like good F-14 pilots grow on trees. You know, when I arrived at the squadron, I defined my flying by his. He made me a better pilot, but I can't tell him that. He can't hear me."

"You know, ma'am, you're alright. A guy tries to jack you up in a stairwell, and you're worried about how he feels. Most folks would just pop him in the nose and be done with him."

"Well, okay, I appreciate that. I was on my way to talk to you. I have an idea for a contest to help morale. I've permission from Halsey, so it's authorized. Anybody in the squadron can enter a design for a new tail insignia for the Black Knights. What do you think?"

"What does the winner get?"

"That's a good question. At first, I thought the winner would get to have the dress plane with the new insignia, but I don't think that's enough."

"The winner gets to have dinner with the skipper in wardroom 1."

"Well, for the pilots and RIOs that wouldn't be a big deal."

"Yeah, but they get the fancy plane. For the enlisted folks it would be huge."

"That works for me. I'm a little worried about the morale of the squadron, Senior."

"I know, I am as well. It helps for the crew to see you around, talking, and stuff. This game will help, too, I think. Who will be the judge, you?"

"No, the goat locker, it will be yours."

"No problem, ma'am. I'll set it up. Just to be clear, only members of the squadron can play, right? Don't want those Felix guys trying to make us the pig fuckers, or something."

Sam laughs, "You have such a delicate way with words."

HANGAR BAY 2

As Sam walks back to the ladder, she sees Newburg walking slowly, holding the arm of a tall man with bandages on his head. "Duck, how are you doing?" Newburg stands straighter and salutes.

"I'm taking MM1 for a walk."

"Of course. Petty Officer Hammond, how are you?"

Hammond slowly straightens up, "I'm getting better, ma'am, one step at time. Thank you for looking after Greg." His face still shows red from the burns on his left cheek and both hands are bandaged. His dungarees and backwards hospital gown show the bandages on his abdomen.

"It's more like Greg's been looking out for me."

"He does that. He told me about your promotion. Congratulations, Commander."

"Thank you. It looks like your healing."

"Feel like I need a damn walker. But I'm glad to be out of medical. Greg is taking me to see the Enterprise. One of my grandpa's brothers served on her."

"Oh, wow. May I join you?"

"Yeah, sure." Sam takes his other arm and helps walk him to the elevator door.

"So, you have family on the Enterprise. My dad was a marine

on Guadalcanal."

"Wow, a marine. Did he get pissed when you joined the Navy?"

"No, actually, he was very supportive."

Greg asks, "What happened on Guadalcanal, Ham?"

Ham rolls his eyes, "High schools suck today," then to Greg, "Bad boys go to hell. Hell, for marines, is Guadalcanal."

Sam says, "Good description. He never really recovered." They stop in front of the open elevator doors and steaming about three miles away is the USS Enterprise. "Well, there she is, the Big E." They stand in silent admiration, then see a blinker flash on the carrier.

OUTSIDE BLACK KNIGHTS READY ROOM

1600, 8 January, 1942

Sam opens the ready room door and catches Puck's eye, motioning for him to join her. Once Eric is outside, she starts walking forward, smiling, "Have you eaten yet?"

"No, I haven't."

"Care to join me in wardroom 3?"

"Absolutely, I understand the pork adobo tonight is excellent."

She grins, "Port adobo, that's the best you can do?"

"I'm sorry, I flopped at improv in college. Thank you for inviting me to dinner."

"Sure."

"I noticed you out and about more. How's it going?"

"I think a little better. I'm still drowning in paperwork." Puck grabs two trays as they walk into the wardroom and hands her one.

"How did Papa take the idea of an insignia change?"

"Well, he wasn't thrilled, but he's letting us do it. He understands we have a major morale problem. I feel for him."

Puck looks at the offerings, "Oh my, instead of the dreaded adobo, it's a meat loaf like substance and mashed potatoes. Dinner is looking up."

"Are you sure it's mashed potatoes? God, do you remember college food? It was a warm up for this."

Puck laughs, "It must be, but I ate well in college."

"Really, how did you manage that?"

Puck grins at her, "Rule 6, only date girls who can cook."

She smiles, "Oh God, a good one. So, what are rules one through five?"

"Now, you're asking me to reveal all my secrets," and to the server, "the apple pie, please."

"Apple for me, too, but may I have mine a la mode?"

The server says, "Yes, ma'am," and piles a couple of scoops of vanilla ice cream on her pie.

"Thank you."

Puck grabs two coffee cups and hands her one. They get their coffee and find a corner to sit. Puck continues, "Rule 1: Don't shit in your own nest."

"Makes sense."

"Rule 2: Never drink alcohol, period."

"I'll bite."

"Too many Indians turn out to be alcoholics. We lack the 'just get drunk' gene, or something. I'm not above the statistics, so I never drink, no matter what."

"Okay, Rule 3?"

"Rule 3: Work first, socialize second. I wasn't there to get a degree in human sexuality."

"Right."

"You asked."

"Just curious. I get it, because I followed the same rule."

"Rule 4: Guys are judged by their friends, so don't hang out with jerks or bums."

"Huge, haven't thought of that one, but, I think it's the same for women."

"Rule 5: Never concoct an impressive 'get laid' story. If I'm not good enough as I am, then they are not worth my time."

"Damn, you've got it all thought out, haven't you?"

"Rule 7: I borrowed this one. You can't fix stupid, so don't even try."

"There's that. Is that all, Puck?"

He grins, "No, college had ten commandments."

"Oh, ten rules, excuse me."

"Okay, never mind. I'm not trying to torture or offend you."

"I'm not offended. I just think the whole thing is both cool and amusing. I'm teasing you, Puck."

He smiles, "Okay, chalk it up to baggage from a bad relationship, which brings us to Rule 8: Never date a girl who needs a relationship more than you do. She turned psycho-needy."

Sam laughs, "Man, you had a hard life. Oh, and that last one is actually true in reverse, as well."

"Hard life, not at all. I only lacked female companionship when I wanted too. Recall Rule 3"

"So, you had to beat them off with sticks. Is that what you're trying to say?"

"I didn't beat them off. Well, except Carla, but she was psycho, like I said. Look, I know I'm not Robert Redford, but I studied at a pretty liberal college. All the co-eds wanted to date Tonto. At the time, it seemed the thing to do. I even tried to convince myself I was cool."

"Where did you go to college?"

"Cal-Tech, class of '87."

"Oh, I'm a Cal-Tech alum, too, class of '84. We were there at the same time."

"AE?"

Yep, AE. You?"

Puck grins, "CS. This is so 'Navy'. I have a BS in CS at Cal-tech. There aren't any words in it."

"You're so right. You know what they stand for, right?"

"Of course, bull shit, more shit, piled higher and deeper."

"Yep, that's it. So, where were we?"

"What?"

"Which rule are you up to?"

"Oh, Rule 9: Cause no harm."

"Good one, I like that."

"I was a jerk and hurt a decent girl to show off."

Sam looks at him for a moment, and nods.

"Rule 10: Stand against the little tyrannies in life, whenever you see one. It makes standing against the big tyrannies easier. And, Rule 11: Respect the little guy. We are all little to someone."

"Puck, that's eleven. Am I missing something?"

"Oh right. Eleven was in flight school."

"Wow, that's very cool, Eric. I like your rules."

"Some seem a little outdated now, but they have served me well so far."

"I don't see them as outdated. They make sense."

"I'm adding new rules, like, 'Don't tell your pilot where to go', and 'Know thine buttons to touch'."

She laughs, "You were right. We needed this."

"I'm working at it, Samantha. I want you to understand that I am."

"I'm sorry I've been such a hard ass."

"You've kept us alive, so far, but I think it's going to get harder. So, we need to get better."

"You're right, that they may have jets and haven't been able to deploy them yet. It has me worried."

"You know, I could be dead wrong."

"Yeah, but erring on the side of caution is a good thing. I mentioned it to Halsey during the check ride, but his intel staff dismissed the whole thing. I'm going to bring it up to Holtz, too, and see what he says."

"I agree, I just can't shake the feeling."

"Ever since you brought it up, I can't shake it either. It makes sense."

"More coffee?" and Puck gets up and refills their cups. When he rejoins her, "You know I had a professor ask me about Little Big Horn. I told him I was descended from a survivor of that battle. He told me no one survived that battle."

"He actually said that?"

"Yep, I told him the Indians did."

Sam laughs, "That's too much. It goes to show, doesn't it?"

"It shows that most still can't see Native Americans as people." He pauses, "I guess, I'm not thinking, either. I know you are proud of your family. My tribe didn't kill any Hunts at Big Horn, did we?"

Sam chuckles, "Not that I know of, we're from east Tennessee. My family is still getting over the recent unpleasantness with the north."

"Isn't the South still getting over that, um, unpleasantness?"

"Yeah, they're still fighting it, every battle. Going over and over it, worrying it like a dog with a bone. Unfortunately, it's still fresh for a lot of people. We're still fighting it, but it's getting better."

"Not in this time. I expect you'll find it is worse now."

"Do you think?" She pauses, watching his face, "You know, I have a photo of my great, great, grandmother. It's like looking in a mirror. She held off a detachment of Yankee soldiers with two dogs and a shotgun. They thought they were going to get her last horse and the last of the provisions. They say I'm just like her. Of course, when my mother says that, she doesn't mean it nicely."

"You have the grit."

"I hope so. I would like to think I make her proud."

"I look up to my grandfather and great-grandfather that way. I only knew my great grandfather when I was little. He played with me. He made learning fun. I remember that."

"Are you descended from anyone at Wounded Knee?"

"I think so, we sometimes look at descendants a little different, and few people survived the massacre."

"I read the book, quite an eye opener."

"We get the story with our mother's milk."

"That I understand, sort of like learning about the Civil War battles at the dining table with grandpa."

"We have a lot in common, Samantha. We both love, and serve a country that tried to destroy our ancestors."

"I never looked at it that way before, but you're right. Well, I've got a lot to do still before head finds pillow. A busy day tomorrow. Remember, we have ready 5 at 0400."

"I'll remember, thanks for dinner, Samantha."

"Thank you for the conversation. I enjoyed it."

CHAPTER 42

GYM, 03 LEVEL AFT, 1800

9 January, 1942

Sam is sweating, running on a treadmill in shorts and a t-shirt, when Lt. JG Lyle 'Packs' Boxter walks in with a towel slung over his shoulder. He sets up the treadmill next to Sam's and starts running. After a few minutes, "Skipper, I owe you an apology. I've been an ass."

She looks at him and pulls the head phones off, "What?"

"I owe you an apology, ma'am. I've been a jerk, and I'm sorry."

"No, what do you mean about being a jerk. I haven't seen it."

"It's true, and I'm sorry. Any chance I could fly with someone else?"

Still running, she bites her lip, "Okay, after our workout, see me in my office."

COMMANDER'S OFFICE BLACK KNIGHT SQUADRON

Sam is doing paperwork when Packs walks in, "May I shut the door?"

"Yes, get some coffee and sit down." Once he's settled, she asks, "Okay, talk to me."

"Ma'am, I'm Mormon. My church all but outlaws women serving in the military. I bought into the vitriol that Book was spewing. I know now, it's crap. You're a good boss and one heck of a pilot. I'm sorry for what I've done, and I would like to fly with someone else."

"I understand. I'll see what I can do, but no promises."

"He has it out for you, ma'am. I don't understand why, really, but it's like he's obsessed."

She nods, "Yeah, I'm worried about him, and I'm sorry you're caught in the middle. I wish there were more I could do for you, right now."

"That's the problem, ma'am, someone has to fly with him."

"That is the problem."

"You know, ma'am, at least the two of us work okay in the air. I'll put up with him for now, but if he doesn't come around soon, you'll have to do something about him."

"I know, Packs, be careful, and thank you," she stands to shake his hand.

"I will be, ma'am, I will be."

COMMANDER'S OFFICE BLACK KNIGHT SQUADRON
0800, 10 January, 1942

Sam focuses on the paper she's reading, a proposed test procedure for repairing and testing electronic cards that are normally replaced and sent out for repair. She's startled by a knock on her door, and a tall, thin, black senior chief in BDUs walk in, "A word Lieutenant Commander Hunt. I'm Senior Chief Hoffman, the ships Chief Master at Arms."

"Yes, Chief, how can I help you?"

"One of my men caught one of your sailors in a page 13 violation of a direct order."

"Really, Chief, sit down, and talk to me."

"I prefer to stand. I will be submitting a full report and requiring that he be brought to Captain's Mast as soon as possible. Discipline must be maintained."

"Chief, I said sit!"

The chief sits at attention. "It's a clear violation, ma'am, nothing for you to do, but discipline your member."

"Chief, until I know everything that is going on, I'm not doing anything. I want it in detail."

"One of your sailors, Petty Officer Joseph Cervella, was caught in a fan room with a female from Reactor Department. They were there for sexual purposes in violation of the page 13 order signed by all crew members. He's being held in the brig now."

"So, you caught them in the act, Chief?"

"No, ma'am, one of my masters at arms caught them."

"I see, okay, take me down to the brig. I need to talk to him?"

"Ma'am, we've not completed our investigation yet..." and her phone rings.

"Black Knights, Hunt speaking, how may I help you?"

"Hello, Commander, this is Captain Tucker from Reactor Department. It seems we have a problem."

"Yes, we do. I have the Chief Master at Arms in my office, and unfortunately, I still don't have any details."

"I have the Legal Officer in mine. Can you come down so we can talk this through?"

"Sounds good to me, on my way." Then, "Shall we continue this conversation down in the reactor office, Chief?"

"That's not necessary, ma'am, there is nothing to discuss."

"Let me rephrase, I'm going down to discuss this with Captain Tucker right now. You may join me if you wish."

REACTOR OFFICE, STARBOARD PASSAGEWAY AFT

Hoffman follows her down the four flights of stairs to the reactor office aft of the mess decks. As they walk in they see

Captain Tucker standing with a small female lieutenant. He turns to Hunt, "Thanks for coming."

"I hope we can clear this up."

"I agree," and he turns to the office staff, "Clear the room. Master Chief, you can stay." To Sam, "I think you've met Master Chief Hatzenbeuler?"

"Yes, sir," and puts out a hand, "Master Chief, a pleasure."

"Good to see you again, Commander, though the circumstances could be better."

The lieutenant, a small woman, reaches out a hand, "I'm Lt. Watson, the legal officer."

"Pleased to meet you, Lieutenant, I think," Sam smiles.

Watson says, "Shall we get down to facts? At 0530 this morning, AD3 Joseph Cervella and EN3 Paula Pressman were seen by MA3 Ball entering a fan room on the 02 level, port side. The MA3 apprehended both on a page 13 violation."

Sam says, "That's it?"

"Commander, as I'm sure you know, with men and women serving together, copulation has become a problem. It seems the fan rooms are the preferred spot. MA1 Ignatius is interrogating them right now to find out what they were up to."

Sam takes a deep breath, "Let me get this clear. You don't even have the facts yet, and you're already jumping to judgement?"

"I knew you would be a problem. Airdales always want to buck the system."

Tucker says, "Stand down, Lieutenant! Let me get this straight, and do not bull shit me! When your MA3 Ball opened the fan room door, what exactly were Pressman and Cervella doing?"

"As I understand it, they were fully clothed and talking, but we have reason to believe they were going to have sex."

Sam and Tucker look at each other, then back to Watson. Sam says, "Are we the thought police now?"

Tucker calmly says, "I want both petty officers here, right now."

"I agree." Sam gives Watson a freezing stare, "I'm calling my senior chief," and goes to the phone.

Watson says, "But, Captain, this is a criminal investigation, and we are not done investigating..."

"Enough, Lieutenant. Let me explain this 06, 03 relationship. I order you to deliver up the petty officers, and you say, 'Yes, sir', and do so. Are we clear, Lieutenant?"

Sam smiles, "Senior Chief, could you please come down to the reactor office ASAP?" She pauses, then, "Aft of the mess decks, starboard side. Thanks."

Watson motions to the CMAA and he leaves. Turning to Tucker, "Sir..." Tucker says, "No."

Sam asks, "Coffee, anyone?"

Tucker answers, "Yes, please, just creamer."

Hatzenbeuler says, "Let me help you, Commander."

"Sure," then, "Lieutenant?" Watson makes a sour face and looks away.

Senior Chief Bond walks in, takes in the scene, and goes to Sam. She quietly brings him up to speed. A few minutes later, the CMAA walks in with AD3 Cervella and EM3 Pressman. Pressman's head is down and Cervella's eyes lock in terror and shame on his skipper's. She smiles at him.

Tucker says, "Okay, this is how this is going to work. Commander Hunt and I are going to ask the questions, and we want straight answers. I want this to be clear, though, we have a lot to cover, so only answer the questions we ask. Do you understand, Petty Officer Pressman?"

She looks up, her eyes alight, "Yes, sir."

Sam looks at Cervella, "Do you understand what he said? Answer only the questions we asked. We don't have a lot of time."

Cervella looks confused, but says, "Yes, ma'am."

Tucker starts, "Pressman, what were you doing when the master at arms arrested you?"

"Um, talking to Joe, um, to Petty Officer Cervella."

"Were you in uniform?"

"Yes, sir."

"What were you talking about?"

"How I miss my momma."

"How did you come to know Petty Officer Cervella?"

"We met on the mess decks. He said his mom makes the best tiramisu."

"Is he your boyfriend?"

"I, um, he's nice, but, um, not yet, sir."

Tucker asks Sam, "May I question your petty officer?"

"Please."

Tucker asks, "Petty Officer Cervella, what were you doing when the master at arms arrested you?"

"Like she said, we were talking."

"Were you in uniform?"

"Yes, sir, full flight deck uniform."

"What were you talking about?"

"About family and home, you know. About how we'll never see any of them again," and he tears up.

"How did you come to know Petty Officer Pressman?"

"We met on the mess decks, like she said. We got to talking about home, and I guess I bragged about my momma."

"Is she your girlfriend?"

Joe blushes, "I would like that, sir, um" and turns to Pressman, "Please?"

Tucker turn to Watson, "As you see, Lieutenant, you have a simple case of two sailors that are homesick and embarrassed to talk about it openly." Palm out, he moves his hand in front of him, "You will drop the charges and move along."

Watson grimaces, tight-lipped, "Yes, sir," and leaves with the CMAA.

Once the door closes, Sam says, "Well done, sir." Then composing herself, "Okay, you two, the Captain got you off the hook. Now, we deserve to know what this is really about."

Abashed, Joe says, "What we said was true," he looks down, "but she wanted to see inside the cockpit of an F-14."

Tucker says, "Okay, and so?"

Joe gets even redder, "Well, we made a deal. I let her sit in number 212, 'cause its seat is safed right now, and well, she, um, she…"

Pressman, blushing furiously, "I promised him oral sex, but I couldn't do it."

Joe says, "She didn't, honest."

Tucker and Sam look at each other, desperately trying not to laugh. Tucker says, "Shall the judges retire to my office to discuss this matter?"

Sam nods, "Absolutely."

Once in the office, Tucker says, "I can't help but think they are so cute. But, we have to do something."

"I know, they are cute, and Joe is such a baby. The thing is, they are the tip of the iceberg. We all miss our families."

"I know I do, but what to do?"

"The punishment has to fit the crime. Oh, by the way, sir, if some of your people are that interested, we can do guided tours."

"That's it, we make each of them conduct training for the other department on what they do. Make them work at it."

"That works for me, sir. I have a question."

"Yes?"

"Why was Watson so hot to string those two up?"

"You need to keep your ear closer to the rail. I have no facts, but speculation is she is having an affair with someone on board, so she needs to seem tough on sex."

"Oh my. Thank you."

Tucker puts out his hand, "I know Klindt had a good relationship with you. I hope to continue that good rapport."

She shakes his hand, "I like the idea of nukes and airdales getting along. I made good friends in the brain trust and I miss them."

"Shall we break the bad news?"

"Yeah, they've sweated long enough. Good coffee, by the way."

"You can't have my yeoman."

CHAPTER 43

OUTSIDE HUNT'S STATEROOM

1100, 10 January, 1942

Sam's walks toward her stateroom, smiling and humming. Captain Van Zandt approaches, "Commander Hunt?"

"Yes, sir?"

"I understand you are still sharing a stateroom rather than moving into the squadron's CO stateroom?"

"Yes, sir, is that a problem?"

"Oh, no, Commander, it's a solution. Admiral Halsey has a larger than normal combined staff. We parked one of them on the Long Beach, but if we can use your stateroom, that solves everything."

"Your staff guy is welcome to it."

"Thank you." Captain Van Zandt walks away, and she enters her stateroom, "Congratulations, Gloria, you're officially stuck with..." Gloria, at her desk, hands over her face, is crying. Sam puts a hand on her shoulder, "What is it, baby? Do you want me to leave?"

Gloria blows her nose, shaking her head, "Can we talk?"

"Sure, honey."

"It's stupid, I know it's stupid, but...I forgot what my Jerry smells like."

"Yeah, it's not stupid."

"It is. If I knew we were going back, it wouldn't be so bad, but I'll never see Jerry again." She struggles to hold back her tears.

Sam squats down next to her, keeping one hand on her shoulder, "Cry. You need to. You've been holding back for too long." Gloria wraps her arms around her friend and lets the tears flow.

After a bit, she pulls back and wipes her face with a tissue, "What a stupid thing this is, my Jerry will be born in a few years and grow up to be just as awesome as I remember. But, by then, I'll be old with wrinkles and boobs that hang to my knees."

"Yep, your boobs will get that bad. I understand."

Gloria swats her, laughing, "You're not supposed to agree."

"It's a good thing being a member of the itty bitty titty committee. I don't have to worry about that."

"You don't now, but a few more years of 9 g's and you might be able to toss them over your shoulder. Thanks, Sam."

"I know it's hard. I really miss my brother, but it's not the same."

"You know, there are thousands of guys on this boat who are now single, and I won't touch any of them. It would just confirm the rumors. Guess, I'm stuck with batteries."

Sam laughs.

CHITOSE AIR FIELD, JAPAN

0800, 10 January, 1942

Lt. Koizumi sits in a meeting with his new squadron, twenty-four hand-picked pilots, some from the future. Time travel, he can't understand it, but he loves his F-15 fighter. It flies like a dream, with power beyond anything he could have conceived. He soaked up the information about his new aircraft, wanting more, but today is an intelligence brief. His thoughts wander until the intelligence officer, Major Miyamoto, says, "We have intelligence from Oahu that indicates Admiral Nimitz has seen the new American aircraft carrier. The Enterprise task force has sortied from Hawaii for an unscheduled trip, and we have a report of several large jet aircraft flying into Hickam Field. The jet carrier has not pulled into Hawaii yet, so it's whereabouts are unknown."

Colonel Nagasawa asks, "What type of jets landed at Hickam?"

"Two were the large fighters, and two were personnel transports."

"Then at that time, the carrier had to be within about 500 miles of Hickam."

"Sir, we understand from previous briefings, that the aircraft have well over a 1,000 mile range."

"And does Hickam have jet fuel to refuel them?"

"No, sir."

"Then, 500 miles, no pilot flies at the edge of his range. You plan a safety margin." He counts on his fingers, "We know it isn't Pearl. We know the Enterprise has made an unscheduled movement. We know the carrier is either undamaged, or only lightly damaged, in our last attack. It is also very unlikely they know about this base. We know the United States launched a carrier attack with medium bombers against Tokyo this year. I conclude that Admiral Nimitz has ordered an attack on our home islands. We must prepare him a surprise."

Major Miyamoto says, "Colonel, you assume much. We cannot know the intentions of Admiral Nimitz. Risking an attack of the home islands would be bold. Everything we know about him indicates he is cautious."

Nagasawa continues, "Cautious, yes, but intelligent. He may

worry that some amount of technology in Japan has also come back in time. The Japan I know in 1990 was very pacifistic. He would assume we would not have war fighting capability, and should we have it, those brought back in time, would refuse to use it. We outnumber the Americans two to one. Still to be victorious, we have much to plan. This must be an all-out effort to sink the carrier. We sink the carrier and the Americans are lost."

03 LEVEL PORT SIDE, USS CARL VINSON

1210, 10 January, 1942

Gloria and Sam are walking toward the ship's library, "Sam, why did Thud want to see us?"

"I don't know. It's a mystery to me." They meet Swede and Gandhi at the athwartship passageway and Swede asks, "Thud?"

Sam says, "Yep," and they walk into the library together. Thud waves at them from the study area where he's sitting with Puck, GQ, and Speedy. He has Jane's 'All the World's Aircraft' open to Japan.

Thud says, "Thank you all for coming. It means a lot, really."

Swede says, "Thud, can you get to the point?"

"Yeah, um, Puck and I have been talking, you know, so we're studying the Japanese Air Self Defense Force, you know, just in case. I tried to share what I found with intel, but they wouldn't listen. I hope that, well, maybe you guys would want to know what Japan brings to the fight if an airfield came back in time."

Sam says, "You have our undivided attention, Thud. Continue."

"Well, they have five major bases. Their main fighters are the F-4E and the F-15J. They have a total of two hundred seventy-eight F-4s, and two hundred twenty-three F-15s. That is a potential of five hundred aircraft, but we know the planes are spread out among five airbases. Not all the bases are the same. So if an air base came back in time, we would be facing anywhere from sixty to one hundred twenty-five Japanese F-4 Phantoms and F-15 Eagles. I think the air wing needs to know."

Sam asks, "You spoke to intel. Did you talk to Captain Holtz?"

"No, Spike, that would be jumping the chain."

"Thank you."

Swede says, "It's a long shot, but seeing as we're here, they may be as well. Is the Japanese F-15 the same as ours?"

Thud says, "No, they are the same airframe and engines, but congress didn't let the avionics and targeting systems be sold with them."

Sam says, "That's a plus. Good job, Thud, good job. I'll push this up the chain. Regardless, when we sortie, I want to carry the Phoenix missile. I'll ask about having the ready 5 birds rearmed now."

GQ says, "Cool. With the Phoenix we can kill them before we're in the same time zone. The design of the F-14 is based on carrying the Phoenix, and with its 100+ range, it's a big advantage."

CAG'S OFFICE

1740, 10 January, 1942

Sam walks into Papa's office and stands waiting as he finishes reading a report. He looks up, "Sit down, Spike. What's up?"

"Packs asked to be reassigned to another pilot. Is there any way we could swap pilots around with the Tomcatters?"

"Why does he want to change?"

"He's having trouble with Book's attitude about women, especially me."

"I would normally entertain this, but we are only a day or two from striking Tokyo. After the strike, we can swap them around. For now, I've arranged for Book and Packs to fly with the Tomcatters, and a Tomcatter, Ensign Tommy "Wingnut' Urland to fly with the Knights. Groovy isn't thrilled, but he gets it. It's the best I can do."

"Yes, sir, I understand. Sir, another thing, I'm still worried about Japan possibly having jets."

"I know, Hunt. The staff has decided they don't, though, so there isn't much we can do."

"I want to load two AIM-54s on each bird, in case I'm right."

"Don't waste a Phoenix on a zero, Hunt."

"We won't. Can I load them?"

"Yeah, go ahead."

BLACK KNIGHTS CO'S OFFICE

1000, 14 January, 1942

Sam, walks into her office and sees a note on her desk, and reads it: Bureau number 626 has issues. Come see, soonest. P. White. She walks into the squad room, "Where is 626?"

Lt. JG John 'Gunner' Harden says, "That's my bird. It's in the hangar, port side by the RHIB sponson. Why?"

"Thanks. It looks like there might be a problem. I just got a note from Chief White saying there are some issues. I'll let you know what I find out."

"Damn, I just got the radar working again. I'll be down when I finish this report."

Sam replies, "Excellent," and heads out. The ship is steaming closer to Japan every day and the status of aircraft problems is increasingly urgent. No one wants to miss the big show because their bird is down. When she gets to the plane, she sees a tool box near the left engine, but the engine access panel is closed. Not seeing anyone near the bird, she calls out, "Chief?"

A pillow case comes down over her head, blinding her, and strong arms grab and lift her from the deck. Shocked, all the air leaves her lungs. She feels herself being dragged. Forcing herself to remain calm, she knows she is in deadly trouble. Her assailant lets go with one arm, still holding tight with the other, keeping her feet off the deck. As he lets go, she goes limp and stomps his left instep. Growling in pain, he punches her in the right kidney. Screaming in agony, her world goes briefly gray.

Then she hears a door shut, and he grabs her with both arms again. Pushing her face down over a metal object, she recognizes Carleton's hate filled voice, "Go ahead and scream, bitch. We're all alone." Holding her down with one hand and his weight, he reaches under the pillow case for the zipper of her flight suit. The movement frees her arms a little and she lashes out, grabbing for his hand, and stomping on his foot. She gets his hand in an Aikido wrist lock and twists his wrist. He manages to pull his hand out, breaking the lock. "You want it rough? Okay, bitch."

She feels the flat of a knife, as he cuts the back of her flight suit. As she feels the knife leaving her skin, she stomps his foot again, twisting to get out of his grasp. He growls and punches her in the buttocks, "You'll pay for that, bitch." He tears the back of her flight suit, exposing her. She hears a door open and Chief White shout, "What the fuck? Get off her!" Carleton releases her.

She tugs off the pillow case, spins around, and sees Carleton bury his knife into White's chest. She registers the shocked look on White's face and lunges for Carleton as he pushes White off his blade. Reaching down, she grabs Carleton's left ankle, pushes the heel of her right hand against his left heel, and twists his foot.

White slumps to the deck, his back against the RHIB lifting arm. The knife goes flying, as Carleton fights to keep from falling. She continues to lift his leg, twisting and pulling back until his right leg comes off the deck, causing his face to hit the non-skid. She lets go and drops onto the small of his back with her right knee, forcing the wind out of him. Then she grabs his left hand and locks it up in san-kojo, applying pressure until his shoulder begins to dislocate.

Chief Gellar and two master at arms run onto the sponson, and she shouts, "Chief White's been stabbed!"

Gellar runs to him, putting his hand on his wound, trying to stanch the blood pouring out. White is gasping for breath, bloody foam running off his lips. "Chief, hang in there, we've got you."

MA3 Anderson says, "Ma'am. Ma'am, let him go. We have this."

MA2 Pickering on his radio, "Whiskey Golf Niner has a medical emergency in the aft port sponson."

Sam says, "Cuff him first."

Carleton shouts, "She attacked the chief and me, arrest her!"

Gellar says, "Bullshit! See her flight suit? The mother fucker tried to rape her!"

Sam nods, "Bobby is right. His prints are on the knife."

On the radio, the security officer asks, "What is the nature of the emergency, Whisky Golf Niner?"

Carleton, gasping in pain, "She's lying."

"Whiskey Golf Niner has a medical emergency."

Bells start ringing, followed by "Medical emergency on the aft port sponson. Now lay the medical emergency response team to the aft port sponson."

MA3 Anderson surveys the scene. Sam's cut and torn flight

suit, exposing her underwear, the stabbed chief, and her holding down an otherwise uninjured officer, and pulls out his hand cuffs. He bends over and cuffs Carleton, saying, "You have the right to remain silent..."

When the cuffs are on, Sam moves to White. Gellar is applying pressure to the wound with his now blood-soaked flight deck jersey. Tears run down his cheeks, "Stay with me, Chief. God damn it, Chief, stay with me."

Sam puts her hand on White's cheek, "Stay with us, Paul, stay with us."

White coughs up more blood, struggling, "You're a good one, Spike."

Gellar, "The medics are on their way, stay with us."

He coughs again, pain ravaging his face. "Take care...of...her...Bobby."

Sam, "No, Chief. Chief...I love you."

Paul smiles at her and his eyes go blank. Gellar shouts, "No! No! No! Damn it, no!" Wrapping his arms around his friend and mentor, Bobby sobs. Sam puts her arm across his shoulders, her head bowed. The only sound on the sponson is Bobby crying.

Corpsman run onto the sponson as Anderson and Pickering lift Carleton to his feet, his hands cuffed behind him. They watch, not wanting to leave. An HM1 leans between Bobby and Sam, placing two fingers against Chief White's throat. After a moment, he says, "I'm sorry."

Then on the 1MC, "Pilots, man your planes. Pilots, man your planes. Now launch the strike package." They can hear the sound of big guns from the escort cruisers firing.

Gellar says, "Ma'am. Ma'am, go. Make his death worth something."

Sam nods, "Yes, Bobby, take care of him for me." As Carleton is lead away, she runs for her stateroom, the back of her flight suit flapping open.

SPIKE'S STATEROOM

Sam hastily changes into a clean flight suit, her hands shaking so bad, she can barely pull up the zipper. She squeezes her fists, trying to control the shaking, and manages to tie her boots. As she shoves the torn flight suit into her locker, all her gear tumbles out of the pockets onto the floor. Then she grabs her helmet, G-suit, gun and vest, and snags the utility tool, combat knife, panties and diaper off the floor, finding only one of the granola bars with her shaking fingers. She runs out the door, leaving the rest of the granola bars she normally brings along on long flights.

OUTSIDE MEDICAL

MA3 Anderson and MA2 Pickering guide Carleton through the door to medical. Book is quiet, cooperative, and solemn. Pickering yells at the nearest corpsman, "Get a doctor. The lieutenant is going to the brig."

A few minutes later, Dr. Hastings walks out, "Okay, what do we have?"

"The Lieutenant is under arrest and we're taking him to the brig. We need you to do the physical."

Dr. Hastings looks at a relaxed Carleton, "Take the handcuffs off, son. He looks harmless enough, and he's an officer. It's not like he can get away."

Pickering shakes his head, "He's dangerous, sir. He knifed a Chief."

Hastings draws a deep breath, "You listen to me, MA2, this is my medical. I'm the officer and you're the petty officer. You damn well do what I tell you, or you'll get arrested. Do you understand me?"

Pickering turns to Anderson, "Go get the legal officer." He

turns back, "Sign the order, sir, and he's all yours."

Dr. Hastings signs the order sheet, and Pickering removes Carleton's cuffs. Carleton swings his right fist, punching Pickering square in the face. As the petty officer staggers, he backhands Hastings, knocking him to the floor. Pickering reaches for his gun, but before it can clear the holster, Carleton grabs his gun hand, forcing it down, and with his right hand, chokes the petty officer, crushing him against the bulkhead. Pickering's head makes a dull thud against the bulkhead and he slides down into a heap on the deck. Carleton turns, kicks Hastings in the head, and runs for the flight deck.

CHAPTER 44

FLIGHT DECK FORWARD OF ISLAND, USS CARL VINSON

520 MILES EAST OF TOKYO

1132, 14 January, 1942

The A-6s are launching as Spike runs toward her plane. Shrugging into her vest, carrying her helmet and G-suit in one hand, her flight suit is still partially unzipped, showing her green t-shirt flecked with blood. Puck sees her run up, a red mark and more blood on her face. "Here let me help you," and pulls up her flight suit zipper, and takes her helmet so she can get her G-suit on. "Are you alright?"

"I'm fine," refusing to look him in the eyes.

Puck nods, "Just like Doolittle, we've been discovered by a fishing boat."

"Okay."

By the time they're settled in the cockpit, Thud's plane is moving. A yellow shirt motions her to start her engines. She flexes her hands a few times, and starts into the familiar check list with Puck. Once the engines are running, the yellow shirt motions them forward to one of the catapults. In ten minutes, they're in the air.

On radio, "Tomcatters to assembly point Whiskey. Black Knights to assembly point Viceroy. Night Riders to assembly point Viceroy…"

Puck says, "Okay, Spike, it's on. Guess they're sticking with the plan and we'll escort the A-6s. Let's keep our eyes peeled for traffic."

On radio, "Puck, Speedy, I'm with you."

"Roger, Speedy."

CARL VINSON FLIGHT DECK

Packs is waiting impatiently as Book comes running up, "Where were you? We have a war to fight. Bird is pre-flighted, so let's go." As Book climbs into the cockpit, he sticks his head down below the seat, and Packs asks, "What now, man? Let's go!"

Book disconnects Packs from the intercom and radio by cutting a wire under the radio access panel, then sits upright, saying, "I dropped my pen. Okay, I'm ready." They strap in, start their engines, and are moved to a catapult.

Packs asks, "How did you get the shiner?" But, there's no reply. He tries again, "Great, the biggest fight of my life and the damn bird is glitchy." They launch and head to assembly point Whiskey.

KNIGHT 1, ENROUTE TO ASSEMBLY POINT VICEROY

"Are you okay, Spike?" She's silent. "Spike, talk to me. You have blood on your t-shirt. I know you didn't cut yourself shaving. What happened?"

"Not now, Eric."

"It has to be now. We're flying toward Japan. What happened?"

"Chief White is dead."

Puck digests that news, "What happened? Are you hurt?"

Spike, in a flat voice, "I'm fine."

The sixty miles to assembly point Viceroy are chewed up pretty fast. As they approach, there are already six F-14s and eight A-6s orbiting. Lizard, Pappa's RIO, on radio, "Knight 1,

Eagle 1, you have Knight Flight with Thud, Swede, Hot Pants, Gunner, and Wingnut."

Puck answers, "Roger, Eagle 1," then on intercom, "What happened, Samantha? We need to be talking?"

Eagle 1 continues, "I'm leading them in, and I want you above and behind to pounce where we need you. You are Knight Flight. I am Eagle Flight. Felix will be doing a fighter sweep up forward of us to draw off attackers."

Puck says, "Roger, Eagle 1," then on intercom, "Hot Pants and Swede just showed up. They are outside, high and behind."

"Thanks, Puck."

"Are you going to tell me what happened?"

On radio, the A-6 commander, LCDR Carl 'Booby' Johnson says, "Viceroy flight, this is Viceroy 1, sound off," and all twelve planes report in. Booby says, "Gold Eagle, Viceroy 1, Viceroy Flight is assembled."

"Viceroy 1, Gold Eagle, roger."

Puck says, "Knight Flight, sound off."

Gandhi, "Knight 309." GQ, "Knight 894." NOB, "Knight 626." Speedy, "Knight 212." ENS Douglas 'Cuddles' Grant, ENS Tommy 'Wingnut' Urland's RIO, "Knight 224."

Puck, "Gold Eagle, Knight 1, Knight Flight assembled." Then, "Sam, please understand, I want to help you, but you have to talk to me."

Lizard, "Gold Eagle, Eagle Flight assembled."

CDR Todd 'Groovy' Miller, "Gold Eagle, Felix Flight assembled."

LCDR Mark 'Faster' Harder, commander of the EA-6Bs, "Gold Eagle, Magic Flight assembled."

Lizard, "Gold Eagle, the strike package is airborne and ready to push off."

Halsey, "Roger, Eagle. This isn't the time for speeches. Go

make us proud. Good luck and good hunting."

Puck says, "We're strung out in right echelon. Let's make the turn."

Spike, "Roger, turning." The forty aircraft are in formation; Felix in front, followed by Eagle, Magic along each side of Viceroy, then Knight Flight, flying at 600 knots to Japan.

As they settle on course, Puck, "Your head isn't in the cockpit, Sam. Let me help you. Please, tell me what happened."

"It's hard, Puck. It's really hard."

Softly, "I know. You have to come back to me, please."

"Carleton tried to rape me, and he killed Chief White."

An edge of rage in his voice, Puck, "You know it wasn't your fault?"

"Doesn't matter, he's dead."

"Sam, it wasn't your fault."

"Feels like it."

"I know it does, but it isn't your fault. Please believe that."

"Thank you, Eric, I'm trying. Please, just keep talking to me."

"Can you talk about it?"

"What's our position?"

"250 miles out, Sam. When you share your pain, it allows me to carry some of it."

"I don't want you to have this pain." Then, "You're right," haltingly, she tells him what happened.

At 100 miles, they pick up faint radar signals. At 80 miles, Puck, "Okay, I'm pretty sure they have us on radar."

Spike, "Call it out. I need you to keep my head here, okay?" Puck informs the flight.

At 60 miles, they hear "Tally ho," from Felix.

Eagle 1, "Strike package, commence dive." All the aircraft in

Eagle, Viceroy, and Magic flights dive.

Knight Flight stays at 5000 feet above Viceroy until they are engaged, then, Puck, "Knight Flight, commence dive." The six aircraft angle down, throttling their engines back to stay in position. At 45 miles out, Puck, "Illuminate?"

"Yes."

Puck, "Knight Flight, illuminate," and all six powerful AWG-9 radars come on at the same time. "Spike, we have a lot of slow movers trying to intercept our boys. Let's bump up our speed and see if we can expose their bellies for Eagle."

"Roger, Puck."

Puck, "Knight Flight, 900 knots." They quickly break the sound barrier in their dive. Twenty Japanese fighters pull up to meet them, and as they do, Eagle Flight fires a salvo of AIM-7 missiles, and five aircraft disintegrate. Closing the distance, Puck, "Got tone. Two," then on radio, "Fox 1. Fox 1." Spike fires the two AIM-7 missiles and one flies home as they follow it in.

Puck, "Splash one," then "Two Zeros right, turning into the merge." Spike rudders over slightly and pulls the trigger. The lead Zero explodes in front of her, flame and debris flash immediately in front of the cockpit. The aircraft shakes violently, and as her canopy clears, they're pointed toward the sea. The left engine has flamed out, warning lights flashing, and Spike says, "Fuck!" Back in the moment, her hands fly through the drill of restarting the engine, while she applies left aileron to stop the spin, and pulls back on the stick to pull out of the dive. "One is out, restarting one. Sorry Puck."

Puck smiles, relieved, "Welcome back, Spike."

As the engine relights, she pulls back on the stick, rolls on the throttles and, "We're back in the fight."

Speedy, "Spike, Spike, you okay?"

Puck, "Yes, Speedy, we're good."

She pulls up to avoid crossing a Zero, takes a hasty gun shot at another and misses. He flies into Thud's cross hairs, and explodes. Puck, "Thud is below and right. I lost the others."

"Puck, where are the '6s?"

"11 o'clock low."

She tips her bird, looking for the attack planes and Tokyo Bay spreads out below them, with Yokosuka on the left and the dry docks of Hodogaya and Konan directly ahead. It's actually beautiful, with small craft moving among the larger cargo and naval vessels. A battleship or heavy cruiser is underway off Yokosuka and anti-aircraft fire puffs in the air. "Okay, got 'em."

"Zero crossing low."

She barrels rolls to miss the Zero, lines up her gun, and "Guns," making her third kill of the day. "Where's Thud?"

"Behind and left, Spike. Zeros, 3 o'clock low, closing the Intruders," and she rolls into a dive after them. Puck, "Tone," then, "Fox 1. Fox 1."

Spike fires her last two Sparrows at the Zeros. Then, Speedy, "Fox 1. Fox 1," and two more Zeros explode. Another flies into the cloud of debris from his squadron mate and also explodes.

On radio, they all hear the call, "Felix 541, Gold Eagle, return to base."

Rolling out of their dive and seeking more targets, Spike and Puck hear a clear tone from the ALR-67 radar warning receiver. There's a missile locked onto them. Spike pickles off chaff and flares and maneuvers violently, "Missile. Where?"

Speedy, "Spike, break hard left. SAM launch. I see a SAM launch."

"Grunt," and Spike rolls left, pulling a 9 g turn and pickling off more chaff and flares. "Thanks, Speedy," as the Nike J missile passes safely behind them.

Speedy, "SAM launch. A-6 above Yokosuka. Break right. Break right!"

Viceroy 5 drops four bombs on a heavy cruiser in dry dock. Lt. JG Brian 'Bismark' Duncan hears the warning and tries to find it. The Japanese Nike J missile flies at over Mach 3, and by the time he sees it, it's too late. The missile detonates just forward of the A-6, and it explodes in a fireball. His wingman says, "Bismark's hit! Bismark's hit!"

They all hear again, "Felix 541, Gold Eagle, return to base."

Spike "Puck, who's Felix 541?"

"Fuck, it's Carleton. He's flying Felix 541."

Then, Lt Mike 'Too Tall' Mohr, flying Magic 417, "Where's the SAM launcher?"

Speedy, "West of Yokosuka on a hill."

Too Tall, "This is Magic 417 starting the music. Everyone stay clear as we engage."

Lizard, "Gold Eagle, Eagle 1, what's the problem with Felix 541?"

A third missile fires at a high-flying F-14, but the powerful USQ-113 jammer on Magic 417 comes on, and the missile loses track and spirals down to the sea. Too Tall closes to 10 miles before launching an AGM-88 HARM missile at the radar control station of the SAM launcher. Going Mach 2, it impacts in less than 30 seconds. The control station disappears, and Too Tall, "Magic 417 to all units. Got the fucker. Can someone destroy the launchers?"

"Eagle 1, Gold Eagle, Felix 541 is ordered to return to base immediately."

Speedy, "We're in position. Want to do a strafe run, Spike?"

Puck, "Too Tall, we're in. Speedy, we're on your wing."

"Gold Eagle, Eagle 1, understood. I'll cut him free when I find him. Things are busy here."

Thud and Spike roll their aircraft nearly inverted and dive on the launchers. Thud lines up on the right launcher and Spike takes the left. They each fire a burst with their 20mm Gatling guns, and Thud's goes up immediately, with secondaries. Spike hits one missile, causing sparks, "Shit, missed, grunt."

As they pull away, Puck, "No, you didn't. It just took longer to go up." Behind them the launchers are ablaze, "Thud is high and right."

Then, "All units, Felix 1, fast movers inbound from the north. 90 miles out, at angels 40. Say again, fast movers."

Lizard's shocked voice says, "CAG says, Viceroy wrap it up and get out of here. All fighters engage."

LCDR Harding, Magic 1, "Eagle 1, want us to stick around and jam?"

"Magic, Eagle. Negative, Faster, you're too slow to play with these boys. Get your people clear."

Spike climbs and turns north, and Puck says, "Thud is right, high and behind. Hot Pants and Swede are closing us at three miles out" On radio, "NOB, what's your position?"

NOB, "I'm over Tokyo with Wingnut."

Puck, "Gunner, we're climbing for angels 40 over Kawasaki, heading north. Come east some so we can join."

"Roger, Puck."

Spike, "How many, Puck?"

"I count 40. It's a target rich environment and we have two Phoenix's on the rails."

"Set up a coordinated strike."

Puck, "They are Bricks, F-4s. We'll fire AIM-54s on my mark."

"GQ has tone." "Speedy has tone." "Gandhi has tone." "NOB has tone." "Cuddles has tone."

Puck, "Puck has tone. Volley Fox 3." They fire the twelve

Phoenix missiles at the same time. The Phoenix accelerates to over Mach 4 as it climbs up out of the atmosphere. The F-14s close their targets, sending mid-course updates to the missiles. Wingnuts missiles lose lock and plummet to the ground.

Spike, "These are F-4s. Remind them we can out turn F-4s."

Puck says, "Okay, Knights, remember, we can out turn these guys. Get in close and knife fight."

Bubba, Felix 1's RIO, "We are at 25 miles and closing. Where are your missiles, Knight 1?"

Puck, "Our Phoenix's will beat you there, Felix 1. Go ahead and close."

The AIM-54's, their fuel expended, drop down and hit the unsuspecting F-4's. Two of the missiles end up targeting the same aircraft. Both of Spike's missiles hit, then 4 more explode, as the Japanese F-4's turn to meet Felix Flight. There are 33 F-4's left as Felix Flight calls out, "Fox 1. Fox 1."

"Spike, Wingnut, my radar is out."

Puck, "Wingnut, pull out and escort Viceroy home."

"No way, Puck. My gun still works."

Spike, "Let him stay."

Puck, "Okay, Wingnut, stick together. This is a fur ball."

Spike, "Lighting burners."

Puck, "Thud is right with us, Spike, low and right."

Four Japanese F-4s turn toward the Knights, missiles dropping from their wings. Puck, "Missiles inbound. Chaff. Chaff."

Spike hits the chaff and inverts in a dive, the rest of the Knights following. Then Ghandi, "Fox 1."

Puck, "The Phantoms are diving on us, Spike. We broke lock."

Then, "Smooth is hit. Smooth is hit."

Spike completes a split S, and climbs, "Where are they?"

Puck, twisting his head, "8 o'clock, crossing left. Thud, above and behind."

"Climbing." A F-4 crosses in front of them a half mile away and she rolls left, lines up the shot, "Grunt." The AIM-9 Sidewinder growls in her ear, and she fires.

Puck, "Fox 2."

The F-4 rolls wing level and climbs as the heat seeking missile chases after it. Her missile loses lock and falls. Spike rolls right and follows him up, "Shit, Puck, this guy knows how to fly."

JAPANESE F-4

Lt. Colonel Hachirou Oshiro came back as the duty officer

in the 133rd fighter squadron. He, like his colonel, is fighting to prevent Hiroshima and Nagasaki. He has another thing in common with Colonel Nagasawa, they're both graduates of the American Red Flag Fighter School. He's diving on a F-14, when he sees another one invert and pursue. To his RIO, "Watch the enemy, Jurou. Tell me what he is doing," pulling his plane past vertical, giving up on his attack.

Lt. Jurou Yamada, two weeks ago a ship board radar technician, "He is following, climbing."

"Let us see if the American knows anything," and snap rolls back upright, beginning the vertical scissors, then snap rolls again, and pulls down.

KNIGHT 1

Spike recognizes the scissor and follows a bit lower, planning to get inside the next turn. Then, the Japanese pilot reverses into a dive, and she rolls up 45 degrees, slows the left engine, and rudders hard over to follow, "Grunt." She rolls and pulls again in a diving scissors, gooses both throttles in and out of afterburner, quickly closing the distance, thinking he'll break out of the scissors again. He does, changing direction 45 degrees left. She finds herself below and behind him as he goes vertical. "Grunt," and pulls a 9 g climb, triggering a the 20mm cannon, "Guns, guns." Her rounds stitch a line of holes across the right engine and wing, and the F-4 starts bleeding fuel and bursts into flames.

JAPANESE F-4

Lt. Colonel Hachirou Oshiro pulls the ejection handle for the first time in his career. As he comes to in his chute, he sees the F-14 winging away.

CHAPTER 45

BLACK KNIGHTS OVER TOKYO, JAPAN,

14 January, 1942

Spike pulls up, gaining altitude. Puck, "Thud is on someone high left crossing."

"Okay, grunt," wrenching her bird into a turn to help her wingman, "See any more targets?"

"There's a few bugging out north, but we don't have the fuel to pursue."

Bubba, Felix 1's RIO, "Anyone see chutes for Smooth and Chaos?"

LCDR Norman "Oyster' Osterman, his XO, "Yes, Bubba, they both have good chutes. We're watching them down. They're going to land feet dry."

"Understood."

Spike sees Thud two miles away following a F-4 as it falls. Speedy, "We stitched him in the engines, why doesn't he eject?"

Spike "Anything out there, Puck?"

"No threats."

"Call for fuel status."

"Okay, Knight Flight, fuel check."

The flight checks in, all near bingo fuel. Puck, "We're near bingo. Let's head for the barn. Eagle 1, Knight 1, Knight Flight is bingo and returning."

Nothing, then, "Knight 1, Felix 1, Eagle 1 has damage. His radio is broke. Acknowledge, Felix Flight is also RTB."

Puck, "Roger, Felix 1. Eagle Flight report in."

Eagle Flight checks in with near bingo fuel. "Knight 1, Eagle 916, near bingo fuel and escorting Eagle 1." Knight Flight and Eagle Flight join up and turn east, slowly climbing to 45,000 feet, to conserve fuel. In their wake, they can see several ships burning and a huge columns of smoke over a tank farm and shipyards.

Puck, "Knight Flight is feet wet."

Spike, "Puck, have Jedi take the boss straight back to the ship. Have Swede take over Eagle Flight as Knight Flight 2."

Puck, "Stinky, escort the boss straight back to the ship."

"Puck, Stinky, acknowledge. Escort the boss to the barn."

"Swede, take over Eagle Flight. GQ shift to Eagle with Swede."

Gandhi, "Understood, Puck, will do."

GQ, "Acknowledge, Puck, shift to Eagle."

Puck, "Gold Eagle, Knight 1, re-designate Eagle Flight as Knight Flight 2."

"Knight 1, Gold Eagle, understood. Eagle Flight is now Knight Flight 2. Felix 1, Gold Eagle, mark the status of Felix 541."

"Gold Eagle, Felix 1, he's indicating a radio malfunction. I'm signaling him to return to the ship."

"Understood, Felix 1."

Spike, "He's still out there."

Puck, "I know. Are you alright?"

"I'm a little numb." She digs out and eats her only power bar.

"I think that's normal. We did well, Sam. A little while and we'll be back on the deck." They're quiet for a time. "I'm concerned about Smooth, and especially Chaos. I knew him in school. He's Japanese American, and knows Japanese. He did some schooling there."

Spike, "Where's he from?"

"I think, San Francisco."

Then, "Knight Flight, Arco 4, we have gas in 30 miles at 104 and flight level 35."

Puck, "Roger, Arco 4, good to hear you. Knight Flight come to 104 and descend to 35."

35 MILES AHEAD OF KNIGHT FLIGHT, FELIX 541

When CDR Miller flew alongside his bird, Carleton signaled that his radio didn't work. Groovy signaled back for him to return to base, and Carleton gave the thumbs up. He was frustrated. He'd only killed a couple of Zeros and one F-4 with his Sparrows. That bitch was always somewhere else. He was running out of options, and he knew it. When they get to the fueling point, he takes his turn with everyone else.

COMBAT INFORMATION CENTER, USS CARL VINSON

1343, 14 January, 1942

Admiral Halsey sits in the flag chair next to Captain Johnson. A dark cavernous room on the o3 level in the center of the ship, the only illumination comes from the console lights, the status boards, and the one big screen NTDS display, front and center. The NTDS shows the location of all friendlies on a map that is ocean blue and land tan. Friendlies are marked in blue and enemies in red. It receives inputs from all the modern ship radars and some aircraft. Operators at consoles identify all tracks and keep them sorted out. Halsey asks Johnson, "How many did we lose?"

"Looks like four planes, three A-6s and one F-14. We have some damaged that might not make it."

"If they have to ditch at sea, we have subs out there to pick them up. Any idea how Jap aircraft we shot down?"

"Not right now. I think at least ten of the F-4s and probably twice that number of older aircraft. Once the air group is back on board, we'll do the debrief and download gun camera footage. We'll have better numbers for Admiral Nimitz tonight."

"Overall, not too bad, Captain." Halsey pauses, "What are those red dots on your screen?"

A technician shouts, "Air raid warning north. 48 aircraft, 200 miles north, inbound at 40,000 feet and 600 knots. Sorry, sir. They squawked friendly until I interrogated them. They're Japanese."

Captain Johnson, "General quarters, please. Direct the CAP to intercept. Notify the group. Clear the flight deck."

The distinctive gong sounds throughout the ship, "General quarters. General quarters. All hands man your battle stations. Up and forward on the starboard side, down and aft on the port," gong, gong, gong.

Johnson picks up the 1MC, "Carl Vinson, this is your Captain. We have 48 Japanese fast movers inbound. This is not a drill, so I need everyone to stay sharp and remember your training. Time on top, 18 minutes."

Halsey, "They must have dog-legged out to seas to come at us from that direction. Can we send the F-14s north to intercept them?"

"Excellent idea, sir," then, "Filliator, inform the strike package about the raid. Direct all the F-14s with sufficient fuel to the north to intercept the raid as it returns."

RM2 Filliator, "Yes, sir," and passes the order.

USS LONG BEACH COMBAT

When the alarm went out, Captain Tenzar ordered general

quarters and ran to combat. As he walks in, "Captain in combat." He looks over the displays showing the locations of all fleet units, then phones the bridge, "XO, take us outside the fleet ring and orient us broadside toward the threat." On radio, "Horne, this is Long Beach actual."

"This is Horne actual, go ahead, Long Beach."

"I'm orienting outside the fleet, broadside to the threat to unmask batteries. I need you 1000 yards behind me."

"Understood, Long Beach."

Then, "Jarret, Long Beach actual. I need you outside the fleet 1000 yards in front of me to unmask batteries."

The Jarret, an Oliver Hazard Perry class frigate has SM-2 medium range missiles. LCDR Robert Hilton, "Roger, Long Beach. We are moving."

Tenzar radios, "Fife, Long Beach actual. I need you to orient 5 miles from the carrier on the threat axis. Your point defense weapons are the last-ditch effort. Keep your battery clear toward the threat."

Fife's CO, CDR James Lamoure, "Understood, Long Beach, repositioning."

200 MILES WEST OF TASK FORCE, KNIGHT 1

Knight Flight hears on radio, "Air raid from the north on the Task Force. All Knight and Felix with sufficient fuel are directed north to intercept the aircraft as they return."

Puck, "Gold Eagle, Knight Flight is turning north with ten aircraft. We may need fuel after the engagement."

"Knight Flight, Gold Eagle, understood. We are scrambling everything off our deck at this time. Tankers will be available."

Felix Flight responds, then, "Knight Flight, we are turning north on my mark, turn. State fuel state and load out."

Knight Flight squadron reports in with enough fuel for 40 minutes of loiter, a few Sparrows and Sidewinders, and what's left of their 20 mike. "Knight Flight, Felix Flight, Gold Eagle, you are to form a picket line north to south with 30 miles of separation between each group. Knight north and Felix south. Once they show their exit vector, all flights close."

Puck, "Acknowledge, Gold Eagle, Knight Flight is the north group."

BEEFEATER 1, COMBAT AIR PATROL, 140 MILES NORTH OF THE TASK FORCE

LCDR Jeremy 'Frosty' Winters, CO of the Fighting Red Cocks, is leading an augmented CAP, consisting of sixteen F/A-18s of the Red Cocks and the Blue Diamonds. As they close the enemy, "Okay, Hornets, lock your x-foils in the attack position."

Lt. JG 'Jail Bait' Funk, Beefeater 6, "Red 6, standing by."

USS CARL VINSON, CIC

Halsey, puzzled, "X-foils. What is he talking about?"

Johnson chuckling, "It's a movie quote from 'Star Wars'. We have it on board. Sorry, sir, he's just trying to keep his guys loose."

CAP, 150 MILES NORTH OF TASK FORCE, BEEFEATER 1

Frosty, "Illuminate." Sixteen fighters turn on the AN/APG-65 radars, and Frosty says, "Tallyho 30 miles to our front."

A few seconds later, Jail Bait, "Frosty, they look like Foxtrot one fives."

"Frosty to Hornets. Boys, we're playing with the varsity today. We sold F-15s to Japan. Light burners," and the F-18s accelerate past the speed of sound as they close in the merge.

At 14 miles, they fire their missiles, "Fox 1. Fox 1." Both the Hornets and theF15s are firing AIM-7 missiles. The missiles cross in the air, two hitting each other and exploding.

As the missiles come in, the Hornets fire off chaff and flares, maneuvering violently to miss the missiles. Some of the Japanese AIMs lose radar lock. The F-15 is not as agile, due to the heavy Harpoon anti-ship missiles they are carrying. They're automatic jamming system does spoof some of the missiles, but five Japanese F-15s are shot out of the sky.

BEEFEATER 332

Ensign Walt 'Meat Head' Jones, Beefeater 332, does a quick barrel roll, firing his counter measures and bores on, maintaining his lock. Three out of his four missiles hit, destroying three aircraft. As he smiles, he hears a loud thump against his Hornet. It pitches up, then tumbles. Meat Head calls, "I'm hit! I'm hit! Punching out!" His F-18, hit right between the engines near the tail, and going 600 knots, disintegrates quickly. The rockets under the seat fire off, and his straps tighten, forcing him into the correct posture for ejection. He blacks out as the 20 g's of thrust launch him out of his crippled plane and into the 500 knot slipstream. The chair automatically rights itself, flying him up 500 feet, before it separates. The parachute controls know he's too high to deploy the chute, so he falls until the air thickens.

DIAMOND 928

Ensign Tim 'Water Boy' Beckett, Diamond 928, shoots down two F-15s. His smile of satisfaction quickly changes to panic as he flies into the exploding cloud of shrapnel from a missile. He struggles to control his injured aircraft, "Water Boy is hit! Water boy is hit! Double flame out." He gets his aircraft under control just as a F-15 rockets by, firing its guns.

BEEFEATER 777

"Skeeters hit! Skeeters hit! Punching out." ENS Jeb 'Skeeter' McAllister, Beefeater 777, ejects into the slip stream. He comes to at 10,000 feet, floating under his chute. As he looks around, he can see a column of smoke rising from the water, all that's left of his plane. He screams, "THIS SUCKS!"

BEEFEATER 946

Lt. Laramie 'Six Gun' Morrison, pulls up in a hard 9 G climb, trying to break the missile lock. He snap rolls right, pulls again, then snap rolls around to see the fight. There's a missile heading straight for him. He rolls vertical and pulls again as he feels his aircraft buck in the explosion. All his warning lights flash and go out. The controls freeze and he can't get the stick to straighten.

Frosty, "Six Gun. Eject. Your left wing is gone!"

Six Gun can't hear, along with everything else, his radio is gone. At 5000 feet, with his aircraft falling out of control, he ejects.

BEEFEATER 1

To his left, Frosty sees Lt. Victor 'Cat Catcher' Bibb, Diamond 767, desperately maneuvering to miss a missile. He flies into a cloud of debris caused by a disintegrating F-15, and his aircraft explodes. He's the fourth F-18 shot down. Water Boy is still fighting to save his plane.

The Japanese light after burners and accelerate. The F-18s also light burners, and pursue. The Mach 2.5 top speed of the F-15 soon outstrips the American fighters, which cannot exceed Mach 1.8. "Gold Eagle, Beefeater 1, they are now supersonic. Be advised the Japanese fighters are carrying Harpoon missiles on their rails."

"Beefeater 1, Gold Eagle, acknowledge. Harpoon missiles. Stay clear, Beefeater. We will engage."

"Roger, Gold Eagle. All Hornets turn west and slow to most economical. Water Boy, what's your status?"

"Double flame out, multiple system failures. Hydraulics functioning. Two computers down. I have a fire in number 2 engine, restarting number 1. I pulled extinguishers on number 2 and fire is out." Once Water Boy uses the fire suppression system, his number 2 engine can't be restarted.

"Understood, Water Boy, keep your head."

"Number 1 engine restarted, returning to base."

Frosty, "Gold Eagle, Beefeater 1, we lost Beefeater 3, Beefeater 7, Beefeater 9, and Diamond 7. Diamond 9 is on one engine. Sending coordinates. Did anyone see chutes?"

Jail Bait, "Frosty, they punched out clean and their chutes deployed, all but Cat Catcher."

Frosty, "Water Boy, are you going to be able to loiter? Don't think it's a good idea to fly toward the ship right now."

"Frosty, Water Boy, my bird is stable right now, as long as I keep it slow. I can do it."

"Roger that, Water Boy. Jail Bait, stay with him. Gold Eagle, we got five with missiles and one with guns. Sorry, we couldn't do more."

Forty-two F-15s continue to target with two Harpoon missiles each.

JAPANESE F-15 FIGHTER GROUP

Colonel Ichiro Nagasawa steadies his F-15 into a slow descent, increasing his speed. His Mach needle at 2.0. Looking out of his cockpit, he sees the forty-two planes to his left in echelon. This is the most important battle of the war. If he destroys the big carrier, all of its aircraft are lost, and the technological edge goes to Japan. Then, his beloved islands will never feel the touch of nuclear fire. He can see the American task force clearly on his radar at 120 miles, "All pilots, remember, hold fire until 60 miles."

CHAPTER 46

THE WHITE HOUSE, OVAL OFFICE, WASHINGTON, D.C.

0032, 14 January, 1942

RADM Ren, RADM Klindt, RADM Lee, CDR Richardson, CDR Warren, LCDR Severn, Lt. Hughes, Lt. Barr, and Lt. Denton are all waiting while the Secretary of War, Henry L. Stinson, Secretary of the Navy, Frank Knox, CNO ADM King, and President Franklin D. Roosevelt sit discussing the information they've received. Hughes leans over to Richardson, "Can you fucking believe this, Scott?"

Richardson smiles, "I know."

Roosevelt looks up at them, "Is there any way to prove all this? It seems too fantastic."

Klindt replies, "You could call Prime Minister Churchill, Mr. President. I would assume he'd have been briefed in."

Roosevelt, "Yes, I suppose. Admiral, what time is it in London? I'm afraid I'm not up to the mental arithmetic right now."

All four admirals start to reply, then Ren, Lee, and Klindt fall silent as King continues, "About 5:30 in the morning, sir."

"An indecent hour, but it must be done." He picks up his phone, "Joe, could you get Winston on the phone?" He turns back to the group, "So, you want to re-invent our entire economy, Commander Richardson?"

"Yes, sir, that's the idea. After the war, the economy should soar. During the war, we would have the advantage over every enemy we face. The country that evolves fastest, wins."

The phone rings and FDR picks it up, "Yes?" then, "Winston, I have a rather curious question for you. Did a Doctor Heinlein create a time machine for your Ministry of Defense out in the Australian desert?" He pauses, then, "How do I know? Winston, my friend, I'm speaking right now with the results. That is how." He smiles, "Yes, Winston, I'm quite certain. It seems we have received a 1990 American aircraft carrier out of the event." He waits, "Hmmm, I see. Toyota? Just a moment." He turns back to Richardson. "Did Australia fall to the Japanese? It seems they found a Toyota automobile at the site of the experiment."

The brain trust breaks up laughing, and Ren gets out, "No, sir."

SEAL SQUAD BAY, USS CARL VINSON, 1350, 14 JANUARY, 1942

The SEAL team sits quietly working on equipment and talking when there's a knock on the door. BM2 Steve 'Mac' Cook opens the door. Standing there is a gorgeous brunette in a flight suit, "Are you the SEALs?"

Steve, tongue-tied, stares at her breasts, and she puts out a hand, lifting his chin, "My eyes are up here, sailor."

"Un, sorry, yeah, we're SEALs. Got anything that needs killing? Ex-husband, um, anything?"

"No, Petty Officer, I need swimmers today, not killers."

Ensign Russel 'Triage' Jeremy walks up, "I apologize for BM2 Cook, he was just potty trained recently. What can we do for you, Lieutenant?"

Cargo Britches, "You know the Japanese are attacking, and we're about to have a lot of sailors in the water. We need SAR swimmers."

Jeremy says, "Yes, ma'am, where do you want us."

CB, "I will have someone waiting for you at the island door out to the flight deck. Bring flippers and hustle."

"My boys live in flippers." Then to Lt. Issa, "Abdul, we have a job. Saddle up boys, we're going swimming."

AFT MARK 10 MISSILE LAUNCHER, USS LONG BEACH

GMM1 Curtis George is in charge of mount 2. In the four years he's been in charge, he's actually fired a missile twice. The deck level hatch opens and hydraulic arms lift two white missiles into position. Gmm3 Franks, GMM3 Mont Blanc, GMM2, Wetten, and GMSN Kruger snap the fins into place, giving each a good tug to make sure they're latched. Then, the two missiles slide forward, rotate up, and wait just outside the doors. FC2 Luke does a quick check, making sure the missiles are talking to the ship and the gyros are spun up. He pushes a button to release the launch. The fire controlman in Combat also releases the missile, and the missile doors quickly open and the two short sections of track extend to connect the rail in the missile housing to each arm of the launcher. Then the missiles are pushed out and up on the launcher arms.

After the missiles are safely on the arms, a latch moves down to lock them in place. The rail retracts, and the door closes. From initial order to battery ready to fire is supposed to take 30 seconds. Preparing the next two missiles, they hear and feel the shudder of the first two leaving the rails. When the door opens, the acrid smell of missile propellant wafts in. GMM1 George is listening to the combat on the sound powered phone, "Kick it is the ass, guys. We're shooting down Japs just like Grandpa did."

JAPANESE FIGHTER FORCE, 95 MILES FROM THE AMERICAN TASK FORCE

Colonel Ichiro Nagasawa picks up the targeting radar from the American ships. He recognizes the AN/SPG-55 radar that several 1990 Japanese ships also used. It's only mounted on ships carrying the standard missile, extended range. "We are in range of their missiles. Dive now. Descent to 200 feet and watch for more fighters."

Lt. Koizumi, "I have a missile warning."

"As you dive, you will break lock. Watch and learn."

The SM-1 missiles fired from the Long Beach lose lock as the Japanese fighters dive below the radar horizon. At Mach 2, it doesn't take the F-15s long to reach their launch point. They fire their eighty four missiles at 60 miles and turn west, staying on the deck.

COMBAT, USS LONG BEACH

Captain Tenzar sees the inbound tracks of the missiles separate from the turning Japanese fighters. Their only source of tracking information the E-2C Hawkeye in orbit over the task force. Because the planes are under the horizon, they cannot fire upon them. "BM2, announce it."

On the 1MC, "Vampire, vampire, missiles inbound. Time on top, 6 minutes. All hands stand by to brace."

Until the missiles clear the horizon, they cannot shoot, so they wait. Tenzar looks at the map, "Horne, Long Beach actual, you are out of position, close it up."

Captain Rogers of the Horne, "The attack is already on its way. I'll have to fight where I am."

Tenzar, "Dunlap, Long Beach actual, you are exposed. Move to the other side of the Horne."

LCDR Sherman of Dunlap, "Roger, Long Beach. I will move."

USS CARL VINSON, COMBAT

Halsey, "Why is the Horne out of position?"

"Not sure, sir, looks like that destroyer is masking his batteries."

Halsey on radio, "Horne, this is Admiral Halsey, return to your assigned position."

"Sir, I can fight right here."

"Your batteries are masked by Dunlap."

"Acknowledged, I am moving."

USS JARRET, FFG-33, COMBAT

The frigate Jarret is the smallest ship in the 1990 task force. It's Mark 13 missile launcher is newer than the Mark 10 on Long Beach and Horne. It's capable of firing seven medium range missiles a minute. The incoming missiles are flying on the deck. They will be in range as soon as they clear the horizon. CDR Robert Hilton, CO of Jarret, "FC1, focus on the missiles headed to the carrier."

FC1 Dauntleroy, "But, sir, some of them are aimed at us."

Hilton, "I know, FC1, but our job is to protect the carrier. We've only thirty missiles, let's make them count."

KNIGHT ONE ON PICKET NORTH AND WEST OF TASK FORCE

Spike remembers Jedi and Papa are over the Task Force, "Puck, have Stinky line up for a forward pass."

Puck, "Stinky, Puck, what is your position?"

"Puck, Stinky, over the fleet. Papa is on final."

"Understood, do you remember how to forward pass?"

"Yes! Will do, Puck."

LONG BEACH, COMBAT

Tenzar watches the inbound missile tracks forwarded by the Hawkeye, but the Hawkeye cannot help with targeting. "Damn, four minutes until we can engage. Forty two aircraft, two missiles per plane, eighty four missiles, it's going to be close."

Then, "Long Beach, Knight 916, standing by for forward pass."

Tenzar shouts, "Yes!" He finds the fighters location on the NTDS. "Knight 916, come to course 352, slow to minimum speed and illuminate."

"Long Beach, Knight 916, I'm at 352, standing by to receive."

Tenzar, "Weapons officer, fire missiles on bearing 097 relative, 15 degrees above the horizon, maximum rate of fire."

Ensign Tyler 'Stinky' Lewis, Jedi's RIO, targets the incoming missiles which are flying straight at them, 100 feet above the waves. The Long Beach fires her missiles at a bearing well in front of the F-14. The SM-1ER missiles go supersonic within seconds of firing, peaking at Mach3.5. It takes just seconds before they're flying through Stinky's guidance beam. As the missiles turn to follow the new radar guidance beam, Stinky sorts them out to individual targets and guides them in until they hit. At the same time, the F-14 is flying toward the targets at 160 knots.

Three out of the first four SMs hit, the second salvo is four out of four. Third salvo hits three out of four. "Long Beach, Knight 916, splash ten missiles. We have to circle back to re-acquire. They're getting a little close."

Tenzar, "Understood, Knight 916. Thank you very much. We have it from here." A moment later the incoming missiles finally rise above the horizon, and Tenzar, "Direct fire! Horne and Jarret, engage."

LCDR Roy Smithson pushes the fire permissive and four more missiles streak off the rails. In seconds, three enemy missiles are gone. Then Horne and Jarret begin firing. Salvo after salvo from the three ships hit. Jarret is able to keep up with the two bigger ships. They hit four, then two, then seven.

FT1 Gilbert of the Long Beach, "Captain, failure to fire on mount 1, starboard rail!"

Tenzar, "Eject it and keep shooting. Tell the guys to calm down."

More and more Harpoons wink out on the threat board, but they're still coming. Tenzar, "Damn it. It's math, simple math. Tell the damage control parties to be ready. We're going to take hits."

The Japanese fired 84 missiles at the battle group. Nine failed to ignite or failed to track, falling into the ocean, leaving 75 Harpoons inbound. Knight 916 took out 10 more. The Long Beach, Horne, and Jarret shoot down 48 missiles, leaving 17 Harpoons tracking inbound with 650 pounds of high explosive death.

The Fife has one 8 celled RIM-7 launcher, the Carl Vinson has three Rim launchers, a rapid fire point defense system. The incoming missiles are at 10 miles when they begin firing at any unmasked missiles, and four more go down. Then the Close In Weapons Systems on Long Beach fire. The CIWS two radars target the missiles, then correct it's 20mm Gatling gun, until its rounds hit the target, destroying two more missiles. Last, the chaff launchers on Long Beach fire off, and the SLQ 32 jammer attempts to spoof the inbound missiles. Jarret's and Fife's CWIS and chaff launchers fire as well, but the CIWS on the Horne cannot, because it is masked by the destroyer Fanning.

LONG BEACH BRIDGE

The XO, CDR Arron Grey watched the missile battle unfold from the bridge. The bow is covered in smoke from the missile launchers, and facing the port bridge wing, he can see the missiles coming in as the CWIS starts firing. A missile explodes, then another. He sees one slowly drift downward, growing bigger and bigger. Tenzar on the 1MC, "Brace for shock!"

Grey shouts, "Brace! Brace!" He holds onto the bridge structure with both hands, his knees bent and his mouth open. The first Harpoon hits the base of the box five decks below him. The whole bridge jumps, and his legs piston upward, his knees bending to take the shock. A pair of binoculars lying on a shelf launch into the air, ricochet off an angle iron and hit him in the back of the head, and he falls into darkness.

NUMBER 2 MISSILE LAUNCHER, LONG BEACH

GMM1 George knows the missiles are close when he hears the CWIS fire. He grabs onto the missile rail support in the brace position. The Harpoon hits on the 03 level, just aft of his launcher. His feet leave the deck, but he manages to hold on. GMM3 sails through the air next to him, then the movement stops, and he finds himself on the deck looking at GMM2 Wetten. The bulkhead Wetten was braced against failed and hurled him twenty feet forward against the lift console. There is a jagged piece of metal protruding from his chest, and his legs are splayed at an impossible angle. George looks for the others. Franks is lying crumpled against the port bulkhead. Luke, furthest forward is struggling to stand. Kruger and Mont Blanc can't be seen. Blood is everywhere. Numb, George looks back toward Wetten.

Wetten blinks. Startled, George recoils, still looking at him. Wetten's eyes fill with sadness, and George kneels next to him, taking his hand, "You did good, friend." Wetten smiles briefly, and his eyes go blank.

MESS DECKS, LONG BEACH

MM1 James Walters, the investigator for Repair Locker 51,

braces for shock. After the first hit, the crew start to relax. Lt. JG Sherman Knots, the locker officer shouts, "Stay braced!" Then, the ship is hit again, one hundred feet aft of the repair locker. Walter's feet and legs feel numb, but he manages to keep his balance. The mess deck is a shamble of broken tables, broken picture glass, and fallen bodies. The starboard side fire main springs a leak and sprays water half-way across the deck. Finally, Tenzar, "Relax brace."

From the 1MC, "Propulsion plant casualty, propulsion plant casualty. Scram number 1 reactor."

Lt. Knots, "Investigators out, fix that leak."

MM3 Small, "Lieutenant, we just scrammed out. We're needed in the plant."

Knots, "The SCRAM was caused by a missile hit. I don't want any of you running into a fire. They'll have to fend for themselves until we can get to them. Investigators out!"

BRIDGE, FANNING DD 385

CDR James Calvin Bentley watches the Horne fire missiles from her bow mounted launcher. To his XO, "They're supposed to be fast, but let's take a whack at them anyway. I want to give the guns a go."

The XO, John Patterson, walks aft to shout the orders to the gun control station by voice tube. As the missiles close, he sees the Horne slow. Bentley, "Looks like the Horne is using us as a blanket."

"The new ships need to survive. I don't blame him," Their 5 inch guns begin hammering away.

Bentley, "Tell that to the Long Beach," as he watches the first missile hit the big cruiser. He looks over the Long Beach with binoculars, then turns to look down range. He sees a small dot growing larger, the missile almost invisible except for its exhaust plume. The dot grows, but appears motionless. Even an amateur seaman knows what constant bearing and decreasing range means. "Well, John, it looks like this one has our name on it."

"Yes, sir, we've done what we can."

Bentley lowers his binoculars, "Yes, seems a shame, though." The missile strikes below the ship's funnel aft of the bridge. The 650 pounds of high explosives detonates a split second after hitting directly above number 1 fire room. The blast shreds the funnel, the two boilers, steam piping, and watch standers. The concussive force breaks the keel of the small vessel and sends shards of steel shrapnel all over the ship. The next thing CDR Bentley knows is that his XO is gone. They were standing side by side, and now he's smashed up against the bridge fairing and all that can be seen of his XO are his boots with stubs of leg sticking out of both.

COMBAT, JARRETT

As the incoming missiles fly into the fleet, Jarret fires one last missile. CDR Hilton is watching the missile tracks on the radar. He is shocked when the CWIS above them starts firing. He grabs the 1MC and shouts, "Brace! Brace!" A deafening boom hits the ship and rocks it to port. As Jarret rights herself, the XO calls on the 1MC, "Damage control parties out."

Hilton rings the bridge, "Where were we hit?"

His XO, John Dallas, says, "No, sir. The Phalanx hit the missile, but it was so close we have damage from debris."

CHAPTER 47

BRIDGE, SALT LAKE CITY, CA 25

1407, 14 January, 1942

Captain Ellis M. Zacharias stands solid, looking out at the ongoing battle, his hands behind his back. "Lieutenant Jared, please give me ahead full." The conning officer orders the bell. "Lieutenant Dougherty, please remind our gunners we have friendlies about." To Jared, "Ahead standard, please."

His XO, CDR Art Olmen approaches his captain, "Sir, could I interest you in a helmet?"

Captain Zacharias accepts the offered helmet, with 'CO' on its front, "Art, what do you make of all these new contraptions?"

"Well, sir, if it kills a lot of Japs, I'm all for it. It seems our enemy has his own share of the new weapons. I'm afraid it makes warfare terribly impersonal. We can't even see the fellows who dropped these contraptions flying our way."

The Long Beach is hit, and Captain Zacharias says, "My God, will you look at that!" Beyond the Long Beach they can see more missiles inbound. "Please open fire with the 5's and 40's, gentlemen." A destroyer aft of their port beam explodes. then they see missiles coming at them. The 5 inch and 40mm guns fire in vain. "Well, Art, it looks as if we'll not be spared." The first missile strikes aft and below the bridge, under the number 1 stack. The explosion slams them both against the bridge cowling. Then the second one hits, just below mount 2, the forward 8 inch gun. The ship is still shaking when the third missile hits the aircraft hangar and rocks her to starboard. Zacharias recovers quickly, "Damage control parties out!" He looks around. Olmen is tangled in the CO's chair on the deck, "Are you alright, Art?"

Olmen disentangles himself, "Just some bumps, sir. I'm quite alright."

Zacharias offers Olmen a hand, "Then quit lying about and see to damage assessment. I'll keep us at station and render any aid we ca..." An explosion rocks the Salt Lake City. The bow rises half out of the water, a huge column of debris and smoke rising up. Zacharias finds himself lying near the aft ladder. Deafened, he struggles to his feet, looking for Olmen. He's lying right where he had been, shocked. But he scrambles to his feet and looks forward. He shouts silently at his captain, motioning forward. But Zacharias is looking for his missing helmet, finding it with a large dent in its side. He tosses it aside and puts a hand to his head. It comes back wet with blood. Olmen grabs Zacharias, pointing to the bow, and Zacharias finally looks forward. The Salt Lake City is missing from just forward of mount 82.

BRIDGE, DUNLAP, DD 384

LCDR Leonard Sherman assumed command of the Mahan class destroyer just four months ago in Pearl. He's proud of his plucky little ship. As the missiles rise over the horizon, he orders the 5 inch guns to open fire. The rounds are landing behind the missiles. Sherman says on the voice tube, "Aim short," then shouts to gun control, "Tell Donny to get the 40 going."

"Aye, sir." The twin 40mm AA guns aft start shooting as well, adding their rapid staccato to the rhythmic booms of the 5 inch guns. He's diverted for just a moment as he sees the Long Beach take a hit, then turns back to the threat. At nearly

600 miles an hour, a Harpoon slams into the hull below the 40mm mount, passing well into the ship before it detonates. The force of the blast staggers him, but he remains standing, and calmly says, "Damage control parties out."

He puts his binoculars back to his eyes, looking for more missiles. Seeing none, he looks briefly over the fleet. There's a column of black smoke from the bow of the Salt Lake City and the cruiser, Long Beach, is on fire.

His XO runs up to him, saluting, "Captain, I think we're a gonner, sir."

Sherman looks at Lt. Ulrich, "Stop that kind of talk, Lieutenant. What's the damage?"

"Sir, number 2 engine room is flooding, the hull is bent at the impact point and both shafts are seized. Fires are out in the aft boilers with steam ruptures, and the 40mm is over the side. It's rough, sir."

Sherman looks over the damage from the bridge, and sees the stern moving separate from the bow in the waves. "Yes, XO, I see your point. We're broken. Lieutenant, prepare to abandon ship. I need to call the Admiral."

BRIDGE, USS SAN FRANCISCO

Captain Cassin Young stands on the port bridge wing wearing his helmet and studying the sky to port, his cigarette nearly forgotten in his mouth. His XO, CDR Jenkins, "Sir, you should retire to the conning tower, you'll be safer."

Young lowers his binoculars and looks at Jenkins, "Safer than my men? I do not think so. I need to see in order to fight my ship. You go in there, if anything happens to me, then you must survive. Lieutenant Smith, get the AA guns firing."

"Sir, you're the Captain, you were hero enough on the Vestal in Pearl. Please, take cover."

Young, still studying the horizon, "You won't give up, will

you? The missiles are nearly here. See the Long Beach? Your point is now irrelevant." None of the 5 inch or 40mm rounds they fire hit an inbound missile. A Harpoon hits the San Francisco right below the number 2 turret, and she shakes as a ball of flame erupts. Jenkins in thrown off his feet and Young is staggered. He picks up the 1MC, "Damage control parties out. One hit port side below mount 82."

CENTRAL CONTROL STATION, FIFE, DD 991

On a Spruance class destroyer, the central control station is the heart of damage control and propulsion control systems. Located two decks below the combat information center and three decks below the bridge, the chief engineer is the lord of this domain. LCDR Peter Gregory would like a window. He has a repeater for course and speed near his station. He can feel the ship shudder as the aft RIM-7 launcher starts firing. The ten mile range of the sea sparrow missile means the Harpoons are close. A few seconds later, the CIWS starts firing, and the CO, CDR Lamoure, shouts on the 1MC, "Brace! Brace!"

Just as in training, he and his crew hold on to something solid, waiting. Then the missile hits two decks above with a massive thump. He comes to in darkness. Somehow, he's lying on the deck with no memory of falling. He tries to move and pain shoots from his abdomen to his neck. There's something on top of him, and he can feel pain in his legs. It hurts to breath. Alarms are flashing and the propulsion and auxiliary control console has smoke pouring out of it. He can feel a fire somewhere behind and smell its acrid smoke.

The only person he sees is HT1 Gorki, lying lifeless a few feet away. Then he feels a breeze and looks up to see daylight. Odd, CIC and the bridge should be above him, not daylight. He sees movement and someone in firefighting equipment walks toward him with a light. The investigator shines his light over the damage and Gregory can see more bodies. Then the light settles on his face, "We have a live one!"

CIC, USS CARL VINSON

Halsey and Johnson watch the attack unfold on the screen. The surreal images of little dots moving across a screen representing death and destruction captivate Halsey. Watching the outbound missiles meet the inbound tracks, causing both to wink out, he asks, "Do you think we'll get them all?"

"I doubt it, sir, but we'll get most of them." They watch as inbound dots merge with the Long Beach, and then with other ships. "Long Beach reports two hits. She's on fire, sir."

"Very well, inform Eightballer 1, there may be sailors in the water."

"Yes, sir."

Looking back at the threat board, he picks up the 1MC, "All hands brace for shock. Brace. Brace." They feel a sharp jolt. Still watching the threat board, Johnson says, "Relax brace. Damage control parties out. Now muster the rescue and assistance detail in hangar bay 2."

"Captain, PRIFLY, we have wounded birds inbound. Can we land them?"

"Did the missile FOD the deck?"

The air boss, CDR Forrester, "Sir, I don't think they can wait."

"Right, receive them, but walk down the deck as soon as possible."

BLACK KNIGHT ENLISTED BERTHING, USS CARL VINSON

The missile hits just below the forward port CIWS sponson, obliterating the control station and starting fires in the 03 level berthing and the 02 level store rooms and ventilation spaces. Hammond is the only one in the Black Knight berthing spaces when the missile hits. Kicked out of medical, with nowhere else to go, he'd gone to the squadron berthing.

Then he hears "Brace! Brace!" on the 1MC. "Shit! Not again." He assumes the brace position against an upright, holding as tight as he can with his burned hands. The missile hits about sixty feet from him, throwing him onto a chair, then onto the deck. Raising himself up to his hands and knees, dazed and half-blinded, he sees flames outboard.

"Here we go," he pushes himself to his feet, and stumbles too the fire hose storage rack. He grabs it, and holding the nozzle in the crook of his arm, throws out the hose, trying to fake it. "It never works right," so, he walks along the hose, kicking it straight, until it's safe to charge. Then he opens the plug valve, holding tight to the nozzle.

Blood is running out of his bandages as he gets water to the nozzle. He pulls back the bale and starts spraying down the fire, shouting, "I'm not losing another ship, damn you!"

ON APPROACH TO CARL VINSON

Ensign Tim 'Water Boy' Beckett is sweating in his helmet, but he can't wipe it out of his eyes as he struggles to control his bird. He has only one engine. If he fails to catch the wire on the first pass, there will not be a second. There is just not enough power. He lowers the landing gear and slows his air-craft, and the whole plane starts shaking. On the downwind leg, he calls in, "Gold Eagle, Diamond 928. Is my gear down?"

"Roger, Diamond 928, your gear is down."

"Understood, my gear indicator failed to light. Making the break."

"Do you want the barricade, Diamond 928."

"Negative, there are wounded birds behind me. I'll make it or I won't."

"Roger, call the ball."

"Roger, ball, 41."

Beckett's bird slams onto the deck, catching a 2 wire. As he hits, an engine access hatch swings down, scraping and crumping against the deck, throwing sparks and igniting the fuel pouring from the damaged engine. As he rolls forward, a yellow shirt motions him to stop and fire crews rush toward him, laying down foam. The foam floods his running engine and it flames out. With Tim holding firmly on the brakes, they soon have the fire out. They hook him up to a tractor and pull him out of the landing area. When he finally opens his canopy, he can smell the acrid smoke from his own aircraft mingling with the smells from the missile hit forward.

JAPANESE F-15 FIGHTER GROUP,
80 MILES NORTH OF THE TASK FORCE AT 5000 FEET

Colonel Ichiro Nagasawa slows his fighter to subsonic to conserve fuel, slowly climbing to altitude for the long flight home. "Tighten up the formation and keep your eyes outside the cockpit. We are going to face more fighters and these will be angry, because we are destroying their home."

KNIGHT FLIGHT, 110 MILES NORTH OF TASK FORCE AT 35,000 FEET

With most of their medium and long-range missiles expended, the Knights know they are going into a knife fight. Then, "All units, Ghost Rider 207, the Japanese are climbing out of angels 5, at 300 degrees. They are 30 miles in front of Knight Flight."

At twenty miles, Spike orders, "Invert and attack!" The fighters invert and pull down in a reverse Immelman. Like gyre hawks, they pounce on the Japanese, breaking the speed of sound. The enemies only option, go vertical to meet them.

Calls of "Fox 1," and "Fox 2," can be heard as Knight and Felix flights use the last of their missiles. Several F-15s are hit, one losing a wing and spinning out of control, shedding parts as it falls.

Puck, "Our squadron is all in a line right." They merge at Mach 1.8 with the climbing F-15s.

Speedy, "Guns. Guns," as they fire at a '15 as it flashes by.

Gandhi, "Don't waste ammo, Thud. You can't hit anything at this speed." Then the F-15 Thud fired upon catches on fire, staggers in the air, and falls.

Spike, "Grunt," and they pull out of the dive to pursue the F-15s. As the g's ease up, she sees the falling enemy plane, "My God, that boy can shoot!"

Puck, "Lucky he didn't fly into his target. Spike, crossing left, high."

She rolls left, "Grunt." As the F-15 she's chasing rolls wings level and starts to climb, she pickles one off, "Fox 2." The missile flies right up his left engine and detonates, taking most of the tail surfaces with it and the '15 pitches forward going into a death spiral.

Then LDCR Todd 'Groovy' Miller, Felix 1, "Spike, Felix is in. Watch for us."

Puck, "Roger, Groovy," and the fight devolves into a classic fur ball.

Speedy, "Spike, you have one on your tail, break right."

Spike, "Grunt," and rolls right, pulling 8 g's into a horizontal barrel roll.

Puck, "He overshot. Thud is on him, high and left."

Spike reverses left, rolling in and out of burners, "Thud is in a sandwich."

Puck, "Thud, you have one on your tail."

Thud, in a tight left turn, trying to line up a shot. A second F-15 is trying to line up on Thud. Spike rolls into the same turn, trying to line up on the second '15. In a 9 G turn,

Speedy, "Almost there."

Spike, "Tell Thud to yo-yo when they break right."

Puck, "How do you know..." The lead '15 rolls right, just as the trailing one does the same. Puck, "Thud, yo-yo right." Thud rolls right and up, into a barrel roll. As he climbs, the rounds meant for him, pass below. Spike fires her last sidewinder at the following '15 and watches it explode. Puck, "Shit Spike, you're good."

LT. JG Truman 'Johnny' Walker, "Bug is hit! Bug is hit!"

Spike, "Thanks." She climbs to miss debris. Another F-15 passes near her in a dive. She inverts and gives chase, "Grunt."

Puck, "Thud is back on the lead '15, 5 o'clock high."

JAPANESE F-15

Lt. Kenzo Koizumi saw his first missile fly straight into an American fighter. He smiles as it explodes. He inverts and dives at the Americans below him. He isn't worried about his wingman because he is flight lead. It's Yosho's job to keep up. Passing close to an F-14, he sees it invert and knows it is giving chase. He rolls 45 degrees and climbs into the yo-yo. The F-14 stays with him, so he repeats it, varying the exact angles, trying to throw it off.

KNIGHT 1

Spike completes the first yo-yo, closing the '15. Puck, "Thud is up three thousand. I don't see a wingman. We're clear to get this guy."

Spike quickly inverts, adjusts to the new line the Japanese is taking and nearly has the shot, "Next pass, I'll have him."

Puck, "Thud got his!" They hear the tone of a targeting radar and he twists his head to see behind, "Break right!"

Spike rolls the bird, pulling right at 9 g's, "Grunt." She drops chaff and flares, "Where is he?"

Puck, "A '14 on our 6. What the hell?"

Spike, "Fuck!" Wrenching her fighter in a tight barrel roll, she pops up in a scissors. As she climbs, she sees tracers pass beneath them, "It's Carleton."

JAPANESE F-15

Koizumi is amazed. He knew he was in trouble, and then another F-14 engaged the one on his tail. He pulls up into a large yo-yo to let the American pass beneath him. As the lead fighter climbs, he sees a chance to roll in behind the trailing one.

KNIGHT 212

Speedy, "Puck, who's on your ass? We're coming." Thud inverts and dives to aid his wingman.

JAPANESE F-15

Colonel Nagasawa is inverted above the F-14 and sees it dive. He sees two F-14s in the yo-yo and another F-15 trying to engage. He knows the path he must take, and dives after his next target.

KNIGHT 212

Thud lines up to join the fray below him. Speedy, "Break right! On our 6, Thud!" Thud pulls right, goes wing level and starts to climb, applying afterburner to keep up his speed. Speedy, "He's still on us, man. Do something, man!"

FELIX 541

Book misses the first shot and follows Spike through the barrel roll, climbing in the scissors after her. Her violent maneuvers are keeping him from lining up a shot. Behind Book, Packs is frantic. His radio isn't working. He pulls off his mask and screams, "What are you doing, man? What the fuck? What the fuck? Knock it off! What the fuck!"

Book ignores him and continues climbing through the vertical scissors, chasing the bitch. He sees an opportunity as they both lose air speed. He knows she's going to have to roll over the top soon. One more scissor. Instead, she slows both engines, opens her air brake, and rapidly bleeds speed. "Shit!" He shoots past her. He cranks his head around as he rolls over the top, then into a Cuban 8, ignoring the shouts behind him. Rolling upright in a dive, he adjusts to get back behind her, pulling left. Then Packs sees the side of the other F-14, recognizing the aircrafts number and the Japanese flags on the fuselage.

KNIGHT 1

Spike pulls out of the left snap roll, straightening back into level flight, hitting the burners, and diving to gain speed. Puck, "He's coming back at us 10 o'clock high."

"I see him." She pulls toward him in the merge at 400 knots, manually rolls her wings back and reduces her throttles to three quarters military. As Book flashes by, Puck twists his head around, "He's climbing into the vertical scissors." She lays on full afterburners, and with no missiles and much of her fuel burned, accelerates like a rocket. As Book rolls, expecting to see her crossing him, she's rolling onto his 6.

FELIX 541

Book inverts out of the scissors, looking for Spike. He sees her in his mirror. Packs, frantic, is looking behind at the F-14 behind them, "It's Spike, you son of a bitch. You're trying to kill her!"

JAPANESE F-15

Koizumi has been trying to get on the six of either one of the F-14s. As they maneuver, he could not. Still, he marvels at their skill. Then he sees a possible opening and he rolls in.

KNIGHT 1

Spike's on Book's six. He tries to invert and dive, then twists to climb again, and Spike follows. Puck, "We have a '15 coming in at 9 o'clock." Book snap rolls 270 degrees to the right, then pulls into a tight right turn, and Spike stays right with him. Puck, "The '15 is behind and outside." Spike rolls wings level and pulls up into an Immelman. Puck, "Book, there's a '15 on our six. Break right!"

JAPANESE F-15

Koizumi chooses the plane still in the turn, and fires his last missile.

FELIX 541

Book hears Puck's call on the radio, ignoring it as a trick. Packs, "Missile! Break right! Break right!" Book looks over his shoulder seeing missile exhaust, starts to break, then feels the missile hit behind him. The aircraft lurches violently and goes into a flat spin. He's thrown forward into his straps by the centrifugal force, unable to reach the ejection handle. Looking up, he can see the smoke from his aircraft spiraling above as they fall. He somehow manages to get his head around to see Packs. His RIO, closer to the center of gravity is still able to move. He meets the eyes of his RIO. Packs looks at him with calm loathing.

Book grunts out, "Eject! Eject!"

Reaching his hands up against the spin, Packs grabs the ejection handles, pulling them toward him. Charges built into the canopy detonate, lifting it up and away from the aircraft. The canopy is designed to fly up when the airflow normally passing over the fighter would push it clear behind the plane. But the airflow in a flat spin behaves differently. Instead, centrifugal force throws the canopy forward. The RIO's seat fires first, launching Packs at 20 g's, and he passes out. He just misses the canopy as he flies 300 feet above the spinning fighter. When Book's seat fires a moment later, it hits the canopy. The chair gyro compensates for the collision and continues to fly up. It separates at the programmed time, so his parachute can activate a few seconds later at 5000 feet. As the two chutes drift down, the F-14 crashes belly first into the ocean at over 200 knots.

CHAPTER 48

90 MILES NORTH OF TASK FORCE, JAPENESE F-15,

14 January, 1942

Koizumi can't believe his luck. The Americans devastated his squadron in the Philippines and now he has downed two. He pulls up to engage the other '14.

KNIGHT 1

Inverted, 1000 feet above the F-15, Puck, "Book is hit! Book is hit!" On intercom, "A '15 is coming after us." Spike snap rolls left, pulling the '14 into a high G turn, "Grunt."

Puck, "He's crossing, 9 o'clock."

She snap rolls upright, going vertical, "Grunt."

As she begins the climb, Puck, "He's coming vertical to meet us. It's a vertical scissors."

She pulls past vertical in the scissors, and again rolls upright as the '15 crosses 100 yards ahead. Then, pulling the stick to her belly, "Grunt," she rolls again to orient with her target as he pulls past vertical. Spike closes on his six as she follows him up.

JAPANESE F-15

Koizumi straightens his roll into the next scissors, but the American is not crossing him. He looks in his mirror and sees his adversary on his six. Giving up the scissors, he continues around in a loop, rolling out in a dive at full afterburner. The

American is still behind him, then he remembers the maneuver he saw. He cuts his left engine, using rudder, elevator, and ailerons, to turn sharply.

KNIGHT 1

Spike says, "Grunt," continuing in a tight 8 G loop, keeping the '15 visible. As the F-15 pulls out of the loop into a steep dive, she sees his burners light, so she lights hers. The Japanese '15 is about three quarters of a mile ahead when she sees his left burner go out. She rolls left and rudders left slightly, firing ahead of the turning plane. The rounds hit behind the cockpit and the fuel cell explodes. The F-15 tumbles and falls. She pulls out of the dive, inverts, and watches the '15 all the way to the water. "That's my maneuver, you bastard." She sees Book's and Pack's chutes nearing the ocean.

Puck, "I think Thud is way above us. Nice flying, Spike. Are you okay?"

"I'm tired. Where is he?" She starts to climb at full military.

KNIGHT 212

Thud is in a vertical scissors with another '15. They climb at full afterburner, twisting in the air, neither able to get a line on the other. Five scissor cycles and they're passing 35,000 feet. Thud is down to 280 knots, the '15 about the same. As his fighter comes vertical, Thud throttles back, bleeding airspeed rapidly, and takes a quick shot. The Japanese pilot spins in the air and most of Thud's rounds miss. Nearly out of air speed, Thud goes to full military on the right engine, easing back on his left as his craft begins to fall. The thrust imbalance slews the aircraft around and he starts to dive. As he gains speed and control in the dive, Thud sees his target 2000 feet lower and several miles away. Speedy, "We have no more fuel, compadre. Let us go back to the rancho. We can drink Dos Equis and chase wee-man."

"Speaking of women, where's Spike?"

They hear Puck, "Gold Eagle, Knight 1. We have two chutes in the water 90 miles at 293."

"Acknowledge, Knight 1. We have a helo 15 minutes out. What is your status?"

"Gold Eagle, Knight 1. Bingo fuel and sans missiles. Stand by for Knight Flight." Then, "Knight Flight, SITREP."

Gandhi, "Angels 5 and 75 miles from home. Bingo fuel with a few new holes. We're flying ok."

GQ, "Bingo fuel and escorting Swede."

NOB, "Bingo fuel and damaged at angels 12, 80 miles from home. We need a tank."

Cuddles, "Bingo fuel, with NOB."

Speedy, "Bingo fuel at angels 35, 90 miles out. Where are you, Puck?"

Puck, "About 15 beneath you." The rest of the squadron checks in, all bingo fuel. "Gold Eagle, Knight 1 request tanker support. We have ten thirsty birds."

"Knight 1, continue on course, 125, and climb to angels 30. Arco is enroute."

Puck "Okay, guys, give me your numbers." They report their fuel state. Those with the lowest amount fuel first.

JAPANESE FIGHTER GROUP

Colonel Nagasawa shepherds the remnants of his fighter wing to the northwest. Twenty aircraft are all that remain of the forty-eight that left Chitose Field. The price was high, but the prize of destroying the American carrier worth it. If only it could be avoided. The emperor had explained to him that people's blood was raging on both sides of the Pacific, and nothing but blood could quench the fire. It's even possible he had killed Americans he had befriended. The last one he fought was good, skilled, quick thinking, and innovative. He reminded himself of the necessity in an attempt to keep the bile from rising in his throat. He muses on the rightness of the old saying, 'War is hell'. "New Wind Flight, this is your leader. Please give me your fuel state."

IN THE WATER 90 MILES FROM THE TASK FORCE

Packs swims to Book, the waves lifting him, so occasionally he can see his pilot. With his life jacket inflated he can only do pitifully small strokes. Then he hears the beat of rotors and stops, looking up. Well aware of how small a man is in the water, he digs out his dye marker and tears open the bag. Soon all the water around him is fluorescent green. He feels the sting of water whipped up in the down draft and a SAR swimmer drops near him. The SAR takes one powerful stroke and is beside him, hooking him into a harness. As the SAR works, he shouts in Packs ear, "I'll have you aboard in a jiffy." Then he's hoisted from the cold water into the colder air, and in moments he's in the chopper and strapped in.

Then the SAR comes up with Book. Book's head is twisted and dangling at an impossible angle. They crew closes the door, and Packs watches them put Book into a body bag. The SAR turns to Packs, "Are you hurt?"

"No, I'm okay."

"I'm sorry about your friend." Packs just shakes his head.

KNIGHT 212 OVER THE TASK FORCE

1635, 4 January, 1942

Thud and Speedy get a good look of the fleet as they approach. Columns of black smoke rise into the afternoon sky. As they get closer, they see a heavy cruiser missing its bow and being tended to by a destroyer and another cruiser. The Long Beach is engulfed in flame. A destroyer's bow rises straight up as it sinks. Another has nothing but a bit of stern sticking up as it slips beneath the waves. Helicopters are out, picking up survivors. The Spruance class destroyer, Fife, is also burning. Two destroyers alongside it, spraying water on the flames. The Carl Vinson, a bit to the east to keep wind over her deck, has smoke rising from her port side. Thud, "My God, we got hammered!"

Speedy, "The Vinson, too. Damn, brother, damn."

Thud, "You think the deck has FOD?"

"It's been awhile. Probably not. Just land easy."

Thud chuckles, "Yeah, right."

KNIGHT 1

Puck, "You okay, Sam?"

"What?"

"Are you okay?"

"I'll need your help to get home."

"Sure, Sam," then, "Gold Eagle, Knight 1, two to marshal."

"Roger, Knight 1. Enter downwind at 1000. Be aware that the smoke is making the ball tricky. You're behind two foxtrot on eights."

"Understood, Gold Eagle, turning down wind. Speedy, we'll make the first break."

Spike, "No, get him down."

Puck, "Okay," then, "Speedy, why don't you go first?"

"Understood, Puck."

"Did we do well today, Eric?"

"I think so, Samantha. Watch your speed."

KNIGHT 212

Thud, "Speedy, are we good compadre?"

"Si, Senior Thud. We kill the bad guys, and now we will drink the Tequila under the stars."

"If only we had some. Making the break."

"Knight 212, Gold Eagle. Call the ball."

"Roger ball, 49."

Speedy calls out the altitude until they hit the deck, catching a 2 wire.

KNIGHT 1

Puck, "A little fast."

"Knight 1, Gold Eagle. Call the ball."

Spike, "Got it."

Puck, "Roger ball, 48."

Puck calls the altitude, "500, 400, faster Sam, 300, 200, on 100," and the '14 slams into the deck, catching a shaky 1 wire. After she idles the engines, a yellow shirt starts giving directions, but she doesn't respond. "We need to move, Sam. Stay with me a little longer." She bumps the throttles, following directions. Puck sees her head bobbing, "We're out of the way, set the brake." He opens the canopy and unfastens his harness. The yellow shirt runs up, shouting, "You need to park it."

Puck, "Use the tractor, she's done." Stepping out of the cockpit, he reaches past her and shuts down the engine, "It's a good thing I do my homework." As the engines spool down, he undoes her harness. They're moving the tractor into position as Handy runs up, "How many ki...um, sir, is she alright?"

Puck takes her helmet off and tosses it into the RIO's seat. Gently, he takes her face in his hands, looking into her eyes. They are sunken and she's having trouble focusing. He physically lifts her from the cockpit and lowers her to Handy. Thud and Speedy run up. When her feet touch the deck, she collapses. Handy and Thud grab her under the arms. Puck climbs down and sweeps her up into his arms, "Thud, Speedy, post flight the bird for us, please?"

Handy's eyes are huge, "Is she okay?"

Puck, "Later." He walks toward the island. Fluffy, just stepping out onto the flight deck, sees Puck carrying the skipper. He turns back and opens the door.

Captain Van Zandt is standing just inside, "Is that Commander Hunt? Admiral Halsey needs..." and Fluffy pushes past the staff captain, "Later, sir." Keeping ahead of Puck, he opens doors and bulls people aside.

Puck carries her down the starboard side ladder. She puts her arms around his neck and tucks her head against his chest like a child. He carries her all the way to medical, with Fluffy acting as lead blocker. They walk into the chaos of medical, and a corpsman with a clip board asks, "Name and injury?"

Puck, flatly, "Commander Hunt. Assault, rape, dehydration, and exhaustion."

The corpsman shrugs, "Get her some water and a nap, we're swamped."

Fluffy grabs his uniform and lifts him up, "She needs care."

The corpsman says, "Go ahead and beat me, we're still swamped. Her injuries are not life threatening. Take care of her yourself."

Puck, "Put him down, he's right. We'll take her to her stateroom and get some water down her. Then, we'll put her to bed."

MESS DECKS REPAIR LOCKER 51, LONG BEACH

MM1 Walters makes his way aft on the second deck, his

oxygen breathing apparatus ready, but not on. The smoke in the passageway seems to be coming from the ventilation. He sees the repair 6 investigator open the door to the enlisted berthing area. He waves and turns around. On his way back, he checks the athwart ship passageway. He pulls off a glove and puts the back of his hand to the bottom of the non-water tight door; it's warm. Then he checks the middle of the door; it's warmer. He tells the line tender with him to report back a hot door, giving the location. Then, he hears a crash on the other side of the door and steps back toward the mess deck as flames flicker out of the ventilation ports near the overhead. He reports back to Lt. JG Knots, "Go check the main deck, assess, and get back to me. Fire team out, attack aft, port side."

Walters climbs a ladder, again checking the hatch, and it's cool. He and his line tender climb through the scuttle, barely fitting with their OBAs. On the main deck they find themselves in another athwart ship passageway. They check the hatches port and starboard to the 5 inch gun magazines, then the library door, and they're all cool. Going into the library, he directs his battle lantern's beam into the gloom. Nothing is burning, but paint is beginning to peel from the aft bulkhead. He yells at his tender, "Go tell the locker officer we need to keep the library bulkhead cool and protect the books."

MM3 Small, "There just books."

Walters grabs him, "They tell our future, idiot. Go tell him." He continues walking forward to check the XO's and other senior officers staterooms. He's checking the door when a lieutenant runs down from the 01 level. He grabs Walters, "Get a fucking fire hose. The wardroom is on fire!"

"But, sir, I'm an investigator."

The LT grabs him by the OBA straps, pushing him against the wall, "THEN FUCKING INVESTIGATE WITH A HOSE!"

Small climbs up out of the scuttle. Walters says, "Go tell Knots the wardroom is on fire and I'm manning a hose." He pulls the one and half inch hose off its storage camel back and fakes it out by stringing it back and forth across the deck so it won't kink when it's charged. He puts down his face mask, fires up his OBA and tests it. Then, charging the hose, he holds the nozzle tight in his hand. Dragging the hose behind him, he climbs the ladder to the o1 level and pushes open the wardroom door. He sees fire everywhere, and several places where the overhead has collapsed. Opening the nozzle, he sweeps it back and forth, laying down high velocity fog.

CHAPTER 49

USS CARL VINSON, 03 LEVEL PORT SIDE

Puck climbs the four stories up to the 03 level with Sam in his arms, Fluffy continuing to lead block. She looks at Puck, trying to focus her eyes, and in a small voice, "Puck, put me down."

"We're almost to your stateroom."

"No, Eric. Put me down."

"Okay." He puts her on her feet. She wobbles and he steadies her. "You need to rest, Spike."

Fluffy adds, "We got your back, boss."

"I know, Fluffy. Help me to the ready room. I need water and something to eat."

Puck, "Are you sure, Sam?"

Her voice firming, "Puck…Puck, just help me. Fluffy, what… find out the status of our planes. How many can fly?"

Fluffy exchanges a look with Puck, "Spike, we got it. Go rest."

She turns toward Fluffy, raising her voice, "There is no time, Chief. As we speak, the Japanese are planning the next attack. We have to be ready."

Fluffy nods, and heads topside.

USS FIFE, REPAIR 6

Lt. JG Laura Wakefield is crazy busy. She has fires forward in repair 5 locker area and multiple people injured. She managed to get the CHENG back in medical, with a corpsman stabilizing him for medivac. The central control station is ablaze, as is combat and the superstructure up to the bridge. It's a mass conflagration drill come to life. A petty officer runs up to her, "Ma'am, I need you forward."

"I'm busy," then to a phone talker, "Tell locker 1 and 2, I need all the hoses they can provide working aft."

BM1 Coats tries again, "Ma'am, the chief can do this. I need you forward."

She turns to him, "Petty Officer Coats, I'm busy. B.U.S.Y. BUSY. If I don't get this right, we'll lose the ship. You got it?"

Coats stands his ground, "Ma'am, the whole ship needs you. Not just this locker. YOU are in charge!"

She looks at him baffled, "What?"

"Ma'am, the CO, XO, DCA, and Weapons Officer are dead. The CHENG needs to be medivaced off. You're it. You are the commanding officer of the USS Fife. Let the locker chief do his job and start doing yours, ma'am."

She looks around and shakes her head, "Do we have contact with higher?"

"Not yet."

"Okay, okay. Does the 1JV still have contact fore and aft?"

"Yes, ma'am."

"Okay, Coats, you are now my conning officer. Go forward, establish coms with the power plants, aft steering, and the helicopter control station, and keep us from hitting anything. I'll be aft at Helicon. They have a radio there. MOVE!"

VF-154 READY ROOM, USS CARL VINSON

Thud walks in, his face tracked with tears and anguish. The rest of the squadron start arriving for the post brief. 'Johnny' Walker asks, "Thud, have you seen the skipper?" Thud looks at him, staring, but not seeing, then shakes his head, no.

"Hey, what's going on, Thud?"

Speedy, coming in behind Thud, "Just drop it, Mi amigo, comprende?"

Gunner and his RIO, NOB, com in laughing. But a couple of steps in, pause, taking in the quiet. Gunner asks, "Hey, Thud, where's the skipper?"

Speedy, "She's okay. Just drop it."

"Okay, man, chill."

Swede walks out of the XO's office. All the aircrew are in the room except Spike, Puck, and Packs. Thud exchanges a look of silent understanding with Speedy. Thud says, "Lt. Carleton tried to shoot Spike down out there. He nearly succeeded when I couldn't get to her. Carleton was shot down, I think, by a Jap. Book went around the bend and tried to kill Spike and Puck. And...and...and I couldn't help them." The room is silent.

Puck leads Sam into the ready room. She is very unsteady on her feet. Puck, "Somebody get her some water and some food." Swede grabs a water bottle and throws it to Puck, who catches it offhand, opens it, and hands it to her. He helps her into a chair at the front.

Sam takes a long pull of water, and looks around the ready room, eyes still unfocused. She sees Thud. "Thud, you did your best."

"A wingman is supposed to protect his partner. I failed you."

Puck, "Not at the expense of your own life, Thud. I only caught bits of what you were doing, but the Jap you tangled with was damn good. Carleton lost. You're right. A Japanese sidewinder got Book. We got the Japanese. There were two chutes, so Book is going to survive for court martial."

Thud, still crying, "Spike, are you hurt?"

Sam rubs her face, "Just exhausted and thirsty. Thud, I'll live. You did your best." Looking up at all her people, "You all did." Her voice firming up, "Okay, where are we? Right now, we need to prepare for a second strike. Which of you have undamaged birds?"

USS SALT LAKE CITY, BRIDGE

Captain Ellis Zacharias stands at the port bridge wing with a loud hailer. At his elbow is the bridge phone talker and the OOD. The Chester, CA 27, is alongside offering aid. The destroyer Mugford, DD 389, is on the other side spraying water on the fires forward. Captain William Handy Hartt, Jr. of the Chester shouts, "Salt Lake City! We stand by to take on your crew."

"We're not done yet, friend. I have three fourths of a ship to fight with."

"What do you need?"

"I need pumps, shoring equipment, and fire fighters." The last is drowned out by the noise of a helicopter. The OOD, "Captain, the Carl Vinson is sending an assistance detail. Shall I land them on the stern?"

"Yes, John, that will do. Have them coordinate with the DCA."

Down in the bowels of the Salt Lake City, BT1 Rivera is neck deep in water operating a valve. As the ship rolls, his head goes under, but he stays with it. As his head clears the sloshing water, he gasps for air. Then he works his way to the ladder, "Go tell the DCA that the starboard main can be repressurized." As he works his way to waist level, he shouts, "Send down the eductor. The main is coming up in a bit." Something bumps against his leg. He pushes it off, looking up the stairs. But the ship keeps rolling and the thing bumps into him again. He looks down and sees the lifeless eyes of BT1 Grady staring up at him.

He hears a shout from above, "Eductor coming down." He grabs the heavy salt water operated pump and lowers it into the water.

BRIDGE, USS CARL VINSON

The RO, Captain Tucker, stands beside Captain Johnson, "Sir, we were lucky. We lost the forward port CIWS, its control room, some fans and supplies. We have smoke damage to an air wing berthing, but that's about it. The fires are being overhauled and the ship is fully functional. Casualties are two dead, eight wounded, and one re-wounded."

"Re-wounded?"

"Yes, sir, one of the Stoddert survivors who was badly burned. He was staying sick in quarters because medical had no room for him. He opened the wounds on his hands and got a couple of new burns fighting the fire. Good thing he did, too. We could have lost number 2 catapult."

The BMOW announces, "Admiral on the bridge."

Johnson, "Two dead and nine wounded, and you call that lucky?"

Admiral Halsey, "I do, William, how long until we are ready to counter-attack?"

"The aircraft are mostly on board now, and being rearmed and refueled. It'll be about thirty minutes, sir. Where do you want to hit?"

Halsey, "We took losses, but we hit them good. I want to attack the air field the jets flew from. Your radar plane had them returning to Hokkaido. I'm told there is only one military airfield there. I want to blow them to hell."

BLACK KNIGHTS READY ROOM

Sam sits at a table writing. A phone talker sitting next to her reports, "Knight 309 is patched and flight worthy."

"Very well, we have six birds..." She pauses and takes a breath, "Swede, put together a flight and report to Combat." She's handed a glass of water and she downs it, "Thank you. Swede, four AIM-54s on each bird, ok?" We don't want to play with the F-15s if we don't have to."

Swede, "Roger, boss. Get some sleep."

"Swede, I'll sleep when we're clear." She pauses again, stretches her shoulders and absently eats a granola bar. She rubs her eyes, "Swede, what's the status of 224?"

Puck, "Spike, Swede left. You need to sleep."

Irritated, "When we're clear," and nods off. She comes to, shaking her head, "Focus. Puck, what's the status of 224?"

"They're replacing a section of wiring. It should be up anytime."

"Are the aircrew not on duty, resting?"

"All but you and I. Spike, you need to sleep."

With effort she focuses on her RIO, "Lieutenant Hawke, I need to make sure we are ready to fight. It's my squadron, and mine to do."

"Yes, ma'am."

BRIDGE, USS CARL VINSON

Captain Johnson stands near his chair talking to Admiral Halsey and drinking coffee when a petty officer walks in, "Request to enter the bridge with dispatches." The conning officer, "Granted."

They young RM2 walks up to Halsey, handing him a clipboard, "Sign here, sir." Halsey signs, the petty officer hands him an envelope and leaves.

Halsey opens it, "Damn it to hell. It's Nimitz. There is to be no follow on attack. He's ordering us to patch ourselves together and return to Pearl. Damn it! Anything new on the Salt Lake City?"

Johnson sips his coffee, "They're still fighting it. From what they said, the missile hit didn't directly cause the damage. It somehow triggered a secondary explosion, which blew the bow off."

"Something detonated the mount 1 magazine. We need to figure that out. Anyway, put out to your pilots to stand down until morning. I want a radar plane and four fighters airborne all night. I'll tell Enterprise to keep patrolling, too. We need to start back home."

BLACK KNIGHT READY ROOM

Sam is still at her desk, working. Her head bobs down and she catches herself, takes a drink coffee, and starts reading again. Captain Holtz walks in with a handful of papers. Seeing Puck, "The flight schedule, Puck, could you post it?"

"Yes, sir."

Papa pulls up a chair and sits down, "How are you, Spike?"

She struggles to focus, "I'm too wiped out to fly, but...but, I got six planes ready and three more almost ready. Swede is ready to lead. We're ready for the next strike, sir."

"There won't be another strike. We're heading back to Pearl...Spike, I'm sorry."

"What?"

"I know what happened. What Lieutenant Carleton did. What he did on the sponson, and in the air. Look, I knew he was melting down. I knew he hated you. I should have figured it out. I, um, I should have done something."

"Sir. Sir, he'll pay for what he did. It...it isn't your fault."

"Sam, Carleton is dead. His neck was broken during ejection."

Sam is startled, "Um, damn, okay, sir. Sir, it wasn't your fault. How could anyone know he would...that he would try to hurt me. That he would kill Chief White."

"Spike. Samantha, what happened out there? Did you shoot him down?"

"No, sir. No. He was so focused on us, he forgot the Japanese. Sir, what about Lieutenant Boxter?"

"He's in medical, but he'll recover. Are you going to be okay, Samantha?"

"I'm...I'm tired, sir. God, sir, we lost people. Good people. How do I deal with that?"

"We keep going, Samantha. We've a lot of war in front of us. We fight to survive each day and trust the guys above us know what they're doing. Each day, we change everything that happened before."

"I know, sir. But, are we changing it for the better?"

"Yes, Samantha. You. I. All of us. We're making a better future."

THE END

THE STORY CONTINUES IN

DIVIDED WE STAND

BOOK TWO OF

THE FIGHTING
TOMCATS

GLOSSARY

16: VHF channel 16 is the international emergency channel.

1MC: General announcing system. Ship wide loud speaker system.

(Number)K: Fuel state. K for thousand pounds.

AB1: Navy enlisted rate and rank. Aviation Boatswain's Mate First Class (E-6).

AD: Naval aviation rating. Aviation Machinist.

ADC(AW): Naval enlisted rank and rate, with warfare badge. Aviation Machinist Chief, Air Warfare specialist (E-7).

ADM: Admiral. Naval Officer rank (O-10). Also used colloquially for Rear Admirals Lower and Upper, and Vice Admirals (O-7 through 9).

AGL: Above Ground Level.

Ahead (Bell): The standard bells, or speeds of a ship are ahead 1/3, ahead 2/3, ahead Standard, Ahead full, and Ahead Flank. The number is the amount of revolutions per minute of the shaft.

Ahead Flank Emergency: Order to come to the fastest ahead speed as fast as possible. See Bell.

Air Boss: The ship's force air department head. The air boss commands all operations on the flight deck and hanger deck.

Amphenol: Multi-prong electronic or electrical connection.

AN: Naval Enlisted non-designated aviation rank. Airman (E-3).

AOCS: Enlisted rate and rank. Aviation Ordinanceman Senior Chief (E-8).

Arco: When an aircraft flies as a refueler they are given a special call sign. Usually the name of a gas station chain.

ASROC: Anti-submarine rocket. A torpedo delivered by a rocket.

ASW: Anti-submarine warfare.

Auto-gyro: An emergency landing technique that uses the wind blowing through the helicopter rotors to keep them spinning, then uses the collective to slow the bird's descent at the last moment.

(AW): Naval specialist Badge. Air Warfare Specialist.

Back (Bell): Astern bells are Back 1/3, Back 2/3, and Back Full.

Back Full Emergency: The fastest astern bell to be answered as fast as possible.

BDU: Battle Dress, Utility. The basic Army and Marine uniform.

Bell: The speed a ship is traveling at: Ahead they are Ahead 1/3, Ahead 2/3, Ahead Standard, and Ahead Flank. Astern they are Back 1/3, Back 2/3, and Back full. In an emergency the order given is ahead flank emergency, or back full emergency which is a command to go as fast as possible.

Bearing: Compass or relative bearing in degrees from 0 to 360.

Bingo Fuel: Near the minimum to safely return to base.

Binnacle List: List of people sick or injured. Every unit and division maintains the list and turns it in daily.

Blow: Submarines use ballast tanks to surface or submerge. By blowing high pressure air into the tanks water can be displaced and the vessel surfaces.

Blue Tails: Nick name for the VAW-122 Griffins. VAW-122 flies the E-2C Hawkeye radar plane.

Blue Water Ops: Carrier operations beyond reach of alternative air fields. You land on the carrier or swim.

Boatswain's Mate of the Watch (BMOW): In charge of all the lookouts, the helm and lee helm. The BMOW pipes (whistles) required ships announcements. The BMOW is also in charge of all lookouts.

Boiler: Boilers generate the steam for propulsion, electrical generation, water distillation, and other uses.

Bolter: An aircraft missing the arresting wire.

Bridge: The ship's navigational control center. Where we drive the ship. The Officer of the Deck (OOD) is in charge except when the CO is present. The Conning Officer directs the ship's course and speed. The Boatswains Mate of the Watch (BMOW), Quartermaster of the Watch (QMOW), Helm and Lee Helm are stationed here.

BTOW: Boiler Technician of the watch. Senior watch in a boiler room.

BT1: Navy Enlisted rate and rank. Boiler Technician First Class (E-6).

BT2: Navy Enlisted rate and rank. Boiler technician Second Class (E-5).

BT3: Navy Enlisted rate and rank. Boiler Technician Third Class (E-4).

CAG: Commander Air Group. The CAG is in charge of all the air squadrons attached to the ship. The CAG is the counterpart to the ship's commanding officer. The carrier CO is always the senior.

Call the Ball: The Landing Signal Officer asks the pilot if they can see the Fresnel lens that shows the correct glide slope for landing.

CAP: Combat Air Patrol. A fighter mission to circle an area ready to defend the fleet.

CAPT: Captain: Naval Officer rank (O-6).

CATCC: Carrier Air Traffic Control Center. This center controls all aircraft within 50 miles of the ship and manages take offs and landings.

CHENG: Chief Engineer. Engineering department head.

CMAA: Chief Master at arms. A senior cop on a Navy ship.

CDR: Naval Officer rank. Commander (O-5).

Combat: Weapon's and communications control center on a naval ship. The CO goes to combat during battle stations (General Quarters).

Decimal: On radio the word 'Decimal' is used to indicate tenths. Thus, fuel at 9 decimal 2 is 9,200 pounds. Fuel is always given as weight.

Division: Naval organization. Naval units are divided into Departments and Divisions. Divisions are functionally oriented units with all the enlisted members typically of one rating.

ELT: Navy Enlisted trade. Some MM's are qualified Engineering Laboratory Technician (Nuclear). They are chemistry and radiation specialists, though they also stand normal mechanical watches.

EM1: Navy Enlisted rate and rank. Electrician's Mate First Class (E-6). Electricians operate the electrical distribution system on the ship, and also maintain all the electrical equipment.

EMCS: Navy Enlisted rate and rank. Electrician Senior Chief (E-8).

EMP: Electro-Magnetic Pulse. A powerful change is the magnetic field. An EMP could damage or destroy electronic and electric gear.

Engine Room: Space where the main engines, electrical generators, and water distilling unit are located. This equipment is operated and maintained by Machinist Mates.

ENS: Ensign: Naval Officer rank (O-1). Junior most officer. Sometimes called a butter bar for their rank insignia which is a single gold bar.

EOOW: Engineering Officer of the Watch. Watch stander in charge of the propulsion plant. Normally a Lt. on a nuclear ship. Sometimes a senior or master chief on conventional powered ships.

ETA: Estimated Time of Arrival.

F-14: The Tomcat. An all-weather interceptor and fleet defense fighter.

Faking hose: Laying out a hose or line in parallel lines so the hose can be safely charged or the line let go without jamming.

Far CAP: Combat Air Patrol. Far CAP is a defensive position away from the fleet.

Fire room: Location of the boilers in a fossil fueled steam ship.

FN: Navy Enlisted rank. Fireman (E-3). A non-designated engineering striker. If designated his rate would precede his rank.

FOD Walk Down: Walking the flight deck looking for FOD (Foreign Object Damage) that could damage aircraft.

Fuel state: How much fuel you have on board in thousands of pounds. (10 decimal 1 = 10,100lbs.)

'G's: Gravities. One 'G' is equal to normal earth gravity. Two is twice earth gravity etc.

General Quarters: The call to man battle stations and prepare the vessel to fight.

Gertrude: Nick name for a short range underwater phone.

GMM1: Navy Enlisted rate and rank. Gunners Mate Missiles, First Class (E-6). Gunner's Mates operate and maintain the weapons on a ship. The rate is split between Gunner's Mate Guns (GMG) and Gunner's Mate Missiles (GMM).

GMM2: Navy Enlisted rate and rank. Gunner's Mate Missiles, Second Class (E-5).

GMM3: Navy Enlisted rate and rank. Gunner's Mate Missiles, Third Class (E-4).

Gold Eagle: Radio call sign for the USS Carl Vinson.

HT1: Navy Enlisted rate and rank. Hull Technician first class (E-6). HT's are Damage control and repair experts. They also operate the sewer system on the ship.

ILS: Instrument Landing system. An aircraft system that helps pilots line up with a runway they cannot see.

Khaki: Slang term for chiefs and officers because they wear khaki colored uniforms.

Knight 212 (or any number): Call sign of fighters flying for VFW-154, the Black Knights.

Landing Signal Officer: A pilot positioned near the rear of the carrier to help guide pilots in. The LSO also grades landings.

Laze: Use a laser to designate where ordinance is to drop.

LCDR: Naval Officer rank. Lieutenant Commander (O-4).

LPO: Naval position. Leading Petty Officer is the "Foreman" for a division. Usually and E-6.

Lt.: Naval officer rank. Lieutenant (O-3).

Lt. J G: Naval Officer rank. Lieutenant Junior Grade. (O-2.)

MACS: Navy Enlisted rate and rank. Senior Chief Master at Arms (E-8).

Magic 1: Call sign for an EA-6B Prowler, radar jamming aircraft of VAQ-133 Wizards.

Master Chief: Naval Enlisted Rank (E-9).

Mini Boss: The air boss's assistant. They divide the observation duties in PRIFLY.

MM1: Navy Enlisted rate and rank. Machinist's Mate First Class (E-6).

MM2: Navy Enlisted rate and rank. Machinist's Mate Second Class (E-5).

MM3: Navy Enlisted rate and rank. Machinist's Mate Third

Class (E4).

MMCM: Naval enlisted rate and rank. Machinist's Mate Master Chief (E-9).

MMFN: Navy Enlisted rate and rank. Machinist's Mate Fireman (E-3).

MMOW: Machinist's Mate of the Watch. Senior watch stander in an engine room.

NAM: Navy Achievement Medal. A medal for individual meritorious accomplishment.

NAVSEA 08: Designation for the leader of the U. S. Navy Nuclear Power Program.

Navy Expeditionary Medal: Medal issued for service in a combat zone designated by congress.

NTDS: Naval Tactical Data System. A system that shares sensor data with other ships.

MW: Megawatt. One million watts. 1,000,000 watts.

O-2 Plant: The oxygen generation plant which removes atmospheric oxygen and compresses it into liquid oxygen used by medical and as pilot breathing air.

Officer of the Deck (OOD): In charge of the operations and navigation of the ship underway. In port the OOD is in charge of the ship's duty section and all operations during their watch.

Operation Praying Mantis: Battle in the Persian Gulf between the U. S. Navy and Iran in 1987.

Op-tempo: Rate of operations over time.

Passageway: Navy speak for a hallway.

Petty Officer: Colloquial phrase for an E-4 through E-6. Generally, it is only used by officers or master at arms who are about to correct the Petty Officer's behavior.

Phoenix: AIM-54 Long range air to air missile.

PQS: Personal Qualification Standard. PQS is the system used by the Navy to qualify sailors to do their jobs.

Propulsion plant drills: Nuclear operator training practicing possible casualties and problems. Continues training is the reality of most sailors.

PRI-

FLY: Primary Flight Control. The highest deck in the island structure where all flight deck operations are managed.

QAO: Quality Assurance Officer

Quartermaster of the Watch (QMOW): In charge of providing navigational information to the OOD and Conning Officer. The QMOW is required to keep the ship's position updated on paper and electronic charts.

Rainbow side boys: The traditional side boys for a senior visitor, only wearing the various flight deck colored jerseys.

Reactor Auxiliary Room (RAR): The RAR is the space where the reactor support and monitoring equipment is located. It shares most of the same functions that a fire room in a conventional vessel would have.

Rear Admiral Lower Half: Naval Officer rank. One-star Admiral (O-7).

Rear Admiral Upper Half: Naval Officer rank. Two-star Admiral (O-8).

RIM-7: Rail launched intermediate range air to air missile. Sea Sparrow.

RIO: Radar Intercept Officer. The RIO operates the radar and weapons system in the back seat of the F-14.

RM1: Navy Enlisted rate and rank. Radioman First Class (E-6).

Roger Ball (Number): Roger ball means the pilot can see the Fresnel lens glide slope indicator. The number is the total weight of the aircraft in thousands of pounds.

RTB: Return to Base.

SAM: Surface to Air Missile.

SAR: Search and Rescue.

SLQ-32: Called the "slick 32" it is a multi-function radar jammer.

Snap 2: Early supply computer.

SOB: Son of a Bitch. Even cuss words have acronyms.

Squawked: Identification, friend or foe (IFF) Code signal.

ST1: Navy Enlisted rate and rank. Sonar Technician First Class (E-6).

ST2: Navy Enlisted rate and rank. Sonar Technician Second Class (E-5).

Switch Gear Room: Space where the electrical distribution system is operated. EM's stand watch in Switch Gear.

TACAN: Radio beacon aircraft use to find the carrier.

TARPS: Tactical Airborne Reconnaissance Pod System. A camera system mounted on a hard point and controlled by the RIO.

Terawatt: One quadrillion watts. 1,000,000,000,000 watts.

TG: Turbine Generator. An electrical Generator powered by steam.

TG/DU: Turbine Generator and Distilling Unit watch.

Thwarts ship passageway: A hall way aligned from side to side rather than forward and aft.

TLD: Thermal Luminescent Dosimetry. A radiation measuring device to monitor crew exposure.

VHF: Very High Frequency. A line of sight radio.

Vice Admiral: Naval Officer rank. VADM (O-9).

Wave off: Order to abort a landing and go around.

Yankee Search: Active sonar search.

YNSN: Naval Enlisted rate and rank. Yeoman, Seaman, (E-3).

XO: Executive officer. Second in charge of a vessel or unit.

X-Ray: Material condition X-Ray. Lowest level of water tight integrity. Only set during a work day in port.

Yoke: Material condition Yoke. Middle level of water tight integrity between X-ray (in port on work day) and Zebra

(Battle Stations).

Zebra: Material condition Zebra. Highest level of water tight integrity

MM1 Maki is a U.S. Navy veteran with twenty years of active service. A nuclear field machinist mate who served on the USS Carl Vinson, CVN-70, and two cruisers. During twelve years of sea time, MM1 Maki circumnavigated the earth once, transited the Panama Canal three times, served on the USS Carl Vinson during Enduring Freedom, and earned multiple campaign awards. S.R. Maki has a background in criminal justice and accounting.

See us at Fighting Tomcats.com

Email us at RoseHillPress17@gmail.com

Made in the USA
Middletown, DE
08 March 2023

26393285R00285